YAF

53452
Canton Public Library
403 Lewis Street
Canton, MO 63435

September 2004 Thompson Gale $25.95

53452

KITH, TRYSTAM
TROUBLE IN THE FOREST:
A COLD SUMMER NIGHT

TROUBLE in the FOREST

BOOK 1:

A Cold Summer Night

TRYSTAM KITH

Five Star • Waterville, Maine

Copyright © 2004 by Trystam Kith

All rights reserved.

This novel is a work of fiction. Names, characters, places and incidents are either the product of the author's imagination, or, if real, used fictitiously.

No part of this book may be reproduced or transmitted in any form or by any electronic or mechanical means, including photocopying, recording or by any information storage and retrieval system, without the express written permission of the publisher, except where permitted by law.

First Edition
First Printing: August 2004

Published in 2004 in conjunction with
Tekno Books and Ed Gorman.

Set in 11 pt. Plantin.

Printed in the United States on permanent paper.

Library of Congress Cataloging-in-Publication Data

Kith, Trystam.
   Trouble in the forest / by Trystam Kith.—1st ed.
     p. cm.
   "Five Star first edition titles"—Bk. 1, t.p. verso.
   Contents: bk.1. A cold summer night
   ISBN 1-59414-224-6 (hc : alk. paper)
  1. Knights and knighthood—Fiction. 2. Forests and forestry—Fiction. 3. Middle Ages—Fiction. 4. Outlaws—Fiction. 5. England—Fiction. I. Title.
PS3611.I88T76 2004
  813'.6—dc22   2004047084

For

CHERYL,
CHRIS,
and
TAMARA

THE UNHOLY TRINITY

FACT: Richard Lionheart bankrupted England twice in his thirteen-year reign.

FACT: Prince John was left with the job of bailing England out of his brother's profligacy the only way he could—by raising taxes.

FACT: Prince John possessed over 300 books and had read them all.

FACT: Unlike the Norman rulers before him, or the next four to come after, Prince John actually spoke the language of the common English people, as well as French, Latin, Greek, and Roman Vulgate (early Italian).

FACT: There were outlaw bands all over England.

The rest is myth, legend, speculation, fictional devices, and outright lies.

PROLOGUE

How the Season Faded

In the warmth of summer, the forest remained cool and shadowed, removed from the brilliance of the clear skies and the heat of the day by the tangle of branches and the profusion of the leaves. The Hart had taken dominion over the forest's vastness at the Summer Solstice, releasing the Bear from the task of stewardship. This year there was a chill in the air, a cold at the back of the wind that promised a hard winter ahead. More noticeable in the shade of the forest than in the warm glare of open lands: Beyond the trees the ploughed fields presaged a bountiful harvest, one that would provide sustenance for all through the lean months of winter.

But within the depths of the forest another harvest was taking place, this one as deadly as the orchards and fields were life-sustaining. Misgiving haunted the Hart as he made his stately way through the sun-spangled glades and tremendous thickets and huge groves of oak and yew and beech and willow and ash, for he could sense the forest was changing; something stirred within it that would forever change it. Already it seemed less familiar to the Hart than it had during his tenure the previous year, and that brought an apprehension that dismayed him. Never in all his reign had the Hart wanted the Boar to hurry his coming, but now, with the forest alive with sinister whispers, he would not have protested surrendering his sway before the Autumnal Equinox, a time that on this glorious summer afternoon seemed terribly, terribly distant.

1.

How Word of Trouble was brought to deSteny

"There is trouble in the forest," said the warden as he pulled his cap from his head and tugged at his hair to show respect. His deeply lined forehead was shadowed in grime and there was mud on his leggings and his cote. The tears on his sleeve indicated he had come in haste and that he hadn't taken the time to make himself presentable. He stared down with embarrassment at the decorative tiles newly inlaid in the stone floor, afraid to smirch it. He did not look at the other man in the chamber.

"Trouble?" echoed the master of the castle, the man responsible for defending it against all enemies. At thirty-one, he was a former Crusader and an experienced administrator with a reputation for fairness. His thinning hair was badger-grey, his eyes a soft, dark-gold color. There was a scar on his jaw and another on his left hand, and he had a small birthmark on his neck that looked like a smear of blood. He set aside his stylus and gave his attention to the warden, hoping to determine if the trouble required the attention of Sir Gui, or if he could manage it himself, an arrangement both he and Sir Gui preferred. He put his sheets of vellum under a weight in the shape of a miniature skull. The room was dimming anyway, and his eyes were beginning to ache. Neither the torches nor the oil lamps had been lit yet. "What kind of trouble? Poachers again? Or the Old Ones?" Poachers were an old annoyance, hardly worth reporting, but the warden was punctilious about it. The Old Ones rarely caused more than minor problems.

"Not exactly," said the warden unhappily, doing his best to conceal his unseemly fear. "That is, there's poaching, that's certain, and the Old Ones keep to their ways, but this is something else. It is more than deer and swans. It is—" He crossed himself, just in case. "It's new, and it's—" He struggled to find the word. "It's wrong." Then he fixed his stare on his wooden-soled boots so he would not have to see the wrath he knew was in Hugh deSteny's eyes.

But for once Hugh deSteny was not angry. "How do you mean, wrong? Do you mean against the law, or worse?"

"Both," whispered the warden. "It's more than the deer and the boar, master. It's isn't just game." He seemed to have difficulty finding the words. At last he blurted out, "One of my men is missing."

"Outlaws, do you think?" suggested deSteny.

"At least," said the warden, growing braver. "Outlaws who have more at stake than simply robbing travelers."

DeSteny picked up his stylus and held it between his fingers, rolling it back and forth. He had caught the underlying note of panic in the warden's voice. "Tell me what you mean, Chilton," he said emphatically.

"I don't know what I mean, and that's the worst of it. I haven't seen anything of the like before now. I knew I had to bring it to your attention, in case I come across more of them." He shifted his gaze to the pale afternoon light beyond the narrow windows. "And I hope I never do again. Naught of those creatures. No."

The master of the castle heard him out. "Is it so terrible?"

"Yes." Saying it made it worse instead of better. "Yes, it is." He crossed himself again, just in case.

"Why?" DeSteny leaned forward across his writing table.

"Because," said Chilton, "it's not—" He stopped. "It's not natural. There were crofters found, a whole family, in their hut. They were all dead, and so pale they looked like cheese. Each of them had such a look fixed on his face as I never want to see on the dead again. Lord preserve me from it. They looked as if their souls had been taken from them." He fought down the taste of bile at the back of his mouth. "All of them had bites on their necks. And nothing else."

"How do you mean, nothing else?" deSteny asked, the first stirring of apprehension in his gut.

"Nothing else," the warden repeated. "No look of a fight, no other wounds, just the ones in the throat. They were enough."

For the first time deSteny allowed his worry to show. "What kind of bites? Big ones, like a wolf would make?"

"No, master. Little ones, just four small holes, like a cat had nipped them—here." He put his fingers on his own neck to indicate where the crofters had been bitten. "Here and here, like little fangs. Nothing really torn, the way beasts do when they're hungry, or the cuts the Old Ones make with their flint knives. Very neat, careful-like. You wouldn't think it would kill them, or drain them. But they didn't have enough blood in them to cause death-bruises. Pale as linen and cold as marble. We looked them over, to be sure there weren't other wounds, like a poignard in the ear or a poker up the arse, though neither of those wouldn't take all that blood, and half the body would be blue with death-bruises. But there was nothing more. Only those two sets of holes. They're not enough to drain them of blood, those four little holes on their necks. Unless—" His voice rose, trembled, and stopped. He could not continue.

DeSteny finished for him. "Unless it was taken from them deliberately." He got to his feet and strode the length of the stone chamber, appalled at what he was thinking. Memories of his time in the Holy Land flooded back, and along with them an abiding sense of failure that always accompanied these unhappy recollections. Surely the evil which had cost him so much there had not come to England? He could not rid himself of the fear-certainty that it had. "When did you discover these crofters?"

"Yesterday. We sent word to the White Friars, and brought the dead to them, as we ought. They examined the dead, but would not do anything more. They said they could not bury them in sacred ground, not the way the crofters died. They claimed it was unholy, and would not anoint them because they were already damned. Once they saw the bodies, they were most determined to keep them outside the village." Chilton crossed himself a third time. "The abbot said I should tell you about it."

"He was right," deSteny agreed. "What have you done with the bodies?"

The warden shrugged. "What else could I do? I left them outside the village walls, a league or so from their croft. I couldn't do naught else, not without the permission of the monks, which I couldn't . . . The pigs have probably got them."

"If you are fortunate, they have," said deSteny with sudden emotion born of the memories he would just as soon not have. So much had changed for him since that first time he saw the kind of bites the warden described.

"What do you mean, master?" asked Chilton, feeling a crawling, cold sensation make its way up his spine.

"I mean, it would be best for all of us if those who died as you described were devoured before they can do more mischief." He slapped his hand on his thigh and resumed pacing, his thoughts still caught in the far-off sands near Jerusalem.

"How long will it take to reach the village where you left these crofters?"

"Half a day's ride, same as to the croft," said the warden. "If there's no rain. It'll take longer if the creek's up. But the signs are for clear skies for a few days more."

"We go there tomorrow morning," deSteny decided aloud. "We leave at first light. Be ready to lead us. I will command a mule for you to ride." He folded his hands and for a heartbeat or two considered doing something he had not done in years—praying. "Are you certain we can reach the croft in half a day?"

"If we leave early, we should be at the croft by noon," said the warden. "It's not a hard ride from here."

"Noon. Very good. I would not want to venture to that place late in the day, not if your description of the killing is accurate." He saw the distress in Chilton's stance, and knew he would have to shore up the warden's courage. "I saw something of the sort in the Holy Land, if what you say is accurate. Such killings are best investigated in full daylight. Once dusk falls, the darkness hampers everything. If there is any danger of it happening that we will be there at evening, I must know so that none of us will have to be out-of-doors after sunset." DeSteny tried to make himself chuckle at these precautions, but it would not come. All he achieved was a kind of snort. "You may go to the kitchen. You have done excellent service, Chilton. I will see you are rewarded."

The warden tugged at his forelock again and put his shapeless hat back on his head. "That's right gracious of you, my master."

DeSteny nodded to indicate he heard this. "And tell my page I want to talk with him." He motioned the warden away, then took flint and steel from his capacious sleeve and set a spark to the oil lamp that stood on his writing table. The little wisp of flame did little to diminish the darkness. "It could be nothing, a disease, or a curse brought on the crofters," he muttered to himself, and was unconvinced. "To have come so far . . . But many have returned from the Holy Land, and a few would be all that are needed to . . . It needn't be that, but the wounds . . ." He sat down and picked up his stylus again, and the wax tablet where he made notes. After a moment of reflection, he began to write.

"You sent for me?" Nicholas Woodhull was an ambitious young lout whose younger-son father had followed King Richard on Crusade, leaving his family to manage as best they could. Nicholas had gone into service when he was seven and had scrambled his way from waiter to page in the intervening five years, making the most of every shred of opportunity that came his way. He had not forgotten that his rank by birth was superior to deSteny's, and took as much advantage of it as he could when they were alone.

"Yes," said deSteny. "I am going into Sherwood tomorrow. There are crofters who have been killed there and I must determine—"

"Will you take me with you?" asked Nicholas before deSteny could finish.

"No," said the master of the castle. "I will take a dozen men-at-arms, though. And the warden, Chilton. Notify the Marshal that I want to depart at dawn. Sir Humphrey may accompany us if he likes, but I do not require it. This is no work for the Marshal, in any case." He looked at his notes.

"And Sir Gui? Do I carry a message to him?" His eyes shone at the prospect of being allowed to attend the lord of the county.

"No, not yet. I will make him a report, if it is necessary,

when I return." Not, he added to himself, that Sir Gui would pay much notice to it, as it concerned only crofters, whose rank was just slightly higher than serfs. "We will want horses for all the men, and a mule for the warden. And one for a monk, as well. I will ride my sorrel mare." Experience had taught him this was the prudent thing to do—he did not want to be in a bad situation on an unfamiliar horse. "I will want to talk to that Trinitarian who came here last week. The one from Whitby."

"He is in the chapel," said Nicholas. "Or he was a short time ago."

"Fetch him for me," said deSteny, adding in a firm voice, "I want this done at once, Nicholas."

The youth looked briefly sullen, then bowed his head a little and hurried away, leaving deSteny to finish the notes to himself; Nicholas, as was true of most of the minor nobility, was wary of those who could write.

DeSteny had lit two more of the oil lamps by the time the Trinitarian friar came to him, and he had begun to make notes on what he had been told of the trouble in the forest. He favored the monk with an impatient click of his tongue, then said without any pleasantries or introductions, "What do you know of a thing that kills with a bite?"

There was no sign of distress at this sudden question, only a hesitation while the monk considered the question. Then the Trinitarian crossed himself and said, "Many things bite, Sheriff. Even men, from time to time, if they are driven to it, or if they are mad." The monk was a short, stocky, square-faced man in his enveloping red habit of his Trinitarian Order, not yet middle-aged though his tonsure made him look older than his years. There was a staunch dependability about him, as if he would be reliable in a fight. His speech was flavored with the rough accents of the north.

"So they do," said the master of the castle, appreciating the friar's calm answer. "Many things bite. From lice to lions." His smile was harsh. He put his hands squarely on the table and levered himself to his feet. "But what of things that kill with a single bite on the neck? Do you know of those?"

The friar regarded the Sheriff with alarm. "I know they are dangerous, whether they are wolves or something worse. We hear stories, we monks, in our wandering. I have kept close to towns because of the tales." His eyes narrowed. "And it isn't wolves, or asps, is it? You would not bother to ask me about wolves."

"No, it isn't wolves," deSteny allowed.

"Worse luck," added the friar, taking hold of his rosary as if it were a dirk. "We might need a priest then, to deal with it."

DeSteny nodded. "That we might. We will have to see. And it is why I will need you to accompany me tomorrow morning. We are going to see if these monsters have killed a family of crofters."

The Red Friar put up his hand. "I am not prepared to exorcize the place. That is a job for a priest, in any case."

DeSteny began to pace. "It is," he agreed uncomfortably. "But you are the best we have here, with our two priests gone to the Holy Land." He frowned suddenly. "We could send to London, if we had time, to ask for an exorcist. But I fear we haven't time enough for that, not if it is as dire as it seems."

"Not if crofters are being killed," the Trinitarian agreed slowly. "I can bring the Host and Holy Water and Holy Oil. It should help, if there is any contamination of the place. And I can bury the dead safely." Burying was one of the chief tasks of monks, who were permitted to administer

Last Rites to the dying as well as tending to the burial of those who hoped for salvation.

"If they can be buried. The White Friars would not do it," said deSteny. He watched the Red Friar bless himself and utter a brief prayer to guard against evil.

"Did they? How? When that is their task?" He placed the tips of his thick fingers together. "How unlike the Carmelites to refuse."

"Will you bury them?" asked deSteny.

"If the dead can be buried, I will." The Trinitarian regarded deSteny with interest. "And if they cannot?"

"Then," said Hugh deSteny with a sigh, "we will need more powerful help than you or I can provide."

"Amen," said the Red Friar.

2.

How the traveling Scholars fared in Sherwood

They had left Wallingford's protecting stone embrace not long after dawn with the intention of reaching Saint Stephen's Priory by nightfall, a group of scholars and a mounted escort to guide and protect them on their journey; it was a precaution taken by most travelers and ordinarily it would have been sufficient to keep them from danger. But one of the horses had stepped on a rusted knot of iron and had to be led while his rider rode double with another one of the armed escort, slowing the progress of the train. So it was that they were still four miles distant from the Priory when the last of the light fled the forest, leaving them in darkness under the black canopy of leaves.

"I don't like it," whispered their leader, a young officer whose experience was largely confined to training and drill. He looked around at the dense shadows and blessed himself like a child afraid of the dark.

"Nor do I," said his sergeant, who was missing an eye and an ear, victims of the same Saracen arrow. He reigned in his horse and motioned to the party. "It will be hard-going from here to the Priory."

One of the men sneezed and crossed himself.

"How much further?" asked one of the scholars, whose command of the language of England was poor.

"Too far to go tonight," said the sergeant, as much for his young officer as for the scholars. He felt the trees loom above and around him like the tremendous hands of a cruel giant, hands that might close upon them at any instant.

"We should have left Maeslen and his horse to make their own way," grumbled one of the men-at-arms.

"Not on the Prince's business," countered the sergeant with an uneasy hitch to his shoulders. "And not in any company of mine. If we break our numbers up, we do nothing but insure our fall."

The young officer, whose name was Renard Widley, took up the same tune. "We will not separate. Our only strength is in our numbers." He did his best to sound as if he believed this.

"A wise plan," said Aylmer deGlisson, the oldest of the scholars, a greybeard of nearly fifty years who had studied in Paris and Rome and was said to know all there was to know. He had a Norman father and a Welsh mother and had spent more than ten years in the Holy Land. "To do otherwise would cause a double risk, in reducing our numbers and in alerting any outlaws that we have less force than when we started out."

"So you have not spent all your life with your nose in a book," said Orlan Royce, the most experienced guide of the escort.

"I would not be truly educated if I had," countered deGlisson. "The world instructs as much as the word does." He managed to smile at his own wit.

Sergeant Ballard made a quick gesture for silence. "We don't want to invite every miscreant from here to York to follow us, hoping to pick off our stragglers."

DeGlisson touched the saddlebags on his mule. "What outlaw would prey on books, do you think?"

"There are those who would hold you, deGlisson, and your fellows, for ransom. And they would get it, as well, knowing how the sentiments are at court, the Prince given so much to reading." Renard Widley could not hide the rancor of his words.

"Let's not bicker," suggested Sergeant Ballard, aware that they had more pressing trouble on their minds. "It's not for such as us to decide these things."

"Right you are," agreed Widley. "Let the courtiers tend to the court." He stared up at the branches above them. "There will be a little light for a short while longer. Perhaps we can find a glen or a shrine where we may make safe camp for the night?"

Privately Sergeant Ballard thought it was a desperate notion, but he could not come up with an acceptable alternative. He did his best to make the others want a better means of finding safety. "What say you, Royce? Is it best to press on?"

"In the forest it is always best to keep moving as long as you might," said the guide. "The trail is narrow but we can make it out. As long as there is a path to follow, it would be best to continue to travel. We might yet reach the Priory."

"How will you know the way?" asked deGlisson, without any sign of fear. "You cannot see the stars to show you."

Royce laughed once, a harsh sound in the deepening twilight. "I have been on all the paths of this forest since I was old enough to toddle. If I cannot find my way in Sherwood at night, you may nail my hide to the drawbridge." He rubbed the stubble on his chin and made his horse move forward. "These animals know the way better than any man does. They will take us safely to the Priory."

There was a moment of nervous quiet as the rest of the party considered what they had heard, though it was obvious that they had little option but to continue on.

It was as if night were muffling the travelers in engulfing

silence, for speech among the members of the party became desultory as the darkness increased, eventually ceasing completely, so that the clop of hooves and the jingle and squeak of tack were the only sounds made as they kept on. It made their passage eerie in the gathering darkness as the woods thickened around them. Somewhat later, the purling of a stream provided a descant to their travels. Then a rustle on the far side of the stream brought the little party to a halt.

"What was it?" whispered Widley. His nervousness communicated itself to his horse, which was sidling and sweating.

"An animal," said Royce, a shade too quickly, adding obscurely, "It is on the far side of the stream, thank God."

As much as four of the men in the party wanted—all for different reasons—to find out why that should be a welcome thing, no one said a word. After a long, hushed moment, they moved forward again, the horses picking their way with a finickiness born of fear, the men tense in their saddles.

Then there was a bridge ahead, where the stream took a turn to the east. Widley motioned to the party to stop again. He swung around in the saddle to make certain all the scholars were still with them. "Is it safe to cross, do you think?" he asked Royce when he was satisfied no one was missing.

"The bridge will hold us," said Royce. "It may not be much, but it is strong enough for our wants."

"And the animals?" Widley demanded, not trusting the evasion Royce offered. "What of them?"

Sergeant Ballard spoke up confidently. "The men-at-arms can deal with the animals. It is the least of our difficulties."

"Would the animals not cross the bridge, in any case?"

asked deGlisson, who was aching with fatigue. At his age, he needed his rest, and tonight promised him very little.

Royce mumbled an answer that no one dared to ask him to repeat.

"What if we rest here?" asked Penrod Lugenis, the best-known of the scholars. "Surely we can stand guard through the night and give the alarm if it is needed? If we keep a fire burning, we should be safe."

"The animals might cross over. Even with the horses hobbled, we could not soon enough be in the saddle to defend ourselves and our mounts," said Maeslen, who was still chagrined at having his horse go lame.

"What should we do, then?" asked Sergeant Ballard, hoping Widley would make up his mind quickly. It was a bad strategy to remain here dithering while the night dragged on. There had been warnings given about being abroad in the forest at night. It was said that worse than outlaws hunted the unwary. Creatures of damnation so terrible that the devils did not want them in Hell were rumored to prowl the heart of Sherwood.

"Let us keep on," said Widley, urging his horse on so abruptly that he nearly slammed into the rump of Royce's mount. Both horses squealed, the lead animal kicked, Widley's mare put her ears back, prepared to teach Royce's gelding some manners.

With a number of sharp jabs with spurs and loud, inventive oaths, the two men brought their horses under control, and turned them in the direction of the bridge.

Perhaps it was the hour, and perhaps it was a last remnant of resistance from her denied flight, but Widley's mare balked at crossing the stream. She planted her hooves and refused to budge in spite of the use Widley made of his spurs. No amount of tugging on her reins would get her to venture one step farther. Finally he moved her back so that the rest could pass, then dismounted, prepared to lead her across.

The mare neighed in protest, reared abruptly, and broke free of Widley's hold on her rein. In the next instant, she had whirled and bolted away, down the narrow trail.

"A thousand demons seize her!" Widley shouted after his escaping horse. Feeling himself a total fool, he looked apologetically at the rest of the party, all waiting for him on the west side of the stream.

"Get up with Royce," called out Sergeant Ballard. "Hurry!"

Ordinarily Widley would not have taken an order from the sergeant, but at present it struck him as the most sensible thing to do; he was glad he didn't have to make the final decision. Wishing his fleeing mare every hardship he could envision, he trudged forward, through the horses and mules and riders, making his way toward the sturdy brown gelding Royce rode, prepared to mount up behind. He had almost reached the animal when he noticed dark figures emerging from the mass of the forest, a number of men with longbows and quarterstaves. He was too surprised to be immediately frightened, and so he failed by two heartbeats to give the warning that might have saved his company.

At the head of the men was a tall, thin fellow with a mass of white hair, making him look like a wraith or malign spirit. He held a boar-spear in one hand and a short sword in the other. He approached the scholars and their escorts, unafraid though he was on foot. The first swipe of his sword bit deeply into the neck of Royce's gelding.

The horse screamed and his legs buckled, throwing Royce and Widley to the ground and causing chaos among the others. Horses panicked and tried to run, but the wood was too dense and the trail too narrow for this to happen, so the animals bucked and kicked and shouted as the dire men from out of the shadows closed in on them. No one riding was able to divide his attention between his mount and these sinister figures.

Aylmer deGlisson was tossed by his mule, and huddled under the thrashing legs of the other animals, his hands clapped to his head, his prayers lost in the cacophony around him. A hoof struck him in the ribs and he fell full-length on the ground, certain that he would be killed by the horses—hoping he would be killed by the horses.

And then the rest of the forest pack was upon them, as relentless as they were ravenous. They seized men-at-arms and scholars without hesitation, falling on them with the ruthlessness of the famished. The hot-copper scent of blood filled the air as the outlaws savaged throats for the rich, life-bearing stuff that welled and spouted there, drinking with a deepness that defied satiation. Those who were not attacked first were stupefied by what they saw, and lost precious time and with it any prayer of escape. More outlaws came to reap the carmine harvest their fellows had begun. They were without fear. Even when one of the attackers was all but run through with Maeslen's lance, he met his end with a desperate courage that bordered on eagerness. None of his companions came to his aid.

Now blood steamed in the night air, making a deadly fog around the carnage as the forest men fed. No rout of starving wolves had ever so ruthlessly plundered a hapless peasant family as these fell men pillaged the travelers.

As the last of line ran from his veins, Sergeant Ballard was grateful that there was no more light than the scattered moonbeams from above the trees. He did not want to see the ruin he knew was all around him: he could smell it, and that was enough to tell him that the predation was unspeakable. At least the Saracen arrow which had robbed him of his eye and ear had been honorably fired in battle. That was a cleaner loss than what was happening here. He was distantly aware of the figure of Penrod Lugenis being lifted onto the shoulders of one of the attackers, and he could find a trace of pity for the scholar. To be fodder for these beasts! He found it unbearable.

"Did any escape?" asked a voice that seemed to come from the bottom of a well.

"Only the lame horse, and it will not go far," answered the white-maned apparition who led the appalling band.

"Shall I go after it?" asked the first voice.

For an answer the leader gestured at the stream and gave a snort of contempt.

It was the last sound Sergeant Ballard ever heard.

3.

What deSteny found in the Forest

Unlike his men, Hugh deSteny bathed every morning, washing himself briskly in cold water. It was a habit he had picked up on Crusade and had not abandoned in spite of the odd looks he received from those who feared he had joined the followers of Mahamot, who were known to wash often, and who still desecrated the Holy Sepulchre, to the shame of all Christian chivalry. This morning was no different, and as he rubbed himself dry with a length of old linen, deSteny tried once more to prepare himself for what he feared lay ahead. Blocking the deep fright that rose in his mind, he did his best to concentrate on ordinary things. He had pulled on his leggings and tugged his acton over his head when he heard Nicholas at the door. "What is it?" he asked.

Nicholas entered without being bidden. "They are waiting for you in the courtyard, the men-at-arms and the warden. They are growing impatient. Also your clerk is in your study. He said you ordered him to see you away this morning. Why you should want him, I cannot guess. But he is there, nonetheless." He scowled in displeasure, making it abundantly clear that he thought he should be the one so distinguished and not the clerk. "It's not right, you taking him. I ought to go with you into the forest. You may need a page, or a messenger, not a scribbler."

"Your father would not like it if anything happened to

you and I cannot afford the blood-price. You are not going with me." DeSteny reached for his tunic of chain mail and bent down to slide his arms and head into it. Then he rose, letting the steel links settle over him of their own weight. It was a technique he had perfected while in the Holy Land when he had no one to serve him as squire: men of his position and rank did not often have squires to arm them under the best of circumstances, and the campaign in the Holy Land was hardly that. "I don't know how dangerous this will be, and you would be a hindrance in a fight."

"What fight?" demanded Nicholas. "You are going to look at dead crofters. The men say that outlaws came and slit their throats. You're taking men-at-arms. I would not be in any danger with you."

"Possibly not," said deSteny. "But if it came to a fight, you would be in the way, and that isn't desirable."

"What if I should ask Sir Gui to give me leave to go?" It was a blatant challenge, but deSteny was not willing to accept it.

"Sir Gui would think it very strange for you to want to examine a dead crofter, youngster. Sir Gui might hold it against you." That was the least of it, for he had often heard Sir Gui upbraid his Bailiffs and Sheriffs for devoting too much time to the foresters and crofters. "It would not gain you the favor you seek."

Nicholas pouted. "How am I going to advance if you hold me back this way? You never allow me to show my worth."

DeSteny slung his scabbard over his shoulder and fixed the band diagonally across his chest so that he could easily draw his sword over his right shoulder with his right hand; he was no belted knight, to carry his sword at his hip. As he reached for his helm, he signaled to his page. "There are more ways for you to advance than risking your life against outlaws, or through force of arms."

"They're all slower," complained the youth.

"But they're safer, and where's the use of advancement if you're in your grave?" said deSteny. "Come. Bring me my gauntlets."

Nicholas shrugged as he picked up the metal-studded leather gloves, fondling them with mingled respect and envy, longing naked on his young face. "How long do you think you'll be gone?"

"We should return before nightfall," said deSteny, leaving his chamber without ceremony. He was moving ahead of the page, going down the stone corridor toward the stairs. "If we are not back by noon tomorrow, a second party of men-at-arms will have to be sent to search for us. Be certain they have priests with them. Don't attempt to rescue us without soldiers to escort you, and don't separate in the forest. Simon has my instructions." He hastened down the stairs, going quickly in spite of the weight of the chain mail.

In the courtyard twelve men-at-arms stood with their horses, ready to ride, their mounts fresh and impatient to be off. The leader of the men was a scarred veteran of the wars against the Saracens, a man nearly forty with a marked limp and three fingers gone from his left hand. He nodded to deSteny and touched the edge of his chain-mail coif in a show of respect. "God give you good day, Sheriff."

"And you, Wroughton," said deSteny. He looked around. "There's Chilton, who will show us where we must go. Where is our Red Friar?"

"He's at prayers," said Wroughton in some disgust. "Getting his Holy Water and Holy Oil and all the rest of it."

"Good," said deSteny.

Chilton, already mounted on one of the two mules in the courtyard, regarded the men-at-arms uncertainly. "Yes. It is good."

DeSteny glanced from Chilton to Wroughton. "Pay attention to what he says," he recommended to the men-at-arms. "He has been where we are going, and he will guide us to the croft. Otherwise we may become lost in the forest."

"Why do you want to make such a fuss about dead crofters? Crofters die all the time, just like the rest of us," declared Wroughton, cramming his helmet onto his head and muffling the last of his remarks.

"Because they matter," said deSteny, knowing his point of view was shared by few others in his position. "And if they were killed unlawfully, we are obliged to avenge their deaths." He took a bit of pear from his wallet and held it out for his sorrel mare, smiling faintly as she ate it.

"You want to rid the forest of outlaws?" Wroughton asked and started to laugh. "Well might you hope to do so."

"If outlaws are all we must rid the forest of, then we may count ourselves most fortunate." There was a sharpness in deSteny's reprimand that caught the attention of the other men-at-arms as well as Wroughton's.

"Those who prey on the King's game are not only men," said Wroughton, beginning to look worried. "It isn't fitting for us to hunt boar and wolves and bear. That's for the King to order."

"That it is," said deSteny, and looked around for his clerk. "Simon," he called out to the lean-faced Jew who kept his records for him. "Be sure that if we do not return, the message I wrote out last night is delivered to the Prince as fast as courier can reach him. Send the courier with an armed escort, to be certain he arrives at Windsor." He pulled his helmet into place and adjusted the strap under his chin.

"I will," said Simon, bowing with more respect than deSteny's rank deserved.

"Yes. I know you will," said deSteny before he swung into the saddle. "And keep that boy Nicholas out of my things. I don't want to come back to disorder." He indicated the page with a ponderous nod. "If he will not learn to read, he is not permitted to tamper with anything on my writing table."

"As you wish," said Simon, a bit more nervously, for it was known that deSteny's tolerance of Jews did not extend itself to his men. "I will comply with your orders, on my oath."

One of the men-at-arms spat.

"It is my order, and he is my clerk," said deSteny. He was about to add something more when he saw the Trinitarian friar come bustling out of the side door into the courtyard, a silver pyx clutched in his hand.

"I regret arriving late, Sheriff," he said hurriedly to deSteny with a quick, short bow. He held up the pyx, explaining, "I wanted to be fully prepared. In case we must tend to the crofters' burial."

"I am pleased you are so, for we may need all you have, and more," said deSteny. "It is what I asked of you." He indicated the second mule. "You know how to sit one of these animals, don't you?"

"I've done it before," said the monk with a resigned air. "You lead the way and I'll strive to keep up." He tugged himself into the saddle, placing the pyx ahead of him on the high pommel. "God bless our endeavors today," he declared, crossing himself and waiting while the men-at-arms did the same.

The last to comply was Hugh deSteny. "If we are ready, then it is time to go," he said, rising in his stirrups so that he could turn in the tall saddle. "All right, men. Single file, at the trot. That includes you, Friar," he called out, then gave the order to the warder to open the gates for them.

Wroughton raised his hand to bring his men up behind him as the little party moved through the gates of Nottingham Castle, across the moat, and through the town toward the outer walls.

The gates yawned open to the encouraging cheers of the artisans and their apprentices who maintained shops near the gates as the Sheriff and the men-at-arms sallied forth to meet the dangers of Sherwood Forest that lay ahead of them, a vast green wilderness that stretched across the middle of England, from the fen country in the east to the Welsh mountains in the west, north to the city of York and south to Huntingdon and Cambridge. Few roads went through it, and few towns other than Nottingham and Lincoln flourished within its borders, for the forest held sway in the center of the island as no armed force or religious company could. The heart of Sherwood was so dense that it was said no sunlight reached it for months on end. Fortresses, castles, and monasteries were scattered through it, isolated and precarious, as well as crofts and hamlets, but for the most part, it was the realm of wild animals and outlaws.

"Watch carefully. We do not want to be distracted," deSteny ordered as he led the way into the first ranks of the trees and the speckled, twinkling light. The shadows were long around them with the rising sun at their backs so that they rode in their own darkness. Their passing silenced the call of birds and the rustle of animals in the undergrowth, and only the clatter of their mounts' hooves and equipment gave sound to the morning as they stormed the great, green stronghold.

They kept to the main road for nearly three leagues, and

then Chilton indicated a narrow track turning to the northwest, toward the deeper part of the forest. "Down that way, a distance." He trembled as he said it. "You will have to ride single file. The track is poorly cut."

The men-at-arms slowed their horses from a jog to a walk, and left the main road for the path leading to the crofters' hut.

"It is not far ahead," Chilton was pale now, and he started at every noise. "We will come to the hut before we reach the hamlet." He clung to the reins as if the leather would protect him.

"Is it on the path?" asked deSteny.

"No, just off, a furlong or so. The track is marked if you know to watch for it." He looked around at the deep gloom under the green canopy and felt himself a stranger in the place, though he had been warden here for more than fifteen years. Now he was an intruder, and he strove not to shiver. "I will tell you when to turn."

"I hope the track is no narrower than this, and no more wild than now," said Wroughton, half in jest, half in earnest. "These branches are hazard enough. They could sweep a reckless man out of the saddle. Not one of us would want to be lost here on foot." He glanced uneasily toward the end of their little group to where the Trinitarian rode, his face ruddy with the effort of keeping his recalcitrant mule moving at the same pace as the rest.

There was a rustle and snap of breaking branches, and then a doe with two half-grown fawns at her heels bounded effortlessly across their path, vanishing noisily into the undergrowth on the other side of the path. Four of the horses brought their heads up in alarm, one of them whinnying uneasily. "They're nervous," said Wroughton, patting the neck of his big bay gelding as the horse sidled.

"They're sensing something other than deer," said deSteny. He had had the crawly feeling of being watched since they rode into the woods. He guessed it was useless to look for the watchers, for they would not be readily found.

Finally, half a league or so further on, Chilton pointed to the left. "There's the way to the croft, that little path there; you can see it just beyond the fallen beech tree," he announced in a cracked voice, and swung the head of his mule in that direction. "It is not far now. The track to the croft isn't long. The buildings are on the far side of the dell." His relief was apparent, and deSteny wished he knew why.

The path was mottled with sunlight and well-kept, the underbrush nibbled back by the crofters' two nanny goats who provided milk for cheese. These, along with a dozen pigs turned out in a fenced area to eat the acorns and new shoots under the oaks, constituted the entire wealth of the crofters, who had lived in a two-room tie-beam timber house with a small kitchen-and-creamery on the far side of the narrow court centered on a well. For a crofter, it was a prosperous establishment, one that many others might begrudge the holder.

DeSteny swung out of the saddle as the party drew up in the little courtyard. "We might as well water the horses and mules while we have the chance." He removed his helmet and held his mare's reins as he looked around the croft. Empty hardly more than two days, it already had that vacant, neglected look of abandoned places, and it made deSteny ill-at-ease to be here; in a year it would be overgrown and crumbling. Thrusting his worst fears out of his mind, he made himself attend to the task at hand, taking a brisk tone to ask Chilton, "Where did you find the bodies?"

"In . . . in there." The warden was still on his mule, as if he expected he would need to escape at any moment.

"In the house." DeSteny pointed to the door, which stood ajar. "Inside, not out."

Chilton nodded.

Wroughton was already drawing a bucket up from the well, and motioning to his men to dismount. "Horses first, then you," he reminded the men-at-arms as the bucket came into view. "Men stand thirst better than their mounts."

DeSteny pulled off one gauntlet and dipped his hand into the bucket, drawing out a cupped-handful of water that he held under his mare's nose, and smiled as she licked his palm eagerly with her soft tongue. When she had got all the water, he filled his hand again and gave her more.

"You spoil that mare," Wroughton chided him. "You treat her like another soldier. She's just a horse."

"She has taken good care of me. I will take good care of her." He knew his men regarded his fondness for his mare as one more in a long list of eccentricities.

"How many were there? Bodies, I mean," asked the Red Friar as he got off his cantankerous mule, taking care to hold the pyx protectively.

"Six." Chilton ticked them off on his fingers, using his thumb twice. "The man, his woman, three children, and an old woman, probably the man's mother, though she may be an older sister or an aunt."

"And no sign of a fight," prompted deSteny. "Nothing is overturned or disturbed, and not one of them has weapons in hand."

"No, they haven't—none that I noticed," Chilton answered, dismounting reluctantly. "Nothing was disturbed. The furniture was not in disorder. I hauled the corpses away in their cart. I used the goats to pull it."

"Did you know the crofter?" asked deSteny, realizing he

34

should have inquired some time before now.

"I . . . had met him a time or two," Chilton lied clumsily.

DeSteny let this pass. "And you took the bodies to the White Friars in the hamlet nearby."

"Yes, to Chefford," he answered, becoming fearful again. "The White Friars have a chapel there, at their friary."

"I know," said deSteny gently, reminding the warden he was familiar with the area he was called upon to administer.

"Then you will know the way to the hamlet," said Chilton, glancing around in distress.

"I suppose so. It is north of here, as I recall." He motioned to his men. "Wroughton, you stay out here. The rest of you, come with me. You too, Red Friar."

The crofters' house was in fairly good repair, the walls not too sooty, and there were three big pots fronting the hearth, attesting to the success the family had enjoyed. There was a roll of rough blankets near the hearth that would serve one of the household, probably the old woman, as a bed at night. A sturdy table and four open-backed chairs stood in the center of the larger of the two rooms, another sign of prosperity, as was the long-handled rendering pan which the crofters used to prepare tallow. Half a dozen two-tined hayforks hung on the wall near the door, and beneath them, a large, square, brass-bound chest stood conspicuously locked.

"They can't have been thieves. They would have carried that off," said Hamlin, the most promising of the men-at-arms.

"Very likely," said deSteny, his spine feeling chilly as he looked around the room again. "Let us go into the other room." He nodded toward the length of woven cloth that separated the two rooms.

It was divided into two levels, with a ladder leading to the loft where the children slept. There were piles of blankets to show where the crofter and his woman slept. Another chest held their few clothes.

"Chilton," said deSteny in a flat voice. "Where were the bodies?"

"In the main room, all but the youngest child, who was in the creamery, turning the cheeses, or so I guessed," the warden answered. "The man and his wife were laid across the table; the old woman was on the floor, in a heap, like cast-off rags. The other two children were in the chairs, bent backward." He crossed himself, looking unhappily at the Red Friar. "There is no blood to mark the places. They hadn't any left."

The Red Friar opened his pyx and took out the Host, which he broke and placed on the center of the table, murmuring a prayer in bad Latin.

"This should not take long," said deSteny, and signaled his men to leave the house. "Make sure you bless the hearth and the door, and any other entrance to the place, including the windows," he added to the Trinitarian.

"Certainly," said the monk, a little huffily at having his work explained to him. "I will not take long."

The courtyard was not light enough to ease the sinking spirits of the men-at-arms. Hamlin spoke for them all when he said, "So it isn't outlaws who killed them."

"It would seem not," said deSteny, watching the Red Friar pause in the doorway to make the sign of the cross in Holy Water on the thick planks, reciting prayers while he did.

"What about the pigs?" asked the warden. "What's to be done with them?"

"Have them rounded up and turned over to Sir Gui, as

death-taxes—that will save us a great deal of trouble," answered deSteny, aware of how avaricious Sir Gui could become over such matters. "So that any relatives will not have to forfeit the holding to pay them." As he said his, he thought it unlikely that anyone would want to keep this croft again, not after such deaths the crofters had suffered.

"Do we go to Chefford?" asked the warden, a bit too hastily. There was sweat on his brow and he was breathing as if he had just run two leagues over rough ground. He was holding the mule's stirrup as if the animal might bolt without him.

"I suppose it would be wise," said deSteny. "We must find out if the bodies were buried, and where." He looked around the courtyard again. "We don't want to be abroad late in the day, not this day."

"No, we do not," said the Red Friar with unmonk-like alacrity. He clutched the pyx to his chest and went to mount his mule.

4.

How the Monks received the Bodies

Like most Orders of monks, the Carmelites were known by the color of their habits: White Friars, as the Trinitarians were Red Friars, the Dominicans Black Friars, the Austins and Franciscans Grey Friars, the Order of the Blessed Mary Pied Friars, the Victorines Blue Friars. The abbot who met deSteny and his men at the chapel door to Chefford tossed back his white hood and regarded the armed men with disapproval.

"And what," he asked by way of opening when deSteny had dismounted and removed his helmet to show his peaceful intentions, "does the Sheriff of Nottingham want with me?"

DeSteny did not rise to the challenge. He tucked his helmet under his arm and met the abbot's stare levelly. "My warden tells me that you refused to bury a family he brought to you two days ago."

"That I did," said the abbot with a sharp glance at Chilton. "Though why he should report it to you, I do not know."

"He reported it to me because he is sworn so to do, and well you do know it, Regis de Bonpont," deSteny replied, using the abbot's full name deliberately to remind the man of worldly obligations. "He is mindful of his duties, though it seems you are lax in them. He would have to tell me if outlaws had robbed a crofter, as well, or killed deer without the Prince's warrant, or taken money from your chapel."

"The dead had no blood left in them," said the abbot bluntly. "I am certain that they would contaminate consecrated ground."

"Though you have the task of burying the dead," deSteny reminded him. "It is your service to God, in your Order."

"True enough. But what if they are not truly dead? It would be a sin to bury such as were not dead." The abbot was pleased to see the distress in the faces of the men-at-arms.

"It may trouble you," said the Trinitarian, urging his mule up to the front of the line, "but if you will show me where the bodies are, I will try to lay them to rest."

The intense rivalry between monastic Orders flared as Carmelite and Trinitarian faced each other. At last the abbot indicated the smaller of the hamlet's two gates, the one facing the stream that gave the place its name: Chefford meant goat-crossing. "They were put to lie there. If you want them guarded, you must do it yourself. If the bodies are still there and uneaten, you may attempt to put them in their graves, face down, Red Friar."

"Well enough," said deSteny for them all. "How were the bodies left?"

"With woven mats around them. We showed them that charity, little as they deserved it." He held up his hand to bless deSteny's men, but stopped before he could complete the gesture. "What will you do? We will not allow the bodies back inside the gates."

DeSteny did his best to contain his ire, though his frown was portentous. "No, you would not, would you?" He rocked back on his heels and considered what was best to do. "Very well, if we find enough to bury, we will put them beyond the walls, if that will satisfy you."

"Yes. It must," said the Carmelite abbot.

The Red Friar stared hard at the abbot of the White Friars. "You are supposed to do this work."

"For those who die in Grace, or through misadventure where Grace can be hoped for," said the abbot sternly. "These were neither of those things. There was only damnation in their ends."

"Well," said the Red Friar with a meaningful tap on his silver pyx. "God may see it otherwise."

The Carmelite shrugged and drew his hood up. "It is time for mid-day prayers," he said, and without any further remark withdrew into his chapel.

"What do you think?" asked deSteny as he remounted his sorrel mare. "Do you want to go through with this?"

"I want to put the Devil to rest, if I can. I must do all I can," said the Red Friar. "And I want these miserable corpses to be at peace in Christ. I will do whatever I must to bring those two things about."

"Very wise," said deSteny as he saw Wroughton and his men cross themselves for protection. He had long since given up such petitions. "You lead the way to where you left the bodies," he ordered Chilton. "If you can find the place."

With most of the people of the hamlet in the field, Chefford looked deserted, though two spotted dogs roamed the center of the hamlet and barked as deSteny and his men passed by. In response to this alarm, a woman put her head out of the windows of one of the larger houses and watched them attentively, saying nothing. From behind her, within the house, a baby began to cry loudly.

"Is this the gate?" deSteny asked as Chilton pulled his mule up in front of the double doors in the hamlet's stockade.

"It is," said Chilton, clearly reluctant to pass through it. "They should be on the other side, laid out next to the wall."

"Then let's go through," deSteny said, and signaled Wroughton to dismount and open the gate.

As they passed through the opening, the Red Friar said, "On a river like this, they could moat the hamlet easily."

"Yes," said deSteny. "It would mean more protection, and from more dangers than outlaws."

Chilton pointed along the base of the wall to rolled reed mats. "There they are," he said, sounding relieved.

DeSteny halted the party. "Best to get to work, then," he said with a trace of reluctance, and dismounted again, securing the reins to one of a group of rings set in the wall. He approached the reed mats carefully, not wanting to disturb any animal that might have come to feed on the flesh of the dead, or something worse. Nearing the first of them, he heard the distinct scuttle of rats, and averted his eyes as a dozen dark, furry shapes scurried away from the more distant rolls. Carefully he leaned down and flipped back the end of the mat. He stared at what he found. "Empty," he said quietly, then directed his attention to Chilton. "Who lay here? Do you remember?"

The warden was pale and he stammered when he answered. "Th-the man. That was the crofter."

"Ah," said deSteny. He motioned to the Red Friar. "Do something, will you?"

"I will put Holy Water on the mat," he said, though there was little conviction in his voice that suggested he thought this would accomplish anything.

"Good." DeSteny continued along to the next mat—it, too, was empty.

"The mother, the old woman," said Chilton, his hands shaking visibly on the reins.

"And this one?" asked deSteny, finding the third roll untenanted. "Who was put here?"

"His woman. The oldest child is next, and then the younger two." Fear had taken a strong grip on the warden and he squirmed in the saddle, communicating his unrest to the mule he rode.

"Empty. Not even bones. They are gone," said deSteny when he reached the next roll. "What were the rats feeding on, if these are empty?" He found the answer in the last two mats. The younger children lay there, the voracity of the rats and the first signs of decay already changing them into alien creatures. "Friar, tend to them."

The Red Friar complied with alacrity, hurrying to anoint them and pray for their souls. When he was done, he got to his feet. "They'll have to be buried in water, I fear, in order to ensure protection for them, and us."

"I suppose you're right," said deSteny, who had been thinking the same thing. "We will have to carry them to a faster, deeper river."

The men-at-arms were not pleased to hear this. "We can bury them here, facing down, with hawthorn in their graves," one of them said.

"It might not be enough," said deSteny, with unhappy memories mastering his careful thoughts.

"What about their heads?" asked the Red Friar reluctantly. "We should cut them off, and then they will be still in their graves."

DeSteny sighed heavily. "Yes. We could do that."

"Then we ought to," said Wroughton. "The horses will not tolerate carrying rotten bodies."

The Red Friar crossed himself. "I will use the sword, if you like." He had a firm jaw that just now was clamped to granite determination.

"I would not want to do it," said deSteny. "But if it must be done, then—"

"It is necessary," said Wroughton, his voice rising. "With the father and mothers gone, and the oldest child. And no sign of them. They cannot be left this way." He looked around as if he expected the early afternoon shadows to stretch out and surround them.

There was a silence between them all, as massive as the walls of Windsor.

Then the Red Friar bent down and rolled the first of the bodies out onto the ground. He held out his hand to deSteny. "Your sword."

Slowly deSteny pulled it from the sheath over his shoulder, and handed it to the Red Friar. "Go ahead," he told the monk, and turned away so he would not have to watch the children being decapitated. He heard the whistle of the sword and the solid thunk as it severed flesh and bone.

"This one can be buried now, face down," said the Red Friar, addressing deSteny. "I've done all that I can."

"You heard him. Make two graves," said deSteny. He knew his men thought him faint-hearted for not watching the friar cut the head off the child, but he had seen—and done—more than his share of that in the Holy Land. He watched as Chilton handed a shovel hanging on the side of the wall to Wroughton, indicating the area where the graves were to be dug.

"This isn't my work," Wroughton protested, not wanting to be stuck with the menial task of digging.

"I'll do it," said deSteny, glad to be doing something. He held out his hand for the shovel and set to work, his chain-mail weighing on him as he labored. By the time he had made a grave big enough and deep enough for the first child, the Red Friar had the second ready, and was reciting prayers over the bodies.

"Put them both in the same hole," Wroughton recommended, squinting up at the sky. "Otherwise we'll be in the forest come sunset."

This timely warning alerted deSteny as nothing else could. He held out his hand to Chilton, to be helped out of the grave, then gave a long, steady look at the Red Friar. "What do you advise, Brother?"

"I think it would be best to be away from here. The men are right. If we linger here we face the chance of being caught in the forest when the sun goes down." The Red Friar crossed himself and looked at his pyx. "I could anoint all of you for the journey. That might give us a little security."

"If we are hunted by what I fear most," said deSteny, "we should avail ourselves of everything that might guard us from harm, even if it means using methods the Church would not endorse." He glanced down at the two children's bodies. "Tend to them."

The Red Friar got on his knees and set the two pathetic corpses in the grave side by side, turned so that they lay prone and not supine, their heads set under their feet, also facing down. After sprinkling Holy Water on the wretched bodies, he made the sign of the cross over them and rose to let deSteny cover them with earth.

"What do you think? Are they at rest?" deSteny asked the Red Friar as he hurried to complete his work.

"They are, if God is good," said the Trinitarian, with emphasis on "they." He indicated the mats. "But regarding the rest of the family, I do not think so, not after—" He gave deSteny his sword again, the blade wiped clean.

"Nor I," agreed deSteny as he slipped the weapon across

his shoulder and into the scabbard. "It troubles me." He resumed his work with the shovel.

The Red Friar crossed himself. "Any sensible man would be troubled, given what has happened."

"Truly," said deSteny, and shaded his eyes to look at the angle of the sun. "We will leave not a moment too soon." He shoveled the last of the earth on top of the children. "I have heard nothing of missing travelers, not recently."

"Nor have I. But if they are missing, it may be that there has been none to look for them, and anyone who has searched—"

"Might suffer the same fate as the ones searched for; yes, he might," deSteny finished for the Red Friar.

"Lamentably," said the Red Friar.

DeSteny put the shovel back on the wall. "We can leave now."

"Not quite yet," said the Red Friar, opening the pyx again and taking the time to mark the cross with the Host on the foreheads of each of the company. That done, he nodded to deSteny and scrambled onto his mule.

Last of all, deSteny mounted his sorrel mare. "For Nottingham," he said, and set off along the worn track.

5.

How deSteny returned to Nottingham

By the time the Sheriff's party reached the main road, Sherwood was darkening, the long shadows making the undergrowth denser than it was, and turning the canopy of beech and oak to a cloaking mass more menacing than storm clouds. With the fading of the day came a wind, blowing as if to extinguish the last of the light; it was cold and cutting, touching the men to the marrow, leaving them worn out with shivering. The undergrowth rustled and the branches flailed. In addition, the men were growing increasingly uneasy, and their mounts shared their distress, shying at noises and balking at shadows more often than they usually did. A fox darting in a thicket or the whistle of a falcon overhead made horses and riders start in alarm, and the mules became more fractious.

"I don't like this," muttered Wroughton as he watched a badger scurry out of their way. "It's too late. We should have left Chefford sooner. It will be dusk by the time we are out of the forest."

"Possibly," said deSteny. "But we must keep on, or we will have to camp for the night." His sorrel mare was restive, and he did his best to calm her. It would not do to have her bolt here in the forest.

"How far is it to Nottingham?" asked the Red Friar from his place at the rear. "We can't have missed the turning, can we?"

"No more than a league or so," said Chilton in the lead, his words sounding harsh. "We will be at the edge of the trees shortly."

"And not a moment too soon. Look at the sky," said Wroughton with feeling, nodding once toward the fading sunset streamers in the clouds over the trees. He crossed himself and pressed his legs into his horse's sides. The horse walked faster.

The other men-at-arms were doing the same thing, urging their horses to pick up speed to hasten their departure from the encroaching darkness. DeSteny lifted his hand to try to hold them back, for he feared that once their flight began, they would not be easily stopped, and would end in a rout. His efforts were useless, for his mare had caught the apprehension of the others around her and was anxious to get out of the trees as the most skittish of the men. When deSteny tried to hold her in, she began to sweat and tremble, pulling on the rein and tossing her head.

At the rear of the group the Red Friar's mule adamantly refused to walk any faster no matter what the monk did to urge him on. Gradually the distance between the men-at-arms and the Trinitarian increased so he was a length, then two, then five behind the rest. When a bend in the road was reached, the party from Nottingham vanished altogether, and it seemed to the Red Friar that the only sound in all of Sherwood Forest was the determined plod of his mule's hooves.

How dark it had become! Vast shadows loomed around him, devouring the last of the daylight. The Red Friar clutched the pyx more tightly, trying to take confidence from the presence of the sacred article. He muttered part of a Psalm but stopped when he heard the tremor in his voice. Then he tried to make his mule walk faster and attempted to shout to the Sheriff and his men, only to discover his throat was too dry and too tight to do more than croak. In growing terror he began to recite his prayers: *"Salva me, Domine, de morte et daemonae. Libera me de ira . . . iram? Sequestra me de . . ."* He could not keep the Latin phrases in his mind, though he tried over and over, unable to recall the rest of the petition no matter how he tried. *"Salva me de morte in aeternam . . . aeternam."*

The mule continued to pick his way along the track in stolid rhythm, untroubled that the rest so far out-distanced them. Then he stopped, his long ears turning, his head coming up, nostrils flaring as his back went rigid. His neck craned out, tense, and sweat darkened his flanks. He gave a sudden, terrified bray, bucked and reared to rid himself of the weight of the Red Friar, then bolted at a jarring, uneven canter, leaving the Trinitarian lying on the ground, stunned, the pyx fallen from his grip.

Dazed as he was, the Red Friar realized the forest was alive—alive and malign. He tried to summon his strength to rise, to find the pyx, to pray, for from the deep, dusk-green shadows there emerged the figures of men, half a dozen of them, as if their bodies were being born directly from the trees. Each man was holding weapons, each baring fangs more ghastly than their longbows, cross-bows, knives, and swords.

Two of them approached the Red Friar, taking care to avoid the pyx where it lay on the ground, its silver top open and the last of its precious contents degraded and scattered, useless to anyone.

"Too bad," said the nearest of the figures, with a lupine grin.

The Red Friar could not summon up the fortitude to cross himself, and his soul filled with anguish.

"Never tasted a monk's blood before," his tormentor went on. "Do you think I'll like it? Or will it be too holy for the likes of me?" he asked the Red Friar with counterfeit sweetness as he knelt down.

A sharp command interrupted him. "Not yet, Will. He's mine by right." One of the shadow-men stepped forward, a tall, arresting figure with a mane of white hair and eyes that shone like a wild animal's, flashing red instead of gold. His lips curled back in a ferocious smile. "Welcome to Sherwood, Trinitarian," he said in bad Norman French. "Good of you to join us. And you will join us."

The rest of the band chuckled at this, though to the Red Friar, it sounded more like a growl than a chuckle.

"*Libera me de morte, Domine. Salva me!*" the monk cried aloud, suddenly finding his voice at last.

"Don't bother God with that. Let us answer your prayers. We'll save you from eternal death. Won't we?" And with that he reached down and seized the front of the Red Friar's habit, plucking him to his feet as easily as if he were lifting a lamb, and not a sturdy, grown man. "You will be one of us now, in our damnable life everlasting. Rise from the dead to live among us." There was no mercy in this creature, only cruelty and encompassing pride. He was amusing himself with his prey.

The Red Friar struggled futilely, battling the cold dread rising within him as much as he feared the shadow-clad, white-haired demon who glared balefully at him. He tried to call on God, but the words failed him, and his soul ached. His captor apparently sensed the Red Friar's emotions, for he winked before bending his head to sink his teeth deep into the monk's neck, attaching himself there so that none of the monk's blood would be wasted. The Trinitarian gave a single, despairing howl as he felt the fangs pierce his flesh, then went slack in the monster's arms, all resistance gone.

Around them, the grinning men watched in envious, respectful silence as their leader made his kill.

Far ahead on the trail, deSteny turned in the saddle at the appalling cry that came eerily through the trees, as if journeying ahead of the wind. His mare tugged against his hands and whickered her distress. The others were momentarily transfixed by the hideous wail, and looked to deSteny for reassurance.

Then the monk's mule, lathered and panicked, hurtled past them and set all the rest of the party careering out of the woods in horrified disorder, the Trinitarian's mule still well in the lead. They rushed past the cluster of wood-cutters' huts at the edge of the trees, struggling to pull in their mounts by the time they reached the gates of Nottingham. One of the men managed to catch the Red Friar's mule and hold its reins. Exhausted now, the mule did not protest.

"Where's the monk?" asked Chilton, averting his eyes from the panting, riderless mule.

"Back there," said Wroughton, cocking his head in the direction of the forest. "He dropped behind a while ago."

Hamlin crossed himself. "In the forest? Still?"

Chilton went white about the mouth. "But—"

"He has the pyx," said one of the men-at-arms. "It will protect him."

The rest made reassuring, guilty mutters, except for deSteny, who had turned his sorrel mare back in the direction of Sherwood, and was now listening intently.

"What is it?" asked Chilton, who had also noticed something odd about the place. "Do you see—?"

"I don't know," deSteny admitted as he fought the urge to go back into the forest in what he already knew would be a foolish and futile effort to save the Trinitarian. Reluctantly, he turned away from the trees and started toward the town.

The gatekeeper appeared at the portcullis to identify them and let them into Nottingham. He looked at deSteny and the men with him and bit back the complaints he had been about to heap on them. He noticed that the monk who had gone with them had not returned, an ill omen most certainly. Whatever they had encountered in Sherwood Forest had left them profoundly shaken, and they would not welcome his animadversions at this time, as appropriate as they might be, and richly deserved as well. So he stood aside and let them go by him, then tugged the gates closed and set the massive bolt back in place with unaccustomed alacrity, his spryness coming from a sharp prickle of horror that raised the hair on his arms and the back of his neck. Something was out there that must, at any cost, be kept out. He had the conviction that he had to be quick getting the gate shut, or place all of Nottingham in grave danger, and as much as he wanted to take pride in what he did, all he experienced was bone-melting relief.

As they clattered up the high street, the men-at-arms began to look askance at what they had done, and the things they had seen that day. Inside the walls of the town, it was hard to believe that so much evil could lurk nearby.

"Do you think we have to confess this?" asked Wroughton as they reached Nottingham Castle.

DeSteny did not realize at first that Wroughton was talking to him, so lost was he in his own ruminations. He shook himself and said, "Confess? To fearing the Devil and his servants? What is the sin in that?" As he spoke, he could not rid himself of the chagrin he now felt at his lack of courage.

"But the Red Friar is still—" Chilton began, striking to

the heart of deSteny's self-recriminations.

"He knew what the risks were, and he undertook to face them, according to his vows," said deSteny more loudly than was necessarily. He looked toward the moat of the castle and the watch-post where the Marshal and his Guards kept their posts. He signaled to Sir Humphrey to lower the draw-bridge for them, and waited for the first clank of the chain. Suddenly he wanted very much to be back in his own quarters, with the consolation of his seventeen books to take away the humiliating sense of defeat that clung to him like an odor. His head ached and his muscles felt knotted. His appetite had deserted him. He did not want to think of food, not after this day.

"Do you think the Red Friar will be all right? The outlaws won't want to harm him, will they? Not a man in Orders? It's not as if he would do them harm, is it?" asked Wroughton nervously as the draw-bridge began its ponderous descent. "I mean, being a Brother, and all, he'll know what to do, won't he? To protect himself from . . . them. He is a monk. He'll be safe—won't he?"

DeSteny could only look at him.

Wroughton turned way from deSteny's gaze, mumbling, "No, I suppose not." He fell silent as the draw-bridge completed its descent and they prepared to enter the castle. "What are you going to tell Sir Humphrey?"

"That we investigated the murder of a family of crofters," said deSteny brusquely, reminding himself that it was true. "We did our best to see the bodies received proper burial."

"And will that satisfy him?" Wroughton asked, not willing to admit how badly shaken he was. "He may want to know more."

"Then he will have to ask someone other than me," said

deSteny, his voice sounding far away even to his own ears.

"But will he accept what you tell him?" Wroughton persisted, as if afraid he would be held accountable for what happened in Sherwood.

"Perforce. I am still Sheriff," deSteny answered abruptly before he got out of the saddle, moving as if every joint ached. The trouble, he knew, was not in his sinews or bones, but something far deeper, something he thought was forsaken long ago in the abattoir of the Holy Land.

6.

What Sir Humphrey learned

Sir Humphrey looked at the bedraggled company of ragged men who straggled up to the watch-post, their faces drawn with fatigue, their bodies moving as if against heavy weights, their garments in tatters, blood marking their footsteps. They were an odd sight for mid-morning on a fasting day, when most of the town bustled with preparations for Market Day, three days hence. The townspeople averted their eyes from the newcomers, crossing themselves to preserve themselves from whatever had happened to these unfortunate men. The most senior member of this group was all but carried between two of the younger men. There were fifteen of them in all, and all carried swords thrust through their belts, showing rusty stain of recent use.

"Let them in," Sir Humphrey ordered his lieutenant, the young Gawain deBracy. "They are not dangerous to us. They need our help, by the look of them. It is our duty to aid them—we are Christians, after all."

The young man-at-arms shouted to those manning the narrow gate of the watch-post, just at the edge of the moat that separated Nottingham Castle from the town itself. The wooden gate creaked open, and the first of the men staggered through, and all but collapsed as he came to a halt.

With a quickness rare in a man of his age and portliness, Sir Humphrey came down the stairs from his observation post. He would have to explain about these men before questions could be asked, and he would have to know what calamity had befallen them in order to accommodate their needs to his. As Marshal of the Castle and the Town, he would be held responsible for their safety. When such pathetic men as these arrived in Nottingham, he felt moved to act promptly so that he could not be faulted by Sir Gui, or the more demanding Hugh deSteny, or made to take the blame that these men had come to grief. He went up to the nearest of the men and addressed him with more urgency than respect. "Who are you and what happened to you?"

The nearest man had a great bruise on the side of his face as if he had been struck with a club. He could only shake his head and point to the man next to him, whose hands were scraped and grotesquely swollen. "We were set upon by outlaws."

"In the forest," finished Sir Humphrey. "How recently?"

"Last night, as we were making camp in the clearing with the shrine to Our Lady of Perpetual Prayer. You know the one?"

"To the south, six or seven leagues," said Sir Humphrey, impatient to hear more. "How did it happen?"

The wounded man shook his head as he tried to bring himself to speak. Finally he marshaled his thoughts and said, "I don't know how it began. First there was no one, and then a dozen men came out of the trees, like shadows at the start, and then . . . worse than wolves." He crossed himself.

The man beside him with the injured face began to weep, keeping his jaw tightly clenched.

Sir Humphrey could see now that these men's clothes had been of good quality and he began to suspect that they were merchants traveling together for protection. He would not be able to dismiss their troubles as minor or unimportant. He would be expected to account for their misfortune, since he was supposed to keep such things from happening at all. He mumbled a concerned phrase or two and passed on to one of the less obviously hurt. "You were set upon by outlaws last night. Will you tell me how it came about?"

The man, whose eyes were dazed in a face grey with exhaustion, turned to Sir Humphrey. "They were demons, demons and devil, not any outlaws I have ever known. They were not interested in our goods, though they took them and our mules quickly enough. Our lives were forfeit, not our merchandise. They wanted only to have us. Us! Nothing else mattered!" He trembled and moved toward the wall as if needing something to hold him up.

Sir Humphrey followed after him. "What did your mules have? What were you carrying?"

Distantly the man answered, "Cloth, for the most part. Cloth and thread. And hides for shoemakers." He made no complaint of their loss, which struck Sir Humphrey as odd, for merchants were known to wax irate at the deprivation of a single item of trade, not matter how small or unimportant. "It was hideous. Those men. They attacked us as if they would kill us." Without warning he fell to the ground and lay there, twitching.

Aghast, Sir Humphrey stood over the man, uncertain of what to do, fearing that the merchant had taken madness from his attackers and was now dangerous to everyone near him. He bellowed to his men to tend to the fallen merchant and turned to one of the others, a meaty youth with rings on his fingers. "What about the outlaws? Did you notice anything about them? How were they armed? How many of them were there? Didn't you have men-at-arms to escort you?"

"We had two," said the young man in a pain-roughened voice. He was favoring his right leg and there was blood on his clothing. "They were cut down first. And they fell quickly. These outlaws knew what they were about. No one could have prevailed against them. No one. They came after the men-at-arms, four or five of the outlaws to each man. The men-at-arms had no chance to defend themselves before they were . . ." His face went ashen. "They were gutted, like deer or sheep. They had set aside their mail, you see, and had only their actons. Any sword could go through an acton." He crossed himself. "I never want to set forth in Sherwood Forest again. Once I return home to London, I will not travel the Great North Road for as long as I live."

Sir Humphrey believed him, and thought it strange that a merchant would make such a vow when he depended upon travel to make his trading worthwhile. He left the young man and sought out another of the merchants, a man nearer his own age and looking marginally less ramshackle than the others. "What can you tell me about the outlaws?" he asked, regarding the merchant with keen attention.

The man shook his head as if still unconvinced of what he had seen. "They were like no outlaws I have ever encountered in England. Nor have I seen their like in France. Only in the Holy Land have I encountered any fighters as bloodthirsty as these men are. And the outlaws have less pity in them than any Islamite." He crossed himself and tugged his sword out of his wide cloth belt. He made a show of wiping the blade to rid it of its stains, and then rested the tip between his feet, his hands resting on the wide quillons. "They were relentless, and lacked any sign of fear. Never have I seen an attack like theirs for fearlessness. Nothing kept them off long—not wounds, not blows, nothing."

"There were a great many of them," said Sir Humphrey.

"No more than fifteen or sixteen, I should say. Well-trained by the look of them. And with a leader who was the most ruthless of the lot, a great, tall, lean man all cloaked in dark green, so that the shadows and the leaves would hide him. In the battle his cloak was thrown off, and I saw that his hair was very light, like chalk. And he had teeth like a lion, with long fangs. You may not believe me, but it is the truth, as God will witness."

"I don't question your answers," said Sir Humphrey, though he did. "I will send for the farrier, to set your bones," he went on more loudly to all the merchants.

One of Sir Humphrey's men-at-arms took that for an order and hurried off, heading in the direction of the garrison stables.

"We walked all night, for we were afraid that if we stopped or slept those creatures would be upon us once more and we would not live to see the morning." The merchant hefted his sword. "Had I not faced pirates before, I am certain I would have suffered as much as the rest of the party. As it is, I hope never to face those creatures of Sherwood again."

Sir Humphrey thought about this. "How many of you actually fell?"

"Other than our men-at-arms, five," the merchant reported. "And we lost a sixth on the way here in the night. He fell into a fast-running stream and we could not save him."

"Unfortunate," said Sir Humphrey, starting to think. He realized he would have to arrange for these merchants to be escorted back to London as soon as possible. He could not have it said that the garrison of Nottingham could not keep a band of outlaws at bay. As to the far-fetched reports of the outlaws' ferocity, well, anyone would say such a thing if attacked at sunset by determined killers. It was a hazard that any traveler had to accept on the Great North Road. The dangers were so well-known that many were used to the risks and regarded them with an air of tolerant amusement. He would have to make sure his men were instructed to make jests about the more extreme accounts, so that rumors would not start, let alone spread. It was bad enough that these merchants had been robbed, but it would not do to allow the people of Nottinghamshire to worry about wolfish ruffians attacking any traveler at will. He signaled to one of his nearest men-at-arms who was not busy with the merchants. "I will want you to carry a message to the Sheriff in a short while. He must be told about this."

"Of course," said the man-at-arms. "I am at your service."

"When you report to him, tell him just as much as matters—that robbers set upon the merchants in their camp. Add nothing else. To report these fantastic accounts would serve no useful purpose, but to bring scrutiny from the Church." He made his last words heavy with import. "That would not serve us a good turn."

"No, it would not," said the man-at-arms readily enough, wanting no trouble for the garrison.

"So. Have Waterman go to the Cistercian priory and ask the abbot if he will take in these men. Tell the monks that misfortune has befallen the travelers. The Cistercians are supposed to succor travelers, aren't they? Let them take the merchants in, for charity—God knows they are in need of succor." Sir Humphrey wanted to send the merchants away from the castle as soon as possible, so there would be no occasion for questions that might embarrass him and his men. It was bad enough that the merchants were attacked in the part of the forest that was supposed to be under his control; he had no intention of taking more blame upon himself than he had to.

"That I will," said the man-at-arms and turned on his heel to do Sir Humphrey's bidding.

Reassured, Sir Humphrey went to the side of another of the merchants and asked him to tell him about the attack, adding, "I find it hard to believe that these outlaws could overwhelm you as completely as I have heard. You are stout fellows. You had weapons, didn't you? How many of them were there? You seem to be a prudent enough man. I should think with guards in your company, you could have fought them off."

"Not those outlaws. They are worse than wolves. They are worse than famine. They were worse than the ocean in a storm," the man said grimly. "They were on us—us, not our goods—like the Devil's own. Nothing escaped their attack. Ravening beasts they were, seeking blood with a fury beasts cannot match. A few went for our horses and mules, but most of them came for us." He looked down at his ruined clothes. "The forest did little of this, or our flight. Most of it was done by the outlaws."

Sir Humphrey acknowledged this absurd assertion with a slight nod and the request that the merchant tell him how he recalled their escape from the outlaws, all the while determining how to make his report so that none of this would be to his discredit. After all, he reasoned, outlaws attacked merchants from time to time, and these outlaws had taken mules and horses and cloth, and murdered the merchants' escort. It made sense that the victims would magnify the events, being unused to combat as they were. Doubtless he would be doing the merchants a service not to repeat their exaggerations, for it would only bring derision upon them later.

Satisfied that his decision about his report would prove best for everyone, Sir Humphrey swung around to see the farrier hurrying forward, his two apprentices trailing along behind. Soon, thought Sir Humphrey, it would be out of my hands. And by the time deSteny learned of this event, he would have the whole account ready, and his position protected. There would be no inquiry beyond the usual, and Sir Humphrey would retain the prestige he had worked so hard to achieve.

7.

How Sir Gui charged deSteny

Nothing annoyed Sir Gui deGisbourne as much as bad news, and never more than when it came from Hugh deSteny, since he knew of old that his Sheriff did not approach him on minor matters. He was not in humor to have bad news today, and he took it badly that the Sheriff had come to wait upon him. Pulling at his neat, little beard, he met deSteny with his best forbidding frown as deSteny went onto his knee and kissed his hand as a sign of homage. He pulled his hand away at once and fixed deSteny with a ferocious glare.

"Very well, Sheriff, what is it this time? I had better warn you that I am not inclined to be lenient today," he said without any exchange of pleasantries. He leaned back in his chair and fixed deSteny with his most penetrating stare, to show how much of an imposition this audience was.

"I would not have come if I did not require your authorization to undertake a necessary operation," said deSteny, using the phrases he had been rehearsing for more than a day. He got to his feet and stood very straight in front of his elegant and decadent superior. "I would not ask if I were not convinced that we must act quickly or face greater dangers than already exist."

"Yes. So I gathered from your message. My clerk read it to me as soon as I came in from hunting, though I confess it has left me confused." He had the knack of being able to look down his nose at someone standing above him, and he used it now. "What is this danger that has you—of all men—in such a dither? It's not the merchants, is it? Sir Humphrey already told me about them."

DeSteny reminded himself that he was not going to let Sir Gui aggravate him, no matter how insufferable his attitude might be. Much as he hated being characterized as one who dithers, he bore it as best he could. He made his countenance expressionless. "No, this is not about Sir Humphrey, not directly. You have not been on Crusade, have you, my Lord?"

"You know very well I have not," said Sir Gui impatiently. "If this has more to do with disabled soldiers returning, well, I am heartily sorry for them, of course, but they are the King's men, not mine, and they must look to him for their livelihood. I am not one to attach another man's vassals." He waved his hand to indicate that this was his final word on the matter. "Though that would mean following him back to the Holy Land, wouldn't it?" He grinned at his own witticism.

"It is not a matter of soldiers," said deSteny with all the patience he could summon. "Or not the soldiers you mean." He paused and launched into the purpose of his coming. "On Crusade we learned of those who have become servants of the Devil, men who were dead and not dead, men who made prey of other men in the Devil's name. They drank the blood of the living to make them one of their depraved numbers. The Greek priests told us of them, and how they must be fought." He had not believed what he had heard, not at first, he reminded himself, so Sir Gui's incredulity should not amaze him. He himself had required proof, and only when he had it did he seek the aid of the Orthodox priests.

"I will not sponsor an expedition to Greece," said Sir Gui, fingering his fashionably pointed beard.

"I will not ask that. I only want to tell you of this danger, newly arrived on our shores." Again he waited, thinking that this jeweled and velvet-clad exquisite was a disastrous choice to rule Nottinghamshire. He might come from a distinguished line, but he had done little to add to his family's distinction. But King Richard had given the fief to Sir Gui shortly after gaining the crown, and Sir Gui had been a man of distinction ever since, elevating his whole minor-nobility family to positions of importance and sparking great ambitions in his father. Many another family had done the same, and though Hugh deSteny disliked the results, he understood the impetus. Detesting his task, he went on, "It seems, from what I have been told, that the Devil's servants we were warned of in the Holy Land have come to England."

"How is that, pray?" asked Sir Gui as if he were heartily bored of the whole matter. He stifled a yawn to make his point.

Beginning to worry that his task was in vain, deSteny pressed on. "I have lately seen dead crofters who had been killed by the Devil's servants."

"Oh. Crofters. Well, they are . . . they are crofters. How can you expect them to defend against marauders?" He gave deSteny another look of displeasure. "If you are here because of a few dead crofters . . ."

"Not that they are dead, my Lord," said deSteny, "but because of how they died." He let this sink in, and added, "They were all drained of blood, my Lord." He knew he should not tell Sir Gui that the bodies were missing: Sir Gui was repelled by accounts of desecration of the dead.

"Someone murdered them, do you say? Or slaughtered

them like hogs." Sir Gui raised his eyebrows, anticipating an answer. "There are marauders from Greece killing crofters?"

"Hardly marauders, my Lord," said deSteny. "They are creatures who were once men, as other men, but who were seduced in death to the Devil's cause, and do his work in the world."

"Murdering crofters," mused Sir Gui. "Not what one would expect of the Devil. He is supposed to prefer finer game."

Now deSteny was hard-put to control his temper. "Killing anyone who has the misfortune to come upon them after dark. They do more than rob, they care more for shedding blood than taking plunder." He tried to find a way to persuade Sir Gui of the horror he had witnessed. "They prey on hapless travelers, as well—"

"But you said you had found dead crofters," Sir Gui interrupted.

"Yes. The warden found them and quite correctly came to me. But more than crofters, travelers are in danger. Those merchants who were attacked by outlaws who stole their goods might well have lost much more than that, had they faced these creatures." He took a long breath. "These men who are no longer men are strongest in the night, but they can be powerful in the day as long as they are on their native ground. Anyone in Sherwood cannot think himself safe while these . . . these servants of the Devil are abroad."

"Tell me, deSteny, why do you bother me with this? Surely you and Sir Humphrey can deal with these miscreants. He has assured me the garrison is sufficient to make short work of a band of outlaws." He reached out and poured himself a cup of wine from the jar sitting on his table, very pointedly offering none to the Sheriff.

"I doubt we can manage this with the forces we have at hand," said deSteny with very real worry coloring his tone. "We will need more men-at-arms."

"God's wounds, deSteny, I judged you a sensible man, not such a credulous fool, to be jumping at shadows," exclaimed Sir Gui with heavy irony. "What has come over you, to permit a few outlaws to unman you? You've dealt with such miscreants before. Let Sir Humphrey take care of it, if you are not willing to."

"If it were only a few outlaws, my Lord," said deSteny, knowing that it was useless, but unable to stop himself. "These are not outlaws as we have seen before, men who rob only goods and gold. These creatures take everything: goods, gold, life, and soul." He saw that he had not persuaded Sir Gui. "They could endanger every man, woman, and child who sets foot in Sherwood."

"Then be rid of them. Hunt them down and kill them. Go into the forest and do your job. That is what your garrison is for, as I should not need to remind you." Sir Gui coughed delicately. "I cannot now afford to pay and equip more men, nor can I enlarge your fortifications. Everything is so costly. You know how much Prince John has raised the taxes, and with all the silver coming in from the Lowlands, the value of our coins shrinks daily." He took another long draught of wine. "It isn't possible for me just now to provide more men, or armor, or horses."

"Then at least ask the Bishop of Lincoln to send us two or three ordained priests. We have only two in Nottingham, and one is crabbed with age." It was a desperate plea, one he hated to make.

"Priests?" scoffed Sir Gui. "Why priests? What good are they?"

"They are trained to battle the Devil and his minions.

Many of them have seen this evil before. They may do more to protect Nottinghamshire than all the men-at-arms in the Holy Land. My Lord, your people will suffer if you do not provide me with some means to strike back at our enemies." He wished now that he had brought Wroughton or Hamlin along, to add the weight of their observations to his petition.

"If it will make things easier for you, Sheriff," said Sir Gui with no attempts to hide his disdain, "I will have my clerk send word to the Bishop of Lincoln, though I cannot say what his answer will be."

"I thank you for it, my Lord," said deSteny, resisting the urge to yell at Sir Gui, to castigate him for his indifference in the face of danger. Somehow he managed to hold his tongue, though he burned to challenge Sir Gui for his thoughtlessness. He bowed stiffly. "You have been all kindness to hear me out."

Sir Gui accepted this compliment with his usual grace. "It is good of you to say so. But I am troubled that you brought this matter to me. I would have thought you were more prudent than to be so distressed by these new outlaws. Greeks or not, you know how to deal with them, and if you do not, Sir Humphrey does." This last was and illveiled threat, a reminder to the Sheriff that he served at Sir Gui's discretion and pleasure.

"I cannot help but be alarmed, my Lord," said deSteny flatly.

"Um-hum." Sir Gui considered his answer and nodded once more. "Very likely not. And finding murdered people, even crofters, is unpleasant. You get the report from the warden and let him notify the White Friars. Then leave it to the monks. They do it for love of God." This last made him giggle. "Oh. You had better know, for it will be called in Banns soon. It seems I am to be married." This was announced with all the enthusiasm of a man revealing the news of his exile.

"May God show you favor in your bride, my Lord," said deSteny, startled, but recovering quickly.

"She is acceptable to my father and I am to hers. I believe it is all arranged now." He lifted his shoulders to show the negotiations were out of his hands in any case. "I have not met the lady yet."

DeSteny thought that it was possible Sir Gui's bride might be disappointed in what her father had chosen for her, but he said, "May it be a felicitous time for you both. How very fine for you and your House. May she give you many healthy sons. May you have long years together. May your union be a happy one."

"Thank you," said Sir Gui grandly. "A man of my position must carry on the name and my only brother is a monk in France. The burden falls to me." He showed a resigned face. "Therefore it is my obligation to provide grandsons for my father."

"Such is the duty of sons," agreed deSteny.

Sir Gui made an ironic toast with his cup. "My bride— Marian deBeauchamp."

In spite of himself, deSteny was impressed that Sir Gui's father had managed to find such a well-born wife for his son. "An excellent family."

"Yes, they are," said Sir Gui. "I will expect you to escort her from Nottingham to here, with all appropriate deference."

"That I will," said deSteny, aware that this might give him another opportunity to ask for more men-at-arms to drive the new menace from Sherwood. "And count it an honor to render such service."

"Most certainly," said Sir Gui unhappily. "I thought . . ." His voice grew soft. "There would be more time before my father made these arrangements."

"The more time to provide your family with sons." DeSteny said this with an inner satisfaction, for he was still annoyed at Sir Gui's refusal to grant him the men he needed, and he was not above exacting a price for his disappointment.

"So my father tells me," said Sir Gui. He drank the last of his wine and poured a little more, and drank that down. "Pity, that we have such poor vines here in England. Our wines are inferior to those of Burgundy. It is very costly to bring wine from France now that Prince John taxes every barrel of it."

DeSteny thought how many men-at-arms could be paid and equipped for what Sir Gui undoubtedly spent on wines, and he cringed. "It is very hard, my Lord. Though Prince John is doing what he must to maintain England for King Richard. As you say, keeping men-at-arms is costly, and he has an army to provide for."

"Still, the taxes are ruinous," insisted Sir Gui, staring off into space. "If my towns and tenants would pay more of the sum demanded, I would not have to make up the rest. I have the right to demand more of them."

The last thing deSteny wanted to do was become any more Sir Gui's tax collector than he was now. He managed his response carefully so that Sir Gui would not be offended by having his will thwarted by the Sheriff of Nottingham. "You know what your duty is better than I, but as one who hears the travail of peasants, I don't think it would be wise to make such demands, my Lord, not when things are so precarious in the negotiations for King Richard's ransom. The people are not happy over what they have come to think of as the rapacity of the Crown. You could find them unwilling to provide more than they do now. The people are already paying money to the Church as well as to you and Prince John, and their silver, when they see silver, goes no further than yours."

Sir Gui poured his cup full again. "No matter. No matter. I was only speculating." He indicated the door. "I will consider what you have told me. And my clerk will write to the Bishop of Lincoln tomorrow, or the day after." He did not smile, concentrating instead on the wine in his cup. "I will let you know when my bride is to arrive here. I will send my herald, so it will be official."

"May God give you many healthy sons," said deSteny with a bow when he reached the door.

"Yes. Let us pray He does, for my father is counting on it," said Sir Gui with maudlin self-pity as deSteny closed the door on him and strode away down the corridor.

8.

How the Red Friar fared in Sherwood

The brightness hurt his eyes, boring into his skull like torturers' knives, and the sound of the near-by stream turned his stomach. The Red Friar rolled onto his side in an attempt to shield his face from the brilliant sunlight spangling its way through the trees. He groaned as he moved, for he had never before felt so overwhelmingly weak, or so filled with lassitude that sapped his will along with his strength. As much as he wanted to be out of the direct sun, he was unable to urge himself to action.

He noticed the pyx still lying discarded on the road, and his first impulse was to reach for it to save the sacred vessel from further desecration. But when he attempted to touch the silver, chapel-shaped box, his fingers burned and blistered, and he was taken with a bout of queasiness that made him glad his stomach was empty. He drew his hand back, hissing as he did. Why should the pyx burn him? And why should he pull away from it? That troubled him. And he could not remember hissing before. He tried to put it down to his unaccountable weakness, telling himself that he would have sworn he was stronger, but this inner protestation seemed as feeble as his body was.

"He's coming around," said a voice not far away. "Should I—?"

"No," said another, deeper, with greater authority. "He

will need no prodding from any of us. He will come to himself shortly."

The Red Friar looked up and saw the white-maned devil of the night before. "Welcome, little Brother, to our band." He grinned, showing more of his sharp teeth than was strictly necessary. "Welcome."

A peculiar lassitude took hold of the Red Friar, as if he had no will of his own. He felt his hand extend as if tugged by invisible strings, and though he wanted to scream when the outlaw's fingers closed around his own, he could achieve nothing more than a whimper, which made his fright all the greater.

"Look at him," said the white-haired creature. "He's afraid of me." The man laughed. It was a grating sound that had only the dreadful joy of battle to lend it merriment. "Never mind, Red Friar. You will get used to it. And when the thirst is on you, you will understand." He tugged the Trinitarian abruptly to his feet. "We need you more than fodder, or you would be as dead as those crofters whose children you buried yesterday. We need someone who can read, someone who can approach travelers without rousing their suspicions. A Red Friar is perfect."

The rest of the band made low sounds of agreement.

The Red Friar stared at the leader, fascinated by the evil emanating from him. "I don't know . . ."

"You will learn. We will teach you." He signaled to one of his followers, the one who had first spoken when the Red Friar woke. "Come. This is my lieutenant. He is Will. Will Scarlet. We are blood relations, he and I." The two outlaws shared their sinister amusement without any sound.

Will Scarlet bowed to the Red Friar. "It is good to have a monk among us."

The Red Friar wished he could run, but there was no

way to move that did not seem impossibly dangerous.

"And I am called Hood, for I never let open sunlight fall on me. My name is Robin. These are my men. All of my men are as I am. As you are now, Red Friar." He went on as if addressing a child, as he gestured to the others. "That fellow there, the one in the smock, is the man you were planning to put to rest with his family. That is the crofter. We call him Hendy for he came so readily into our hands. His oldest son and his woman are with us as well, at our stronghold. They arrived there three nights since. The two men with the crossbows were men-at-arms, escorting merchants on the Great North Road. We took a few of the merchants, but they did not have anything useful, beyond their lives. We put them to rest. In case you were wondering what became of them."

Suddenly, as he realized the enormity of his disaster, the Red Friar began to tremble, and he sat down quickly, his head bent toward his knees. He wanted to pray but all the words had fled him, and he could manage nothing more than *"Pax vobiscum,"* which he repeated several times, all the while fearing he would vomit.

"Prayers won't help you now, Red Friar. You are seeking relief in the wrong quarter. In fact, they will serve to make you feel worse if you persist in them. Prayers are useless. They could be dangerous, as well, if you try to call upon those who are our sworn enemies." He reached down, his long, white fingers like the legs of a tremendous spider. Gently he patted the Red Friar on the head. "Come. Get up. Up! You will feel better when all is explained to you."

The Red Friar could not imagine that. He tried to crawl away from Hood only to discover that his will was insufficient to the task. He looked up at the sinister figure above him. "What have you done?"

"Made you one of mine," said Hood, unable to keep from gloating. "My first Friar. I had hoped there would be something unusual in your blood, but there wasn't." He regarded the Red Friar narrowly. "Stand. We cannot remain here much longer, with the sun rising higher in the sky."

For reasons that baffled him, the Red Friar made haste to agree, scrambling erect as if at the order of the Pope. As soon as he was on his feet once more he swayed, feeling light-headed. If he had been standing next to anyone but Hood he might have reached out for support, but he could not bring himself to do that.

Hood did it for him. "It will take time for you to recover your strength, and when you do, you will have more than ever you possessed before. You will, however, be mine from this day on. You will be one of my band, and you will obey me utterly." He gave the Red Friar a direct look that could not be escaped.

"They will send men-at-arms against you. The garrison at Nottingham will come to end your power here." He had hoped it would be a threat, but he listened to himself in despair, for there was nothing but subservience in his tone. Despair went through him like a hot wind.

"Men-at-arms. How frightening," said Hood with no trace of fear about him. "We will have to be ready for them."

"But—" the Red Friar could not keep himself from protesting.

"Let them send the garrison. We need their blood." He howled with something that might have been laughter, and the rest echoed the sound, the ululation filling the forest and sending birds and game scattering for leagues around them.

"They are well-armed and will hunt you down," said the

Red Friar, seeking for a menace that would instill in Hood a tenth of the terror the outlaw leader instilled in him.

"Let them try," said Hood, and started off into the deepest part of the forest, not bothering to look back to see if his men were following him.

The Red Friar told himself he would resist, he would not join the other at Hood's heels. He would not become one of that devilish band. But as he issued these stern mental instructions, he could not keep from trudging off in the wake of the others, moved by a force he was unable to conquer.

Somewhat later they arrived at the heart of a dense tangle of thicket, and discovered three ancient oaks growing up and through a vast boulder. At the base of this stone a number of tie-beam huts had been erected, with a great fire-pit in the center of the huts. Two dozen men and half as many women waited beside the fire-pit, a deep, unending hunger stamped on every countenance.

"There is trouble coming," Hood announced as he strode to the foot of the boulder. "We must be ready for it."

The men and women listened in silence.

"Tonight, when we rise to hunt, I want every one of you to seek out a single place where you can go to ground, if you must. I want us to be able to scatter in an instant, and disappear into the forest when we are threatened. I will summon you from your lairs when it is safe. No man-at-arms can find us if each is hidden alone."

Will Scarlet added, "If we are attacked, we must not be captured. Remember how terrible the craving is when it is denied. If they kill us, we have nothing to fear, but captivity must be avoided."

"Only when we are able to fall on the men-at-arms and overpower them should we engage them in combat, and take what we need from them when we have triumphed. It is not to challenge their valor or honor. They are not our enemies. They are our food. They are livestock," said Hood with very little emotion.

The Red Friar listened with growing dread.

"And in that regard," Will Scarlet went on, "we now have two more mules to trade with the crofters who are willing to aid us. We can provide them with the things they need, if they will protect us."

"If they refuse, or fail in their tasks, we will exact a price," said Hood in the same flat voice as before. "And they will pay that price in blood."

The people gathered around him howled again, and to his dismay, the Red Friar found that he, too, was howling.

"It is going to be a good night for hunting," announced Hood. "There are crofters who have told their warden about us, and they must suffer for their insolence. The man has four sons and three daughters, and two sisters who live with his family. We will take them all, and kill them when we are done, so that others will know they will not become one of us if they betray us—they will die."

Again the bestial chorus sounded.

"Sleep for the day, save for you who are to guard us. And at sundown we will march for the croft. It is six leagues away. They will be sleeping soon after sundown, and that will make our work easier. We will be there before midnight." Hood's satisfaction was compounded of arrogance and will. He did not look at any of his followers as he trod off toward the largest of the huts, closing himself away from the loud acclaim of his band.

"Come, Red Friar," said Will Scarlet, amused and forbearing at once. "You will need rest. It is getting too bright for us." He indicated the hut next to Hood's. "You can share my roof for the time being." He smiled. "Don't touch my harp, though. I will tolerate many things, but not that."

"Your harp?" asked the Red Friar, shocked afresh at this revelation. It was as if he had discovered that Belial was a gifted stone-cutter, or Asmodeus an orator.

"Yes." He made a gesture of encouragement. "You see, I am a troubadour. Or I was, once. I came upon Hood in the dungeon of Ely Castle, and I was imprudent enough to let him out, being as we are remote kindred. I was told he was a killer, but the lord of the castle had not paid me as he had promised. I thought it would be a good idea to set my distant cousin and his enemy free, to show the lord I would not let him get away with fleecing me and remaining unscathed. Hood agreed, when I told him my plan." He shook his head slowly. "He was on me like a cur on a rat."

Stunned by this information, the Red Friar followed Will Scarlet into his hut.

9.

How deSteny sought Aid

Anxiously now, Hugh deSteny read over the letter he had written, trying to determine if the tone was right. There was so much he wanted to convey, and he had so little certainty that his account was convincing. But he had to have help, capable help, informed and intelligent help, in order to defeat the Devil's servants. Sir Gui was useless in this battle, deSteny knew it. If there was to be any chance of defeating the evil in Sherwood Forest, he would need a better ally than either Sir Gui or the Bishop of Lincoln, who was a venal and worldly cleric disinclined to believe in undead creatures preying on the living. It would take more than belief to triumph, in any case. It would take knowledge and the capability to perform rites and rituals powerful enough to blast the soul. And there was only one man in all England with enough true scholarship to prevail against these outlaws: John Plantagenet, Prince of England.

To deSteny the letter seemed, on this second perusal, to be lacking in purpose and without any real persuasive power. There should have been special language that could convey everything he had in his mind. But he could think of no other way to tell of what he had seen and what he feared without making his missive seem like the ravings of one gone mad, or the carking of a fool. No, he decided, it was probably best to leave the account bare and unelaborated, so that the stark report would not depend on eloquence or dread for its impact. He signed his name and office, sanded the parchment, rolled it, put a cloth band around it, and dripped sealing wax over parchment and band, then pressed his Sheriff's ring into the hot wax, leaving a sharp impression. Done, he summoned his page. "I need to talk to Wroughton. Bring him to me at once."

Nicholas Woodhull stared at him. "Why do you want to see him?"

"Bring him here, whelp, or I will see that you have cause to regret it," said deSteny, who was in no mood for Nicholas' posturing.

"My father—" began the page.

"Your father will have the pleasure of finding another place for you to serve, caitiff, if you do not carry out my orders, and at once." Had he been dealing with a man, and not a boy, he might have slapped the writing table for emphasis, but aware of Nicholas' youth, he only raised an admonishing finger. "And do not think I will not set you back to him, in disgrace, if you defy me again."

Chastened, Nicholas looked down at his feet. "I will get Wroughton for you, Sheriff. At once."

"Yes. Now," added deSteny, pressing his advantage. He watched the gangly boy hurry out the door. Left alone, he tried to convince himself that his letter was strong enough, and made the danger apparent without such language as must alarm any clergy who might read it. It was tempting to write another letter, but that would mean using another precious sheet of parchment, and that would not do, for it would draw attention to the predicament he faced, putting it into a more sinister light than was seemly. It was true the danger was real, but he had not yet confronted the peril for himself, and did not want to have his judgment questioned. In matters like this, he had learned that reserve was the wiser course: men panicked so readily at the mention of the undead. Little as he liked it, he would have to rely on messengers to deliver his letter without mishap. He was still frowning as Wroughton came into the room, leaving Nicholas hovering near the door.

"You wanted to see me, Sheriff?" He was sweaty and red in the face, the result of having his morning fighting practice interrupted.

"Yes." He leaned forward, arms braced on the writing table as if to guard his sealed letter. "I have a necessary errand for you to perform, and it must be done quickly, and with great care and discretion. I want you to leave by noon today."

The urgency in his voice caught Wroughton's attention. "What is it?" he asked with none of the impatience he had shown a moment before.

"I need you to choose six men, men you trust, brave, strong men, to ride with you to Windsor, carrying a message for me to the Prince." How could he describe the courage they would need should they fail? He tapped the tips of his fingers together.

"To Prince John?" asked Wroughton, astonished at the idea. "Not to Sir Gui?"

"Sir Gui has other things to do just now," said deSteny, thinking of Sir Gui's coming marriage and his determination not to become engaged in any disputes that would detract from his place at court. "In this instance, it must be Prince John."

Wroughton was much perturbed, but all he said was, "If that is your order, Sheriff."

"Yes. It is. And these are my instructions. You are to obey them without cavil." He paused to be certain he had Wroughton's full attention. "You must go as fast as you can, and only in daylight. Do not let yourselves be caught on the road at night. Seek out monasteries and churches for your nights' rests. I cannot have the message lost, and not to—"

"The outlaw bands—no I think not. That would be very bad," said Wroughton quickly, realizing deSteny's intent. "We will do as you command. Fear not, where errands to Prince John are required, every precaution and courtesy will be observed. I understand your motives, sir, given that you act without the instructions of Sir Gui. Whatever the matter may be, the Prince will not have to wait for Sir Gui's alarms. I will choose my men carefully. I'll see they'll all be well-armed. And our mounts will be the strongest." He stood up straight and did his best to smile. "It will be a fight, won't it, Sheriff?"

"Yes, Wroughton, I very much fear it will. But not on the road to Windsor, if we are to have any chance of prevailing," said deSteny, adding in an undervoice, "and it is not of our making."

"No, sir," agreed Wroughton, crossing himself.

After a noticeable silence, deSteny copied the gesture. "I want you to leave every place you stop at first light. Do not dally once the sun rises. And do not press on when sunset is near, not when you may find shelter close at hand. I would rather you take two days longer to deliver the letter than have you fall to the outlaws and fail to deliver it altogether." He paused to let the importance of this warning fix itself in Wroughton's thoughts. "Very well. Get your provisions at once, and have the farriers re-shoe your mounts. I don't want anyone lost because a horse casts a shoe."

"It will be done," said Wroughton. He stared at the letter lying between deSteny's elbows. "Is this what we must deliver?"

"Yes," said deSteny, his right hand moving to cover the parchment. "Never let go of it, day or night. Keep it next to your heart, and let nothing happen to it, or all of Nottinghamshire will pay the price of it."

"The price is a high one, and so is the prize," said Wroughton, pleased with himself for being entrusted with such an important commission.

"More than your life is worth, Wroughton," said deSteny, his dark-gold eyes catching the light and shining like new bronze.

"It's the way of rulers to demand," Wroughton observed with more nonchalance than he felt. He looked at the letter again, not daring to touch it without permission.

"And for those who serve them to obey," deSteny agreed, and continued more somberly. "I would like to hope that you will arrive without incident, but I cannot assume you will have no impediment. Therefore, make sure Father Andrew blesses your weapons and presents each of you with a pyx to wear, which none of you are to remove until you arrive at Windsor. Do you understand me?"

"I trust I do," said Wroughton, growing eager to hold the letter.

"And I," said deSteny, and handed the letter to Wroughton. "Do not crack the seal. It must be received intact or the Prince will not be pleased." Worse, he thought, he might not credit what he read.

"I will guard it with all care." He slipped it inside his camise, next to his skin. "I will secure it with a band before we depart."

"Better yet," said deSteny with a decisive gesture, "get an underbelt and wear it against the small of your back. That way, if you have a fight, there is little chance of it getting damaged." As he thought of the dead crofters, he discovered his faith in such measures was lacking.

"As you wish." Wroughton prepared to go, then paused. "Do you want me to report to you before I depart?"

"No. Dispatch a page to me as you leave. I want no delays. It will be noon before long and you must be beyond the walls of Nottingham by noon." He made a sharp gesture to send Wroughton on his way.

"God defend us all from evil," said Wroughton, blessing himself as he turned on his heel and strode to the door. "I will place this in the Prince's hands myself. I swear it on the blood of my mother and the honor of my father."

"I will not hold you to that oath, if you are attacked. Your safety must come before all else but this letter. If you cannot reach Windsor yourself, make sure one of your men takes the message for you. It is essential. Fail in this, and it were better to have been taken by the Saracens than to return to Nottingham."

Wroughton's face changed little but his eyes took on the glazed shine of a fever. "It must not happen," he declared with such simple determination that deSteny at last believed him. "We will be away before noon." He no longer felt he was being hurried beyond all sense. He saluted and departed.

DeSteny watched Wroughton go, his face shadowed with worry. He hoped that the sight of the crofters would impose restraint on Wroughton, who was inclined to be too much on his mettle. After a short while he sighed and rose from the table; slowly he walked to the window, where he stood looking out beyond the roofs of Nottingham to the vast expanse of Sherwood Forest. It was huge and virtually unbroken by turrets or steeples. Not so long ago he thought of the forest as a sea, with the brave port called Nottingham holding firm against it. Now the trees seemed a relentless, besieging army, every uncertain shadow concealing an enemy, every thicket an engine of war, and Nottingham the hapless fortress standing alone against its green might.

One of the women of the castle, her expression and tongue blurred by the mead she had drunk a short while ago, came to the door and leaned in, her gates-of-hell sleeves revealing more than her arm as she reached toward him. "My good lord Sheriff," she called out to him, her long hand extended in his direction. "You have a burdened look. Come and let me ease you for an hour."

He smiled but signaled her to leave. "Not just now, Vidonia," he said, his dismissal softened by a rueful smile. "I have my burdens and may not yet put them down."

She made a petulant moue. "You never have time for me, or any of us. One might think you have no taste for—"

"You are all so charming that I cannot choose among you." He said this readily, the excuse an old one. "It would hardly be wise for me to favor one and not the others when you are all so deserving."

Now she was pouting, and she struck out at him the one way she could. "You know, they say you were wounded. The women all say it, and some of the men as well. That while you were in the Holy Land, you had your satchel cut from your staff, and you are no longer able to do the act."

"Surely you know that to stop the deed being done, the rod must be taken as well as the satchel," he said brusquely, adding, "in the East, such a man is prized by women whose husbands are long absent, for that man cannot fill her belly. It is also said of such men that they may continue the act much longer than those who are entire, for they do not release seed. Do not seek to compare me with those men." He watched her, asking himself suddenly: why not? What held him back? It was so long ago that he had abjured the rest, why did he cling to this one last—

Vidonia cut into his thoughts. "You might as well be a priest!" she scoffed. "Not that they aren't the randiest of all."

It took him a moment to shake off the shock she had given him. He did his best to smile at her. "That they are," he agreed, and went back to his table. "Now, lady, leave me to my gloomy thoughts."

She came and leaned across the table toward him: he could smell the honey of the mead on her breath. "Show me, lord Sheriff. Show me how you are a man."

He stared at her. "Not now, Vidonia. Unless you want outlaws to lie atop you in nights to come?"

"Outlaws!" She moved back as if he had slapped her. "How could such a thing happen?" With a grand gesture that was only slightly out of control, she swung around and left him alone in the room.

10.

What Wroughton found on his Journey

"God protect me." Wroughton stood at the small monastery window, looking out at the encroaching night. He shivered and blessed himself, trying to hold his thoughts at bay, for it would do him no good to anticipate the worst while he slept here. The hospice of this monastery, which had seemed a bastion against all evil in the late afternoon, now felt to him like a fragile egg in the land of serpents. It would take so little for outlaws to breach the walls. He did his best to banish that prospect from his apprehensions, and came near to succeeding until the Vespers bell rang a second time, reminding him that the last of the light would shortly be gone. The cautions Sheriff deSteny had issued, so over-circumspect at the time, he now realized were barely adequate to the risk they were taking.

"Good Sir Messenger," said one of the Grey Friars, coming up to him with a show of deference. He held the door open. "The Abbot of Saint Coemgen wishes me to ask you to join him at table."

"Does he?" said Wroughton, his uneasy gaze flicking about the gathering shadows, trying not to see faces in their depths. "Well, I suppose it would be correct. It is very good of him to extend such an invitation, of course." He looked at the monk who had approached him, and said, "This is somewhat unusual, taking us in as you have; you Austins are not often keepers of hospices, are you?"

"No, not often," said the monk, his manner diffident but his voice stern. "In such a place as this, it is fitting that we should keep watch against the darkness." He touched the rosary that hung from his belt. "Better to serve here and welcome travelers than to take our chances in caves and solitary cells, which afford no protection beyond prayer."

"Doubtless," said Wroughton with feeling. "The forest being what it is, it is dangerous enough within these walls. Outside them—" He did not say anything more.

"If you will follow me?" said the monk, indicating the corridor behind him. "He is waiting for you."

"Very good," said Wroughton, and fell into step behind the monk. His thoughts, as he went along the hall, were dreary. He had not considered at the beginning of the journey that the woods would encroach upon him as they had begun to do. It was as if the world had contracted to this endless realm of brush and trees. He cleared his throat and stared at the rough crucifix at the end of the corridor, and for him it now seemed more important that the thing was made of wood than that it depicted Christ at the moment of His Sacrifice.

The Grey Friar led the way to the refectory door, and stood aside, permitting Wroughton to enter ahead of him, so that no taint of pride could be attached to his piety.

Everything about the refectory was familiar in a skewed way. The plank tables and benches were like those in the barracks mess, where Wroughton and the other men-at-arms ate when they were without wives or other women to provide for them. The fare was as plain as soldiers' food, but lacked the generous sections of meat, offering instead leeks and turnips. And the silent ranks of monks were so eerily unlike the roistering bonhomie of fighting men that Wroughton had an uncomfortable moment when it seemed to him that he was in the company of ghosts, or the damned, and not living men at all.

The Abbot Ambrose rejoiced in austerity, which had spread his fame over half of England: he was gaunt with fasting and hoarse from reciting prayers through most of his waking hours. It was said that his knees had calluses thick as the knees of camels from long hours before the altar in the chapel. It was known he drank only water and ale brewed by his monks, which he called The Living Breath of God in honor of the Host. This Abbot Ambrose was held in superstitious awe by those who traveled the Great North Road. He motioned to Wroughton to join him, and as soon as the solider was at his side, he began to intone the blessing of the evening meal, which consisted of a single loaf of bread, a single salted fish, and a third of a wheel of cheese per man, less than half of what Wroughton's men were used to. As the abbot continued his prayers, Wroughton contemplated the meal and hoped that in the morning his men would not be exhausted by hunger. With the ground they had to cover tomorrow, he did not want the men-at-arms accompanying him to succumb to fatigue while within the shadow of the forest.

No speech was allowed during the meal, and no lingering at table was tolerated, so it was not long before the monks put their hands in their laps and waited for Abbot Ambrose to dismiss them, admonishing them all to be vigilant in the preservation of their souls, "For the forces of evil are everywhere and they do not hesitate to seize the lax." Aware of their situation as guests, the soldiers remained in their places, fidgeting, until the abbot rose, blessed them all, and admonished them to pray for the redemption of all mankind.

"Thank you," said Wroughton, wanting to show his

respect to the abbot. "My men and I are grateful for the protection your abbey gives us, and the diligence of your prayers, from which we benefit."

"The abbey provides no protection, nor can it. We have no stout, high walls to hold off attack, nor soldiers to man them. We have no weapons beyond our knives. Only God provides protection, through the intercession of His saints and Our Lady in this place of perdition, where the Devil has room to roam." Abbot Ambrose regarded Wroughton severely, his eyes brilliant with an emotion that was more than zeal. "The world is full of falseness and evil, and while we are here none of us is proof against it without Grace. We rely on the protection of Heaven in this world, and the Mercy of God in the next."

"Then thanks be to God," said Wroughton, determined not to be put off by the man. He could feel the Sheriff's letter inside his acton like a live animal, or a plate of hot metal pressed to his spine. The leather belt holding it in place suddenly felt too tight. "The Prince will thank you as well."

Abbot Ambrose spat with contempt. "Not he! He spends his time reading. Reading, if you will! They say he has more than a hundred books, perhaps as many as two hundred, and that most of them are secular. It is said he sends men into the world to seek out more books for him, that he might increase their numbers, not content with what he has. It is a sign of trouble. What sort of work is it for a Prince, to read? What will become of his people if he falls into error from it, as he must?"

"It is the work of the state to study, perhaps, given the troubles of the time," said Wroughton, wanting to avoid an argument.

"The state should be run in accord with God's Rule, not

out of the texts of men who can think of nothing but ways to poison the world with doubt," said Abbot Ambrose, and turned away, his condemnation almost a visible presence around him. "God should be the test of all things. Then there would be no more trouble."

"Perhaps it should," said Wroughton, hoping to recover some degree of dignity. "And it may be that our mission will bring the Prince nearer to God's way," he suggested, addressing the abbot's back.

"Then I pray your mission will be a success," said the abbot without looking at Wroughton as he left the refectory.

"Not much joy there," said young Simkins, coming close to Wroughton in the corridor leading to the cells that had been assigned to them for the night.

"No, not much," said Wroughton.

The monks around them frowned at hearing this: speech was forbidden to them after their meal, and any taint of enjoyment was regarded as the greatest sin. From now until midnight only prayers would pass their lips. At midnight, they would have Mass, and then retire until sunrise, when prayers would begin again. It was a life Wroughton found stifling beyond all enduring.

Simkins and Piers came to the door of Wroughton's assigned cell. Both of them were eager young men, bold and strong, good with horses and the passage of arms. Piers spoke first. "Are we to keep watch tonight?"

Wroughton had already thought this over, and he answered promptly. "Yes. There are six of you. Two keep awake until midnight, then two more until dawn, when we must leave." He had removed his leather tunic and was now only in acton and braies. "Tomorrow night, the two who slept all night tonight will stand guard, and I will relieve them."

"But this is holy ground, isn't it?" protested Simkins.

"Won't the prayers of the monks guard us? Grey Friars are noted for the strength of their prayers."

Wroughton rubbed his short beard. "I hope they will, but I cannot take chances."

"Truly?" asked Simkins. "Or is this to keep us from falling into habits that will not be acceptable on campaign?"

"That, too," said Wroughton, unwilling to wrangle with these young men. "Get to your duty. And keep your sword at the ready. Do not take the pyx from around your neck, any of you." This last was the sternest admonition of all.

"We heard the orders the first time," said Piers. "None of us want to fall prey to whatever is in the forest."

"See you remember that, all of you," said Wroughton, and made a sign of dismissal.

"Who's to stand second guard?" asked Piers, unwilling to leave quite yet. "Has that been decided?"

"Oh, Cathmor, I suppose, and Newlyn. Let Gaynes and Boden rest tonight." Wroughton was as hungry for sleep as much as he longed for a proper meal, with farsted goose and beef gobbets in new ale. He laid his leather tunic across the end of the cot and indicated the little oil lamp burning in front of the crucifix over the bed. "Morning will come soon enough and we will have to be prepared to leave at first light."

"That it will," said Simkins, and nudged Piers toward the door. "Come soon enough. We'll see to our duty."

"Good," said Wroughton, and dropped onto the cot, feeling the leather bands shift under the thin, straw-filled mattress. He tugged the single blanket up to his shoulder and prepared to fade into sleep as his two men closed the door.

But, tired as he was, Wroughton did not sleep. He lay in bed, his mind active with possibilities, and no whispered prayers alleviated his travail. The night pressed in on him like a living, malign thing. He thought half a dozen times that he heard noises in the forest that were more than the sounds of night-wandering animals, or the cry of owls on the wing. Eventually he drifted into a kind of fitful doze, where his nightmares had the substance of his waking thoughts, and he thrashed at the cover, for it seemed to muffle him in dangerous silence. He envisioned such things as he had not encountered since he had returned from the Holy Land, and what his memories conjured up chilled his blood.

In the corridor outside the cells where their fellows slept, Simkins and Piers held their swords by the quillons, the points resting between their feet. Simkins kept himself awake thinking of all the women who would flock to him once he reached Windsor, for word of their heroism would surely spread through the castle as soon as they were inside the towering walls. He thought of the women back in Nottingham who were available to him, and in his imagination the women of Windsor would be more beautiful, more accomplished, more amorous than those he had known before. At sixteen, he was ready to marry, but wanted first to know enough of the world to choose a wife wisely.

At the other end of the corridor, Piers was anticipating the money he would earn from this duty. He might even get enough to purchase his own war-horse so that he would not have to depend on that old hard-mouthed mount his father had left him. Then he would be able to rise in rank. He might even be able to go on Crusade, if King Richard sent for more men to fight with him. Then there would be adventure and loot as well as the opportunity for the advancement he longed for. He was dwelling on the satisfaction he would find in knighthood—for surely he would be knighted for his valor—when he saw one of the monks approaching him, a finger raised in warning.

"Good soldier, God keep you now and in your final hour. In His Name, if you would, come with me?" the monk said, his voice hardly more than a whisper. His grey habit was so much the color of the night around him that he seemed invisible, a portion of the night that had a voice like the wind in the trees.

"Something wrong?" asked Piers, shaken and glancing about uneasily, his pleasant reverie fled.

"Yes," said the monk. "If you will come?"

For a moment, Piers could not decide what was best to do. Then he hefted his sword and followed the monk, taking care to walk softly. He didn't speak for fear of disrupting the prayers going on around him. The monks were fussy about quiet, he knew, thought here in the forest, he would have thought they had more than enough of it.

At the entrance to the chapel there was a small door that led to the sheepfold where the monks' flocks were penned at night. This the monk with Piers opened, and pointed to the meadow beyond the sheepfold. "There is something out there. I saw it moving at the edge of the forest."

Piers was tempted to laugh but found it unexpectedly difficult, as if he had swallowed a fish-bone and it had caught in his throat. "Deer, most likely. Or a goat wandered away from the flock. The deer often graze at night. I have seen them at the edge of the fields around Nottingham."

"We know deer," said the monk more severely. "And they are not the cause of the disturbance." He peered into the moon-limned darkness. "I must be certain I have reason to wake my Brothers."

"Well, if you think there's danger, and you need my

aid . . ." said Piers, all but swaggering. "It is fitting for me to accept any challenge." He hefted his sword with confidence. "I will look for you, if that would please you." These monks were all alike, he reminded himself, men without spines, cowering in the shelter of the monasteries, praying for the return of Christ so that they would finally be safe from harm. When calamity came, they ran for soldiers faster than mice from cats.

"Yes. Do that," said the monk gratefully. He held the door wider for Piers, then stepped aside as the young man-at-arms strode out into the shadowy night. Once he was certain that Piers had gone a short distance from the door, the monk slammed it shut and put the bolt in place. Shivering, he crossed himself and hurried to the chapel to pray for the repose of Piers' body and soul.

The sound of the door closing and the second, more ominous, thud of the bolt brought Piers up short. "What? Ah! No! Open this door!" he demanded of the Grey Friar who had shut him out of the monastery. He swung around, his sword up, and he took three hasty strides back toward the door, intending to pound on it with the pommel of his sword as well as shout. "Open! I am outside!" Behind him, the sheep bleated and milled in their fold.

"Good evening, soldier," said a voice not ten steps away from him, a deep voice, a voice that sounded a wild note, one that summoned up all manner of horrors to Piers' racing thoughts. There was a soft, equivocal laugh that was ineffably vile; it sounded as if the voice were coming nearer.

Piers swung his sword up to the ready, determined to hold his ground with whatever threatened him. "Stand fast! Whoever you are, I am—"

A figure emerged from the darkness, a tall man in a long cloak: the hood was thrown back revealing a mane of bone-white hair. He held out empty hands. In long strides he approached Piers without a trace of fright, though he was apparently at a disadvantage. "The sword will avail you nothing, soldier."

"If you try, you will discover otherwise," Piers countered, using all his will to keep from shaking. His sword felt heavier than he had ever imagined it could, and he suddenly regretted not wearing the pyx as Wroughton had ordered.

"Such foolishness," said the white-haired man, reaching out and seizing Piers' wrist in a strong grip that reached all the way up his arm.

Shame filled Piers as he felt his strength ebb at the white-haired stranger's touch. The sword dropped, and Piers could not contain the moan that rose from the depth of his soul, certain now that he was lost.

"You see?" the man went on calmly as he forced Piers down onto his knees. "These Austins and I have an understanding. I and my men will leave the Grey Friars in peace as long as they provide us with travelers for fodder." His eyes were red, glowing like hot coals as he bent to his work.

Gouts of blood steamed in the cool night air, but they vanished quickly as the followers of the pale-haired creature converged on Piers in a delirium of slaughter, as relentless as wolves, as terrible as tigers.

11.

What Sir Gui commanded deSteny to do

Hugh deSteny regarded Sir Gui deGisbourne with angry disbelief. "But it would be unwise to leave at this time," he protested. Ever since Sir Gui's arrival in Nottingham at mid-morning, they had been closeted together, their tempers fraying as the sun rose high overhead, as if the fire of the noon-day sun heated their humors to dangerous levels.

"Well, I can't have my affianced bride brought here by a company of rough soldiers for her escort. Her father would be displeased. It would not be fitting," said Sir Gui, making an impatient gesture with his pomander. "She would be offended."

"Better off offended than hurt, and if her father cannot bring her himself, he would surely be more pleased to have his men with her than yours," said deSteny, his eyes hardening. "It is not as if there is nothing for this garrison to do. We have duties enough for another company of men. You have not forgot the outlaws in the woods who prey on travelers. We have a responsibility to provide anyone abroad in this shire with a modicum of protection. With Wroughton away, I cannot spare more men for such duty as escorting your bride. It would place Nottingham at risk to have the garrison depleted. Perhaps when Wroughton returns . . ." He let this trail off, hoping it would be enough to convince Sir Gui that he was not being capricious.

"Oh, yes—that errand to Windsor," said Sir Gui in a tone of ill-use. "You sent him off with six men without so much as a word to me."

"Time was my first concern," said the Sheriff. "It would have meant a two-day delay for them, and that might have been too much."

"And because of this . . . mission, you have insufficient men available to bring my bride to me? What a paltry thing you must think me." He scowled. "Am I nothing more than a landless knight, that I have no men to do my bidding? Must I depend upon her father—who is old and ill—to spare his men for this task, which should be mine, as if I were only a country yeoman?" Sir Gui pulled at his short-trimmed beard. "Her father will not like it."

"Very likely not," said deSteny, recovering himself somewhat. "No one wants to send men into Sherwood now that there are so many tales of marauding outlaws." He paused. "All the more reason to ask her father to use his veterans for the work instead of Nottingham's men-at-arms." He knew he would not prevail in this dispute, but he was hoping to gain a little time so he would not have to unman the garrison completely.

"And have it appear I am unable to protect her? That I am unwilling to do her the honor her family is entitled to receive from me? No, I think this would not sit well with Stephen deBeauchamp." Sir Gui's voice rose half an octave and he put his hand to his chest in a show of dismay. "What sort of bridegroom would I be then?"

"I would hope you would be prudent enough to make sure that men she knows give her escort." DeSteny lowered his eyes. "I would like to think her father would not want her to face danger among unfamiliar men-at-arms, so that she would not know whom to trust. It would be wiser to have her with those who have learned to value her for herself than send her off among strangers, who have not determined her worth beyond being your bride, as I fear may be the case in our current arrangement. I would be remiss not to speak of this before undertaking the mission." He was so annoyed with Sir Gui that he might had walked out of the room had Sir Gui not been his superior. There had been a time in his life when that consideration would not have stopped him, but those years were behind him and he could not persuade himself that insulting Sir Gui would achieve the ends he sought.

"A trifling matter. What woman knows soldiers, who is worthy of being called Lady?" He made a performance of scoffing, his face set in furious lines.

"I believe you may underestimate your bride if you think that," said deSteny sharply. "She is a fool if she does not recognize her guards. All the more reason for her to travel with her father's soldiers."

"I know that she was brought up a deBeauchamp, and has not been permitted to know low company," Sir Gui said with a look of condemnation directed toward the Sheriff. "She is said to be of a submissive and noble nature."

"Then you have not met her?" asked deSteny, less surprised than he might have been with a man of different temperament than Sir Gui's.

"I have not had that privilege. Our union was arranged with the good offices of cousins, who knew both of our fathers were seeking a suitable match." He wiped his upper lip with his finger, making sure his moustache was in place. "I am awaiting her eagerly. I have sent word to her saying as much."

"And she?" asked deSteny, thinking she might be disappointed by Sir Gui when they met at last.

"She is charming, virtuous, biddable, sensible, modest, and mild, or so I am told," said Sir Gui, as if reciting these qualities would make the marriage more welcome to him.

"If she is all those things, she is aware of the risks her position imposes upon her, and she is prepared for them. No doubt she has carried a knife in her belt. And she knows every one of her father's officers by name, and the men-at-arms who guard her: you may depend upon it; she has been taught this so that no imposter may impose upon her, and no abduction could succeed," said deSteny, knowing it was useless to argue, that he would not convince Sir Gui to use her father's escort to bring Lady Marian to Nottingham. He was growing tired of this brangle, and sought for a reason to conclude it. "It is nearing time for our mid-day repast. Surely you will honor your men by joining us at table?" he asked, with the certainty that Sir Gui would not.

Sir Gui gave deSteny a hard stare down his nose. "This is not settled, deSteny. Do not suppose that it is. I will expect your men to report to Stephen deBeauchamp's current seat at Arundel, in my name, and to provide honorable escort for my affianced bride. You will order your men to travel in battle-harness, of course, and to display my badge. You will present yourself as my deputy. My bride will have her two maids to accompany her, of course, and whatever servant her father wishes to accompany her. Her father has not yet recovered from the wounds he received in the Holy Land, and that is the reason he cannot bring her here himself." This last concession was offered as a sop to deSteny. "It would shame his wounds to demand more of him than the hand of his daughter."

Knowing it was reckless to challenge Sir Gui, deSteny bit back his most cutting retort and said only, "Then I am to take it that you wish to travel with the men, to lead you escort? Giving full weight to the esteem in which you hold your bride and her family, that is." He had the satisfaction of seeing Sir Gui blanch.

"I?" Sir Gui clapped his pomander to his chest. "Sadly, I fear I cannot. There is much to do here in Nottinghamshire, and I must supervise it. As much as I would wish to present myself to her at her father's fortress, if I were to undertake the rigors of the journey, I would not be able to arrange a welcome for her suiting her rank." He took a turn about the room, agitated and annoyed. "It is fitting that I remain here."

"Fitting?" How delicious it would be to be able to call Sir Gui coward. DeSteny savored the thought even as he gave a short bow to his superior. "I will do what I can."

"And of course," Sir Gui added with a sly look of malice. "I expect you to be leader of that escort."

"Go with the escort?" Now the Sheriff was upset. "That is impossible. My work is here. I have much to do to make this castle safe for your bride. You have said so yourself." The shock of this order rattled him, as he knew it was intended to do.

"In ordinary circumstances, yes, that is true. But these, you will allow, are not ordinary circumstances. And you, yourself, have reminded me that Lady Marian deBeauchamp requires more than simple soldiers to bring her to me, since her father's health will not permit him to undertake the journey." Sir Gui's smile was more a gloat than a sign of approval. He rounded on the Sheriff. "You will do my bidding, Hugh deSteny. You will obey my commands or you will be disgraced. Bad enough that you fled the Holy Land. If you were to fail here, your reputation would fail utterly."

There was enough truth in the threat that deSteny did

not wish to test it. He rocked back on his heels, absorbing the blow and gathering his thoughts. "When did you want us to depart?" It was not as much capitulation as strategic retreat, he told himself. "Since Wroughton is away, I will not have many men to guard Nottingham. I will need to depute my duties while I am gone."

From outside came a loud shout as the guards were changed. It was officially now the middle of the day.

"Wilem deFolleux will do it," said Sir Gui, naming one of the most pampered of his cronies. "He has already said so."

"Wilem deFolleux," repeated deSteny, picturing the languid, effete young man. "But he has never commanded so much as a hunting party."

"This will remedy that lack in him," said Sir Gui triumphantly. He preened as he strode around the room, his pomander held to his nostrils. "You know his birth is beyond question, and his family have long been staunch defenders of the realm. He will acquit himself with distinction, I have no doubt."

This was a sentiment deSteny could not share. "And what if there is real danger while I and my men are away? Do you seriously expect deFolleux to deal with it? How will you defend Nottingham with the garrison halved and a fop to command? If the outlaws should plunder the crofters near-by, or waylay a party of merchants within a day of the gates? What if a monastery should be attacked with no one to go to the aid of the monks? Such things are not beyond possibility, Sir Gui, as we both realize," deSteny declared, his ire building again. "What use would your friend be in such coils?"

"He would bring a dozen of his father's men-at-arms to fill most of the gaps in your absence, so you need have no fear for the town," said Sir Gui, clearly pleased with this clever notion. "And Wilem's father will be content to find that his son has shown himself to be a stalwart leader."

So that was it, thought deSteny. Sir Gui was using this escort duty as a ploy to aid one of his friends. He sighed once. "I will talk to Sir Humphrey. Between us, we will arrange matters." He looked at Sir Gui with ill-disguised disgust. "Since you will have it, I will do as you command."

"Certainly you will," said Sir Gui, and looked around the room once more, and paused, staring out the window. "It gives a good aspect of the forest, doesn't it?"

"Yes, it does," said deSteny. He had mastered his anger, and now he was trying to think of all he had to do in order to prepare for this ill-considered escort of Lady Marian deBeauchamp. Briefly he wondered if Stephen deBeauchamp was as happy with the alliance with deGisbourne as Sir Gui claimed.

"I will expect you to leave in four days, without further dispute. That will be enough time to make the arrangements you consider necessary for the protection of Nottingham, which I expect you to do. You should be able to provision your men in that time, and make the necessary arrangements for the garrison to be placed under Wilem deFolleux in your absence." His smile widened as he regarded deSteny. "Sheriff, you exceeded your authority once, in sending Wroughton and those men to Windsor. Now you will have to bow your neck."

There had been a time, a decade ago, when another man had told deSteny much the same thing, and deSteny had refused to obey. Then he had defied the man giving the order, and paid the price of that defiance. Now he shrugged. "It is your fiefdom, Sir Gui. You must choose if you wish it left in inexperienced hands. You know my warnings, and the reason I have given them. If you decide to leave all Nottingham open to attack, you will be the one to suffer. Your bride may find ruins to welcome her." It was not entirely accurate, but it was near enough to the possible to cause Sir Gui to smart.

"You would suffer as well, I think, you and your men," Sir Gui shot back, color mounting in his face.

Again deSteny shrugged. "Yes," he admitted. "But my loss would not be as great as yours, nor would my blame." He was gratified to see that this time his words had struck deep.

His face stiff with disapproval, Sir Gui inquired, "What would you recommend, then?"

This was the opportunity deSteny had been hoping for. "I would ask to be permitted to assign the men of the Guard and the garrison to support Wilem deFolleux and his troops, so that they will not have to learn afresh all we have discovered in the last weeks."

Sir Gui realized he could not prudently refuse so reasonable a request. "Very well. Make whatever arrangements you think best in that regard."

DeSteny managed not to smile. "Then I will do as you order, and leave from here in four days. Sir Humphrey will serve in my stead"—he trusted the older man would not be too lax, or too eager in fulfilling the Sheriff's duties—"until Wroughton returns, and that should reassure you regarding the safety of the town. I will leave written instructions to that end, so they will be certain to be carried out." He was aware that Sir Gui found the Sheriff's skill in reading and writing suspicious, and at the moment, he used that suspicion. "Wilem deFolleux will work in conjunction with Sir Humphrey and Wroughton. They will advise deFolleux and manage the men-at-arms."

"I assumed Wilem would supervise them all," said Sir Gui, petulance returning to his handsome features.

"You said yourself he has no training in command. No matter how skilled he may be"—and the Sheriff opined the fellow had no such skill at all—"he will have to learn the manner in which Nottingham is defended. It is not something that can be grasped in a day. He will be in no position to invent a defense if it is needed. This is no place to begin such lessons, since much has happened recently that warns of greater intrusions," deSteny reminded Sir Gui. "And given what we have faced of late, you will need someone who is familiar with the trouble in the forest if the town is to be preserved."

Reluctantly Sir Gui nodded. "I will send a messenger to Wilem tomorrow. He will arrive before you leave."

"Well enough," said deSteny, though he did not actually think so. It was, however, the best he could achieve and he recognized it. He bowed. "My men are waiting, Sir Gui. I will speak to them when our meal is done."

"Very good," said Sir Gui, realizing he had gone as far with deSteny as he was likely to be able to do without courting direct opposition. "Let me know the names of the men to go with you. And tell me what you expect those who remain to face. You have insisted; you must acquiesce."

This was not to ensure the men were given recognition or preferred posts, deSteny was aware. Sir Gui wanted to be sure that the Sheriff took the number of men Sir Gui had ordered he have for the escort. "I will. You will have the lists in your hands before we depart. My word on it." That was no concession, for Hugh deSteny had no intention of setting foot upon the Great North Road without a full complement of armed men. He regarded Sir Gui carefully. "Is that all, my Lord?"

"For the moment," said Sir Gui with a dismissing wave of his hand. "I will have to see you before you leave, of course. There are niceties that must be observed, and I want to be sure you know how to proffer my regards. In addition, I have certain gifts you are to carry to my bride. I will entrust them to you the day before you leave; you will be accountable for their safe delivery."

Once again deSteny felt compelled to object. "Surely they may be presented to the woman when she arrives here? Sending anything of great value with an escort is so great a risk, I cannot advise you to do it."

Sir Gui was determined to make the most of the slight accommodation he had gained. "I must present her with the jewels promised by the marriage agreements before she comes here. Her father would be entitled to keep her by his side if I did not provide tokens before she left his roof."

This confirmed deSteny's guess that Sir Gui was not the bridegroom Stephen deBeauchamp wanted for his daughter. He coughed once and said, "I will do all that I may to deliver anything you entrust to me, but I must warn you again that the Great North Road—indeed, all of Sherwood—is no safe place, and anything you give to me may be seized by brigands while we are traveling."

"You will have to make it your purpose to be certain that you do not encounter any brigands or outlaws while you travel," said Sir Gui, as if this were nothing more than a matter of decision and will.

The Sheriff did not know how to respond, so he bowed once again, turned on his heel, and strode out the door, saying as he went, "My page is at your disposal. His name is Nicholas Woodhull."

"Quite a well-born lad to have to wait upon you," said Sir Gui with a trace of envy in his tone. "I wonder that his father should send him to you instead of me. Perhaps he didn't want to seem too ambitious."

"I cannot say what his reason might be for his selection. Inquire of him if you wish to know his reasons," answered deSteny, who knew the cause very well: Nicholas' family did not want his son in the tutelage of a man of Sir Gui's reputation. He closed the door behind him and made his way down to the soldiers' hall, where the cooks were delivering the first of two stuffed pigs to the waiting men. Shouts of approval greeted the arrival of the great spits with their smoking, succulent burdens. Scullions carried in trenchers for the men, and an understeward rolled a tun of ale into the center of the room, broaching it with a single blow of a mallet to the bung.

Sir Humphrey was at his place at the high table, and he motioned to deSteny to join him. "A fine meal, as always," he approved as deSteny made his way toward him. "I'll say this—Sir Gui does not stint on the fare for his Guards and his soldiers. He shows us the regard we have earned, and no question about it."

"Enjoy it while you may. You may not have long to indulge in the pleasures Sir Gui offers," deSteny recommended, gladdened that his insistence on first-rate food for the men was appreciated. It did not matter that Sir Gui was thanked, for morale was more important than credit. He sat down on the chair beside Sir Humphrey, his expression grave. "There is something we must discuss. This afternoon, Sir Humphrey. It is urgent. And it is important," he said quietly as one of the waiters brought a trencher to Sir Humphrey, four huge collops of pork steaming in it. Those at the high table were given such service—the rest of the men were left to scramble for themselves.

"What might that be?" asked Sir Humphrey, instantly

apprehensive. He paused in the act of pronging meat on his dagger.

"Nothing quite dire," said deSteny, making a reassuring gesture.

"Ah, well, then," said Sir Humphrey, securing one collop and lifting it to his mouth. "What more?"

"I have just left Sir Gui," the Sheriff went on. "He has given me orders that I do not think either of us will relish." He made a sign of thanks to the understeward who presented him with his pork-filled trencher.

A heartbeat before he heard that, Sir Humphrey had been enjoying his meal. Now the pork was as tasty as coal and the trencher looked grey. "What might that be?" he asked, feeling trapped.

As the meal progressed, Hugh deSteny gave Sir Humphrey a succinct account of his interview with Sir Gui. As he talked, his meat grew cold and his ale went flat, as was the case with much of his life.

12.

How Wroughton came to Windsor

They were closing the great gates of Windsor when Wroughton and his two remaining men rode through them on lathered horses. It was dusk, and the last glow of the sun stained the western sky blood-red.

The Captain of the Guard waited in the courtyard ahead of them, fists planted on his hips, and an air of extreme irritation about him. This was not the behavior he expected of visitors to Windsor. He made no greeting as Wroughton dismounted and flung his reins to a waiting groom from the stable. Though it was the height of discourtesy, he forced Wroughton to approach him rather than going forward to greet him.

"I am from Nottingham, on urgent business from the Sheriff there; I have message I am charged to deliver," Wroughton said as he went up to the Captain of the Guard. His eyes stung with fatigue and his belly grumbled from emptiness. Although it was the end of summer, his breath made ghosts on the chilly evening air. "It is from the Sheriff of Nottingham. Here. This letter is for His Grace." He patted his chest where the letter lay. "It must be put in his hands and his alone."

"And for that reason you arrive near dark, well after prudent men are within walls," said the Captain condemningly. "What made you undertake so reckless a venture? Why did you not remain in a hostel for the night, and present yourself properly in the morning, when it is safe to be abroad?"

"Because I have lost four men in coming here, and I dared not chance another night outside stone walls, for their sake," said Wroughton, indicating his remaining escort, who were still mounted.

This did not impress the Captain of the Guard favorably. He glared at Wroughton as he signaled the grooms to take the horses to the stables. "What is so desperate that you lose men and manners in this way?"

"The message from the Sheriff describes the trouble," said Wroughton, his expression hardening. He motioned to his men, who were dismounting now that the grooms had come for their horses. "Cathmor and Boden are the only two who survived. I started from Nottingham with six men." He gave the Captain a hard look. "Are you saying I should have endangered these good men for your convenience?"

The Captain did not relent, but his manner softened a trifle. "You are saying you have been set upon?"

"Repeatedly," said Wroughton. "And in places that should have been safe. We would not have made it through at all if we had not lasted out one assault until sunrise." He folded his arms over his chest, as much to protect the parchment he carried as to express his defiance of the Captain of the Guard.

"What places?" asked the Captain, disbelief making him sarcastic. "Crofts with stout walls? Gated towns? Abbeys? Fortresses? Or did you try to make and hold camps for yourself?"

"Do you think we are complete fools? We made no camps. Monasteries, they were the worst. We stayed in monasteries and were not safe," said Wroughton, and let the impact of that announcement sink in before he went on.

"I must hand this letter to Prince John. I am ordered on my honor to present it upon my arrival."

The Captain still had his doubts about Wroughton, but he had been on the rough side of Prince John's tongue more than once and did not relish another such encounter with the King's younger brother. "Very well. He is at table. Since you insist upon it, I will lead you to him now."

"And what of my men?" Wroughton asked, refusing to move while Cathmor and Boden were unaccommodated.

The Captain made a gesture that was almost capitulation. "They will eat with the rest of the men-at-arms. I will allow so much." With that, he turned abruptly and strode away, not glancing back to learn if Wroughton was following him.

Windsor was a huge, echoing, draughty pile of a castle, its fortifications massive, its interior dark and confusing. The odor of smoke was strong from the braziers and the many fireplaces that did little to dissipate the chill of the stones. The corridors the Captain used were lit by torches and occasional trees of oil-lamps, and their smell was pervasive and upsetting to Wroughton, who had seen enough of fire at London when he was young.

Finally they entered a square room where tables were laid for dining, and two dozen men hunched silently over their trenchers, picking bones from the fish-and-fowl dish they were served for their evening repast. The sizzles of fat from the open hearths where venison turned on a spit were the loudest sounds in the room.

Wroughton was so hungry that the odor of the dish made his mouth water as if he were a child and this a feast. Hunger gnawed at him, immediate and intense. He did his best to shut his distraction from his mind as the Captain led him to the high table and bowed with just enough respect to those seated there.

"What is your reason for your coming, Captain?" demanded one of the most formidable figures at the high table, a middle-aged man with grizzled hair and half the fingers gone from his right hand.

This unpromising beginning was ignored. "Your Grace," said the Captain, going on his knee to a slender man of moderate height with regular features in a long face framed by silky, ruddy-brown hair and a short, neat beard. Dressed well but simply, he was no more outstanding than several other men at his table. His most striking features were his keen, deep-hazel eyes under a wide, high brow.

"Captain," was the answer in a deep voice as he rose.

"Your Grace, this man has come from Nottingham on the Sheriff's business, and he claims urgency of commission in presenting himself now." The Captain got to his feet. "Fellow," he said to Wroughton, "this is His Grace, the Count of Mortain and Lord of Ireland, John Plantagenet, Prince of England."

Wroughton had already knelt. "Your Grace," he said, kissing the ring on the large hand extended to him. "I am here as the deputy of Hugh deSteny, Sheriff of Nottingham, who entrusted me with the mission of delivering this message to you. It has never left my person since Nottingham's gates closed behind me." It was undignified to have to wriggle so industriously to get the message from under his belt and acton, but his orders required no less of him. "It has lain along my spine since this journey began," he said as he drew it out of his padding and mail, and handed it to Prince John, saying as he did, "Now I have done as I was sworn to do."

"So you have," said Prince John, taking the letter and looking at its flattened appearance, frowning as he broke the seal, unrolled it, and read the salutation. "An urgent matter requiring knowledge and discretion, and from so careful a man as deSteny. He sent you to me most hastily, didn't he?" He signaled Wroughton to rise. "You have done well to bring this to me, good soldier."

"Will you read it, Your Grace? There is some hasty purpose, or so I have been told. If you will read it?" Wroughton asked anxiously, wishing to know what he had carried that was worth the lives of four of his men. He knew it was incorrect to question Prince John in this way, but he could not help himself.

"Yes. When I am done here, I will give it full attention," said the Prince, no trace of offense in his manner. "Whatever the trouble is, I will learn of it before midnight. I will send for you if I have anything to ask you." It was a dismissal, and the Captain tapped Wroughton on the shoulder, motioning him to leave.

"But the Sheriff said—" He stopped himself before he said anything unseemly. This was not what Wroughton had anticipated, and he hesitated before he stepped back from the Prince's chair and bowed. "I am at your service, Your Grace." It was vexing to be so close and yet not be permitted to tell what had happened on the journey from Nottingham to Windsor.

"Oh. Soldier," the Prince called after him. "To be certain: this is from Hugh deSteny himself, I take it, and not at the behest of Sir Gui deGisbourne?"

Wroughton hesitated. "That is correct, Your Grace."

"Not from Sir Gui. Curious." Prince John rose, making a sign to the others to remain seated. "That puts a different complexion on things," he said, and indicated a corridor at the rear of the dining tables. "If you will come with me, soldier? I will attend to this at once."

"Your Grace?" said the Captain of the Guard.

Prince John shook his head. "No, Pearce, not you. This soldier—"

"Wroughton," he supplied.

"Wroughton," echoed Prince John. "Have food sent to my study, if you will," he went on to a steward who hurried up to him. "Some for Wroughton, too. Drink as well, I would guess. For Wroughton. I will want a clear head, I fear, if deSteny is writing to me." And without other formalities, he led the way out of the dining hall, along another smoky, ill-lit corridor.

This was more than anything Wroughton had hoped, or prepared for. Exhausted though he was, he smiled at this unexpected favor, and did his best not to grin, thinking there would be men in Nottingham who would squirm with envy for such distinction as this, and Sir Gui would not believe that a simple soldier would receive such distinction from the Prince. "Your Grace is—"

The Prince waved him to silence. "You are the one who has braved the forest on this mission. And if Hugh deSteny sent you, it is no minor thing." He reached for a key hanging from his belt as he approached a bolted room. "I will read the whole of the message, and then you and I will talk, Wroughton."

"Your Grace," said Wroughton, all but overcome by the honor the Prince was bestowing on him. When he reported back to the Sheriff, he would have to report everything from this meeting. Men in Nottingham would stand him a drink just to hear what the Prince was wearing.

Prince John unfastened the lock and lifted the bolt, then opened the door. The room was L-shaped, dark, and unlike any Wroughton had ever seen before, lined as it was with shelves, all containing books, great, massive books with leather-and-board covers and closed with metal hasps. A few of the volumes were chained to the shelving for reasons that escaped Wroughton. One of the chained books lay open on a stand, clearly a Testament, for the pages were filled with beautiful illuminations of scenes and incidents that were familiar to Wroughton, and an elaborate cross was at the top of the pages Wroughton could see. He wanted to examine the book more closely, but dared not touch it without permission. The stacks of other books astonished him, for he had not supposed there were so many in the world. His awe was too great to do more than glance at the stands occasionally. For the first time in his life, he wished he could read. Three braziers supplied a modicum of light, hanging oil lamps over a trestle table standing in the middle of the room giving the greatest brightness. Two stools flanked the table.

Prince John sat on one of these, making a negligent indication that Wroughton could take the other stool while he perused the letter, his frown increasing as he read; twice he shook his head in dismay. When he had finished, he read the message a second time, then folded the parchment and placed it on the table, directing his gaze toward Wroughton. "Your Sheriff does well to send you to me. I do not think deSteny is often in error, is he?" He watched Wroughton for his single shake of his head. "If what he reports is true—and I must suppose it is, for I know him to be an honest man—there is cause to worry."

Was this supposed to be a compliment or a fault found? Wroughton could not bring himself to ask Prince John. He nodded and made himself wait for more. "Your Grace," he said, to indicate he was listening. What on earth had the Sheriff said that evoked such concern from the Prince?

"DeSteny tells me that you have seen the trouble in the forest for yourself, that you can describe it for me. Will you tell me about it?" Prince John regarded Wroughton with intense curiosity.

Wroughton coughed once, struggling to find words. He knew he had to say what he knew, but it would have to be to the Prince's satisfaction, and that banished sense from his thoughts and left him with a pervasive panic.

"Let me make this less difficult for you, Wroughton," the Prince suggested with a glance at the folded letter. "It is reported here that, among other things, you came upon crofters who had apparently been drained of blood, and who would not be properly buried. Is that what happened?"

"Chilton reported it, Your Grace, the warden for that part of the forest, the Nottingham precincts. He led us to the croft. A friar went with us, to tend to the dead. There were six of them. The White Friars would not bury them." As he gave his account, the horror of that refusal claimed him again.

"And the friar who accompanied you was lost in the forest? Lost, or did you see him laid to rest?" Prince John prompted him.

Wroughton had the unhappy feeling that the books around him were whispering, for he had never before been in a room that contained so many words. He made an effort to concentrate. "That he was. Lost, that is. It was through no fault of his, or the Sheriff's. The day was waning, and we were all in a hurry to be out of Sherwood. He—the Red Friar—fell behind, and when we noticed this, we were . . . unable to find him again."

"A bad thing," said the Prince, his manner slightly distracted as his thoughts rushed ahead of his tongue. "And there have been other attacks?"

"Yes, and there must have been some we have not yet discovered, given what the tales are on the Great North

Road." He could feel his pulse mount, his temples beginning to pound. "Coming here—I left with six men and arrived here with two." He could not stop the shiver that went through him. "Piers was the first to go, at the Austin's monastery. Then Newlyn vanished the next night, and Gaynes the night after that. I found none of them. They might have vanished at a witch's spell. We were spared on the fourth night, and I had hopes that the worst had passed, that we had moved beyond danger. Then Simkins left the protection of the hostel last night, saying he could hear Piers calling him."

"And what did you hear?" asked Prince John.

"I thought I heard . . . wolves. There were howls. Everyone heard the howls. I tried to stop Simkins, but . . . he went out into the forest. We found no trace of him in the morning, not even his sword or his boots." His voice had dropped to a mutter. He wondered why he should speak so openly to the Prince, who would surely despise him for his failure to protect his men.

"You did not follow him?" Prince John saw the nodded response. "Excellent. Very good."

Wroughton was shocked. "Your Grace?"

"Better to lose one man than two, and your mission was more important than the men lost, or deSteny would have sent you alone," said the Prince, his thoughtful gaze directed toward Wroughton in a mildly distant manner, revealing his preoccupation. He sat a little straighter, his eyes sharpening. "Given all that has transpired, you would have been reckless beyond forgiveness to have attempted to bring back the soldier last night. Or any of the others," he added darkly. "And on your return, stop for no one, not even those you think may be your men. They will be the most dangerous of all."

"But . . ." Wroughton began, and faltered. "The men must be dead."

"They are undoubtedly not alive," Prince John agreed. "Yes. They must be, most assuredly, dead. I have an account in one of my books that speaks of those who die improperly. But that does not mean they lie quiet in their graves." He rose from the stool and went to one of the shelves. As he pulled out a massive, leather-bound volume, he said, "I will have to read more before I can do as your Sheriff asks. But he was right to send you to me."

"He is an honorable man," said Wroughton, convinced that he had to say something.

"That he is, little though he may believe it," Prince John said, continuing to read, placing the open book on the trestle table at the limit of its chain. "In a short while, I will have more questions for you. In the meantime, pray do not interrupt me."

Wroughton bowed, knowing he would never dare such a thing, for it was nothing a soldier would do, not to the man deputized to rule England, Ireland, and half of France. He sat on the stool, feeling as exposed as if he were in a Saracen camp. Just sitting in the presence of the Prince was an honor he had never anticipated, no matter how it made him twitch. Even the arrival of a servant with two trays of food did not lessen his apprehension, for he dared not eat while in the company of John Plantagenet. It was an effort not to fidget, and he did what he could to keep from sighing or tapping his toe.

"Aren't you hungry? The hour is quite late and you have been in the saddle most of the day, haven't you? You must be famished. Why don't you eat?" the Prince asked suddenly. "God in Heaven, man, do not stand on ceremony in this room. You have already rendered me good service and the least I can do is feed you. So long as you are here, you must fend for yourself—I have been known to get lost in reading for hours, as my wife would complain to you, should you mention it."

"But Your Grace . . ." He could think of no way to say it. To imagine Prince John's wife complaining of anything her husband might do was unimaginable.

"You've ridden all day, haven't you? And your bones must ache—I know mine would do. And if you are not hungry, you are ill, which is much worse. I hope you will not have to be physicked." He made an impatient gesture with his fingers. "Eat. No need to wait on form. This is a library, not a court. I have no desire to have you collapsing on me, or thinking poorly for lack of food. This promises to be a long night, and you will have to keep pace with me."

Chagrined, Wroughton bent over his tray, carefully plucking out the morsels of chicken with his fingers and devouring them before he began to pull the trencher apart. It was the best wheaten loaf he had ever tasted, and the chicken was savory and tender, not baked to dryness as most he had had were. Onions flavored the gravy, and a small tub of butter was more delicious than the cheese he was used to. A tankard of dark brown ale helped to slake his thirst as he guttled down the meal. By the time he licked his fingers, Prince John had taken three more volumes from the shelves and was searching though them, marking his place with strips of cloth as he went.

"DeSteny says that these marauders hunt in the dark. And apparently only in the dark. Is this true?" Prince John asked suddenly.

"So it seems," said Wroughton, choosing his words carefully. "The reports have been few, Your Grace, and I am not privy to all of them, but I have not heard of them hunting when the sun is high."

"Ah." He pulled at his lower lip with his long fingers. "I feared as much. Yes. I must concur. Your Sheriff is right to be worried, or so it seems. These are not ordinary outlaws, are they? They do not hunt in the day, or have not been observed hunting in the day," Prince John corrected himself, and went back to his studies, leaving Wroughton to fight off the weariness that threatened to overcome him.

Now that he had food in his belly and stout walls around him, and his duty was done, fatigue picked at him with a persistence of a hungry duck, and he had much to do to keep from falling asleep. His fatigue embarrassed him and he strove to keep his eyes wide open and his expression alert. The warmth of the room was treacherous, and he found it increasingly difficult to resist his exhaustion. Only his precarious seat on the tall stool made him strive to remain awake. It would cause more chagrin than Wroughton could endure to be so shameless as to drowse in the presence of Prince John. So he kept to his perch and did his best to remember his prayers.

It was much later in the night when Prince John interrupted Wroughton's dozing, saying, "This is going to be difficult." He closed the volume open in front of him. "I will need some time to prepare, and I must do so alone. You might as well have the Master Sergeant assign you a place to sleep."

Wroughton, mildly disoriented, looked about the library. "Won't you need someone with you?" He was so accustomed to guard duty that he was ready to serve.

"To protect me?" Prince John suggested mildly. "Here at Windsor? I doubt it. What could assail this place that armed men could not stop?" With that question, he ushered Wroughton out of the door and prepared for serious study.

13.

How deSteny began his Journey South

"In a single column!" Hugh deSteny turned in the saddle and stared back at the road leading from the edge of Sherwood to the gates of Nottingham. He hoped he would see them again, and the town they protected, but he was not certain he would. The forest was too dangerous now for any of them to assume they could cross it safely. The mounted men with him watched him with a variety of reactions, and one of them made a joke that was instantly hushed. "Let us be underway," said deSteny in the tone of one announcing an execution. He faced the forest as he would an army of the Prophet's warriors.

The wood was filled with the calls of birds, the rush of wind, the chuckle of running water, and the countless noises marking the passage of many animals that lived within the forest's shelter. The clatter, jingle, and squeak of men-at-arms were nothing more than another part of the counterpoint that greeted the morning, and one that seemed vain compared to the vast welter of sound in the forest.

"To Arundel," deSteny called out, and set his dun moving forward, noticing already that his mail coif was chafing his neck. By evening, he thought, he would have a blister at least, if not an actual wound, and that he would have to treat with woolfat mixed with pansy. Annoying though it was, it would have to be borne.

Once into the trees, the party moved at a steady trot, covering ground handily for the first part of the journey. The horses had all been chosen for steadiness of temperament and stamina, and the Sheriff hoped they would reach Saint Dunstan's Priory by mid-day, which was more than seven leagues from the gates of Nottingham, and a more than satisfactory distance for mounted men to cover in the space of the morning in heavy forest. It was his intention to cover fifteen leagues this day, and the same the next, if the horses would stand the pace, and they met with no mischance. It was a punishing pace, requiring them to trot half the time, with little allowance for rest. Worry about trouble kept them all moving at a crisp jog longer than they ordinarily would, and they covered three leagues in half the time most riders in the forest would. During the later part of the morning, as the horses began to tire, the Sheriff signaled his men to rein in to a walk.

They arrived at Saint Dunstan's in good time, made a hearty meal there, and were on their way before the monks had finished singing mid-day Mass.

"We should reach Wainford Croft well before sunset," deSteny told his men, as he had done at the meeting on the eve before their departure, when he mapped out the roads they would take. The fortified farmhold was more of a hamlet than a walled barnyard, and the shallows of the river were carefully maintained by the Gates family and their neighbors, for the coppers they charged for helping wagons through the water augmented the earnings of their farming. "They have rooms and will not charge us more than two pieces of silver to house us and our mounts for the night."

"Is there a chapel at Wainford Croft?" asked the youngest of the men.

"There may be," said deSteny, who did not remember

seeing one when he had passed that way two years ago. "If there is not, they will have a shrine where you can recite your prayers. There is one to Our Lady beside the ford. There will be many more as we continue down the road."

The young man sat a little straighter in the saddle. "I am no palmer, to offer Aves at every cross-road shrine. I thought only it would be well to be shriven."

"You were that before we left Nottingham," deSteny reminded him.

"Still," said the youngster.

A scarred veteran of the Crusades laughed harshly. "Blessings won't stop arrows, if it comes to that. Nor swords."

"But they will protect our souls," the youngest man-at-arms said with feeling. "And in this place, our souls are in peril. We all know that." He cocked his chin in the Sheriff's direction as if seeking confirmation. "Those who have died here have not kept quiet after. They do not lie still in the graves, awaiting the Last Trumpet."

"Who says so?" demanded the veteran, who was called Canute, after the great Danish King who had ruled England long ago.

"Everyone," muttered the young man. "No one in the market wants to set foot in the forest between dusk and dawn, not without an army to guard them and an escort of monks. They are all afraid they will become fodder for the Devil."

A few of the older soldiers in the escort laughed, but the laughter was more bravado than amusement, which troubled deSteny. He raised his hand for silence. "If there is danger, better listen for its subtle approach than comfort yourselves with noise if what you dread is abroad. No more jollity, not tonight."

The youngest man-at-arms, Byrle of Penndale, who was not quite fifteen, had the grace to blush under his mail coif. The men on either side of him chuckled at this boyish lapse, though neither of them was older than eighteen.

DeSteny gave an abrupt signal to quiet them, and tried his best to ignore the chafing on the inside of his thighs. Long hours in the saddle at the trot always left him with raw patches, and he was glad to have the salve made for him by Mother Hezibeth: let the Church say what it would against herb women, to deSteny's mind, Mother Hezibeth and those like her were worth a week of Psalms and Masses. He would use her ointment to ease his discomfort, and he would offer it to his men, no matter how much the Church condemned such methods.

It was late in the day when the Sheriff and his men entered the stout wooden gates of Wainford Croft. They were met by wary men just in from the small fields, and their women, who sighed at the badges on deSteny's men's surcotes as much as their numbers.

"Welcome," said the master of Wainford Croft, a man deSteny's age called Hamm of the Gates family, who did not appear sincere in his greeting.

"God show you favor and a bountiful harvest, good crofter, and send you many healthy sons. I am the Sheriff of Nottingham, and these seven men are my soldiers. We are bound for Arundel, on the business of Sir Gui deGisbourne, who is lord here, for you and for us," said deSteny as he dismounted, cursing the aches and bruise he felt gathering in his flesh. "My men and I need shelter for the night." He patted the wallet on his belt. "I have money to pay our keep, and our horses'."

Hamm Gates regarded him slightly less hostilely. "That's as may be. But our cooking pots are not full, and our children are hungry. We have our own to feed," he said, his eyes measuring deSteny and his men, assessing their worth.

"Then coins will help you, come market-day, and a smoked ham will give you a meal for tomorrow. Take them with my thanks," said deSteny, taking care not to let the crofters offend him. "And we will not have to demand anything in Sir Gui's name. You will have meat from his larder and we will be safe for the night." He did not want this to become a confrontation, so he added, "I will tell him of your generosity, and ask that it be considered when his tax collector comes."

"We have little meat," Hamm Gates warned. "If you want venison, you must find it at an abbey, where the monks are allowed to kill deer. We have only goats and sheep, and we cannot slaughter one for you."

"And some of them have horns that do not curl, but antlers that branch," said deSteny evenly, his hands away from his weapons. He regarded the crofters without any sign of disapproval. "I am not here to punish you for poaching. If you have poached, that is not my concern. My mission is otherwise." He felt the collective intake of breath more than he heard it. "You need your goats and sheep alive, I know. And the deer you have killed were doubtless raiding your fields, and you did away with them to save your crops. Let us help you dispose of the evidence, so that if the King's Warden should come, he will find nothing to make him think you have broken the law."

"Is the King's Warden coming?" demanded Hamm Gates, a touch too urgently for an innocent man. "When is he to be here?"

"Eventually—when he is satisfied that all he will find amiss in the forest is poaching," said deSteny, holding the reins of his horse out in suggestion that the animal should be stalled, brushed, watered, and fed. "There are two coppers for the lad who cares for my horse. Two coppers for each of our horses," he added, knowing his men were as tired as he, and the coppers would purchase as much goodwill as grooming. The sum was generous, enough to persuade one of the children to step forward.

A boy of nine or ten presented himself at once. "Two coppers? For caring for one horse? Are you sure?"

"Yes." DeSteny handed him the reins. "He will not bite you if you do not touch his mouth. Clean his feet, too, after he's brushed. I don't want him going lame because of a pebble. Brush the mud off his legs when it has dried. Make sure the saddle-pad is free from dust and any burrs or grit."

The boy squared his shoulders and tugged the horse after him toward the extension on the barn that served as stables.

"He will do a good job," said Hamm Gates, and motioned for the other children to come forward. "You know how it is done: see to the horses," he said.

"Your son?" deSteny asked Hamm Gates as the horses were taken off by youngsters. "A fine boy."

"With your horse? My nephew. My heir, however," answered Hamm Gates, his bluntness mildly surprising to deSteny, who wondered how it was that Hamm Gates had no living sons to inherit his croft. "My late brother's boy."

"A hopeful lad, by the look of him," deSteny observed.

"Thank God for it," said Hamm Gates, then indicated the forty or so people standing around the huge barnyard. "Let us portion out our guests. Each of the houses can take two men. There are eight of you. That leaves only two to sleep in the barn, to guard your horses and your gear. No doubt you can decide who they will be. There is room in the loft. Which might be just as well, for the sake of your horses."

"Canute, then, and Sprague." He pointed to the men-at-arms in turn. "Tonight you will sleep in the hay. Meaghar, you'll keep watch until midnight. Ackerley will relieve you. If there is trouble, sound your alarm."

"Like Our Lord, we sleep in a stable," quipped Sprague, who fancied himself a wit. He was in his middle-twenties and had been to the Holy Land where he had lost four toes, an injury he regarded as a sign of distinction.

Canute accepted the assignment with a sigh. "Are we to keep watch, as well?" His tone suggested that he would rather not.

"I doubt that will be necessary," said the Sheriff, more to keep from insulting Hamm Gates than from any conviction that they were safe here. He coughed and went on, watching the crofters from the tail of his eye. "With Ackerley and Meaghar to guard, you may sleep as best you can."

Meaghar laughed once. "Repose your faith in me," he quipped.

"Men sleeping in stables do not sleep soundly, not even when the loft is full of hay," said Sprague, his rich chuckle bringing a few, faint smiles from the crofter. "We will be alert to any disturbance, without question. If Meaghar or Ackerley should sound the alert, we will be up and ready in a trice."

A few of the escort were becoming restless. Ackerley had his hand resting on the hilt of his sword now, and Delwin had taken to tapping his foot so that his spur jingled. The village made them nervous, and they didn't trust peasants. Now they were out of the saddle, they were realizing how hungry and tired they were. Nottingham seemed very far away, and the road ahead most uncertain. They did not like having to wait while the crofters arranged matters to their satisfaction. DeSteny was aware of this. He opened his wallet and handed over money to Hamm Gates. "Here. For our food and lodging, and the stabling and feed for our mounts." He smiled as he did this, hoping his men would take their lead from him and present a more agreeable demeanor.

Hamm Gates seized the coins at once. "Very well. Assign your men as you think best. You will sit at my table tonight. You and one other." If he wanted this offer to sound gracious, he did not achieve his ends.

"Very well. Hearne, you will keep me company." He knew that Hearne was more readily amused than most of his men, and that he knew more tales and songs than half the minstrels who wandered England; he hoped those abilities would stand them both in good stead during the evening.

The other men waited as various crofters pointed out who among them they would have in their houses. When it was settled, the oldest woman went to the bucket suspended over the little branch of the river that had been diverted to run through a corner of the barnyard. As she watched the bucket fill, she motioned to deSteny to approach. "It is sweet, and clear-flowing," she announced as she offered the water to deSteny and his men. "You may drink it without harm."

"And right welcome it is," he said, drawing his drinking cup from the pouch hanging from his belt. He filled it and drank. "You are fortunate to have good water. When water is foul, then the horses must suffer."

"Good water makes for good beer," one of the crofters said, doing his best to make the occasion a friendly one now that money had changed hands.

"We broached a barrel tonight," Hamm Gates announced, his expression melting into one of pleasant accommodation.

Hearing this, deSteny hoped the morning would not be too unbearable, or the men too slow to rise, but he showed his appreciation, and was glad the awkward moment had passed.

It was some time after supper had finished and the rushlights were burning low that Hamm Gates said, "I must talk with you, Sheriff. It is very important." He had drunk four generous cups of beer but his tongue was not unruly and his eyes did not shine as some of the crofters' did.

DeSteny regarded him with interest. "Yes? What is it?" His two cups of beer had not done more than release the worst knots in his sinews.

"I am . . . troubled." He glanced around as if he feared they might be overheard, though none of his household was paying them any attention—they were caught up in listening to Hearne describe the wonders of London.

"Why?" asked deSteny, and waited for the answer.

"My brother . . . he lost his wife and child . . . to . . . to what is in the forest. Their bodies were frightful to behold, and he had to bury them. It filled him with a grief that was terrible to see. I did not expect such mourning as he has done, for was altered nearly beyond recognition. He was like one gone mad, swearing he would bring an end to the . . . the trouble, or die trying to do it." Hamm Gates fell silent, staring toward the narrow window as if it held something only he knew of.

When he began to worry that Hamm Gates would tell him no more, deSteny said, "Is that all?"

"No," said Hamm Gates, looking embarrassed at his lapse. But he took his time in resuming. "He went into the forest. Alone. We have not seen him since. He vanished. We have had no report of him, and no message, either. He might as well have been carried off to Heaven. Or Hell. And he isn't a man who can easily become invisible. He is large, my brother, much larger than I, more than a head taller and with shoulders as wide as a doorway. His arms are thick as haunches and he can drive nails with his fists. He has been our sawyer and smith for ten years and more, so he is stronger than any of the rest of us."

"I did not meet such a man on the road as we came here," said deSteny, to keep Hamm Gates talking.

The crofter shook his head. "He went to find his wife and son . . . He found them dead, and brought them back to be buried. He saw them into the ground and he swore he would avenge them. He set off from his house with his quarterstaff and his knife, and enough food for three days. That was more than six weeks ago. The monks of Saint Procopius' Monastery, who pray for us, say he is lost."

"Is that why you are worried about him?" DeSteny knew there was more.

"Yes," Hamm Gates admitted as if such concern were shameful. His beer slopped over his chin and he drank again.

"And you have looked for him?" He guessed the crofters would not go far into the forest, but he did not doubt that some effort had been made.

"How far have you gone to find him?" Hearne interjected.

"Not beyond our usual limits," Hamm Gates said, turning away in shame.

"But you do continue to search," deSteny said.

"Yes. And ask travelers if they have seen him. Nothing. A big man, strong. He was always laughing at himself for being so big, but after his family were dead, he stopped. He could not smile, let alone laugh. He swore he would not face the danger of the forest but over running water, so that he could not be taken by outlaws. He carried his staff with him, and he is a powerful fighter with it. The monks told him he could only be safe over running water, and with a wooden weapon." Hamm Gates offered this last as if to approve the prudence of his missing brother. He frowned, reiterating, "He was very good with a quarterstaff. No man for a day in all directions has ever bested him in contest."

DeSteny shook his head. "I have seen none such in Nottingham, but I will ask for him as we go, if you like, and look for him in the villages we pass. I will make inquiries of other travelers." The thought that the creatures in the woods might have claimed more victims chilled deSteny to the bone, and made him hope more fervently that Wroughton had reached Windsor safely.

"If you will, I will remember you to God every night," said Hamm Gates. "Find out, also, if he has done what he swore to do. If he has found what he sought—" He stopped again.

"It might not be wise to have him back, if that is the case," deSteny appended.

Hamm Gates smiled wanly and reached for the spigot on the barrel. "When you inquire, use his name. We call him Little John."

14.

How Much the Miller's Son came Home

In the mill there was a pervasive odor of dampness and the constant groan of the wheel turning in the millrace. The grinding of the stones kept the old building shuddering, but the miller paid no attention to any of it. He had become accustomed to the sound so long ago that most of the time he no longer heard it. But tonight he was alert to every sound around him, for his son was missing, and had been missing for six days: it was being said that he had been carried off by evil sprites that lived in Sherwood.

"Who's there?" he called out in a shaking voice when an unfamiliar clink sounded. He held his breath, waiting for another sound.

A small, black scrap fluttered toward him, and he almost giggled in relief—a bat, nothing more. The miller gave a wobbly smile to the little animal as it flapped upwards toward the thatched roof. There was nothing to fear from the bats, no matter what the priest said about them: the miller had never been troubled by the tiny beasts.

Another sound caught his attention, a sound from outside. It seemed a bit like someone calling his name, but with a rough intonation, harsh and grating, as if the very grinding of the stones had gained a voice and was calling to him. He stood still, listening and concentrating, trying not to hear the water, the mill-wheel, and the turning stones. He moved nearer the door, concentrating.

"Father!" The call was louder, or closer.

The miller could not entirely believe it. "Much?" he whispered, saying his son's name as if praying to a saint.

"Father! Come out! I know you're in there!" The voice was close-by, probably in the meadow by the stream where the mill stood.

This time he shouted. "Much! Is that you, boy?"

"I've come back for you, Father," he answered. "Come out to me."

He could not guess why Much would not come in, and imagined all manner of hurts the lad might have that made climbing the stairs and crossing the narrow bridge into the mill difficult or impossible. It was hard to bear, thinking of his child being hurt, and that ended any sense of caution he might have. He made up his mind at once. "Stay where you are, boy!" he yelled, hearing a muffled echo from the mill itself. "I'll be out shortly."

"I am lonely, Father!" Much called out. "I miss you."

This simple plea tore at the miller's heart and hastened all he did. He pulled his smock over his head, paying no heed to the fine dusting of flour that was deposited on his clothes. Then he opened the door and stepped outside, taking the enclosed torch to light his way. "Ah! My son!"

"Father!" Much sounded more urgent.

The miller hurried along the narrow bridge and clambered down the steep stairs to the ground. He peered into the dark, looking for his son. "Much?"

"I am near, Father," said the young man, seeming to materialize out of the nearest clump of trees.

"My boy!" The miller began to weep with joy. "I thought you were lost to us. Come, my boy. Embrace me."

"That I will, Father, and gladly," said Much, and came up to the miller in a rush, wrapping him in arms that were stronger than the miller remembered. "I have missed you. You don't know how keenly I have missed you." Much repeated as he took his first, deep bite of his father's throat.

The miller jerked like a gaffed fish, his mind recoiling from what was happening. How could his boy, his Much, do this to him? Surely it was a devil that had taken the form of his missing child. It could not be Much worrying his neck. His thought began to blur, and terror built in him as he realized he was bleeding to death.

Much raised his head, and the miller saw his face was smeared with blood, and he called out, "Hurry. He won't last long." Then he resumed his grisly task.

Half a dozen figures came out of the darkness and converged upon the hapless miller, a few of them snarling as they waited for their turn as the pulsing red fountain began to dwindle to a weak stream.

Wolves, thought the miller in an eerily calm way. That is what they remind me of. They are just like wolves. He tried to lift his hand to touch his son, but it was much too heavy, and the effort was unimportant in the fading glimmer of his thoughts. Then he lost consciousness, and a short time later, his life.

Much laid his father down regretfully—he was still hungry—and turned to those who had accompanied him. "I told you I could get him out of the mill."

"So you did," said Will Scarlet, who just now lived up to his name: blood covered his face and hands, bright in the moonlight. "We could not have got into the mill, that's certain."

"He might have been in an iron tower," said Penrod Lugenis, the former scholar.

"Built over running water," said Amadin, who had been a skinner until Hood's men found him. "As safe as a church."

"Safer," said Piers, recalling how the monk had cozened

him out of the monastery into the grasp of Hood."

"Still, he came out when I called," said Much with pride. "Nothing could have lured him out but my voice."

"So you said," Will Scarlet remarked with a trace of boredom.

"Because it is true." Much took a defiant stance beside his father's body.

"The two of you, stop it," said Amadin. "There's nothing worth fighting over."

"You have done what we all do," added Penrod Lugenis.

Much sulked. "No one could find us prey. You all looked and you failed. You were hungry. I told you we would have what we sought. I did that, and I have been one of you for no more than five days, and yet I have brought you to feed."

"And that was good of you, but nothing more than is expected," said Will Scarlet, trying to maintain his composure. "You cannot boast of every kill."

"None of us are allowed to boast of doing what we must," said Marzial deGranville, who had been a Royal Courier until Hood's men had set upon him almost a year ago. "It is not pleasing to Hood."

The others agreed with growls.

"This was my father!" Much insisted. "Doesn't that count for something?"

"Ease of capture, most certainly," said Piers. "As for the fact that he is your father, that is past."

"Because he is dead," said Much.

"Because you are one of us, and all your living ties are for naught," said Will Scarlet.

There was a long silence among the small group of Hood's men. Then Amadin coughed. "We shouldn't linger," he said pointedly. "Someone may come looking for him, and then we would have trouble."

"That's so," said Will Scarlet. "We should return to our camp."

Much shook his head. "Does this mean nothing to you?"

"It means we are no longer famished," said Piers.

Thomas Franklin, who had not spoken until now, observed, "The night is young, but I suppose you're right: we must go back. Hood doesn't want us abroad for long."

"You will tell him what I did," said Much, looking toward the forest. "You know who to tell, and how."

"If you insist," said Will Scarlet, "I will do it."

"He must know my devotion," said Much, beginning to trudge toward the trees. "I have a mother, too, and two sisters. We can return here."

"Not for a while," said Will Scarlet. "Once they find your father, they will arm against us."

"Will he rise?" Piers asked, trying to recall his own transition.

"Not he. We broke his neck," said Will Scarlet.

"Oh, yes. That's right," said Piers.

A moment later they were into the trees and the sight of the mill was lost behind branches. They moved along steadily, as if in daylight rather than under the ashen moon. Along barely visible trails they went, startling badgers and foxes on their way, covering ground with unholy speed.

Midnight had just passed when they reached their camp again, and found a good number of their fellows gathered about a fire, some of them with the bloated appearance that showed they had glutted themselves on the blood of animals. Others showed the lethargy of hunger, and they watched their comrades with the steady, envious gaze of foxes.

"Where's Hood?" asked Will Scarlet, speaking for the half-dozen of his companions.

"Still hunting," said a lean palmer called Clemence. He had taken off his jerkin and was washing blood off his body using water from a leather bucket.

"On his own?" Marzial deGranville asked.

"Who knows?" Clemence shrugged. "You must have found prey to your liking, to return so early."

"That we did," said Piers, sinking down on a log and readying himself for a nap.

"I took them to my father's mill," said Much.

"That he did," Will Scarlet confirmed. "And he drank first." This last was delivered in a cutting tone.

"I caught him. He was mine," said Much.

"We all slaked our thirst," said Penrod Lugenis, no longer interested in the argument.

"But he was my father," Much persisted.

"And?" Penrod Lugnis prodded.

"What's the importance of that?" Clemence asked. "He's dead in any case."

"The importance," said Much with exaggerated patience, "is that I killed him, even though he was my father."

Will Scarlet shrugged. "And Hood killed me, though we are cousins. The only difference is your father will stay dead."

The men around the fire showed a little curiosity about the debate, but most of them were not very interested.

Much stomped over to the well and pulled up the bucket. "I have to wash." He dropped his hands into the water, staining it red.

"So do we all," said Piers. "There are other hunters who will be drawn to the scent of blood." He went to join Much, doing his best to keep the young vampire from blurting out any more claims about his father.

"How long will it take for the Sheriff to find out?" asked Clemence.

"About the miller? A day or two, no more. Chilton should know tomorrow," said Will Scarlet.

"If we made Chilton one of us, we would not have to worry about him," said Thomas Franklin.

"They would just appoint another to his post, and what would be the use of that?" said Amadin. "We know Chilton."

"Besides, if Chilton dies, or becomes one of us," said Penrod Lugenis, "it is likely that the Sheriff will appoint more than one man to guard the forest, and that would not be useful to us. Best to keep things as they are."

"The scholar is right," said Orlan Royce. "When I was a guide, I often encountered Chilton, and I know that his reports are heeded in Nottingham."

Amadin clapped his hands. "That can be to our advantage. Let him try to keep up with what we do, and see how well he fares." His laughter was like the yapping of wolves. "There are more of us than him. We can run him ragged, so that he cannot make a true report, no matter what he may do."

A few of the men made noises of agreement, but most of them were too busy preparing themselves for the arrival of Hood, who would not be pleased if they had not cleaned themselves after the kill.

"Well, just so you think about it," said Much, sloshing water over his head and rubbing his face with his free hand.

Will Scarlet flung up his hand in exasperation. "Very well. We will think," he said, and set about neatening himself along with the rest.

15.

How Hood wrought among the Pilgrims

All day long the Red Friar had tried to remember his prayers, and to repeat them without feeling desperately ill. Now that the sun was going down, the urge to piety had left him, and he was unable even to think about God, for any attempt along those lines left him as wrung out as a bad case of dysentery. He drew his hood over his head and prepared to leave the hovel he shared with Will Scarlet.

"They say there will be ample drink tonight, for all of us. We will feast upon the unwary," Will Scarlet remarked from his bed of straw and lichen. "There are pilgrims on the road, bound for the coast to take ship to France."

"They may be protected," said the Red Friar, recalling the many times he had accompanied such men and women along the Great North Road.

"Not from us," Will Scarlet declared as he flung back the bear-hide rug that covered him. "They are not wise enough to arm themselves against us."

"They carry . . . joined sticks, you know the kinds I mean—the sign of their belief. They have them around their necks, with special beads." This last was hard to get out. "And many of them have . . . that bread on their persons. They carry it to guard them." He wanted to say the Host, but that was beyond his capabilities. He motioned to the troubadour. "Can you ignore such things?"

"Not really. Not I. But Hood can. He is . . . less hampered than the rest of us are. I don't know why, only that he is so. He is the strongest of us, and he has proved it often." He was on his feet now, stretching as much as the low, earthen ceiling would permit. He sighed as his hand brushed a fall of dust from his head. "Might as well be in a grave."

"It is where we ought to be," said the Red Friar. "In a grave, with the . . . protection over us." Just admitting so much left him queasy.

"So we ought, but it isn't going to happen, not to us." Will Scarlet sighed as he prepared to raise the flap of the deer-hide covering the entrance. "Unless there's someone out there smarter and more determined than Hood is, and as ruthless and as strong. Even if there is, he'd have to know just what he was up against, and that doesn't seem too likely."

"Perhaps not," said the Red Friar, rubbing the stubble of his unshaven pate. "I don't like thinking about how we will go on until it's over."

"Neither do I," said Will Scarlet as he left their quarters.

Sherwood Forest was rustling down into dusk. Blue gloom spread everywhere under the canopy of leaves. The men around Hood were emerging from their various dens and burrows, most of them restless with need. All were silent in anticipation of what they know must come. Will Scarlet and the Red Friar joined the others at the side of their leader and waited for him to speak.

Hood's face was unusually gaunt as he stared around the clearing. His cloak hung open so that the faded green of his garments could be seen in the last of the daylight, and the shine from his red eyes was as brilliant as sunset. He stretched with animal thoroughness, sinuous as a cat, and then addressed the gathered men. "Tonight we will feast.

No one will go unfilled. You will drink to the dregs."

There was a sound compounded of hunger, wrath, and longing. It was not quite a howl, but it echoed uncannily through the trees, carrying silence in its wake.

"Not far from here there is an abbey. Most of you know the one I mean, for the Trinitarians. We have been there before, on similar missions," Hood went on, his expectations finding expression in the relish with which he told them. "A party of pilgrims arrived there in the afternoon and sought the protection of the monks. This was granted. The abbot has sent word that his Trinitarians will be at prayers in the chapel from sundown until midnight, and if we come during that time, the pilgrims will be ours to do with as we wish, if we will but continue to leave his monks untouched. They will not bar the gates against us, or set guards on the walls. We will encounter no opposition from anyone, for the wine the pilgrims drink will be laced with poppy, and they will sleep deeply. We will be able to take our fill so long as we are away by midnight."

This time the sound was louder, and a few of the men began to pace energetically.

"There are more than thirty pilgrims, so you will have to stay quiet as you drain them, so as not to disturb any who might have not been touched by the poppy. And you must drain them." He paused, and when he went on his voice was as cold as a hinge in winter. "We cannot have them joining us, so it is best if they are all forever dead. You know how this is done."

"Take their heads!" one of the men shouted.

"Break their necks," said Will Scarlet.

"Put a hawthorn branch down their gullet," said Penrod Lugenis.

"Yes," Hood approved. "Bring the heads you take to me.

All of them. If you break necks, or stuff them, cut off their noses instead, but be sure all are reckoned. I will count them all, to be certain that we have left no one behind to—" He broke off, peering up into the massive darkness. "The man who fails to take a head or bring me a nose when he has fed will be sent away from here, and kept away."

The Red Friar nudged Will Scarlet and whispered, "Where is the disgrace in that?"

Will Scarlet answered as quietly as he could, "The crofters are warned, and they know what to do. It has happened before. For them we are bad enough—they do not want rogues."

"You mean you let the crofters kill vampires?" The Red Friar was shocked.

"Yes. So long as the vampire is not one of us," said Will Scarlet. "They have made the Old Ones as they are."

"But if they can kill us . . . How are we to survive? Won't it be the end of us, to have the crofters kill us?"

"And consign us to Hell everlasting," Will Scarlet reminded him. "You no longer serve . . . your old master. Hood is the source of life and death here."

"I suppose so," said the Red Friar, doing his best to accept this dire situation. Perhaps, he thought, he would be considered a martyr if he defied Hood. But as soon as the notion crossed his mind, he knew it would not happen, and he all but staggered under the weight of his despair.

"The pilgrims will be given the wine with their meal, and they should sleep shortly afterward, with sleepy guards to watch over them," Hood continued. "Their dormitory doors will not be locked, and you will have nothing barring your way. Strike swiftly and allow no one to escape." He pointed up toward the sky. "Bring your swords and your daggers. It is time we were off."

Somehow the Red Friar heard himself say, "I do not carry a sword, nor any weapon."

Hood rounded on him, his red eyes alight. "Then have one or the others do the work, just so long as you bring a head or a nose to me."

It was an order impossible to disobey. The Red Friar nodded dumbly and tried not to look at Hood.

"I am ready to go," Hood announced, holding his sword aloft. It was a signal to the rest of them to prepare for the night. All hurried to arm themselves, and then fell into step behind Hood, making their way through the dusk toward the Abbey of Saints Florus and Laurus which had stood in the forest for more than three hundred years.

The walls of the abbey were thick and its buildings squat. The gates, of iron-bound oak were so heavy that two monks were needed to open them. Hood swung them as easily as a lady might push aside a curtain, and waited while his band trooped into the small courtyard where they stood together until he closed the doors. From the far side of the courtyard came the sounds of monks chanting their prayers. He pointed in the direction of the cells where the pilgrims were quartered. "There. Do not alert them, or we will have a fight and the monks will have to get involved. The Abbot would not like that. He would have to resist us, and those monks under his authority would be in danger." His low laughter was dreadful to hear.

"What must I do?" the Red Friar asked Will Scarlet, hoping he did not know the answer. "How should . . . it be done?"

"You will know," Will Scarlet answered grimly, his features lupine as he started along the corridor leading to the dormitories.

The first of the band was inside the building already, and the rest were close behind. In spite of his best intentions, the Red Friar found himself falling in with the rest, an emotion stirring within him he did not want to acknowledge or recognize. In this place, he should feel his perfidy, and his shame should stop him from taking part in the debauchery. This was his own Order, and he was coming as a thief in the night to steal more than gold. His jaw tightened uselessly against the thirst that had started to rage in his veins, compelling him to go in search of the one remedy that would bring him ease. He could not recall how he had reached the door to the men's dormitory, but he slipped inside and flinched as he caught sight of the crucifix over the sleeping pilgrims' heads. He stumbled forward, suddenly eager to feel the pulse of life under his lips. He leaned over a scrawny young man lying under the single rough blanket provided by the monks, and laid his fingers on the lad's neck.

"Wha . . . ?" the pilgrim murmured, disturbed and about to awaken.

As much to silence him as to feed, the Red Friar abruptly bit away his throat, opening his mouth wide to the delicious, vile fountain of blood, hot, damnable, and delicious. Never had anything satisfied him as that hideous, sweet, red liquid did. No lust, no matter how intense or shameful, had ever worked on him as the slaking of his thirst did now. There was blood all over his face, his habit was gory with it, and still it was not enough. As the pilgrim's veins gave up their treasure, the Red Friar wallowed in his sin and fulfillment, oblivious to the others around him.

A sharp sound brought him to his senses. Will Scarlet was standing by the cot, the lower half of his face smirched with blood, his sword raised, a head dangling by the hair from his belt. "Hurry. Finish up."

"Hurry?" the Red Friar repeated as if he did not understand the word.

"Yes." Will Scarlet pushed nearer. "I'll get the head for you."

The necessity of this act nearly overwhelmed the Red Friar, who held out his hand to stop the blow. "It is profane."

"Then I'll take the nose instead," Will Scarlet offered. "It's all one to me."

"The nose," the Red Friar agreed. "It isn't so bad."

"Truly," said Will Scarlet as he shoved the Red Friar aside. And struck. "There, you see? Nothing easier."

Replete and despising himself for it, the Red Friar permitted Will Scarlet to hand him the young pilgrim's nose. He walked as if overcome with wine, his steps weaving and unsteady as he did his best to keep up with Will Scarlet. Around them the rest of the band was also making their way back from the dormitories to the courtyard of the abbey, many of them dazed, a few of them giggling.

In the courtyard the rest of the band was gathering, many of them moving quickly with excitement, a few lethargic from their over-enthusiasm. Hood was waiting for them, the heads of three youths dangling from his red hands. He waved his men forward, an expression of something hideously like gratification on his lean features. "Is it all done?"

As if responding to the question, the night was sundered by a single scream.

"The Devil!" swore Will Scarlet, his pleasant features blanching beneath the red smears. "The monks will hear that."

"Who is the fool who—" Hood demanded in a voice that left all his band still and silent as if riven by lightning.

The scream had become a high, keening whimper of unmitigated horror.

"It was Much, the miller's boy," said Penrod Lugenis, his tattered scholar's gown engorged from neck to hem. "He has not finished."

Hood stared around, fixing in his mind the faces of those about him. "Yes. Much is not here. Well, he has done his worst. Now I will do mine." The promise inherent in those simple words chilled his men. "Do you—Will Scarlet and the Friar—go fetch Much. Be sure you dispatch his victim, for it would seem he has made a mull of it himself."

The Red Friar trembled. "If you would allow—" he began, only to be interrupted by Hood.

"You heard my order. Did you not understand me? Or do you seek to disobey me as well?" His words were smooth, almost gentle, but none of his men were deceived. "Fetch Much for me. Now."

"Of course," said Will Scarlet, plucking the Red Friar by the sleeve. "Come," he urged in an undervoice as he started back across the courtyard.

"But this is . . ." The Red Friar could think of nothing heinous enough to describe their errand.

"We must do it," said Will Scarlet. "Or he will dispatch us."

"Would that be so terrible?" the Red Friar inquired as they stepped again into the pilgrims' wing of the abbey.

Will Scarlet stopped and turned to the Red Friar. "Are you in such a hurry to burn in Hell?"

The Red Friar ducked his head. "No," he admitted. "But this will only compound our sins."

"The fire is no hotter for a dozen sins than one, and eternity is the same length. You might as well take all Hood has to offer until you stand before God, for until then, Hood is our lord and we owe him fealty," said Will Scarlet and resumed his search for the unlucky Much, following the echoing sounds of fading shrieks.

The Red Friar was not as certain of these doctrinal assumptions as Will Scarlet was, but he was absolutely certain that Hood's wrath was immediate and hideous. He trudged after the troubadour, resigned to their task.

They found the youth on the second floor, in the women's dormitory, cowering in the corner away from the fragile girl he had attacked. As she writhed on her pallet, blood spurting from her mouth and ears as well as the wound in her throat, she continued to cry out, her voice now hardly more than a gurgling rasp. Very quickly her writhing turned to spasms and she twitched with oncoming death. Much shivered at the sight, unable to bring himself to act. As Will Scarlet and the Red Friar entered the dormitory, the look of relief on Much's loutish features turned to dismay.

"No. No. I thought—"

"You thought the monks would find you, didn't you?" Scarlet said as he went to dispatch the girl, standing over her as blood shot from her neck. "It is a waste. Pity."

"It is. I . . . I'm sorry." Much lowered his head. "Hood is angry, isn't he?"

"Yes," said Will Scarlet as he handed the girl's head to the Red Friar. "As you knew he would be. What made you do such a foolish thing?"

"I don't know," said Much, getting slowly and awkwardly to his feet, as if he had suddenly become very old. "It wasn't anything like my father. She was—"

The Red Friar went to his side. "It was mad of you." He had wanted to rebuke Much for his folly but could not now summon up the indignation to do it.

"You'd better come with us," said Will Scarlet, holding out his hand to the miller's son.

"She was just so thin and pale," said Much as Will Scarlet led him out of the cell. "I could tell she was ailing, and doing . . . this . . . was more than she could endure. I . . . faltered when I realized what her trouble was." He paused to lick the spatters of blood from his mouth, then went on as if he might exonerate himself with Will Scarlet. "She wanted God to heal her, that was why she was a pilgrim. She had put her hope in being cured on her journey. I didn't want to add to her suffering. I thought that if I let her bleed to death she would not be so frightened. I didn't drink very much of her blood. It was thin and tasteless. I was afraid she would start to pray if I bit too deeply."

"You are babbling," said Will Scarlet without a trace of sympathy. "It will do you no good."

Much swallowed hard twice, then glanced at the Red Friar, who brought up the rear, the head of the girl still clutched in his hands. "I thought she didn't deserve to die this way."

At that Will Scarlet laughed aloud. "No one deserves this. We do not, nor do those who fall to us. If you start to trouble yourself about who is deserving of our attention, you will end up like a rabid beast." He shoved Much ahead of him and out into the courtyard.

Already there was a pyre of branches prepared for Much, packed tightly so that the fire would be concentrated and burn hot. Hood's band stood around it with quiet purpose. There was a moment that seemed suspended, when no one breathed, and even the monks in the abbey stopped chanting.

"You know what to do," Hood said to Much.

Mutely the miller's son nodded. Then he began to climb onto the pile of branches. No one offered to help him, and no one protested.

"Bring a torch," Hood ordered, paying no attention to the man who rushed to obey. "Put the heads with him."

There was a flurry of activity as the band did as Hood ordered. Two of the heads rolled off the pyre and had to be flung higher onto the branches. The Red Friar strove to think of the holy words to protect these plundered souls, but his head ached as if caught in a vice and all he could do was whisper, "Farewell," to the heads, and to Much.

Hood took the torch from his man and thrust it deep into the branches, stepping back as the first flames sprouted, his eyes reflecting the same color as the fire. "Come." With that, he turned his back on the pyre and walked straight out of the abbey gates, not looking back as the fire's plume suffused the night sky beneath a thickening cloud of oily smoke. The smell of burning meat filled the woods, putting all its denizens on nervous alert, for all of them dreaded fire.

Bringing up the rear, the Red Friar tried to find compassion in his heart for Much, who was bound from this world to the fires of Hell, and was disgusted when he was unable to summon the sensibility required. As he went deeper into the forest, the fire's brightness faded and the Red Friar began to comprehend the depths of his damnation. What caused him the greatest despair was the realization that he did not mind.

16.

How deSteny passed through London

The Great North Road led down to London Town, and past the old, partly ruined Roman fort on the river where ferrymen waited on the west end of the walls of the Tower to carry the men from Nottingham across to the south bank. The town was full and bustling, the traffic increasing as they neared the river. Hugh deSteny and his men tried not to stare at the close-huddled houses that spread out along the Thames for almost a mile, the smoke from their chimneys making the air pungent, although deSteny, and a few of the others, had seen London, and grander cities in other climes. They approached the ferrymen carefully, not wanting to alarm them with all their weapons. The early afternoon sun made the river shine like old silver.

"I am the Sheriff of Nottingham," deSteny called out. "I am on the business of Sir Gui deGisbourne, and we must go over the river."

The leader of the ferrymen—a hulking fellow with a squint and one missing ear—shouted back, "Even men on nobles' business must pay."

"Yes. Of course," deSteny agreed. "The full rate. We're not here to haggle, we've other concerns."

"Very good," said the leader of the ferrymen. "Do your horses balk at boats? I warn you, I won't stand for any kicking or rearing once we're away from the shore. You'll all have to dismount, of course. If you damage my craft, it will cost you six shillings." An outrageous sum, but the ferryman's face was set.

"They do not balk at water, or anything but fire," said Hearne. "Unless your ferrymen are afraid of horses." His chuckle spread through the men-at-arms and brought scowls to the ferrymen's faces.

"How much to take us over to Saint Thomas Southwark?" deSteny asked.

"A shilling for the lot," said the ferryman. "And a pence to each of the men." It was another outrageous price and each of the men knew it. "For each ferry."

"You shall have it," said deSteny without protest. He could see Byrle and Ackerley swell indignantly.

"We can cross Friars' Bridge," Hearne suggested.

"We could swim," Meaghar suggested, only half-joking.

"And pay the Church more?" Sprague countered.

The ferryman laughed harshly. "That's right. You'll pay the friars more for their help over Father Thames than you will pay us."

"But they'll say prayers for us," Canute shouted.

"And we may need their prayers," Meaghar added.

"Then cross with them," said the ferryman. "But if the bridge doesn't hold, don't blame us."

It was well-known that the Friars' Bridge could not support more than two horses at a time, and that alone made the ferries preferable. "We will forego the prayers," said deSteny. "Come. Let us be about it." He signaled his men to dismount and lead their horses. While they settled on the order of their crossing, he rummaged in his leather tunic for the coins to pay the ferrymen. "Four shillings and seven pence," he said, taking out the coins and holding them up for the ferrymen to see. "Here are two shillings and four pence. When we are over the river, you shall have the rest." He rocked back on his heels. "You know I have all the money, for I have shown you the coins."

The leader of the ferrymen scowled but accepted the money and the terms, nodding grudgingly. "All right. But if you cheat me, your lord shall know of it. Get your lot aboard and we'll set off." He took up his position to work the sweep-oar, saying to his assistant, "Look lively now. These soldiers must be on their way."

"Very good," said deSteny, thinking that any appeal to Sir Gui for money from such laborers as these would fall on deaf ears.

Four of the nine ferries were shortly loaded and the boats set out into the river, the sweep-oars sculling them toward the far side and the low-lying wharf of Saint Thomas Southwark, the Abbey sprawling at the edge of the close-built village. The current was strong but the ferrymen knew it well and kept their craft steadily on course.

Delwin's chestnut stamped nervously, but the other horses managed to remain calm for the crossing, although deSteny's dun took exception to a floating log, snorting a challenge and tossing his head as it drifted past. When they reached the wharf, a pair of friars came hurrying down from the abbey gate-house and helped to get the horses up the bank.

After he paid the ferrymen, deSteny gave the friars thruppence each and signaled his men to remount. "We must press on. The afternoon isn't faded yet. I want to be at Croydon before nightfall."

Only Hearne had a good notion of where that was, but the rest looked displeased. Byrle shook his head. "It's getting on. Half the afternoon is gone. We could stop here."

"No," said deSteny. "We must press on."

"But Croydon is a long way yet," said Delwin. "And we

have been pushing our horses for days."

"All the more reason to make haste," said deSteny, swinging up into the saddle and pulling in his reins. "If we go now, we should arrive by sundown."

The men exchanged uneasy glances. "There are said to be robbers on these roads."

"Then keep your swords out and be ready to fight," deSteny recommended. "Tell me how you plan to avoid trouble, morning or evening, if we must travel on these roads."

The men accepted this unhappily, remounting slowly and coming around to follow the Sheriff of Nottingham as he led the way to the Croydon Road.

"Have you ever been here before?" asked Ackerley.

"Many years ago. I went on foot then." DeSteny did not enlarge on his experience, preferring to keep his attention on the road ahead of them. His memories of that first journey were mixed with the later events of his life, and were tender as a new-healed wound.

"Did you have any trouble?" Canute had to shout to be heard from the rear.

"Not from outlaws," said deSteny in a tone that stopped all questions before they could be asked.

As they headed off into the brilliant afternoon, they passed open fields where cattle and sheep grazed and crofters toiled. The country was more open than that to the north, and although forests loomed in the west, here the fields and meadows joined together, making a broad swath of grass and crops through the gentle hills that led toward the sea.

Late in the afternoon they passed a group of pilgrims bound for the South Road to Hastings, and from there to France, where they would join with many others bound for the Holy Land. The pilgrims were glad of the company of men-at-arms and such an important official as the Sheriff, although one of them complained that they needed a priest more, and was quickly silenced by his companions.

"This is a fine beginning to your travel," said deSteny, ignoring the complaint. "You should make a good passage at this time of year."

"Well," said the oldest pilgrim, a fellow in his forties with a slight hunch in his back and the hands of a man who had worked all his life. "If God is good, we will."

"God and the weather," said deSteny.

The pilgrim smiled and shook his head. "That comes from God, as do all things." Around him the pilgrims said Amen.

"Perhaps," said deSteny. "Though I think it may be the nature of things more than God's Will that shapes the weather."

The oldest pilgrim looked shocked and went silent, withdrawing from the side of deSteny's horse in favor of walking with his companions.

"Why did you say that?" Byrle asked deSteny in a lowered voice, hoping not to be heard by the pilgrims. He had ridden up beside the Sheriff.

"Because it is what I think, and because I don't want to be forced into escorting them to the South Road and all the way to Hastings." DeSteny shook his head. "They believe because they are bound to the Holy Land for the sake of their souls, they should be able to commandeer assistance from anyone they meet. They will ask for charity for their evening meal and their lodging. They'll probably get it. But we cannot accommodate them, no matter how much they may want our escort. And you may believe that they do want our escort. We have no obligation to them. Sir Gui is our master and we must fetch his bride. That is our duty."

"True," said Byrle, frowning a little. "But these pilgrims are—"

"They are not our charge," said deSteny.

"No, they aren't," said Byrle unhappily.

"They expect our help," said Meaghar.

"They have need of us," said Byrle.

"That is part of the problem," said deSteny. "Our mission is for Sir Gui and his affianced bride."

"But the pilgrims are on a holy journey," said Delwin, who had been drawn into the debate.

"They cannot turn us from our sworn duty," said deSteny.

"No, I suppose not," said Meaghar.

"Keep your purpose in mind," said deSteny, and turned his eyes to the road ahead while Byrle and the others fell back behind him.

They came to Croydon just at sunset when the sky was filled with red banners, announcing a change in the weather. By then the pilgrims were some distance behind them, and they had caught up with a party of eleven merchants traveling with three men-at-arms; they kept a steady progress that suited deSteny and the merchants with their laden carts and even-tempered palfries ambling along were glad of new company, and the time they shared the road passed pleasantly enough.

"Where are you bound for at Croydon?" the wool-merchant asked.

"Probably the Black Ram," said deSteny.

"A suitable place for fighting men. The tavern has good ale and strong cider. We will probably go to The Cup and Ball. They have better service for merchants, including a small warehouse for our goods." He slapped his thigh. "It is the Black Ram, the Cup and Ball, the Weeping Lady, or the abbey."

"True enough," said deSteny, who had stayed at the abbey in his previous visit to Croydon but doubted that another hostel had been built in the intervening years.

"And you choose the place that suits you best," said the merchant.

Meaghar, who was behind deSteny just now, chuckled. "Do they have bawdy houses in Croydon?"

"Not officially," said the wool-merchant with a lifting of his brows. "There are ways you can arrange these things."

"Are you going to market?" deSteny asked politely, ignoring Meaghar.

"Eventually." The merchant accepted this return to business without any sign of rancor. "For now we are meeting with merchants from the Low Countries and France who have a fancy for English wool, which we have in quantity, just as they have goods we seek. They come twice a year, and they bring gold and other merchandise with them. If all goes well, we'll sell most of our bales and can trade the rest at Canterbury Market before we return to the north-west. I am from Gloucester."

"Good country for wool," said deSteny, who had often met Gloucester merchants at Nottingham.

"But not without hazard," said the merchant with another lift of his shaggy brows. "The forest is a difficult place."

"That it is. Every place has its hazards," said deSteny.

The wool-merchant went along for a short distance without speaking, and then added, "We heard many warnings, coming here. Rumors of trouble in the forest."

"We have heard such rumors, as well," said deSteny.

"Do you—being Sheriff of Nottingham—put any stock

in them?" The speculation in his eyes was tinged by fear.

"Yes, because a prudent man is always cautious and heeds warnings." He made a point of being calm, his manner as courteous as he could make it. "And it is sensible to take precautions on the Great North Road, rumors or nothing."

The wool-merchant nodded. "That is good advice you offer. Thank you. I'll bear it in mind when I turn northward again."

DeSteny wanted to ask what the wool-merchant had heard, but supposed this might make the man suspicious, so he said only, "I am pleased to be of service," and continued on to Croydon and the Black Ram.

17.

How Little John found Hood

He had been wandering through the forest without coming upon what he sought. He had been careful, keeping to the light that protected him, and water that shielded him. When he slept, he took care to find holy ground—anything from a cemetery to a shrine—and kept his crucifix clutched in his hand, and had whispered prayers as he walked. But so many days had passed that he had begun to lose heart, thinking that he would fail in his sworn purpose. At dawn he had risen from his sleeping place among the graves protected by standing stones that had recently been surmounted with crosses. He had slept there before and been satisfied that it kept out all evil, which satisfied him that God would not forsake him in his mission.

This morning was a good morning, not too cold, and he stretched as he rose, wrapping his cloak around his shoulders. He ate the last of the cheese he had earned with a day's labor cutting trees at a remote croft a week since. He scratched his beard, and wished he had thought to bring shears with him as well as his knife; he would soon be as shaggy as a winter pony. Picking up his quarterstaff, he set out for the river half a league away. The songs of birds accompanied him, but he paid no attention to them, for he missed the sound of human voices and the birds were no substitute for hearing his own name spoken. No bird called "John" or "John Gates," and so he shut out their cheerful voices.

As he came to the river, he looked about for a means to cross. The current was too fast for him to swim, and the water too deep to wade, but he was determined to get over to the other side. He followed the bank for some distance, going deeper into the forest than he had ever done, into the closely gathered trees where the light scattered down like small, shining coins into the green gloom. He walked on through the morning and the full light of noon, and shortly after the sun crossed the mid-heaven he found himself on the narrow bank that grew steeper as the trees crowded in closer and closer together.

Finally he came upon a makeshift bridge—two halves of a tree-trunk stretched from bank to bank, offering narrow footing on a stout support—and he looked about before stepping onto the rough surface, making sure he could cross without mishap. He took a dozen steps, going carefully, for although the halved log was thick and sturdy enough to hold four or five men at once, it rocked a bit and the worn surface was filled with splinters and worn bits that made for uncertain footing. Using his staff to improve his balance, he was almost at the center of the bridge when he heard a soft chuckle behind him. He turned and saw a man behind him, dressed in scarlet and holding a dirk in his hand. John kept his place on the bridge but carefully swung around to look at him.

"You are a long way from home," said the man with the dirk.

"How can you know that?" John asked, watching the dirk.

"Because this is a long way from anything," said the man in scarlet. "If anyone is here they are lost." He favored John with an unfriendly smile while he toyed with his dirk. "Am I wrong?"

"I have been searching for someone," said John significantly as he looked at the man. "I know what you are, varlet. I know what you and your kind have done. You are what I have sought."

"Am I?" The man in scarlet tossed the dirk into the air with negligent ease and caught it expertly. "What makes you so sure of that?"

"I know what you are," John accused.

"Do you? And what is that?" Scarlet laughed without merriment.

"You know what you are," John said.

"I am a wanderer of the forest, as are you," Scarlet said with spurious geniality.

"You and your kind are monsters," said John calmly.

"And what do you mean by that?" said another voice at the other end of the bridge. "Do you know or are you guessing?"

John looked around and saw another man, a tall, white-haired man, with his hood flung back to show his pale features, lean and fox-faced, with an air of menace about him that all but stifled the breath in John's throat. He hoped his fear didn't show when he answered, "I know."

"Then you know how reckless you are being," said the white-haired man.

"Hardly reckless." He took a fighting stance and brought up his quarterstaff into a fighting position.

"Then you are desperate," said the man in scarlet.

True though it was, John would not give the two the satisfaction of hearing him admit it. "Come on! If we're going to fight!"

The white-haired man shrugged his shoulders. "That is up to you," he said calmly, but in such a manner that John's flesh crept on his spine.

"If you want to cross, come ahead," John offered,

shifting his stance to the smaller of the two half-logs. "We can pass if we're careful."

"Passing isn't my intention, nor is stepping on the bridge," said the white-haired man. "You are becoming a nuisance, caitiff, blundering about as you have done. The only thing I can admire in what you do is your tenacity, and that, under the circumstances, is far from praise."

John heard him out, his hands tightening on the staff he carried. "Whatever you intend, have at it."

"I think not. I think you must come to me. It is fitting, since he is the one determined to force a fight upon me. He must begin it. Mustn't he, Will?" The white-haired man chuckled, and it was the most evil sound John had ever heard.

"Yes. He must," said the man in scarlet.

"I will do no such thing," John vowed. "If this is to be a battle, let it be here, on this bridge. Over this water." He shifted his stance again, preparing to defend his position on the bridge, and knowing he faced a formidable opponent. He studied the white-haired man carefully, taking note of how he moved and behaved, anticipating a difficult fight.

"We can wait," said the white-haired man. "Eventually you will have to leave the bridge, and when you do, we'll be waiting."

"I'm not afraid," John said, aware of the terror rising within him.

The man called Will sat down on the bank and began to throw small stones into the stream. "You will grow tired, fellow."

"Then I will fall in and the river will carry me away. You will not be able to touch me," he said defiantly, hoping he wouldn't drown, though at the moment, that seemed preferable to dying at the hands of these two unwholesome creatures.

"What a waste that would be," said Will Scarlet, and

glanced over to the other end. "What do you think, Hood?"

"I think it would be a waste," the white-haired man answered silkily. "He is a fine figure of a man, strong and full of life. He may not value that, but I do. And after all his family has given us so far. How shall I repay such generosity?" This was calculated to inspire fury, and John nearly succumbed to it.

"You killed them!" he shouted.

"Unfortunately, yes. We gave your woman the choice of becoming one of us, but she refused. More fool she," said Hood.

John managed to curb his temper, but he could feel his gut tighten and the blood rise in his head and neck. How dared this vile travesty of a man say such things to him? He used his quarterstaff to make a swipe at Hood's head. He had no hope of striking him, but wanted the satisfaction of some gesture before he was wholly caught up in fighting this unnatural being. "May God give me strength against you!"

Hood took half a step back, but whether from actual distress or as a calculated ploy, John could not tell. To keep from being rendered incapable of action, he began to spin his quarterstaff in the French fashion, the whirring it made giving him renewed satisfaction. Squinting up at the trees, he shifted his position a bit, taking care to stay out of the sunlight. "The longer you make us wait, the harder it will be for you."

"So you say," John responded, wanting to taunt his tormentor. "But the water protects me, and the sunlight. If I swim away, I will be in full sun in less than a league. And the water will keep me safe until I reach the light. You daren't follow me into the water, let alone the sunlight, dare you? You'll be burned to ashes." He could not swim, but he hoped he could stay afloat long enough to reach the place where the trees thinned and the river cut through broad meadows, where no fell creature could come in the day.

Hood folded his arms. "And leave your woman and child unavenged? After all you have sworn to do?"

John continued to twirl his staff. "If not today, some other time."

"All cowards say such things," Hood remarked to Will. "Haven't you noticed?"

"That I have," said Will, throwing a bigger rock into the water.

"Do you think you can hit him?" Hood asked Scarlet impatiently.

"Eventually," said Scarlet. "I want to wear him down."

John began to feel a sinking sense of defeat. It had taken him many weeks to find these two, and if he failed to fight them today, it might be a long time before he had such an opportunity again. He swung his quarterstaff again, stopping its rotation and using its impetus to make a strong lunge at Hood, who jumped back, and let out a high, eerie cry as a bit of sunlight touched his cheek. At once a burn appeared there, smoke rising from it as if from an invisible branding iron. It was exhilarating to see that dire creature hurt. John gave a shout of satisfaction and moved a little closer to Hood's end of the bridge. He moved toward Hood, his quarterstaff up in the air ready to strike. As soon as he started toward Hood, a rock thumped into his back, almost knocking him off his feet. He teetered, righted himself, and stepped back to the center of the bridge.

"Such poor judgment," said Hood sarcastically. "To allow yourself to be goaded that way."

"A coward's ploy," John said, breathing too quickly.

"Better than a fool's," said Will, tossing a pebble in John's direction.

"So tell me, crofter, how you come to think you can stop us? We are many and there is only one of you." Hood folded his arms and contemplated John as if he were a prize goat he was planning to buy.

"You took my wife and child," said John.

Will laughed softly. "So we did."

"Yes. And you buried them and mourned. But how could you think to come after us?" Hood shook his head. "Others are more careful of their lives than you."

"Others have done what is between them and God"—he had the satisfaction of seeing Hood wince again—"I do as I must for the sake of my soul."

Will laughed aloud. "I'll tell the Red Friar."

Hood lowered his head. "And what will any of this accomplish? You cannot kill us—it's too late for that. You can only sacrifice yourself."

"But I can kill you," John said. "If you are burned by so little sun, then full light must consume you. I have heard it said that as you are bound for Hell, you burn as a foretaste of it. I know you cannot cross running water or tideland, except when the tide is turning. I know holy water will hurt you, and the cross. I can hurt you with iron, and salt. I know you burn and that wooden weapons will defeat you." He held up his quarterstaff. "This will."

"If you think so, you may try," said Hood, offering a vulpine smile.

"You want to catch me off-guard," said John, shaking his head knowingly. "You think that with one of you on either bank, I must eventually make a mistake. You want me to fall into your hands. I'm not such a fool."

Hood laughed again. "Not a fool, no, but far from wise." He closed his eyes for a long moment, then turned his baleful gaze on John. "You don't know what you're dealing with, for all you've been told."

"You want to distress me," said John. "You want me to let you get hold of me. *Apage, Satanas!*" he ordered, holding up the crucifix that hung on a thong around his neck. He let the end of his quarterstaff rest between his feet.

"Latin," said Hood. "Your village priest must take good care of you. What other things have you learned, I wonder?" He gave a signal to Scarlet. "Don't let him back up, Will."

"What Father Batholomieu taught is no affair of yours," said John, raising the staff with one hand. "You cannot speak of him."

"I can do any number of things," said Hood. "Most important to you now—I can wait." Hood moved a step away to avoid the shifting sunlight.

Without any sign of fear, John addressed Hood. "You are a damnable thing. You will be lost to the world."

"Yes, but long after you," said Hood, the sinister edge in his voice making his intentions clear.

"Shall I rock the bridge?" asked Will, getting up and starting toward the split logs.

"And send him into the water? No," said Hood. "But rock the logs a bit, to keep him off his balance."

"As you like," said Will, and put his foot on the larger of the two halves, giving it an experimental shove, smiling when John had to shift and lean to remain upright. "Yes. I see what you want." He kicked at the end of the half-log—hard—and the wood shuddered down its length.

"Do you think you'll be here at sunset?" Hood asked John.

"I could be. Not that it will help you. The water protects me, or you would have come after me before now. I am safe as long as I am on this bridge. The water will run all night."

John was beginning to worry, trying to think clearly in spite of the terrible dread that was turning his body cold.

"If you join us, you would have nothing to be afraid of," said Hood.

"Except God and the light of day," said John, stepping onto the other half-log as the one on which he stood rocked again.

Will whistled tauntingly, and moved to the second log, grabbing the rough wood and wrenching it. "Step lightly, big man."

Hood watched, his garnet eyes narrowing. "We could use a smith, and your shoulders and your hands say you can do such work. You would want for nothing."

John laughed. "But for life and salvation." He rocked as Will jarred the logs.

"You are not coming off that bridge alive," said Hood. "You will drown or you will come to us. Nothing else is possible."

Using the end of his quarterstaff like a pike, John lunged at Hood. "Then I must drown."

Hood grabbed the quarterstaff and yanked hard, his strength far greater than John's, which surprised John for the few heartbeats he had to try to fight back. But then he fell and his shoulders landed on the end of the logs. An instant later Hood was on him.

From the far side of the river Will Scarlet watched, ravenous and loathing himself for his hunger while he watched Hood feed.

18.

How Marian left her Father's House

The fortress of Arundel was built on old Roman foundations, and so was basically a square-walled fortification with six buildings arranged in a U within the walls. Stables and a small chapel were newer than the rest of the place—the barracks were the oldest two structures inside the walls, one of them now housing the lord, the other all the soldiers and their families.

DeSteny had his men in the courtyard, mounted and ready to leave. He turned to his host and said, "I would feel better if we had a wagon for your niece."

"Might as well advertise a woman, and attract every rapacious rascal from here to York to prey upon her," said the newly installed lord, Reynard deBeauchamp. "No. Her father made his intentions plain. She is to be dressed as a lad and ride with the rest of you."

"A pity he should die so suddenly," said deSteny. "You said it was unexpected, the fever that took him?"

"That it was. But Stephen had forty-nine good years, and not many fighting men can claim so much for themselves. Our brother Oliver died at twenty-three, coming home from the Holy Land, and our brother Nicholas succumbed at age five, from a broken leg that festered. I barely remember him." Reynard deBeauchamp shook his head. "A good man, my brother Stephen, and a credit to the family, but God has His reasons, and it is not for us to ask what they may be. It is the way of the world that men die, and God knows the why of it."

DeSteny stared into the middle distance. "I suppose He must," he said.

DeBeauchamp put his hand on deSteny's shoulder. "It is good that Marian is to be married. With her father gone, she should be with a husband. This cannot be her home as it was when her father lived. A woman alone—it is never a good thing. Women were made from men so that they would always have to be a part of men. It is what God intended." He looked at the black mare his niece would ride. "This is a good horse. It should do her well."

"I'm sure the mare will be fine," said deSteny. He was aware that deBeauchamp wanted to have his niece gone as soon as possible—the girl was strong-willed and held her father in high esteem, far less so her uncle. She criticized Reynard deBeauchamp at every opportunity. "It's her grief that has made her sharp-tongued," he went on in spite of his own prudence.

"Sharp-tongued!" DeBeauchamp spat to show his opinion of her behavior. "She is a proper shrew. My brother would not curb that in her, and this is the result. Well, I wish Sir Gui good fortune with her. Tell him to beat her often or he will have to surrender rule of his house."

DeSteny could not imagine Sir Gui using a rod on his wife—it would be too demeaning for him. No, Sir Gui would be more likely to ignore his wife than chastise her. He supposed that Marian deBeauchamp would be left to her own devices most of the time and treated like a castle hound the rest of the time, fed and indulged but given no special notice. He said, "I shall tell him what you advise."

"Her father spared the rod, you know," said her uncle condemningly. "And look what has become of her." He shook his head. "My sons will be glad to see their cousin gone."

"And so shall I," said Marian deBeauchamp as she emerged from the main house of the fortress. She was a slim girl with only a hint of bosom. This morning she was wearing good quality men's clothes and her brown hair had been cut off short, as most youths' hair was. Judging by her appearance, she might have been a page or an apprentice to a notary. "DeSteny, I am in your hands." Her manner was condescending but subdued. Looking to her uncle, she added, "I wish you joy of my father's fief."

Reynard deBeauchamp contemplated his niece for what seemed a long moment, then shrugged. "It is the right of our family to rule here. You would be the first of us to uphold our right."

"Yes. I know." She went to the black mare and took the reins, preparing to mount. "I am ready."

"Very good," said deSteny, disliking being caught in this family squabble. "When we reach Nottingham, Sir Gui will send a messenger to you with their plans for the wedding, so you may attend."

"Good of him," said deBeauchamp, and watched while deSteny gave Marian a leg up into the saddle. "She rides well enough, I'll allow her that."

"Such a kindly admission," said Marian, making no effort to hide her sarcasm. "Sheriff, are your men ready?"

He indicated the seven of them, saying, "Eight, counting myself. By order of Sir Gui, who is eager to see you."

She laughed. "Did he tell you to say that?"

"Most certainly," said deSteny as he got onto his dun. He took up his position at the head of his men, Hearne immediately behind him, then Marian deBeauchamp. Next came Delwin and Byrle riding side by side. Behind them Canute,

Ackerley, Sprague, and Meaghar brought up the rear.

"It is time," said Marian a bit testily.

"Yes. We need all the daylight we can find," said deSteny. "And the weather isn't going to hold much longer." He looked up at the high clouds veiling the morning sun. "We could have rain tomorrow."

"This is England," said Marian. "Surely you didn't expect sun all the way to Nottingham?"

"No," said deSteny. "But I would like to see the summer last a little longer, since the signs are all for a hard winter."

Marian laughed again, not quite mocking him. "Then why linger? We are not needed here," she said pointedly. She nodded once to her uncle and pressed her heels into her mare's sides.

"Move out," deSteny ordered his men. "At the jog."

"Nothing faster?" Marian sounded disappointed. "The road is not too rutted. We could canter a while, to put distance between this place and us."

"We have a long way to go and we will not get there more quickly if we tire the horses." He offered Reynard deBeauchamp a salute as he passed beyond the gates of Arundel and began the long journey north.

By nightfall they had reached the priory of Saint Honorius of Canterbury, and the hostel the monks maintained for the travelers, where they were received with some disapprobation on the part of the Prior, who looked askance at Marion deBeauchamp, and only consented to giving her a place to sleep if she allowed him to bar her into her cell for the night. "It isn't seemly for a maid to dress as a man," he declared, staring at her as if he expected the worst from her. "She must be kept apart."

"I am willing," she said, accepting the condition gracelessly but deciding to comply with the Prior's orders; it was only one night.

"A bad thing," he said later to deSteny, "letting a woman go about the world in such a guise."

"It was the order of her father, for her protection," said deSteny.

"And she must obey him. I do understand. But her father erred greatly." He folded his hands in his habit sleeves and glared up at the vaulting in the refectory. "I hope this does not bode ill for her marriage."

"And I," said deSteny. He decided to keep his thoughts about Sir Gui and his pretty pages to himself. He was relieved that they had remained at the dining table rather than visiting the chapel. "She is not the sort of woman to comply with—" He stopped himself before he said anything inappropriate.

"You may think it is important to maintain decorum, and say nothing that would redound to your lord's honor," said the Prior, "but we hear many things here, on the Sussex Road near the cross-road with the London-Portsmouth Road: we hear many things." He spread his fingers on the table as much as his knotted joints would permit. "There are almost as many rumors about Sir Gui deGisbourne as there are about the Great North Road."

"And you would like to know if you should believe them," said deSteny.

"They seem—ah—troubling." He waited for deSteny to speak. "Both those about new outlaws and those about Sir Gui."

"With good reason, I fear," deSteny admitted. "Merchants have been set upon more often than in past years."

The prior nodded and crossed himself. "It is more than outlaws, they say."

"It is," deSteny said, but ventured nothing more as much as he wanted to know what the prior had heard.

"Some fear for their souls." The prior coughed. "Devils and imps and worse than that, according to some."

"Perhaps not devils and imps, but dangerous creatures nonetheless," said deSteny, wanting to end their conversation without appearing to retreat. "I think it is wise to be cautious."

"And trust in God," said the prior, giving deSteny a disapproving stare.

"An armed escort is as wise as prayers, perhaps wiser, at least in this world," said deSteny. "I wouldn't offend you for any reason, Prior, but I would recommend soldiers as well as prayers for those bound north."

"I'll keep that in mind," said the prior condemningly. "And Sir Gui?"

"No worse than any other popinjay," said deSteny. "And no better."

"Well, then, I will pray he has worthy sons to follow him."

DeSteny rose. "We must depart at first light, for we still have a long way to go and the weather is against us. I am grateful to you for your hospitality. A suitable donation will be made upon our departure."

"It will buy only Masses and Psalms, not armed men." The prior gave deSteny a look of pitying contempt. "If only you comprehended the power of faith."

DeSteny listened without any emotion. "I'll bear your remarks in mind."

He withdrew to his cell for the night, and paid no attention to his dreams. When he rose at Lauds, before dawn had begun to glow in the east, he made a point of avoiding the prior.

"How far today?" Hearne asked as he saddled his horse.

"Twenty leagues, if there is no rain." It was a demanding pace and both of them knew it. He glanced at the sky, trying to decide if the thickening clouds heralded a storm.

"And if there is?" Hearne took his short military cloak and pulled it around his shoulders, showing that he expected a downpour.

"Then we must try for ten leagues at least. We must cross the Thames in four days if we possibly can. It would be better to cover the distance in three days, but that would mean no delays of any kind." DeSteny placed his saddle-pad on the dun's back and reached for the saddle, hefting it from the stand and lifting onto his horse.

They left the priory as the monks were beginning Prime, bound for London on the Portsmouth Road. They made good time until mid-day, when the skies opened and drenched them, chilling them and making the road slick under their horses' hooves. By nightfall they had gone twelve leagues and needed to stay the night at Leith Hill in a hamlet of crofters. They left the next morning in a steady drizzle, coming to Bishops' Ford on the Wandle before the light faded too much for travel. They went on the next day on the Streatham Road and finally reached London Town.

"Four days," said Marian as deSteny signaled to ferrymen on the opposite bank to come to get them.

"The rain slowed us, but we haven't had to stop because of it," said deSteny.

"Very true," said Marian.

"We have a long way to go," deSteny reminded her.

She gave him a sharp look. "Where will we stay in London?"

"At Nottingham House," said deSteny, as if the choice were obvious.

"My father arranged for me to go to Arundel House near the London Wall," said Marian with such determination that deSteny stared at her. "I would dishonor his memory not to go there, as he wished."

"I cannot leave you in the care of others," said deSteny. "If you are going to stay at Arundel House, then we must stay there as well."

She glared at him. "You're the Sheriff of Nottingham. Why should Arundel House open its doors to you?"

"Why, on your behalf, of course," said deSteny, unwilling to argue with this tempestuous young woman. He wondered if she knew anything of Sir Gui, or he of her.

"Tell me," she demanded, "why."

"We cannot give you proper escort—" he began, only to be cut off.

"You can escort me to Arundel House, see me installed there, then be off to Nottingham House. In the morning, you may come for me." She made a gesture of dismissal.

"And if you should need help in the night?" He studied her square little chin.

"Then you must attend to me," she said without concern.

"If you insist upon this, I must remain with you." He sighed. "I am charged to guard you day and night, which I cannot do from half-way across the town."

She gave an exasperated sigh. "All right. You may remain, but only because Sir Gui would require it of you. Not that I am certain that he is so solicitous of my welfare as you say he is. That is all I can arrange for you, though. Your men must go to Nottingham House. I won't have them be a charge on my uncle." From her expression of distaste, she was as displeased with Reynard deBeauchamp as she was with deSteny.

"Very well. I'll send my men, with Hearne in charge, to

Nottingham House. They will come for us at first light so we may take full advantage of the day. We must have all the light we can." He knew his men would be offended with this arrangement—he was annoyed, himself—but he doubted he could convince Marian to change her mind.

19.

*What Wroughton encountered on his way
to the Great North Road*

It was ten days since his arrival at Windsor that Wroughton was summoned to Prince John's presence. Again he entered the library and found His Grace striding up and down the aisle between the reading benches. He went down on his knee. "Your—"

"Get up, Wroughton, do," said Prince John impatiently. "I have two letters for you to deliver to deSteny. One is for Sir Gui which I want deSteny to see before he hands it over. I have stipulated that in the contents, so Sir Gui will be aware of what I have done. The other is for deSteny himself." He held out two rolled and sealed letters to Wroughton. "If you leave before mid-morning, you can be at Holy Rood by nightfall."

"What of my remaining men?" Wroughton asked, anticipating having to travel alone, and dreading it.

"You will travel with an escort from Windsor, of course. It is fitting that Windsor provide you escort, for you travel on the Court's business now," said Prince John. "Your men will be sent back later, when they may go more slowly, and they will be protected, even as you will be. You must hasten."

Wroughton swallowed hard at this unexpected honor. "Who will be in command?"

"Why, you will, Wroughton. You know the danger better

than anyone." He watched Wroughton kiss the seals on the letters and shove them into his tunic.

"They will lie over my heart every step of the way," he vowed.

"Just so they get to deSteny, they may travel in your shoes for all of me." The Prince stroked his short beard. "The roads must be protected at all costs. England must have safe roads, or we are nothing."

"Yes, Your Grace," said Wroughton, bowing in the French way he had seen the courtiers do.

Prince John held up his hand, forbidding deSteny to depart just yet. "Think about this if you would: there are many men out there on the roads who are in dreadful danger and yet do not know it. How am I best to deal with this? I have an obligation to see them safe. The men are subjects of the King and as such are entitled to protection in his name. Should they be warned, and thereby able to prepare as well as to panic, or should the danger be minimized in the name of keeping tranquility in the land?" He waited a long moment, then said, "I know our people must be guarded, but I fear for travelers who may seem suspicious to others. There is enough mayhem done to strangers as it is. If more suspicions are added, they may well be called to account for themselves in a most unkindly way. It is not acceptable to me, or my brother, to have such misadventure befall traveling men." He went over to the hearth where a small fire was laid. "Well, I shall consider the ramifications before making my preparations to guard the roads. There must be a balance between the protection of travelers from the trouble in the forest and their safety from one another. I cannot have crofters refusing to give shelter to travelers, but I cannot permit the crofters to be attacked by these dreadful creatures."

"Your Grace," said Wroughton, as much to show he was

paying attention than from any lack of opinion.

"Tell deSteny that I am mindful of his plight, and I will do what I can on his behalf. I am aware of the danger in which he stands and I will not turn my back on him or Nottingham. The men remaining here will return in good time, with men who will reinforce Nottingham. I realize Sir Gui will not be pleased, but he'll have to endure it as best he may. Perhaps I will allow him to entertain me for three days. That will assuage any hurt he may feel for being slighted in favor of Nottingham." He gave a single shake of his head. "Men like Sir Gui are the very devil to keep pleased. They speak of their dedication to our absent Richard, and they strive to carve out as much of this island for themselves as they may while he is gone."

Now Wroughton was embarrassed. Even if he agreed with the Prince's remarks—and in a general way he did—he knew it was unseemly to volunteer anything. So he cleared his throat and did his best to listen closely.

"I mustn't keep you. You have far to go today and I should not encourage you to waste daylight—what little there is of it this morning. I trust you have a cloak of oiled-leather to keep the rain off." He held out his hand again, and let Wroughton kiss his ring, then motioned him to depart. "May God see you safely home, Wroughton."

"Amen, Your Grace," said Wroughton as he left the Prince's presence, hastening down the stairs to the main courtyard where an escort of ten men awaited him, eight of them soldiers, one a priest, and one a farrier, to tend the horses. Wroughton got into the saddle on a raw-boned blood-bay, pulled up the reins, and turned toward the main gate where a winch was being worked to raise the portcullis. He peered up at the sky and asked himself if he would be dry by day's end.

The man at the head of the soldiers came up to Wroughton, saying, "I'm Ellenby; I'm in charge of the Prince's men."

"Very good," said Wroughton. "I saw you at bowls, didn't I?"

"I do play at bowls, so you may have." The clatter of the horses' hooves grew louder as they crossed the draw-bridge, and left the comforting embrace of Windsor's stone walls. "I am told you know the way?"

"I came down the Great North Road," said Wroughton, not wanting to claim any expertise he lacked. "There is only that one road, after all."

"True enough," said Ellenby. "But if we should encounter anything irregular, you would recognize it."

"So should you," said Wroughton with feeling.

Ellenby laughed. "As your experience is foremost, then I will rely upon you to serve as our guide in these matters." He swung around in his saddle and called out to his troops, "Moreton, Simmons, Danebraugh, come ride ahead of us. Wroughton is to be protected at all costs, by the order of His Grace, Prince John."

The three men put their horses into a fast trot and took up their positions ahead, making a lozenge formation on the road. The wind had whipped up the trees so that they thrashed their branches and moaned. It wasn't a very comforting beginning to what promised to be a hard ride.

Behind them, a soldier past his first youth but not yet ancient, called out, "I am going to keep my mace ready. No telling what may drop from the trees in such weather."

"Fortesque is right," said Ellenby. "Let every one of you have a weapon to hand." He pulled his dagger from its sheath and brandished it.

Wroughton wondered if he should tell these men that

the foes they might encounter were not damaged by iron and steel, but by wood and holy water. He kept this to himself, trying to maintain the air of a favored messenger rather than a frightened soldier. Taking his short sword, he swung it purposefully, but the sound of the blade cutting the air was lost in the soughing wind. "We have a long ride ahead of us," he said. "We will have to be vigilant all the way to Nottingham."

"So we must," said Ellenby with a kind of cheerfulness Wroughton found off-putting. "We have cheese in our saddle-sacks for mid-day. Evening will see us safe within walls."

The rest of the men shouted in agreement, and continued in under the cover of the trees, keeping a good pace for the first half of the morning, but slowing down when they came upon a party of merchants bound north.

"Will you give us the protection of your company?" asked one of the merchants, a tall, angular fellow riding a white jennet.

"Alas, we are on the Prince's business and must hasten," said Ellenby dismissingly before Wroughton could speak. "You have three armed men to guard you. They should be sufficient if you do not remain abroad past sunset. Do not remain outside once the sun is down, not if you wish to be safe."

"Safe!" The merchant regarded Ellenby with a hard look. "You are the Prince's man, and we pay his taxes—"

"Those are King Richard's taxes," said Ellenby sharply. "The Prince is honor-bound to collect them, for the maintenance of England and the honor of the King. The Crusades have cost a great deal and may continue to do so; Prince John must do his duty to his brother." He urged his horse ahead of the merchants' train of mules, ponies, and jennets. "The man probably hides his money in France or Scotland, so that he cannot pay the full amount. So many merchants do that, and similar things to keep their gold in their coffers."

"No one enjoys taxes," said Wroughton.

"If they are not paid, England is lost to France," said Ellenby with a deliberate curl of his lip. "King Richard owes a mortgage to the King of France, and the French will not forgive a groat of it." He spat and swung his dagger. "Those greedy men think only of their profits."

"And King Richard thinks only of his war," said Wroughton impulsively. "It is good for him to Crusade, but at what cost does he ransom the Holy Sepulchre?"

"It isn't for us to fret over such things, it for us to do our duty to the lords," said Ellenby. "Let the great ones do as they must, for the sake of God and Christ and honor. We have enough to do in our ventures. And all men know this." He pointed to a narrow bridge ahead. "Single file!" he ordered. The men obeyed, and once over the stream, they remained in a column as they moved ahead of the merchants.

Although Wroughton agreed with Ellenby, he felt as if he ought to argue with him, because he so disliked the man's haughty manner. "Should not we be consulted when we must face the dangers?"

"It is our duty to face dangers," said Ellenby. "If we cannot do that, we are less than dust in the road." He fell silent as he pushed ahead of Wroughton and used this as the excuse not to speak with any of the others.

The wood was lively, filled with dappled light and rustling leaves, and the occasional sound of animals moving out of sight, but the impression made by these activities was more sinister than cheerful. The shadows of clouds passing overhead added to the changing light, reminding the men that rain was coming, and casting vast shadows over the green expanse of the forest. The men continued along the road, holding their horses to a slow jog-trot; their gear and tack jingled, squeaked, and clattered, marking their progress as they went on, and rendered Sherwood silent where they went.

"There is a turn-off to Saint Gertrude's up ahead," Ellenby called out a while later. "We'll stop there for a meal and to rest the horses." He grinned. "They make fine beer and good cheese at Saint Gertrude's."

One of the men whooped, the sound echoing and becoming lost among the trees, accompanied by a flurry of birds taking to the air in alarm. The horses pulled and pranced as the men continued to laugh.

"Better conduct, better conduct," Ellenby said. "These are holy women we will ask for food and drink. You cannot behave as if you are in barracks." He chuckled. "Not that nuns don't have their charms."

"How do you know?" Fortesque asked.

"It would be unseemly to tell you," said Ellenby with a smirk. "Besides, the nuns I spoke of as charming are not at Saint Gertrude's."

Another burst of enthusiasm made Wroughton wince. These men were less than worthy of high regard, he thought, but dared not reprimand any of them. It wasn't his right, and it wasn't sensible to be at odds with his guards, so he held his tongue as they left the road for the track that led to the nunnery.

The nunnery walls were partially stone but mostly wood, a stockade topped with an array of crucifixes that was as elaborate as it was imposing. There were a half-dozen serfs working in the small fields where the nunnery's sheep grazed and barley grew. A bell rang as Wroughton and the Windsor guards came into view, and the heavy wooded gates swung open. Habited nuns bustled out of the nunnery to greet the men, and one of them called for a household slave to take the horses in hand.

"Mother Barnaba," called out Ellenby.

An elderly nun with a weathered face came forward. "Sir Willard, you are welcome here, in the name of Christ."

"And amen, good Mother," said Ellenby, dismounting with alacrity. "We have come to ask for a meal and some oats for our horses. Perhaps a small keg of beer to take with us."

"Ah, Sir Willard, you are impertinent, but you shall have what you ask." She tisked as he went onto his knee in a mocking gesture of submission to her will.

"I am unworthy," Ellenby said, and winked at the nun.

As Wroughton got off his horse, he heard one of the men mutter, "She's his aunt. She won't refuse him anything."

"We'll have goose and onions," said another with merry anticipation.

"And double rations of beer," said Danebraugh as he surrendered his reins to the stable slave.

"We might as well enjoy it here. There will be precious little extras on the way north," said Simmons.

"It won't be that bad," said Fortesque. "Wroughton here must know where we will be well-received." He gestured his approval of the possibilities.

A young nun came up to Wroughton. "If you will follow me, I will bring you to the refectory."

"Thank you, Sister," he said and fell in beside her, feeling awkward. "You are good to take us in." That was ill-said, he knew it, but he never knew how to behave around nuns, particularly in the ones in their own buildings. He would rather storm the ramparts of a castle than enter a nunnery.

Ellenby sauntered along beside Mother Barnaba, chatting genially with her, and accepting her affectionate admonitions. "I'm sorry we can only stay for this one meal, but the Prince has ordered us to hasten. We must be about his business as soon after sunrise and breakfast as we may put saddles on our horses."

"You always say that," Mother Barnaba reminded him. "And you always stay the second night."

"We mustn't this time. Prince John would not approve," Ellenby said emphatically. "This man—Wroughton—is under orders to return to Nottingham as quickly as possible and as we are his escort, we'll have to go at his pleasure. If you wish us to remain, it must be with his permission. It is his mission to carry a message from the Prince to Sir Gui, and other lords, and you know how stringent the Prince can be." He glanced over his shoulder at Wroughton. "So we have to depart as soon as our fast is broken in the morning. Unless Wroughton should decide that we must remain the second night, so as not to risk being abroad after dark." His laughter was insinuating as he looked toward his men. "We have a long, hard ride ahead."

"Then let us ease its beginning," said Mother Barnaba, addressing Wroughton for the first time. "It would make us happy to aid you in this capacity. It is past mid-day, and you may well not be on the road again until late morning, tomorrow. You must rest, so why not rest here? Your horses will be well-fed and you will return to the road in fine fettle, and we'll remount those of you who need fresh steeds." She had a hard smile, but one that was difficult to resist.

"Yes, Wroughton," said Fortesque to the Nottingham soldier. "Let us remain here for the second night. We'll be off again after morning Mass."

Wroughton knew he should refuse, but he also sensed that these men would resent his depriving them of the stay here, and so he coughed delicately. "If you must remain, then I suppose I must comply. This place is more readily defended than many, and that will mean something, if we are attacked. I should not go on alone, and if you believe our mission is best served by staying an extra day, then, so be it."

Ellenby cried out approvingly as he entered the refectory. "Then bring on the beer, Mother Barnaba, and cook geese and onions and lamb to serve with your bread and we will be glad of your hospitality, in the name of Our Lord and Our Prince."

"Goose and lamb today and pork tomorrow, with cheese and ale as well," Mother Barnaba promised. "We have new, white bread, too. And we'll send you on your way with mead and smoked venison. Mind you give a little to the cats, for Saint Gertrude."

"Their patron," said Fortesque knowingly. "Small enough token for such a goodly reception."

This was a generous offer and all of them knew it. "You are a good Christian, Mother Barnaba," said Ellenby. "Isn't she, Wroughton?"

"She is most generous." Knowing this was a mistake, Wroughton allowed himself to be convinced, and followed Ellenby to the high table.

20.

What became of Marian deBeauchamp

On the third day north from London, Ackerley came down with a persistent cough that sapped his strength even as it heated his humors. Because of his condition, the party was forced to go slowly, and that put them behind their intended progress for the day. During the night, spent in a croft of pig farmers, his fever worsened, and the headman of the croft told deSteny they would have to take Ackerley away from their hamlet, for he was dangerous to them all.

"Where might he receive care?" deSteny asked.

"At the Trinitarians' abbey of the Holy Sacraments," said the headman. "But he mustn't stay here. Who knows what vapors he has released among us?"

"Yes, he may be a danger to all of us," said Byrle. "He will have to be left with those who can care for him."

"Very likely," said deSteny, hating to have to do this. "Very well. Tell me where this abbey is."

The crofter sighed with relief. "Down the lane just beyond the cross-roads. There is a shrine to Saint Christopher at the turning."

"How far?" deSteny asked.

"Two leagues, nearly. He will be taken in there, never fear. They do not turn anyone away. The Abbot is Harold of Yarmouth. He was once the Sheriff of Suffolk, or some such place." The crofter averted his head as Ackerley was half-led, half-carried out to be assisted into the saddle.

Marian deBeauchamp had already mounted, and she looked down from her horse. "If the man is sick, he cannot remain with us. It won't do to have the men all taking ill. You cannot expect him to ride all the way to Nottingham."

"No, he cannot," deSteny agreed. "Which is why we must take him to the abbey."

"And quickly. This day will not make for easy travel." She pulled her cloak more tightly around her as if to emphasize this point. "There is rain in the air."

"As you say," deSteny responded and gave his attention back to the crofter.

The man almost doubled over to show his regard. "May God keep you safe, Sheriff."

"For now I had best rely on my men to do that, but I thank you for your good wishes." DeSteny watched Canute and Meaghar wrestle Ackerley into the saddle. "I am thankful to you for sheltering us. I trust no misfortune will come upon you on our account."

"No. I should think not." The crofter blessed himself and refused to look at Ackerley again. "You paid us well enough."

DeSteny nodded to show he was paying attention, though he truly had no wish to linger in the hamlet any longer than absolutely necessary. He offered the crofter another two copper coins and said, "For your next market-day, so the people may be merrier."

"You are good, Sheriff," said the crofter as he seized the coins. "May God guard you on your journey."

As the other soldiers said Amen, deSteny mounted up, glancing over at Marian deBeauchamp, who looked unperturbed by all the recent developments. He settled himself into the saddle and moved his horse to the head of the line. "Meaghar, you ride next to Ackerley. Be sure he doesn't fall off his horse. And don't stay any nearer to him than you have to. I don't want you sickening, too."

"That I will," said Meaghar, more resigned than obedient.

"And you," deSteny added to Marian deBeauchamp. "Keep your distance from him. You mustn't enter his miasma. I do not wish to bring you ailing to Sir Gui."

She looked mildly annoyed. "What shall I do? Stay a mile back? Wouldn't that defeat the purpose of your escort?"

"Not a mile, but five lengths at least, to escape the miasma," said deSteny, noticing the heavy clouds crowding out the morning above the trees. "And perhaps Hearne should ride with you. He will serve as your own guard."

Hearne swung his horse around and went back to ride at Marian's side. He seemed neither pleased or annoyed at this assignment, though his horse sidled under him. His face showed no emotion, and his voice was flat as he said, "I will ride with her."

"Very good," said deSteny as he prepared to lead the little party away from the croft.

"Sheriff," called out Marian. "Where are we bound?"

"To the Trinitarians," said deSteny. "They will take care of Ackerley. You may stop there for a meal if you like."

"With such a sick man? With all your worries about the illness, shouldn't we be careful?" Marian asked sarcastically. "I think we would be safer taking our meals in the saddle than with him—don't you agree?"

"I think I must keep you safe at all cost," said deSteny. "So we will eat in the saddle, and you will be able to tell Sir Gui that you were guarded at all times from all evils."

Marian laughed aloud. "Will he care, do you suppose?"

DeSteny was tempted to say no, but he knew she had hit upon something undeniable, so he only responded, "He will be relieved."

Again she laughed. "Oh, very good, Sheriff, very good." She waved him away and looked toward Hearne. "You will be with me, won't you?"

"I will," said Hearne curtly.

With that they followed after the other soldiers in her escort, leaving the crofters behind with their pigs.

The overcast sky was clouding over as they rode along, making the road under the trees so dark that they could not easily see its turnings, or the places where the road was uneven or deeply rutted. In a short while, a slow, sullen drizzle began, and the group rode more slowly, and Ackerley grew worse.

"When we turn for the abbey, you wait at the shrine with Lady Marian," deSteny shouted back to Hearne. "I don't want to take any more chances than we must."

"As you wish," Hearne called. "I hope we can find shelter while you go to the abbey. We're going to get wet."

"If there is any shelter, yes, avail yourself of it," deSteny replied. "This is only going to get worse. I am sure a storm is coming."

"And it should be here by nightfall," said Meaghar.

"Which might as well be now," said Canute. "It is almost too dark to go on."

"But we must," deSteny said sharply.

"Yes. For Sir Gui and for poor Ackerley," Canute agreed with an edge of cynicism in his voice.

"That is all to the good," said Meaghar. "But what are we to do when the storm hits? If we are still on the road, it will be—"

"We will deal with that when we must," said deSteny in a tone that allowed for no argument. "For now, we must keep ourselves in order." He looked back at Ackerley as he swayed in the saddle, humming to himself. "He has to get care—that much is certain. Once he has been attended to, then we will look to the rest of us."

"A difficult situation," called Marian, still ironically amused by their predicament. "Do you suppose the shrine is anything more than a little niche with a statue in it?"

DeSteny didn't answer. He was beginning to worry about the attention they were drawing to themselves by all this yelling back and forth. The most dangerous inhabitants of the forest did not usually move about in the day, but with the sky so dark, it was possible they might now be abroad, and the noise his party was making would bring the night-hunters running. He motioned for silence, and pointed along the road, indicating a downward turn in its angle.

Ackerley began to sing, coughing and sputtering with every breath. *"Western wind, when wilt thou blow, That the slow rain down may rain? Christ, that my love were in my arms, And I in my bed again!"* The plaintive words became ugly and frightening as Ackerley's voice harshened and his breath became so short that he often required two or three to get through a single word of the song; there was no satisfaction, no yearning in the plaintive tune, only a kind of rough determination that turned the lament into a demand. For a while only that ragged singing and the sound of their horses' hooves marked their progress, and finally Ackerley could do nothing but cough.

At last they reached the shrine to Saint Christopher, and deSteny signaled for the turn to the abbey. He called back, "Hearne. We are about to leave the road."

"Very good," came the answer from farther back than deSteny had expected. Apparently Hearne and Marian had fallen a greater distance behind.

"We'll come back to the shrine," deSteny said. "As quickly as we may. Wait for us at the shrine or near to it."

"By mid-day?" Hearne called, repeating his question when deSteny could not hear him clearly.

It was a troubling notion that they were still in the second half of the morning, but deSteny realized it was so. "I hope so. Not much later, in any case. You and Lady Marian keep sheltered while we're gone."

"Very good," Hearne repeated.

DeSteny waved, although he could not see Hearne, and then swung his dun off the road and onto the lane that led toward the Abbey of the Holy Sacraments.

"Looks sturdy enough," said Meaghar as they emerged from the cover of the trees.

Coming up to the stone-walled abbey, deSteny called out for Abbot Harold and his monks. "We have a sick man in need of succor."

A monk appeared in the warder-door and looked at the bedraggled men. "And who might you be?"

"I am Hugh deSteny, Sheriff of Nottingham, and I am bound north on the order of Sir Gui deGisbourne," was his stiff answer. "One of my men has taken a fever and cannot travel any further without doing himself greater injury. We were told that you would take him in and nurse him, so we have brought him here."

"Um," said the monk, and ducked back inside the wall, and a moment later the abbot himself entered the warder-door and greeted the travelers.

"You have brought one of your men to us for care in his illness?" His voice was high and hoarse from years of shouting.

"Someone must care for him," said deSteny pointedly. "I hope you will be good enough to take him in."

"We will do what we can for him," said Abbot Harold.

"Can you get him off his horse, or do you require our help?"

Feeling relief for the first time, deSteny answered, "We can manage, good Abbot." He signaled his men to dismount. "Canute, help Meaghar bring Ackerley down, will you?"

"I will," said Canute, stepping up to hold Ackerley's reins while Meaghar prepared to grab Ackerley as he fell off his saddle. The scrape of metal on metal and a number of half-uttered oaths marked their progress, made more difficult by the rain that soaked their garments and made their mail slippery. Finally Meaghar levered his shoulder under Ackerley's arm and helped him to stand.

"My monks will take him now, and we will do all that we know for his body and we will pray for his soul," said the abbot, swinging the warder-door all the way open, allowing three friars to come out to take charge of Ackerley. "Choose one of your men to remain with him, Sheriff, so that he may have the escort of a comrade as far as the grave, should it come to that," he added as the monks took Ackerley, supporting him among them, and assisting him to walk. "He will need someone to accompany him if he recovers, and someone to bring his things back to his family if he does not."

"Canute?" deSteny suggested.

"I will stay," said Meaghar before Canute could obey. "Go along, Sheriff. Sir Gui is waiting, and the rain is getting worse." He took the reins of his horse and Ackerley's and started toward the abbey gates.

DeSteny stopped him. "When you come north, with Ackerley or alone, travel with others. You should not make your way alone on the road, and if Ackerley lives, he will be weak and of little use in a fight. You must not depend upon him to hold his own against outlaws, or worse than outlaws.

Wait for a train of merchants or a company of scholars and stay with them."

"You are a prudent man, Sheriff," the abbot approved. "You show concern for your men."

"As you must for yours," deSteny said, and waited for Meaghar's casual salute before swinging his dun around. "Thank you, Abbot Harold," he called over his shoulder as his men fell in behind him.

"It is God Whom you should thank," said the abbot as the small company of soldiers departed. He saw the gates open to admit Meaghar and the two horses. "Welcome, soldier, to the Abbey of the Holy Sacraments."

Meaghar accepted the blessing of the monks with proper humility, and then asked directions to the stable. "I will make my bed there, and care for the horses and tack."

"That is fitting. I will give you daily report on this man's ailments. You can be of service to us," said the abbot, and gave his attention to Ackerley.

In a very short time deSteny couldn't see the abbey walls behind him, for the trees and rain screened them from view. Knowing he had done all that he could for Ackerley, he turned his thoughts to making up the time they had lost, all the while admitting to himself that in such weather it would not be possible. As he neared the shrine, he called out "Hearne!" and waited for a reply.

At first there was nothing, and then there came a cry from a great distance. "Here!"

"Where?" DeSteny raised his voice.

The answer took longer and was fainter when it came. "Here!"

"Where? Ahead on the road? Behind?" He was shouting as loudly as possible now, and his throat ached with the effort.

"Here!" The shout seemed farther off than before. It echoed among the trees, confusing the direction it came from.

DeSteny felt the first twinges of alarm. "Canute, you and Byrle go back along the road for a league. Call out regularly. Sprague, you and Delwin ride ahead on the road at least a league, and you call out, as well. If you should happen upon any travelers, ask if they have seen a young woman on horseback—not that I think she is still on the road, but the effort must be made. I will remain here and conduct a search of the woods immediately around us." He dismounted and secured his dun's reins to the edge of the shrine, and signaled to the others to move out.

"Was that voice Hearne's?" Byrle asked nervously.

"It must have been," said Canute, and kicked his horse to a trot, forcing Byrle to follow him.

"But what can have happened?" Byrle insisted.

The question lingered in deSteny's mind—he could not be certain he had heard Hearne in that far-away cry. He stepped off the road and into the underbrush, frightening a red fox that bolted from his hiding place and hurried across the road, its ears a-prick. It seemed an ominous harbinger to DeSteny as he circled the shrine, widening his track with each pass. All he found was Marian's hood lying, muddied and wet, in a small puddle near an out-cropping of rocks. He took this and made his way back to his horse, already certain that Hearne and Marian deBeauchamp were not going to be found.

21.

How Penrod Lugenis was Rewarded for his Prize

The small party of Hood's men got Marian deBeauchamp off her horse as soon as they were sure they were beyond deSteny's search. Hearne they left in a copse of hawthorn, his arms tied and his dazed eyes wet with rain.

"I'd prefer to ride," she said coolly, determined to show no fear to this company of rough-clad men.

"Not much longer, you wouldn't," said Piers. "You don't know what the deep forest is like. Horses are too big, blundering about worse than bears." He looked to his three comrades for signs of agreement.

Penrod Lugenis laughed. "He's right. We go on foot because the undergrowth is thick. Upon occasion, we take to the trees and use them as our pathways."

Marian studied him. "You speak well, and you're clearly an educated man. How do you come to be in such company as this?"

"It is not of my choosing, my Lady," said Penrod Lugenis. "But once I became one of their number, what option did I have, but to live as they do? Your soldier will discover the same."

"Is that what I am to expect?" she asked with a catch in her throat.

"No, it is not," said Penrod Lugenis. "I do not know what Hood will decide about you, but his is the only decision." He drew in her horse and held the reins. "If you will dismount?"

"So you can kill my horse?" she challenged.

"No. It has little value to us, or we should find game in plenty to sustain us in the forest, and only the creatures would know we are here."

"Then what will become of him?" she asked, reluctantly climbing out of the saddle.

"If he is fortunate, a traveler will find him, if he is not, a crofter or a monk will." Penrod Lugenis shrugged. "In any case, it is still summer, and he need not fear wolves, or other hungry hunters."

Marian lifted her head. "He is a good horse."

"Then may he find a worthy master," said Penrod Lugenis as he removed the reins from the bridle and signaled to Piers to take the saddle off. "He will do well enough."

Piers dumped the saddle next to the trail without any regard for its structure. "Done," he announced.

"Very good," said Penrod Lugenis, and slapped the gelding on the rump, then swung his arm to send him trotting away. "He may have a hungry night, but he will not wander long." He studied Marian deBeauchamp for a short while. "Best to worry about yourself, not the horse."

She strove to look indifferent to her fate. "I assume you will hold me for ransom."

"Ransom!" Penrod Lugenis laughed, and, after a moment, the three of Hood's men with him laughed as well. "Why should you be held for ransom?"

"Well, my uncle would pay to have me restored," she said, not convinced of this herself, "and my affianced husband would give a lot for me, as well."

"What good is money to us?" Piers asked, sudden menace in his manner.

"You must have something you want," she said, trying to

maintain a detached attitude. "I am sure you could ask for it."

"What we want we take," said Orlan Royce, and licked his lips.

"If any harm should come to me, no ransom will be paid," Marian said quickly.

"You will not believe that we seek no ransom," said Penrod Lugenis. "And what we want is not what you fear, although you should."

Piers clapped his hands once. "Can we not sample her? Just a taste?"

"If you want to answer to Hood, taste away," said Penrod Lugenis. "You tell me what you expect he will do when he learns of your theft."

The fourth member of the small group of vampires, Clemence, shook his head. "We should all be drained and stuffed with hawthorn and buried face-down at a cross-road."

The other three nodded solemnly, and Piers said, "But I am still thirsting."

"You had your share of her guard," said Penrod Lugenis, and turned, starting away from the others.

"I would have thought you would tie me," said Marian.

"Why? Where would you go? We are now more than a league from the nearest road, and you do not know which way to travel." Penrod Lugenis gave her a long, considering stare. "I don't think you're a foolish woman, to willfully be lost in the forest, which you will be if you do not stay with us."

"But surely there is a monastery near-by, and crofts," she said, her courage faltering.

"Of course there are," said Penrod Lugenis. "And if you know precisely where they are, you might be able to find them, but as you don't, you could wander for days, and not find anything more than trees and bushes."

Marian folded her arms, wishing now that they had let her keep her cloak. "If I thought I could find—"

"But you can't," Piers finished for her. "Come along. We want to reach the camp before nightfall."

They moved off through the forest on trails so narrow and poorly marked that they might have been nothing more than scratches in the ground. They avoided streams, and when they could not, they crossed on stone bridges, for anything less substantial seemed to cause the four vampires acute distress. Marian did her best to keep this in mind as she continued on with them, through the thickening shadows and the fading light of afternoon.

It was sunset by the time they reached the glade where Hood's men kept their camp. A fire had been lit in the main pit, more for illumination than heat, and it served as a place for the vampires to gather as they prepared for their nighttime forays into the woods. Little John, who had been standing guard, gave the alert that Penrod Lugenis was coming back and that he and his men were not alone.

"They have a woman in boy's clothes with them," he announced, his deep, gruff voice carrying easily through the dusk.

The Red Friar had just emerged from his hovel, and he looked about curiously. "A woman? Are you sure?"

"I can smell, can't I?" Little John asked. "You sniff the air and tell me what kind of blood you—"

"And the clothes?" the Red Friar interrupted. "How can you be sure of the clothes?"

"Amelin called in from his post, a short while ago. I report what he said," Little John said bluntly. "Or do you question his senses, too?"

"No, I do not," said the Red Friar. "But it is surprising

that Penrod Lugenis would bring a woman to this camp, that's all."

"It is strange," Little John conceded.

"What is strange?" Will Scarlet asked as he came up to the two.

"That Penrod Lugenis would capture a woman and bring her here," said the Red Friar.

"It depends upon the woman," said Scarlet, and chuckled.

"I suppose," said the Red Friar, and bent to shove another log into the fire-pit. "The nights are getting cold early this year."

"That they are," said Scarlet. "It makes our hunting easier. Everyone wants to find a warm place for the night. All we have to do is seek them out." He glanced up as Penrod Lugenis and his three companions stepped into the light from the fire. "You're creating a stir, fellow."

"Why am I doing that?" Penrod Lugenis asked.

"They say you've brought a woman with you," said Little John.

From all around the camp, men appeared as if they were shadows taking on bodies, or beasts transformed into men.

"That I have. Marian deBeauchamp, the promised bride of Gui deGisbourne, daughter of Stephen deBeauchamp." He stood aside and motioned to her. "Come forward, my Lady."

Marian was tired and cold, and her fear was so pronounced that it was very nearly another companion with the vampires. She held herself well, as she had been taught, but her inclination was to weep, an inward admission for which she silently castigated herself. "Who is leader here?" she asked in a tone calculated to intimidate all but the highest-ranking peers in England.

From the deep shadows on the other side of the camp, a voice said, "I am."

All eyes in the camp turned toward the speaker as Hood himself stepped out of the twilight to stand in the glare of the fire.

"I have come from the Great North Road," Penrod Lugenis said. "This is what I found there."

"Just this woman? Was she alone?" Hood asked derisively.

"No, she was with soldiers, but most of them carried a comrade off to the monks to find him some relief from a fever," said Penrod Lugenis.

"She was left with one man to guard her," said Piers, gloating.

"We made short work of him," said Orlan Royce. "And we left him with hawthorn all around him."

"A reasonable action," said Scarlet. "All things considered."

Hood held up his hand. "You have brought me this woman for what reason?"

"She is of high rank, and she has powerful kin," said Penrod Lugenis.

"All the more reason to be rid of her," Scarlet said with a wave of his hand as if to usher Marian out of their lives.

"Possibly," said the Red Friar. "But she may have advantages, as well."

"That was my thought," said Penrod Lugenis.

"It is a bold decision," said Hood, "to bring her here to me. Did you intend her for me?" His stare fixed Penrod Lugenis as surely as an arrow could.

"Of course," said Penrod Lugenis, a note of uncertainty creeping into his confident tone.

"I see," said Hood, his glare moving to Marian. "I see."

"She can command many things, a woman of her rank," said Penrod Lugenis.

"And for that, you shall have first favor of our next hunt," said Hood, and smiled as the tension that had crackled in the glade as much as the fire finally eased.

Listening to these men discuss her with no more concern than her uncle would show a hound or a bull, Marian could not believe that she could emerge from this safely. She looked about her, seeing the company of men—so much larger than she had anticipated—and knew that she had almost no hope of escape. To her astonishment, she saw Hood approaching her, his white skin and hair making him appear to be a ghost.

"So you are promised to Gui deGisbourne," he said as he came up to her.

"Yes," she said.

"And how do you regard him, your pledged husband?" The mockery in his red eyes revealed his opinion.

"As I would any husband," she said, speaking the truth as bluntly as she could, and hoping it would buy her a quick death.

"And how is that?" Hood tweaked the straight bangs out of her eyes.

She stared at him defiantly, unwilling to show her fright. "As a master who has the right to use me as he would a cur, and probably will. I know my value is in my blood and any sons I may give Sir Gui, and that otherwise, I am no better than any drab in the land, I am purchased just as she is, but my price is higher than hers."

"Your value is in your blood," Hood repeated in ferocious amusement. "That much is true."

She felt a cold grue make its way along her spine, but she held his gaze with her own. "I will not cheapen my name, for then I would truly be nothing more than a drab."

"Why not become a nun, and keep to yourself?" Hood asked, having trouble saying "nun."

"God is as capricious a husband as any, and more uncaring than most," she said bluntly. "I lack a calling."

"Then it is a shame you were not born a son," Scarlet dared to say.

Hood glowered at him. "You're right, Cousin, but you are also impertinent."

Marian turned to Scarlet. "It is a pity, for I cannot remain maiden all my life, can I?"

"And you would rather die than be dishonored," said Hood with satisfaction.

The men in the clearing moved nearer to the fire, as if trying to share its heat.

Swallowing hard, Marian said, "Yes."

"Then you shall have your wish," said Hood, and took hold of her shoulders. "I will not dishonor you, Maid, but I will kill you—for a while."

She stared at him, comprehension just beginning as she felt the flesh of her throat give way under the power of his attack.

22.

How deSteny arrived at Nottingham

The rain had continued for four days, blustery and cold, soaking the forest and everything in it. The road had become so muddy that the horses wallowed as they labored on, and mud came up to their girths. Their progress slowed from seven leagues a day to four. DeSteny didn't push the soldiers, for he was reluctant to arrive at Nottingham, where he would have to admit his failure and accept the punishment Sir Gui was certain to mete out to him, punishment he would richly deserve for allowing Marian deBeauchamp to vanish, along with Hearne. The recriminations Sir Gui would heap on him would be nothing compared to the dismay he felt already: he continually thought back to that dreadful realization that they were gone, and the hours spent searching for Lady Marian and Hearne.

The same questions rankled: What had he missed? What sign had he ignored? What subtle trace had he overlooked? What had become of the two of them? Surely if they had been set upon there would have been some sign—blood, a weapon, broken branches, anything—but aside from the discarded hood, there was nothing.

They were ten leagues from the gates of Nottingham when Byrle spoke up for the first time since their breakfast in a small, run-down abbey. "You couldn't have known. Truly, Sheriff. Who could have?" It was drizzly and cold, and the young soldier sniffed and rubbed at his reddened nose.

"I was charged with her safety," deSteny said. He huddled in his cloak as much for comfort as for warmth. "We know the forest is dangerous. I should have insisted that she remain with us, or kept more of our men with her, or—"

"And who is to say you wouldn't have lost another man?" Delwin demanded.

"I might have done. But she might have been spared," said deSteny miserably.

"So she might. But you did all that any man might to guard her. You wanted to keep her from harm when you left her in Hearne's care." Byrle sounded worried.

"But I didn't. She disappeared," deSteny said, his heart heavy. He wiped the wet from his eyes. "Who knows what has become of her? There has been no word, I take it? No demands for ransom, or any other news of her?" He had some very unpleasant notions about the possibilities, most of which made him cringe.

Delwin gave a gesture of helplessness. "We searched for her and we have asked everywhere for word of her. No one has seen anything. What more could you do without summoning a company of soldiers? And where would such soldiers be found? We were leagues from any fort or castle. What other course was open to us? I don't think Sir Gui wants it known that his affianced wife has vanished. It could lead to speculation that wouldn't please him." He was incensed now, and the more he spoke the more he fueled his aggravation. "You are going to report the . . . incident. You will explain what happened. We did all that anyone could. We haven't abandoned our duty."

"Perhaps you haven't, but I have," said deSteny, feeling a desolation of spirit he hadn't known since his terrible days in the Holy Land.

"No," protested Sprague. Under his helmet his face was

drawn with fatigue and worry. "You have done all that any man might."

"I doubt if Sir Gui will see it that way," said deSteny with an attempt at humor. "He isn't likely to be pleased with this news."

"He may be relieved," said Byrle. "If half the rumors are true."

DeSteny knew he should discourage such talk, but all he said was, "Don't say that where any friar can hear you."

"Why? They gossip more than soldiers do," said Sprague. "But we'll hold our peace."

"Just as well," said deSteny, looking around as the way became more familiar. "The garrison may have realized something was wrong, for we are coming late."

"They'll attribute that to the rain," said Sprague, determined to be hopeful.

"And traveling with a woman," added Delwin. "They won't have sent out scouts for us, not yet, not with Sir Gui's man in charge."

They reached a sturdy, covered bridge and went over the swollen stream. "It's good to be out of the wet, even a little while," said deSteny, knowing the stream protected them as much as the roof did.

"So it is," said Sprague. "I will order a tub of hot water when we get back, to clean off the grime and warm my bones."

"And I," said Byrle.

"We'll all want a bath," deSteny said, settling the matter. He retreated into silence, and his men took their example from him.

Shortly before mid-day, they made the turn for Nottingham, and in a little while, they were out of the forest and riding up to the walls of the city. They were admitted promptly through open gates, and rode directly to the castle, drawing rein and signaling for the portcullis to be lifted. Men on the ramparts hailed them, and, hearing their names called back, raised the gates hurriedly, gathering around them as they came inside the walls, bedraggled as half-drowned cats.

Sir Humphrey was at the head of the men who came forward to meet the Sheriff and his men. He stared, counting the reduced numbers and keenly aware that the woman they had gone to escort was not with them. "Three men missing? Hearne? Meaghar? Ackerley? And—the bride?"

"It's a long story," said deSteny resignedly. He swung off his dun and sighed heavily. "Where is Sir Gui?"

"Heaven only knows. Not here, that much is certain," said Sir Humphrey, rolling his eyes upward. "And Wilem deFolleux! What a fop! You should see him in his silks, his pomander to his nose, parading about: Sir Gui's crony has done little more than wander the castle with troubadours serenading him, play his shawm, and order elaborate feasts. My men have had to go and kill cranes and geese for his pleasure. We had to butcher suckling pigs two nights ago, and they say we'll have to bring in three red harts for him tomorrow, dressed for the spits. Soldiers doing the work of scullions!" His indignation mounted as he spoke. "He has done nothing about the trouble in the forest, and is only interested in the quality of cloth that comes from Nottingham's looms. The most manly exercise he undertakes is hunting, and that only when it is fitting that he accompany Sir Gui."

DeSteny nodded. "In other words, Sir Gui's sort of man." It was an unwise remark, but he made no apology for it. "As you can tell, we had . . . difficulties."

"I supposed something of the sort," said Sir Humphrey.

"What will you tell Sir Gui?"

"As much of the truth as he'll permit, when he returns." DeSteny signaled his men to dismount. "We might as well get this over with. There is nothing to be gained in prolonging our report."

The men obeyed, but slowly, as if they wanted to make themselves less noticeable.

When the grooms came to take the horses in hand, deSteny said, "My dun needs her hooves trimmed and new shoes. The off-side rear one is loose. I can hear it click." This ordinary complaint seemed reassuring, an uncomplicated problem with an easy solution.

"I'll tell the farrier. He'll see to it tonight," said the groom, taking the dun and the roan in hand.

Some of the soldiers not on duty had wandered up toward them, but now hesitated, as if worried they might experience some invisible contagion from the Sheriff and his men. Sir Humphrey regarded these soldiers with scorn. "Do you respect deFolleux so much that you look upon deSteny with scorn? You know how the forest is. Do you believe you could have fared any better? He would stand by you, if you had gone on this ill-omened journey."

The Sheriff regarded the Marshal with surprise. "You are very good, Sir Humphrey," he said. "But these men are right to be dubious."

"Any man who has not faced danger can have no worthwhile opinion, no matter how high-born he may be," Sir Humphrey declared. "If they were not in your company, they can have nothing to say one way or the other. You are not obliged to listen to anything. Keep in mind whose vassals you are. And," he added portentously, "if I learn that any of you have spoken to any of Sir Wilem's court, I will dismiss him from mine. Is this clear? You are all on your honor." The men standing around Sir Humphrey said nothing, although their expressions were eloquent. A few of the men manning the ramparts lifted their pikes to show their support. "Come inside, Sheriff," Sir Humphrey went on, making it obvious that he welcomed deSteny's return. "You must be cold and hungry."

"That I am, and all my men," he said, falling in beside the stout, sturdy Marshal. He was surprised at the support Sir Humphrey had given him, and the polite manner in which he allowed deSteny to take the lead. They entered the keep and started along toward the ward-room. "If there is any punishment, it is mine to take."

"Nonsense," said Sir Humphrey. "It is Sir Gui's doing, ultimately. If he was so worried for his bride, he should have fetched her himself."

DeSteny agreed but held his tongue. "Sir Gui is away?"

"From Nottingham and Gisbourne," said Sir Humphrey. "He is said to be hunting with his cousin." The angle of his brows made it clear that he doubted this.

"A last tryst, do you think?" deSteny asked.

"That would be my guess, for there is not much sport to be had in the forest just now," said Sir Humphrey as he opened the door to the ward-room. "I will have water ordered for a bath. You look numb and there's mud half-way up your legs."

"All of us have had a hard go of it," said deSteny. Then he looked about. "Has Wroughton returned?"

"Not yet," said Sir Humphrey. "I suppose we might expect him within a se'enight."

"For his sake, I hope so. The weather is turning filthy," said deSteny. He went to one of the benches drawn up before a smoking fire. "This is good. It's warm."

"Your men will have hot food shortly, and spiced wine to

get their blood flowing once more. If you want the same, I'll have the page bring you a tray at once." Sir Humphrey sat at the other end of the bench.

deSteny shook his head. "I'll wait until my men have eaten."

Sir Humphrey nodded. "As you wish. This is a shabby way to receive you, no matter what the reason for it." He paused, sighing. "We've lost nine more crofters to whatever is out there," he said slowly.

"Poor wretches," said deSteny, looking over his shoulder as a page came into the ward-room.

"Amen, and may God save them," said Sir Humphrey before telling the page to have the bath-barrel brought. "Make sure the water is hot. The Sheriff has been chilled on his journey. And bring a pot of wine with pepper and ginger."

The page was shocked at this extravagance, but bowed and withdrew.

"I could order your quarters prepared," Sir Humphrey suggested.

"Not until I have got out of these clothes," said deSteny. "Besides, I must suppose that Sir Wilem still occupies them."

"It is time he left," said Sir Humphrey, making no apology for his brusqueness.

"He is here on Sir Gui's invitation, and to do his bidding," deSteny reminded him. "You have an obligation to maintain his hospitality."

"No doubt. But my first duty is to Nottingham, and you are Sheriff here." Sir Humphrey folded his arms. "You are in immediate need of warmth and food. It is fitting that you receive both. And Sir Wilem isn't within the walls."

"Where is he?" deSteny asked, only mildly curious. "You

said he was away, but where?"

"He is also hunting. With Sir Gui." Sir Humphrey's inflection revealed his opinion of this.

"Another tryst?" DeSteny knew he ought to speak up on Sir Gui's behalf, but couldn't bring himself to do it.

"It may be," said Sir Humphrey. "It is your right to reclaim your place, Sheriff."

DeSteny was about to speak, but stopped as the page came back bearing a small tray on which stood a tankard of wine. Wraiths of steam rose from its surface, smelling of ginger and pepper and the warm vines of France. He took the tankard and felt its heat on his hand, so intense it verged on being painful. "Thank you," he said, both to the page and Sir Humphrey. He took a long sip, enjoying the sensation in spite of the discomfort.

Sir Humphrey waited until the page was gone, then said, "Don't wait for Sir Wilem to come back. This is your place. Take it. Otherwise Sir Gui will blame you for all that has happened."

"Not without cause," said deSteny.

"That's as may be," said Sir Humphrey. "You and I know it was foolish to bring a woman into the forest with so small an escort. All it did was alert the creatures within that there was something to find. If he didn't go himself, then he should have sent a proper contingent. The men with you were hardly enough for three merchants, let alone a lady."

"She wore boy's clothes," said deSteny.

Sir Humphrey laughed harshly. "As if that could fool those—those—" He stopped, not finding a word to express what he thought of the marauders. "There is no disguise sufficient to deceive them."

DeSteny nodded and drank more hot wine.

23.

How the Red Friar met an old Friend

Will Scarlet dragged the bench toward the tree where Hearne was tied, head down, ankles lashed to the higher branches; the soldier's face should have been purple, but it was the color of whey, his eyes staring out of darkened sockets like empty pits. His skin was slack and what little was left of his voice came out in a rasp. Here, in the muted light of the deep forest, all the colors were faded, and that added to Hearne's sepulchral pallor. Scarlet kicked the plank into position and straddled it, facing the dying soldier. "Don't fight it, my friend. You can't do anything."

Hearne's eyes opened slowly but were fixed on a distant point only he could see. "Be . . . damned to you." There was almost no breath left in him, but the vitriol of his curse was still apparent.

"Yes, of course," Scarlet soothed, gently touching the blood-matted stubble on Hearne's cheek. "We're all damned here, every last one of us. That's been arranged some time ago." Then he tweaked the ragged edge of Hearne's beard. "Don't fret, soldier. You're near the end. It'll be over soon."

"Not soon enough, no, not soon enough. You should have left me where you abandoned me. I would have been dead within a day," Hearne whispered, his eyes unable to focus on his tormentor. His breath came out in little clouds, mute testament to the warmth that remained in his flesh;

Scarlet's breath had no fog, for he was cold as the air around him.

"Oh, don't say that," Scarlet pleaded. "You have given so much to so many of us. You should be proud of your sacrifice. You nurture us and become a martyr to your faith at the same time. What man could want more?" His laughter had an edge to it.

"Vile!" Hearne tried to spit and succeeded only in sending a thin stream of drool along his face toward his brow. He ground his teeth.

"Don't be so condemning," Scarlet recommended. "You have some time left, and you wouldn't want it to be unpleasant, would you? We can make it so."

Hearne strove to speak, and was able to get out a few fragmentary words, but he could not express his repulsion adequately, and so tried to ignore Scarlet, looking past him to the little grove where Hood's band lived.

"You aren't listening to me, are you?" Scarlet said, amused and offended at once, his youthful features marred by cynicism.

There was a strangled cry from Hearne as his eyes at last picked out the bustling figure of the Red Friar. "You!"

The Red Friar stopped in his tracks, a swift look of chagrin going over his features. Then he steadied himself and continued on toward the soldier. "They have you, haven't they?" He meant this to be sympathetic, but he heard himself, and to his own ears, he sounded as if he were gloating.

Hearne couldn't answer. His eyes fluttered and his mouth trembled.

"You're annoying him," said Scarlet to the Red Friar.

"I don't want to add to his discomfort," said the Red Friar, and castigated himself inwardly for lying so obviously.

"No. You want to drain the life from him," said Scarlet,

chuckling. "Hood wouldn't like you doing that, not while he hasn't finished."

"But he said . . ." the Red Friar began, but could not go on.

"His lady hasn't had her first kill yet. It is fitting that she have this one, considering." Scarlet rose and took a step back. He studied Hearne critically. "He isn't going to last much longer. She'd better get her fill soon or miss out on the satisfaction."

"Perhaps she'll find it distasteful," the Red Friar ventured.

"She may," said Scarlet. "And if she does, she'll starve."

This blunt statement troubled the Red Friar. He glanced over his shoulder, half-expecting to see Hood coming out of his cave in the roots of his hollowed tree. Shoving his hands into his sleeves, he began to pace. "She is new to this life. She may not like it. She is a lady. She isn't used to the hardships Hood's men endure daily."

"Well, she can't go back to her family now, can she?" Scarlet said.

"No," the Red Friar conceded. "But she has to be able to . . . to attack living men and drink their lives. She is gently raised."

"Her late father was a fighter. He went to the Holy Land and he fought the French in Aquitaine. His daughter isn't made of feathers, Friar. She has more substance than you give her credit for having." Scarlet looked down at Hearne. "He won't be able to fight her, in any case. Look at him. He's worse than a dying dog."

The Red Friar had an impulse to pronounce the blessing for the dying over Hearne, but even thinking of those sacred words made him queasy, and instead of pronouncing a blessing, he pointed his finger as if in criticism. He went up to Hearne and said, "I'm sorry it has come to this. You have been a loyal soldier."

Hearne managed to shake his head, but could not speak.

"Is he alive yet?" Hood asked suddenly as he lifted the bearskin that covered the entrance to his cave.

"Yes. For a little while. He is becoming faint," said Scarlet, moving aside so that Hood could see for himself.

"A pity, but still necessary," said Hood, shrugging slightly. "Come, Marian. It is time you made yourself one of us. You don't want to be apart from us, do you? I will make you the crown of my . . . my heart." He held out his hand to someone standing behind him, and a moment later, Marian deBeauchamp emerged, still dressed like a boy, her face glowing in anticipation. "You know what is to be done."

"Yes, my Lord, I know," she said, moving past him and strolling toward the tree where Hearne was tied; her long stride reminded Scarlet of a big cat's rolling gait. "He's proving to be most robust," she approved as she stopped in front of Hearne. "Well met, soldier," she said, smiling a little.

"My Lady," he muttered, torn between duty and fear.

"Yes. Truly." She knelt next to him, her face so near his that they almost touched. "You wanted to preserve me, and preserve me you shall." Her fingers swept aside the disorder of his hair, exposing the top of his neck.

"You mustn't, my Lady," Hearne whispered. "You mustn't."

"But I must," she said, and bent to pull off the scabs that had formed over his wounds. She drank eagerly, and, when the stream faltered, she sucked at the torn skin until she could pull no more from it. Sitting back on her haunches, she shook her head. "There wasn't much left of him."

Hood grinned in lupine delight. "Then we will have to

find you more. I cannot have my Lady go hungry." He pulled his horn from his belt and blew on it, summoning his men from half a league around. While they came in answer to the brazen call, he walked up and down in the space before his cave, impatiently tapping his long, pale fingers on his wolf-skin tunic. As his men arrived, they watched him narrowly, trying to discern the purpose of his muster.

"All but your guards are here, Lord," said Little John when the clearing was full. He still carried his quarterstaff, but he no longer brandished it.

"Good. Very good," said Hood, looking about. "Well, my fine lads, my Lady—who is your Lady—has had her first taste of the eternal food, and she is hungry for more. She must have more or she will go hungry to bed, and this cannot be."

A few of the men hooted derision, but most remained silent and expectant.

Marian deBeauchamp rose from where she had been crouching next to Hearne. "My Lord—who is your Lord—has promised me sport."

This time there was a more enthusiastic response as the men realized that they would participate in the hunt. Will Scarlet lifted his hand in ironic salute to Marian, and she inclined her head to him as if to a courtier.

"Who is in the forest this day? Near enough that we can reach them before nightfall?" Hood asked, looking directly at Little John, whose task it was to know such things.

"There is a party of merchants from the north, all fat and with well-laden mules. They travel with ten armed men and three monks for guards. There is a tinker with his pack, a crofter and his son taking pigs to market, and a small contingent of soldiers from Windsor, judging from the arms on their surcotes. None are more than three leagues away."

Little John almost smirked as he said this.

"The merchants are tempting," said Hood.

"But they are well-armed, and they are bound for the monastery of Saint Hilarion. They may well be within its walls by the time we can reach them. The crofter is small fare, hardly worth our effort for what we would get from it." Little John took a deep breath. "The party from Windsor is most easily reached—it is little more than two leagues away, and they are not moving very fast. One of their number has brought mead for them all, and they are inattentive."

"You say they are drunk?" Hood asked, his red eyes shining in anticipation.

"I say they are well on the way to being so." Little John pointed to Nicholas the Joiner. "You observed them. Tell Hood what you told me."

Nicholas coughed awkwardly. "I saw two large jars of mead being passed among the men. They were letting their horses pick their road. All but one, who was fretful and would not drink. The rest made mock of him for his fears, and, I think, imbibed the more to show him how foolish they thought him."

"He is the one we must stop first," said Hood, and held out his hand to Marian.

"He is riding in the rear, or he was when I saw them," said Nicholas. "We can still separate him, if we plan for it."

"No matter. He is ours." Hood brayed a terrible laugh. "You shall have the pride of kill, my Lady. You will be the one to take his life."

Her face brightened. "You are gracious to me, my Lord."

"Not gracious," Hood corrected her. "It is mete that you should have the most worthy prey." He ducked inside his cave and retrieved his longbow and a quiver of arrows.

"Come. All of you arm yourselves. We may have to fight these men." He pointed to Little John. "Lead the way. We'll keep pace with you."

Little John pointed to one of the many narrow paths that led away from their clearing. "On to the old shrine, and then south on the road. We should meet them within a mile, if they have kept on at the same pace."

"Onward!" Hood ordered, and strode toward Little John, Marian deBeauchamp right behind him. The men sorted themselves out into a single file as they made their way through the dense undergrowth of the inner forest. Shortly before they reached the old shrine, Hood called the Red Friar up to his side. "I want you to go on the road. We will flank you in the bushes. I don't want them put on the alert. A single monk on the road shouldn't bother them—in fact, if you ask to join them, they will probably think you more unfortunate than they." He gave the Red Friar a shove, sending him ahead of the rest.

The Red Friar staggered on the uneven ground and almost steadied himself against the old shrine, but thought better of it, for the Church had consecrated the sacred niche as its own, and the Red Friar knew it would be unsettling to get too near it. He recovered himself and straightened his habit, brushing off as much of the mud and bits of forest matter as he could see. Then he took up his position across the road from the shrine, his hands folded above his slight paunch. He hardly saw Hood's men melt into the shadows around him, but he knew they were there.

A short while later the sound of ambling horses came through the trees. Their tack squeaked and jingled, and one of the men was half-singing a song about an amorous mouse; the Red Friar moved to the middle of the road and stood patiently in the dull light of the cloudy afternoon, waiting for what was coming.

Ellenby was at the head of the party, swaying a bit as they went along. He held one of the jars of mead in his free hand while he leaned back to try to join Fortesque, who rode on his right, in song. Behind them, Simmons and Danebraugh shared a jar of mead, but didn't bother to sing; they preferred drinking to making their presence known in the forest. Moreton and Wroughton brought up the rear, and both of them looked uneasily about.

The Red Friar held up his hands. "Good soldiers," he said as they came up to him. "May your day be blessed."

"Amen to that, good Friar," said Ellenby, slurring his words a bit. He pulled his horse to a halt.

"Well met," said the Red Friar, who could think of nothing else to say.

"Indeed." Ellenby belched. "How is it you're abroad at such a time?"

"Alas, it is for penance," said the Red Friar. "I am supposed to walk from Saint Matthew's to Saint Erconwald's."

"York to London, nearly the whole of the Great North Road," said Ellenby. "What sin have you committed that demands so many leagues of you?"

"It is not fitting for me to say," the Red Friar said, "but to my Confessor." He lifted his hand as if to cross himself, but thought better of it and sighed.

From his place at the rear of the company, Wroughton shook his head and stared. "I know you," he said, "I know you, Trinitarian!" He raised his voice as fear shot through him. "You were the one we lost in the forest—" Without thinking he began to back his horse up, putting distance between him and the fell monk.

"I know you, Wroughton," the Red Friar agreed, saddened that he should have once been friendly with the soldier. "I ask your pardon for this."

"You're one of them!" Wroughton pulled his horse back onto his hind legs and swung him around.

The Red Friar moved forward and seized the reins of Ellenby's horse. "Well met," he said again, with deadly purpose, as he heard Hood's horn order the outlaws to the hunt.

24.

How Wroughton made his way toward Home

Moreton looked about in confusion as he saw Wroughton attempt to bolt just as more than thirty men in green and brown poured onto the road from the thickets and the branches of the trees. The four soldiers on the road ahead of him were surrounded by unknown men, and he knew this meant serious trouble. He quickly decided to follow Wroughton, and tried to wheel his mare, only to find himself caught by four of Hood's men. He drew his sword and struck out at them as they grabbed at his legs in an attempt to pull him out of the saddle.

"Moreton!" Wroughton shouted as he tried to spur his mount away from the chaos. "Follow me!"

"I'm trying!" Moreton shouted as he kicked one of the men near him. His horse sat back on his haunches, squealing in distress, front hooves flailing, scattering the outlaws like autumn leaves. Taking advantage of this, Moreton clapped his heels to his gelding's sides, sending the horse bounding toward Wroughton. An instant later, he drew rein and looked back, compelled to see what had happened to his four companions. He held his horse with hard hands, keeping the frightened animal under strict control as he prepared to give battle. In the next breath, he was upset to discover that his leader had been overwhelmed and that the other three men were also in the hands of the outlaws.

Ellenby was on the ground, half a dozen of Hood's men

around him, holding him down. Hood himself approached the supine soldier, ignoring his curses and threats. He nudged Ellenby with his toe. "It is your hour."

"Never! May God strike you down for this!" Ellenby shouted desperately.

"All in good time," Hood said, his red eyes glowing like living embers. His stride lengthened and he drew all his men around him.

There was a long howl as men took hold of Ellenby's arms and legs, holding him spread-eagled on the ground, holding him in readiness for Hood. Moreton kept his horse still just long enough to see one of the outlaws drop down beside Ellenby and bend over him as the others leaned closer in shared anticipation. The scream that followed goaded Moreton to action and he set his gelding galloping after Wroughton. "Oh, God save us!" Moreton shouted, and a moment later felt a weight on his back as a pair of outlaws emerged from the underbrush, daggers drawn. He didn't realize that he had been stabbed until he felt warm wetness spread down his back from the wound in his shoulder.

Wroughton charged at Moreton. "Get onto my horse! Go!" he yelled as he came up to the other man. "Hurry!" He used the pommel of his sword to brain one of their attackers and had the satisfaction of hearing the bone crack. As the second outlaw faltered, he swung his sword and hacked the fellow's shoulder, all but cutting the joint through, then swung out his arm to help Moreton get onto the rump of his horse. "Hang on!" he bellowed as he urged his mount into a run. The big gelding surged forward as if in his panic he was unaware of his extra burden, and wanted only to escape.

"What were they?" Moreton asked breathlessly. Now

that he was out of immediate danger his wound was hurting him. He could feel the blood running and it began to worry him.

"Outlaws," said Wroughton. "Worse than any." He pulled his horse in to a canter, not wanting to exhaust the animal before he was out of range of Hood's men. "They are dire things, not men at all."

"Did you see—" Moreton began.

"No. Nor did I want to," said Wroughton grimly. He was more frightened than he could admit, and he whispered a prayer as he rode.

"What will they do to the others?" Moreton asked in gasps.

"Kill them, if they are merciful," said Wroughton. "Or, if they are not, those men will swell their numbers."

"How? They are sworn to Prince John and the King," said Moreton. He shifted his hold on Wroughton so that he wouldn't bounce so much, for that was making his pain much worse.

"Not once those men have charge of them," said Wroughton. "We should have hurried. I knew we should have hurried." He began to look for side-roads, knowing that not only was he going the wrong way now, but that the outlaws would be lying in wait for him to make another attempt to reach Nottingham. He also doubted that Moreton could ride much farther.

As if to confirm this, Moreton groaned. "I'm getting weak."

"Hang on," said Wroughton.

"I will," said Moreton with more hope than certainty.

They rushed on, the curve in the road shutting out the dreadful scene behind them. Neither man bothered to look back, although the noises that followed them raised the hair on their necks. They put half a league between them and the slaughter before Wroughton saw a lane coming in from the left, and he swung his horse onto it, pulling him in to a walk and letting him begin to recover from their mad rush.

"Where does this go?" Moreton asked in a thready voice.

"I don't know," Wroughton admitted, ducking his head to avoid a low-growing limb.

"Then why—" Moreton wailed.

"Because we must get away," said Wroughton. "This appears to be a wagon-way, which means it may lead to an abbey or a hamlet, in either case, we'll be safe for a while."

"Are you sure?" Moreton asked, his voice fading to a whisper.

"Of course," Wroughton lied as he peered about into the darkness, his thoughts preoccupied with unwelcome impressions of the dangers around them. He kept on in silence, hoping that Moreton would continue to remain conscious. When he finally caught sight of a stockade, he was weak with relief. "See?" He said more heartily than before. "A hamlet. The crofters will let us in, most certainly."

"Um," said Moreton, as if incapable of thinking of any words.

Wroughton rode up near to the gates of the stockade and stopped his horse. Rising in his stirrups, he shouted, "Hello the gates! Open in the name of the Sheriff of Nottingham and Prince John!" He waited and repeated the summons more loudly, and was finally rewarded by an answering shout.

"How many are you?"

"Two!" Wroughton answered. "And one of us is wounded. I ask you to let us in for the duty you owe your Lord."

There was a longer pause this time, and the next voice

was louder than the first, and less cordial. "Why should we?"

"Because your failure to aid a messenger of the Prince will cost you dearly," Wroughton shouted back.

"If anyone ever learns of it," came the sharp rejoinder.

"It will be known," said Wroughton. "And good service will receive as much favor as poor service will bring censure on you and your hamlet." He hated having to argue with the fellow, whoever he was. "I have a wounded man with me, a soldier of His Grace Prince John. If he isn't helped soon, he will die. Do you want his death held against you?"

"You are not the only ones we must answer to," the voice called back, but there was less defiance in it now, as if the speaker knew he had to concede. "There are others in the forest, and we must answer to them as well."

"No doubt," said Wroughton, not wanting to add that they were precisely the threat he and Moreton were escaping. "But open the gates to us."

"We will," said the voice. "And may God have mercy on all of us."

"Amen," Wroughton said, guiding his horse to the gates and waiting for them to be opened. When the first moaning of hempen hinges sounded, he almost wept. They would be safe at last! As soon as the opening was wide enough, he used his heels to move his horse through the narrow opening and found himself in a small square, surrounded by a dozen men of varying ages. "May God thank you for your charity." He did his best to sound grateful, but could hear annoyance in his voice.

"That man is badly hurt," said the headman of the hamlet, an angular fellow with a blighted right eye and two fingers missing from his right hand.

"We were set upon. By outlaws," said Wroughton. "If

you will see to this fellow's wounds, you will be rewarded in the King's name."

"So you say," the headman remarked, adding something that sounded like, "We touch the benefit of Kings." That couldn't be right, Wroughton thought as he stared at the headman, whose speech was almost unintelligible to Wroughton, for he was not familiar with the dialects of the crofters in this part of Sherwood.

"Am I to stay here?" Moreton asked weakly.

"No doubt," Wroughton muttered, not at all pleased with this necessity. Then he cleared his throat. "How far are we from Nottingham?"

The headman rubbed his chin. "Our way, most of a day, the main road, a little longer."

"Ah," said Wroughton. "And what is your way?" He made a point of speaking clearly and slowly, hoping to get the crofters to speak in the same manner.

"We go about the crofts, of course," said the headman, as if such an answer were obvious. He shifted his speech a little, sounding more like Wroughton. "Your kind would say we go on the by-ways."

"You mean you have a road connecting the crofts?" Wroughton asked.

Lapsing back to his own dialect, "As well shine a chestnut," the headman said, or so it seemed to Wroughton.

"What?" he demanded.

"A way goes among us," said the headman as if speaking to someone nearly deaf, once more using a more cultivated manner of speech, but awkwardly, as if he were not very familiar with the language. He signaled to an older woman at the edge of the curious folk gathered about. "Mother Sibley," he said. "This poor soldier needs your help. What say you?"

The old woman shook her head. "He may stay, but the other must go." She spat and made a sign with her fingers that indicated she thought Wroughton was dangerous.

The headman shook his head. "You heard her. We will care for the wounded man, but you must leave." He folded his arms, saying truculently, as if conceding too much to Wroughton, "You may ride our track to Nottingham. It should be safer than the Great North Road."

Wroughton swallowed hard. "I have a missive from the Prince that must get to Nottingham and the Sheriff. I am sworn to deliver it."

"Then you had better leave at once," said the headman as two of his stalwarts took Moreton in hand, bearing him gently toward one of the wooden houses. "Stay on the track until you reach the river, and then bear to the north—to the left."

"I know which direction north is," Wroughton muttered as he looked about, seeing only implacable faces. "If you fail to care for Moreton, the Sheriff's men will return and raze this place to the ground."

"If they can find us, then they may do as they wish." The headman pointed to Moreton. "But you will want him safe again, won't you?"

"You have sworn to care for him," Wroughton said sharply. "I must know you will do him no harm."

"If any living person can save him, Mother Sibley will," said the headman in a tone that bordered on awe. "She has saved those whose wounds stank of pus and she has made the ill sound again. If your man dies, it will not be on her account."

Little as he wanted to accept this endorsement, Wroughton saw that to protest more would be folly for him and dangerous for Moreton. "Very well," he said. "But if anything should happen to him that is not on account of his wounds, you will answer for it."

"As we have for the crops and the hunt," said the headman bitterly. "Get you gone, soldier. The longer you linger the nearer to night it is, and the more dire the hunters that will be abroad in the land." He ducked his head as a kind of afterthought, as if he had only just realized this might be expected of him.

"The Sheriff and his men will know of this." It was more bluster than threat, but Wroughton could not keep from uttering it.

"Then you had best be on your way, to tell them. They will not hear it on the wind," said the headman, turning his back and adding an incomprehensible string of words that to Wroughton seemed to be, "Cats darling frober say." The other crofters exchanged knowing nods and one man winked.

Keenly aware that there was nothing more he could do, Wroughton swung his horse around. "I will not forget this. I hope you will have no call to regret this day's work."

"Nor we," said the headsman, signaling his men to close the gate behind Wroughton.

It was dim enough under the trees for Wroughton to have some difficulty picking out the narrow track that led eastward through the close-growing trees. He started his big gelding walking, and hoped they would find shelter for the night at an abbey or monastery, for he was beginning to think that the crofters might be in league with the baleful outlaws. At least the nuns of Saint Gertrude knew their horseflesh, he reminded himself in an attempt to feel reassured. He was tired and frightened and cold, but he made himself go on along the unknown road, alert to every sound as the dusk closed in around him.

25.

How Sir Gui's return to Nottingham was planned

All through the morning rain fell steadily, so that by midafternoon all the forest was drenched. Roads were morasses of mud that sank cart-wheels to the axles and horses to their knees. Those few travelers who slogged through the city gates were caked with mud and soaked to the skin. The odor of wet wool and horses permeated to every portion of Nottingham Castle, combining with the strong scent of burning oak from all the fireplaces, and the slight mustiness that came with the pervading damp.

Hugh deSteny sat in his study, a book of accounts of various ancient battles open before him, but presently unread. He had dismissed Simon some time ago, saying he would review all the records that had been prepared for him when he was more attentive, and Simon had been forced to accept this. DeSteny was deeply preoccupied with his own thoughts, none of which offered him any semblance of comfort or optimism. He was overcome with a sense of his own failure, for he had been unable to bring Marian deBeauchamp to Sir Gui. At the time he had almost been willing to believe he had done his duty, but the last two days, since he had returned to Nottingham, doubt had eroded his convictions and now he was convinced that he had betrayed the trust of his Lord, Sir Gui. He sighed and looked down at the page before him, the stilted Latin providing no refuge for him. "Horatius would despise me," he mumbled as he quickly turned the pages of that hero's sacrifice, holding the bridge against the Etruscans. "Lars Porsena would have nothing to fear from me." A cup of what had been hot spiced wine stood near his elbow, now cold and tasteless. He could not bring himself to drink it.

"What do you want to do about the merchants bound for York?" asked Sir Humphrey from the doorway. He was looking the worse for wear and his voice was raspy.

DeSteny looked up apologetically. "What did you want, Sir Humphrey? Forgive me. I wasn't attending."

"The party of merchants who arrived from York at noon. What shall we do about housing them?" He sneezed and wiped his nose with his sleeve. "Sir Wilem left no instructions when he departed this morning to hunt." The tone of his voice revealed his opinion of Sir Wilem as a hunter.

"You should be in your bed, Sir Humphrey," said deSteny, noticing for the first time that the Marshal had fever spots in his cheeks.

"And who is to do my work? Not Sir Wilem, I think. Nor any of his cronies. They couldn't marshal a flock of geese, let alone a town. Sir Gui is not careful in choosing those who are to defend his interests." He sniffed, only in part because of his cold. "He is a feckless sort, callow and self-indulgent. He will not view Lady Marian's circumstances as unfortunate. When he returns, he'll call for musicians and cooks, not either of us. He has no sense of his duties here."

"No, Sir Wilem does not," deSteny agreed. He rose from his chair. "But you are ailing, and I would not want to be the cause of your illness worsening."

"You aren't," said Sir Humphrey. "That's God's Will, not yours."

DeSteny said something noncommittal as he fussed with the ties on his short leather cloak. "Still. You should be in the care of a nurse." He took a step back.

"I think I should be on duty, that's what I think," said Sir Humphrey, settling the matter. "Not that I don't appreciate your concern. I am grateful for it." This was more a concession to courtesy than a reflection of any genuine feeling. "About the merchants? What shall we do?"

"They are entitled to a place to stay. Do they have money?" deSteny asked, putting aside his fretting.

"Not a great deal. They are taking goods to market, not coming from it." He coughed, looking embarrassed. "When they return, they will have money."

"They are not willing to stay in a hostel or an abbey?" DeSteny shook his head. "No. I suppose not, with all their goods—too much chance for theft, and they are, as you say, bound to market. Is there any room at the taverns?"

"There is some, but not as much as they would like," said Sir Humphrey. He looked down at his feet. "A courier arrived a short time ago."

"A courier? From whom?" deSteny asked, preparing himself for more bad news. "Sir Wilem?"

"Sir Gui deGisbourne. He intends to come here tomorrow to claim his bride. He is bringing four red deer and two boars for a feast, and dozens of birds to be roasted, and two barrels of fish. We are enjoined to supply the rest. He will expect a grand occasion—you know how he is." Sir Humphrey shook his head slowly. "He says he wants to show his bride a proper welcome. We must tell him what has happened."

"So we must," said deSteny heavily. "Very well. I will prepare my report for him. I thank you for this timely warning."

"He also says he is bringing twenty men with him as guests, to add to his welcome of Lady Marian to Nottingham," said

Sir Humphrey, more miserably than before.

"Then we must be ready to give them good welcome, whether she is here or not," deSteny told him with a fatalistic hitch to his shoulder. "I will see if Sir Wilem has any preferences in this, and then I shall set about making ready." He did his best to infuse his voice with encouragement, and failed singularly. "The onus is upon us. If Marian deBeauchamp isn't here, that doesn't excuse us from our obligations of hospitality."

"Indeed not," Sir Humphrey agreed, and coughed again.

"Sir Humphrey," deSteny told him. "Get you to bed, at once. Having you ailing will not please Sir Gui, and I have more than enough to displease him as it is."

Sir Humphrey shook his head. "I will, but not yet. I have orders to give for Sir Gui's reception. Once that is done, I will do as you recommend. My woman will tend me." He cocked his head. "You could do with a woman, Sheriff."

DeSteny laughed once. "But what woman would have to do with me?" he countered, and nodded his dismissal to Sir Humphrey. "May you mend swiftly."

"Amen to that," said Sir Humphrey as he left the room.

Alone, deSteny began to pace, his frown deepening. He had lost men and Sir Gui's bride, and little though he anticipated a happy marriage for the two, he knew this disappointment would be held against him. Striding down the room, he paused at the window to look out at the forest, his sense of being besieged increasing as he looked at the green gloom in the sullen rain. Where was Wroughton? he asked himself. What had become of the men who rode with him? The longer they were absent, the more troubled he became. He put the tips of his fingers together and did his best to calm his thoughts, but without success.

"Sheriff?" The young man in the doorway was one of the

under-stewards, a long-faced boy called Geoffrey. "Sir Humphrey said you have need of my service?"

With a sigh, deSteny gave up his fruitless ruminations and gave the youngster his attention. "Sir Wilem is gone to join Sir Gui in the hunt, has he not?"

"So I have been told," Geoffrey answered carefully. "I know nothing to the contrary."

"Then we must suppose it is true," said deSteny, certain that Sir Wilem would relish telling Sir Gui of his missing affianced bride, and the Sheriff's role in her disappearance. "They will be here tomorrow, I understand."

"That is what we were told," Geoffrey repeated. "We are supposed to prepare suitable festivities for them." He looked up at the ceiling. "Under the circumstances, what should they be?"

"A very good question," deSteny said, shaking his head. "They will not want a happy occasion, for the circumstances are far from joyous. But his company are worthy of our best efforts, and we would be remiss not to provide the ceremony to which they are entitled." He rubbed his face as if hoping to awaken some inspiration that had thus far eluded him. To his astonishment, it worked. "So it may be best," he went on with unexpected confidence, "if we ask the Bishop to perform a Mass upon Sir Gui's safe return, in which protection for Lady Marian may be sought. Then a suitably grave feast will follow, with only musicians for entertainment—no jongleurs, no baiting of cocks or bears, no dancing. That should achieve a balance that offends no one." This last seemed unlikely, but he said it with the same determination as he had the rest of his plans.

"As you say," Geoffrey remarked, looking relieved. "Shall I send for the Bishop to come to you?"

"No," said deSteny, who suddenly wanted to be out of

his study. "I'll go to him. I will speak to him myself." He pulled the hood of his cloak up and reached for his gloves. "I suppose I must find him at Saint Stephen's?"

"So I would suppose," said Geoffrey, stepping out of deSteny's way and slightly averting his eyes.

"Well, I'll try there first," said deSteny.

"Shall you want your horse, Sheriff?" Geoffrey asked.

"No reason. I'll walk. It will do me good," he said, and strode off down the corridor toward the stairs. By the time he reached the courtyard, he was almost convinced that he had managed to make the best of a dreadful situation. He left the castle and went along the wide, boggy street toward Saint Stephen's Church, the oldest church in Nottingham still used for services. The firm line of his mouth showed his resolve as he entered the building and stood in the narthex, a double row of thick columns leading down toward the altar. He flipped his hood back and looked about the dim, incense-laden interior for a monk or priest to help him.

"Sheriff?" said a voice behind him. "This is unexpected." His accent was that of the aristocracy, for he was a third son of a minor courtier, and had been raised for the priesthood from youth, although he still had the manner of the nobility.

DeSteny turned about and saw Father Raleigh Lorimer standing near him, his habit damp on the shoulders, suggesting he, too, had just come in from the rain. "Good day to you, Father," he said a bit awkwardly. "Is Bishop Tilton receiving?"

"He is at prayers just now, but he will be through shortly." Father Lorimer regarded the Sheriff with open curiosity. "How is it that you wish to speak to him?"

"He and I have matters to discuss," said deSteny, deliberately oblique.

"If you were to impart to me what they are, I might be able to alert the Bishop so that he may prepare for your discussion." He had a somber expression that turned sour as he spoke. "You are not often at Mass, are you?"

"I have many duties that curtail my religious exercises," said deSteny in a tone his men would have recognized as discouraging more remarks. Very few churchmen had ever challenged him about this, preferring safety to orthodoxy.

Father Lorimer was not one of his men, or a cleric of a squeamish nature, and he decided to pursue the matter. "You should set the example to all the rest. You have an obligation to show your men the way. If officers of your position are lax, how can your men be expected to do anything more than say a *Pater Noster* once a day?"

"That is your concern, Father, if you will pardon me for saying so. My duty is to preserve their bodies—their souls are your concern. Just as you have taken an oath to God, I have sworn to uphold the King and his nobles, and that is where I will devote myself." Although he was dissatisfied with himself for answering the prelate in this abrupt way, he was unwilling to be caught up in useless apologies and explanations, so he shouldered his way past the stiff-necked priest.

"You may find that the Bishop will expect more of you than that," Father Lorimer warned as he watched deSteny go toward the altar and the chapels behind it.

"That is for him to say, Father, not you," deSteny countered as he walked past the altar with only the slightest hint of a blessing or a genuflection. He soon saw the Bishop in the Lady Chapel, flanked by two Pied Friars of the Order of the Blessed Mary. They all were bowed in prayer. DeSteny stepped back from the doorway, not wishing to intrude, and certain the prayers would shortly be over.

The ringing of a bell brought the Bishop to his feet and

the monks to his side, tending him as if caring for a sick calf. He blessed them both, then waved them away. "What is it you wished to see me about, Sheriff?" he asked, coming out of the Lady Chapel with alacrity.

DeSteny had been preparing for this moment, and so did not hesitate. "I was hoping you and I could arrange for a proper celebration of Sir Gui's arrival here. I am sure you understand the difficulties inherent in this occasion." He saw Bishop Tilton nod, and went on. "I know we must show proper regard for the lamentable events in Sherwood, and we must also receive Sir Gui with appropriate display. So it occurs to me that a Mass, said in thanks for his safe arrival, and for Lady Marian's protection and deliverance, would be welcome to all."

Bishop Corby Tilton was as much a politician as a spiritual advisor, and he weighed this suggestion carefully. "Two Masses, I think," he said in a measured tone. "One upon Sir Gui's arrival—thanksgiving, of course. It will be fairly brief, but a good display. Then, after the banquet—and I am sure there will be a banquet, won't there?—yes, I thought so—we will have a second Mass for Lady Marian. This Mass will be Solemn and with all the augmentation that is allowed, so that the gravity of the situation is fully appreciated. No one will find fault with such arrangements, not after I have given the homily, which I will deliver in language that will address the dangers she faced in coming here as well as all the efforts that will be needed to rescue her. That should answer all the questions that may arise." He rocked back on his heels, mentally reviewing this plan. "The banquet should not be too grand."

"I agree," said deSteny, pleased to have someone with the same understanding as his own. "Musicians only to entertain."

"And no bawdy songs, only doleful ones," said the Bishop. "Sir Gui may not quite approve of that, but it is fitting."

"That it is," said deSteny, almost allowing himself a little sense of relief. "What will you require of me for the Masses?"

"I think it would be best for me to take a short while to meditate. I will send you my answer later today." He was about to dismiss the Sheriff when something more occurred to him. "Do you know when we are to expect Sir Gui?"

"Tomorrow, weather permitting." He held up his hands to show he had no ability to change this. "Should we pray for rain?"

Instead of being amused, Bishop Tilton turned a disapproving look on deSteny. "Best not to jest about God's work in God's House."

DeSteny ducked his head. "I meant no disrespect."

"Well, and fighting men are not gentle in their ways," the Bishop said, relenting. "I will give you the benefit of the rigors of your profession."

DeSteny managed a bit of a smile. "Each profession has its own demands."

"And God knows the whole of them," said the Bishop. "Look for my messenger after sundown. I will strive to have a plan in place by then. Brother Erwin here"—he pointed to the older of the Pied Friars—"will bring my thoughts to you."

"I do read and write," deSteny reminded him.

Bishop Tilton nodded. "Yes. I recall hearing that. An odd accomplishment for a man in your position, if you will pardon my remarking upon it."

"You may remark upon anything you like, Bishop Tilton," said deSteny, and with that, made his escape.

26.

What became of Wroughton in the Forest by-ways

Wroughton had spent the night in a goat-shed, the animals gathered around him in the pesky way of goats. He now knew why they were considered animals of the damned, and in the morning, when he wakened, he saw that they had made a feast of part of his cloak. Struggling to his feet, Wroughton drove the goats back, and opened the small, high window to look out into the morning. He saw rain, heavier than the night before, but with less wind driving it.

 He stretched and scratched at his chin, and wished he could have a glass of ale and a wedge of cheese, as he would do in Nottingham. His joints ached and he felt heavy-headed, but he attributed this to sleeping on three heaps of straw, and the damp. It was too frightening to think he might be ill, for he knew sickness could mean death. He saw the horse the nuns had given to him standing haltered under the eaves of the sheepfold, a short distance away, and was perversely glad that his mount was out of the rain. It would have slowed him down more than he wanted had he had to wait for the gelding to dry. He looked about for the crofter, and noticed that three small children had emerged from the nearest house, two of them headed in his direction, running through the puddles with eager enjoyment.

 "You!" the older child shouted. "You! Get up! It's morning."

 Wroughton worked his shoulders to ease the kinks that

had settled in there during the night, then he went to the door and let himself out into the wet day. "I am up. I thank you for the safe accommodations."

The taller child laughed. "It is only because you are the Sheriff's man. We want no trouble here."

So young and yet so canny! Wroughton thought. "You shall have none on my account," he told the boy. "I have given your father my word on it."

"Just as well," said the boy, and walked past Wroughton to deal with the goats. Wroughton saw a pile of hay had been dropped for his horse, and he was pleased that the crofter had been willing to do so much. He rubbed his eyes, wanting to get the last of the sleep out of them, and prepared to knock on the door of the crofter's hut.

The crofter anticipated him by a breath or two. "May God send you good day," he said rather formally to Wroughton.

"And to you," Wroughton replied, taking a copper coin from his wallet and giving it over to the crofter. "For your generosity."

"You are most kind," said the crofter as if speaking to a cleric. "We see few strangers here from one season to another."

"Even with the crofters' track?" Wroughton asked, wondering if they would offer him anything to break his fast.

"Crofters aren't strangers; we know whom among them we can trust," said the man. "Sheriff's men are another matter." He walked a few steps to the midden and relieved himself into its steaming mass.

"True enough," said Wroughton, doubting if he ought to do the same. "I think it would be wise if I were to leave shortly."

"Yes," said the crofter. "It is a way to the next hamlet,

and still a long ride to Nottingham."

"Can I reach it today?" Wroughton asked.

"Today?" The crofter gave it his consideration. "I should think you could, if the river isn't too high. If you have to go along to the bridge at the Abbey of Four Crowned Ones of Rome, that will slow your journey. You should stay with the Blue Friars in that case."

"Ah," said Wroughton. "Victorines. Well, I shall keep all you have told me in mind." He decided he couldn't ask for food outright, so he suggested, "Is there any cheese or smoked meat I could purchase from you? If I am to travel a long way today, I want to be sure of a meal."

The crofter laughed. "You may have some cheese. You can get smoked meat at the next hamlet. We call it Four Oaks, since there are four oaks inside the stockade."

"I'll keep that in mind." Wroughton did his best to conceal his disappointment. "How am I to find this place?"

"Stay on the track and bear to the left where the road meets another." He gestured to the right as he spoke.

"Which is it?" Wroughton asked, confused by these contradictions.

"To the left," the crofter said, again gesturing to the right.

"North or south?" Wroughton attempted to get better information.

"East. Toward Nottingham," said the crofter as if it could be the only answer. He signaled to one of his boys. "Hey! Bring a mug of goat's milk to our guest."

The boy coughed and said he would.

Wroughton fetched out another copper from his wallet. "For the goat's milk," he said.

Again the crofter took it. "Much appreciated."

"I should go as soon as I may?" Wroughton suggested.

"The goats will be milked shortly." The crofter pointed toward a three-sided shed. "Your saddle is in there."

"Yes. I recall," said Wroughton. "I can be away directly, then." He started toward the shed to claim his saddle.

"Very good," said the crofter, then went to let the sheep out of their fold and into the pasture outside the stockade.

Wroughton brought his saddle and put it on the horse, tightening the girth enough to be snug but not tight enough to interfere with eating. He checked the bridle to make sure the bit hadn't shifted during the night. Then he patted the horse's neck.

The boy came up to Wroughton and held out a wooden mug that was almost full of warm goat's milk. "This is for you."

"Good," said Wroughton as he took the mug and drank its contents down. He tossed the mug back to the boy. "I'll be under way." He busied himself tightening the girth and when he was satisfied, he climbed up into it, gathered up the reins, and rode out of the hamlet.

The rain dripped through the trees and soaked into Wroughton's cloak. At least the water would hold the fell outlaws at bay, he told himself, and did his best to ignore the discomfort of getting slowly sodden again and kept his eyes on the narrow track through the forest.

Then the path he was on ran into the slightly broader trail that went two directions away from the narrow way he was on. Left or right? Which way should he turn? It was dark enough that he could not readily reckon which direction was east—if indeed east was the way he should go—so he looked along the path as if to determine which seemed the most traveled direction, but could not discern anything specific that suggested which was the way for him to choose.

At last he arbitrarily chose the right-hand direction, and rode down the track for some distance, not at all convinced he had selected the proper course. He was just about to turn back when he saw a stockade ahead and a broad meadow with a number of fenced pastures in it, reminding Wroughton that he was eager for some smoked meat, or a haunch of veal at the least of it. A herder out in the fenced pasture caught sight of him and lifted his staff in what seemed to be recognition, or a signal, a gesture that encouraged Wroughton to push his horse to a trot as he came up to the gates, now standing open. A few fingers of watery sunshine penetrated the clouds overhead, lending a brightness to the hamlet that was almost supernatural.

"Hello!" he shouted, rising in the stirrups.

There was no answer from inside the walls.

"Hello!" Wroughton yelled again, looking about. He waited, then called out, "I am coming in. I am the Sheriff of Nottingham's courier." With that, he nudged his horse to action, and ducked his head as he rode into the village. He saw the four oaks the crofter had mentioned, and he spoke up. "I was told I could get smoked meat here. I have coins to pay for it."

No one came forward.

Wroughton got down from his horse and walked up to the four oaks around which the huts of the hamlet were clustered. He kept his full attention on the various dwellings and other buildings, not yet wary, but becoming uneasy because of the continuing silence. "Is anyone here?"

"Yes." The voice behind him shocked Wroughton so much that he jumped. "Most of us are gone to market."

Wroughton swung around and saw a man of advanced years in a worn woolen smock and leather leggings leaning on a short staff, his head turned slightly away in the manner of men whose ears were keener than their eyes. "Good day to you, crofter," he said, being as courteous as he knew how to be. "I hope God has shown you His Grace." He waited to see if the holy name caused any perturbation to the crofter; when it didn't, he went on. "A bad day for marketing, with the rain and all."

"Good day, courier," said the old man. "You are a long way from the Great North Road." He made this observation with the suggestion that this was a suspicious circumstance. "As to the market, it is the time for selling the lambs and kids of last spring that they do not want to keep through the winter." He waggled his eyebrows. "It is now, or we must wait until spring, and the new lambs and kids."

"I suppose it must be so," said Wroughton, who didn't think that the crofters wouldn't all go to market in such weather.

"They had a chance to travel in a group, for protection," said the old man. "I and two shepherds are kept here to watch."

"Thank God for their prudence. Many of my companions were set-upon by brigands." Wroughton made sure that he crossed himself in thanks for his delivery.

The old man shook his head. "No one is safe in these times." He chuckled nastily. "Not even a man wearing mail."

"No," said Wroughton, feeling uneasy. The emptiness of the hamlet troubled him, and now he regretted coming here. "If all your people are at market or in the pastures or the forest, I'll press on to the Victorines' abbey of the Four Crowned Ones of Rome. God give you a good day, old man."

"The monks will not be able to help you," said the old man with an emotion suspiciously like satisfaction. "It is all they can do to care for themselves. They had a fire in their barns and half the abbey is in ruins."

"When did this happen?" Wroughton asked, feeling slightly ill.

"Two days since," the old man told him. "They were fighting off night creatures and their torches started a fire in the hayloft. We smelled the smoke here."

Wroughton blanched. "The bridge? What of the bridge?"

"The shepherd who brought us this news said nothing of the bridge," the old man informed him.

"Do you know anything more about the road to Nottingham?" Wroughton doubted it was wise to ask, but he also believed that he had to find out as much as possible for his own safety as well as for the protection of his mission.

"Only that it is long and narrow," said the old man, leering at Wroughton and trying to bring him into focus. "Like the grave."

Wroughton got back on his horse and swung the animal around, going toward the gate, and thinking that he would be glad to be in Nottingham barracks again. He was beginning to shiver, and he couldn't persuade himself that this was only because the air was chilly. There was a tickle in his throat and an ache in his head that didn't bode well for tomorrow, and his shoulders ached in the steady, relentless way that warned of worse to come. He stifled a sneeze and headed off along the track, telling himself it was his imagination that he was being watched. In spite of what the old man said, he kept on toward the abbey of the Four Crowned Ones of Rome, wanting to get over the river before nightfall, for he was convinced that he would be safe once he had running water between him and the Great North Road.

The rain had picked up again, and there was a blustery

wind thrashing the branches of the trees so that any movement in the undergrowth was covered or disguised by the encroaching storm, and this, too, contributed to Wroughton's unease. He ducked his head and huddled into his cloak, but none of it helped him stay warm or dry.

By the time the abbey came into view, Wroughton was thoroughly miserable. His hands were cramped on the reins, and he could tell by the uneven walk and the nodding of his head that his mount was going lame. At another time he would have dismounted and led the animal, for it belonged to the nuns at Saint Gertrude's and for their sake he would have cared for the gelding with more concern. But in this place and at this time he daren't dismount, or slow their progress more than was already the case. He peered through the wet afternoon and was able to make out the blackened gaps in the walls that spoke eloquently of fire.

"I think it might be best to go over the river at once," Wroughton said to his horse. "It would be unkind to impose upon these friars just now." Hearing himself speak, he felt more decisive. "The monks will need everything they've salvaged." The gelding nodded, and although Wroughton knew it was from lameness, he took it as agreement. "Yes. I was hoping you would see it the same way I do."

Coming closer to the abbey, Wroughton saw that there was no one about. He thought perhaps that the monks had gone to seek shelter in another abbey or monastery, and resigned himself to being alone. "I'm sorry," he said to the horse as he turned toward the bridge and prepared to go across. "I'll dismount on the other side, and give you some relief."

The sound of the hooves on the bridge seemed unnaturally loud as they crossed over the swollen river. As soon as he reached the other side, Wroughton dismounted and pulled the reins over the gelding's head in order to lead him. He felt a bit dizzy as he started off, but he steadfastly ignored his discomfort. He wanted to get out of the forest before nightfall, and so he struck out at a brisk walk, trying to make good progress as he went along the rutted path. At least, he told himself, he no longer felt cold. The walking must be warming him. If only he didn't ache.

He came to a fork in the road and after a long hesitation, took the wider branch, and hardly noticed when the curve took him once again back toward the heart of the forest.

From his vantage-point in a near-by tree, Fortesque shot an arrow toward the next grove where a dozen of Hood's men were waiting. He would show them he was as worthy of feeding as any of them. Poor old Wroughton, he thought, to have come so far and tried so hard, and yet to be destined to fail in his mission. He would shortly have to report back to Hood, to describe where Wroughton was bound, but after, he would have the opportunity to reap the reward of his devotion. He climbed down from the massive oak and fell in behind Wroughton, determined not to be deprived of his first major kill.

27.

How Sir Gui Ordered deSteny in Regard to Lady Marian

Because of the rain, Sir Gui was delayed by three days, and he didn't arrive at the gates of Nottingham until late on the first dry afternoon—a time of glaring sun and a brisk, icy wind. His group of guests rode behind him, most of them looking more bedraggled than they wanted to, for in spite of the cessation of the rain, the weather had taken a toll on them. Sir Wilem had lost two of the feathers from his cap, leaving him with only one to add dash to his clothing, leaving him looking like a molting bird. Sir Gui had on his finest cloak—the one lined with ermine fur—and wore it with the hood up against the bluster. The soldiers who provided them escort were more sensibly dressed: leather actons under their chain-mail and leather cloaks over it.

Sir Humphrey admitted the party as soon as it arrived, and rang the bell announcing Sir Gui's presence, while apologizing that they had no one to sound the trumpet for him. The bell was as much of a warning as deSteny was going to get, and he heard the tocsin as if it were the knell of doom, or a summons from Heaven for the just to appear before the Lord. The first sound alarmed him and he dropped his stylus, betraying the state of his nerves. As the ringing ceased, deSteny rose from his writing table and pulled on his surcote, belting it with his sword-girdle and fastening it with the buckle he had been awarded for valor so many years ago. He hoped Bishop Tilton was ready to begin the service they had agreed upon.

Sir Gui entered the keep and dismounted, calling for a groom to take his horse—a showy red roan with a handsome head—and shouted for a steward to summon his bride. "For I am come to begin our marriage celebration," he announced with grim determination, and strode toward the door into the Great Hall.

DeSteny came down the stairs from his quarters, trying to still the qualms that had taken hold of his thoughts. He paused one step from the main floor, and faced Sir Gui as he came in. "God give you good welcome," he said.

"So He will when I kiss the hand of Marian deBeauchamp," said Sir Gui with a practiced smile. "Where is she?"

"As to that, Sir Gui," deSteny said heavily, inwardly cursing Sir Wilem's cowardice, "God alone knows." He saw the frozen expression in Sir Gui's eyes and he went on. "I regret to have to tell you that she was taken from us during our travels, and although we have searched for her, our efforts, so far, have been to no avail. Every effort has been made to find her, and I am sure we will find her eventually."

"Do you say so?" Sir Gui asked dangerously.

"Yes. It is my vow to find her for you," said deSteny.

"How very honorable of you." His sarcasm was cutting.

DeSteny saw they were being observed and decided to do his best to minimize the gossip that was certain to follow this meeting. "Perhaps we should go to my study, Sir Gui, where we may discuss this more fully."

"If you mean to prevaricate—" Sir Gui began.

"No; I leave that to your courtiers," the Sheriff interrupted him sharply, taking the risk of offending Sir Gui. "I believe I will serve you better where we may be private." He started up the stairs as if anticipating a sharp reprimand.

None came. "Oh, very well. Who wants to give the servants any more food for gossip than they have already," Sir Gui muttered, and maintained a steadfast silence until deSteny's study was reached. "If you do not satisfy me, Sheriff, it will go the harder for you," he warned as he took deSteny's chair.

"We were unlucky. One of the men was unwell, and it was not considered prudent to expose Lady Marian to the illness," deSteny began.

"Better a fever than to be spirited away," said Sir Gui.

"We lost men trying to protect her, but she was, as you have said, spirited away from us," deSteny went on. "And by such spirits as I have good cause to dread—all men do. We tried to find her, but—"

"Spirited away!" Sir Gui accused, flinging his hands into the air. "You make it sound as if the Devil sent his minions to take her from you."

"It seemed that way," said deSteny. "You know what those outlaws are capable of doing, or you should. If we had had enough men, she would have been safe. But I've warned you about those pernicious creatures. You knew it was hazardous to send her into the forest without at least a dozen men to guard her." He didn't raise his voice, but there was a sharpness in his tone that made it seem he had.

Sir Gui's face was thunderous. "How can you tell me this?" He looked around as Sir Wilem came into the study door. "This is a fine show of service!"

"Have you need of me, cousin?" Sir Wilem asked with a half-smile that might have been charming if he hadn't been so tousled by the wind.

"Come in," he gestured. "Hear what this caitiff has to say."

"We should have had a larger escort. Or if you had allowed it, I could have asked for men from Arundel to accompany us," said deSteny, stung by Sir Gui's epithet. "We did all we could. We cannot fight those creatures the way you fight armies."

"That is all well and good, for who shall say you didn't put forth your best effort." Sir Gui glowered at deSteny. "You may make any claim you like, and I must, perforce, accept it."

"You cannot believe I would equivocate about such a serious matter. You seem to think that we didn't do everything in our power. We did so poor a job that men died for your Lady Marian," said deSteny. "Good men, loyal men. Yet perhaps all of us should have died, so you would never know what became of her, and them."

"So you say," Sir Gui muttered.

"They died in your service, Sir Gui," the Sheriff persisted. "They deserve your good opinion, even in defeat. They gave their lives to try to guard Lady Marian—what more can any man do?"

Sir Gui shook his head. "You must defend them, for your own sake. It is no less than I would expect of a man of your sort." He paced two steps away, then swung back. "This isn't settled, deSteny. I will require a full account from you, and from my cousin as well. Don't bother with excuses, just tell me how this all came to pass."

Stifling a sharp retort, deSteny said, "The Bishop is ready to offer a Mass now, and another after we have dined. It is fitting that we go to Saint Stephen's at once."

"You are trying to postpone our discussion," Sir Gui accused; he poked his fingers at deSteny. "I will not have it."

"I am hoping not to offend the Bishop," deSteny countered.

"How convenient, that the Bishop should demand our attendance," said Sir Gui with such sarcasm that deSteny winced. "I suppose you worked this out between you," Sir

Gui went on. "You and he have decided to thwart me?"

Sir Wilem made a sound that wasn't quite a giggle and waggled his fingers derisively in deSteny's direction.

DeSteny was doing his best to maintain the decorum that was required of him. "I am deeply sorry to have to tell you these things, but I will not lie to you, and I give you my word that I am greatly troubled that we were unable to protect her for you. She deserved to be brought to you without harm and without insult. It was our sworn duty, and we were unable to fulfill what we pledged to you."

"Indeed! At least you acknowledge so much. I reckon it is little enough, but there!" Sir Gui flung open his cloak. "Nothing can be done now to undo what has been done. So let us go and recite the prayers. You will then explain to me how your men failed you, and, how it is that you are alive to tell me." He gave a furious laugh. "You and the Bishop are in agreement, so who am I to say anything against your plans? Why do you bother asking me anything?" He signaled to Sir Wilem. "Come. Lend me your support. If I must go through this travesty, I must have someone to sustain me." He laid his hand on the elegant young man's shoulder in a proprietary manner. "You must stay by me, Wilem. I depend on you." He shot a critical glance at deSteny.

It was an effort, but deSteny was able to collect his thoughts and assume a respectful demeanor; he could not rule his temper and that galled him. His head ached and he was finding it hard to concentrate. "I will institute a search and will find out all that I can about what has happened to her."

"Yes. You will." The implacable sound of Sir Gui's remark was flavored with petulance, which deSteny knew boded ill. He took up his leather cloak and prepared to accompany Sir

Gui to Saint Stephen's. "Shall I walk with you?"

Sir Gui gave him a long, contemptuous stare. "No," he said in quelling accents. "You will not walk with me. You will go before me, and see that all the men of this castle do me the honor I deserve. They will have to do much to show me that they are not to blame for Lady Marian's abduction, and so they shall learn before they eat their next meal." He tapped the jeweled hilt of his dagger that protruded from his belt. "I am in no frame of mind to allow any show of disrespect."

"The soldiers here would not do so," said deSteny, feeling his heart thumping in his throat, for he had heard tales of Sir Gui's capricious cruelty, and could not bear to think of it being visited on any of his men, not after so many losses among their ranks.

"So you say." Sir Gui motioned to deSteny to precede him. "So, if I should happen to see any hint of it, you shall answer for it. Do not suppose that I am unaware of your view of me, Sheriff. That rankles, as it should, for you are my inferior." He frowned. "It is more than enough that I should lose my affianced bride. I will not allow anyone to slight me, especially not an old Crusader like you." His arm was still around Sir Wilem's shoulder. "Help me bear my disappointment."

"No one will slight you, for Lady Marian's sake, if no other's," deSteny said as he left his study and started down the gallery toward the stairs to the ground floor.

Sir Gui came after him, still contriving to keep his hold on Sir Wilem. "How shall I explain all this to my father?" He looked directly at deSteny. "You shall explain, Sheriff. I leave it all to you."

DeSteny lowered his eyes. "I shall, of course, do just as you wish, Sir Gui," he said with as much humility as he could summon up. "Perhaps he will advise me how I might go about finding her and returning her to you."

"She has been gone too long to come to me; surely that is obvious, even to such as you," said Sir Gui sharply. "You will have to send her back to her uncle. It is no longer possible for us to wed. How can my family be sure of any heir she might give me? So many days in the hands of miscreants, well, what must have happened? How can I accept her as my wife when she has been so compromised? No one would expect it." He stroked Sir Wilem's cheek. "What do you say, cousin? Should I accept her, or shall I return her to her family? Um?"

"I say you would be wise not to marry her now she has been in the outlaws' hands for so long," said Sir Wilem, not quite smirking.

They were almost on the ground floor when deSteny thought of something that might serve to soften Sir Gui's implacable disapproval. "Sir Gui," he said, "are there lands promised in your marriage contracts?"

"I believe so. Why?" Sir Gui pushed his finger at deSteny. "You are not going to find an excuse for your failure, are you?"

Ignoring that sally, the Sheriff held up his hand in a display of useful thought. "If we are fortunate enough to find Lady Marian, you may want to complete the marriage, at least for the sake of the contract, rather than disavow your pledges," he said, mulling the possibilities in his mind as he spoke. "The Lady Marian has a good marriage portion, or so it has been rumored. You need not lose that, along with the woman. Your father would appreciate salvaging at least that much of his arrangements for you."

Sir Wilem sniggered. "It will also make you look less lax, Sheriff."

"This is not for my benefit," said deSteny. "I was trying to find a means of saving the purpose of the marriage without compromising your line."

"How do you mean?" Sir Gui asked, trying to follow what deSteny was proposing.

"If I can succeed in finding her, and you are willing to marry Lady Marian, for the sake of the contract, you could then live apart and not have to relinquish her marriage portion." DeSteny waited until Sir Gui cocked his head in thought. "Your father would not have to give up the advancements he had secured for you, and you would not have to live with your wife because she was away from chaperonage too long to have her assuredly a maid."

Sir Gui nodded slowly. "A wise notion, Sheriff," he said after he had thought the suggestion over. "After the Mass we will speak more of this. I will send you to my father tomorrow, and you will present to him the terms you and I will agree upon. You have shown yourself not wholly lost to good sense." He turned to Sir Wilem. "How does this strike you, Wilem? Doesn't it seem an apt resolution to the problem that confronts us?"

Sir Wilem wrinkled his nose as if he had come upon a noxious odor. "I suppose the Sheriff is right. You cannot have this woman to live with now." It was difficult to determine if this made him pleased or annoyed.

"Yes." Sir Gui regarded the Sheriff narrowly. "Well, you know what you must do. If you cannot convince my father of these things, you will have failed me twice, and matters will not go well for you." He made an emphatic gesture before he shoved deSteny aside, and, with Sir Wilem close at hand, strode out into the pale rays of afternoon sunlight.

28.

How Hood laid a Trap for Wroughton

The Red Friar laid his hand on Fortesque's shoulder. "You'll get used to it, in time. Be patient and it will come to you," he said heavily. "I managed to become accustomed, and it is far more against my vows than yours."

Fortesque sighed. "I never thought I would end up in a nest of vampires, and be forced to become one of them." He shook his head. "But I suppose no one does. I wanted to achieve recognition and glory, for my family. My father was a younger son, and so his portion wasn't great, and my mother had only a modest inheritance. They spent much time and money on supporting my efforts, and working to advance me; I am a younger son, and I am the only one of my brothers to come so far, although my oldest brother may become an Abbot one day. My two younger brothers have not yet reached an age to show their promise." He stared up into the branches. "Now, all that has been for naught. None of my brothers will be able to accomplish as much as I have."

"You don't know that for certain. You may be seen as a martyr," said the Red Friar, wincing a bit on the last word.

"Not likely," Fortesque exclaimed.

"They only know you were lost while on escort duty," said the Red Friar. "And the forest is known to be dangerous."

Fortesque allowed himself to be comforted. "It may be so," he allowed. "And if it is, I will be pleased for the sake of my father and brothers. However I don't think this will be enough to enhance our reputation." He rose and stretched, looking around the nearly deserted glade where the enormous stumps of ancient oaks provided shelter for Hood's men. "What if I should be recognized?"

"Then you will do well to be certain those who see you do not live to report it," said Little John, coming up behind them and stretching hugely. "Silence them, and be fed. Not a bad bargain." Now that the sunny autumn day was drawing to a close, the outlaw camp was coming to life, and Little John set about adding kindling to the great pit where they kept a fire going through the night.

"You must be prepared to face old comrades as your enemies; we are your comrades now, not they, and you can rely only upon us," added Will Scarlet. "Think about the men you fought with and turn their strengths against them. You know them better than I do. What would they do to you, if they were aware of your current state?" His easy, cynical smile caught Fortesque unprepared.

"But Wroughton—Surely our bonds, forged in battle, would be stronger than any—" Fortesque began, but could not continue.

"Do you truly think so?" the Red Friar asked. He put his hands together over his wide belt. "Think about it: would you have hesitated to strike down one of us when you were still alive?"

Fortesque considered his answer. "No," he said at last, very slowly.

"Then you would do well to assume that your comrades will do what you would do, were you in their position," said Scarlet. "Keep that in mind tonight when we take to the byways of the forest."

"Will that be soon?" Fortesque asked, troubled at the

hunger that flared in him. "We must be swift, if we are going to find Wroughton tonight." Without being aware of what he was doing, he licked his lips.

"Soon enough," said Scarlet, with a sickle of a smile curving his mouth. "We're all getting peckish, none more than Hood himself."

The Red Friar rubbed his stubbly jaw. "It is no good trying to deny it, much as we may wish to," he declared. "This is one time when the flesh rules the . . . the . . ." He struggled for the last word, "soul."

Scarlet laughed out loud. "As you say, Trinitarian." He sat down on a split log that served as a bench. "Were it up to me, as I was before, I would not have to do this, but I lost that part of my nature when Hood gave me his."

The Red Friar nodded slowly, and looked around in surprise as Little John left off tending the fire. "What is it?"

"Hood took everything from me. Everything. He corrupted my body and suborned my soul, and made me thank him for it. He gave me back his black heart to fill my emptiness. So that all I have now is his," he said, his deep voice choked with emotion. "It is true for all of us, Fortesque. You'll see that, in time."

Fortesque stared at the little flames catching the wood in the large pit. "I think I have fallen into Hell."

"No, not yet," said the Red Friar. "That is for later." He looked away and caught sight of Lady Marian deBeauchamp striding across the clearing, a vulpine smile curving her lips; he watched her with an emotion that was almost regret. "Look at her. She has taken to this life quite well."

"That she has," said Scarlet, a little envy in his remark. "And I suppose we should all be grateful for it." He glanced at the woman, who was still in boy's clothes. "How could she have wanted this life?"

"She was Sir Gui deGisbourne's affianced wife," said Fortesque.

Scarlet laughed. "So they say. Sir Gui married, though." He cocked his head to show his skepticism.

Fortesque bristled. "They were plighted."

"Do you think she was pleased?" Scarlet asked, and motioned them all to silence as Hood emerged from his quarters.

Hood went to the fire and brought his horn up to his lips. He blew a loud, unmelodic summons that was swiftly answered; his men erupted from their various shelters, hastening to gather at the fire. "The day is almost over," he said when most of his company stood around him. "And there is a man abroad in Sherwood whom we must make our own before he can reach the edge of the forest. Fortesque has told me where our quarry was bound. We must reach him tonight or lose him."

There was a moan of displeasure, and Little John folded his massive arms over his chest in blatant dissatisfaction.

"Why not kill him?" Lady Marian asked. "We could all have some then."

"He is little enough—one man for all of us," said Scarlet.

"We may need him for later, as a guide or in some similar capacity. In fact, I intend that he should render a double service to me: sustenance now and treachery later," said Hood with a peremptory flourish of his hands. "We have foes, strong foes, and we must be ready to confront them."

Scarlet laughed. "What foe could defeat us?"

Hood rounded on him, red eyes smoldering. "You know of whom I speak. So do you all."

"I don't," Fortesque whispered and was hushed by the Red Friar.

There was a mutter of unease that moved through the gathering like wind through branches.

"So tell me," Hood went on, "who is willing to come with me after this poor, lost soldier? It should be a good chase, if nothing else."

A roar of assent arose, and Scarlet laughed more loudly.

"Then take up your bows and your staves and strike out for the Abbey of the Four Crowned Ones of Rome. We will begin our chase from there. Scarlet, you and a dozen men take the north path, Little John and another dozen, the south. I'll go by the middle way with Lady Marian and all the rest. Be careful, for this man we hunt is alert to the danger we are to him. When you find the man, if you find him before I do, you may subdue him, but you are not to drain him. Anyone who fails me in this will lie under the cross-roads with hawthorn through his heart. This soldier Wroughton is marked by me to become one of us." He pointed to Fortesque. "You will guide me." He signaled to another of his men. "You, scholar, you will stay behind to watch the fire. See it remains burning while we are gone."

Had he still been living, Fortesque would have blushed; as it was he turned a pasty shade that made his face look splotched with white lead. It was troubling to be so conspicuously singled out and he felt embarrassed even as he contained his pride at this distinction. Since the blood had stilled in his veins, he turned a pasty shade that was tinged with green. "It will be my honor to hunt with you."

Hood shook his head. "So untruthful," he murmured even as he signaled Fortesque to come to his side. "You detest me."

"I . . . fear you," Fortesque admitted as he moved forward reluctantly.

"Such is the beginning of wisdom," said the Red Friar

softly as he fell in behind Hood, Fortesque, and Lady Marian. He didn't bother to watch the others disappear into the undergrowth, for he had grown used to this facility in the last month.

"So, young Fortesque," Hood said as he set foot on the narrow path leading away from the clearing, "when did you last see Wroughton?"

"I saw him settled to sleep last night. He was on the other side of the stream that runs through the forest past the Abbey of the Four Crowned Ones of Rome. He was in a hunter's cabin, his horse tied to graze. I think the horse was lame, for he favored his off-side front foot. I couldn't see if the joints were swollen; it is also possible he was throwing a splint. In any case, he will not be able to ride away." Every word seemed treason, but he could not keep himself from revealing all to Hood.

"This is most promising. We can drain the horse if nothing else is available." Hood glanced toward Lady Marian. "It's not as if he can run away, if he's lame."

Marian tossed her head. "Let me have the man first. For the love you say you bear me. It is your right, but cede it to me."

Hood went a short way in silence. "All right," he said. "Since he was part of your escort, you may claim him. Take him as tribute for your loss of a husband. But be certain that you drink only a little of his blood. There are others as deserving of his bounty as you are. You may want it all, but you must not—"

"I know," she interrupted. "I am not to take more than a mouthful or you will not be able to imbue him with your nature." She was mildly annoyed.

"Tell me," Fortesque began apprehensively, "why do you wish him to be with us?"

"I've explained that," said Hood shortly.

"But it seems . . . so arbitrary." Fortesque frowned deeply.

"Do you say I have not the right?" His question was a sinister purr.

"No, no, of course not," Fortesque answered hastily.

Hood spoke with exaggerated care. "I need Wroughton for the same reason I need you: to serve as bait for a larger catch."

Fortesque nodded. "I see." He considered this and then made bold to ask, "And whom do you hope to catch with Wroughton?"

"Why, the only one the length and breadth of Sherwood who can harm me—Hugh deSteny, the Sheriff of Nottingham," said Hood, and heard Lady Marian's light laugher as he lengthened his stride and hurried into the darkness.

29.

How deSteny began his Chase

"Mount up!" the Sheriff called as he climbed into the saddle. He was riding a big-shouldered bay gelding so dark he looked black when not in direct light; the horse had been provided by Sir Gui, and he was a handful, mincing and bouncing in an excess of vigor while deSteny gathered in the reins and brought him under full control. The Sheriff hoped this pent-up friskiness indicated stamina, but, knowing Sir Gui's taste in horses, he wasn't sanguine about the prospects.

Three of his own men and three of Sir Humphrey's obeyed deSteny's command, one of the men—Twitchell—shouting out "Courage for the Right!" which was Sir Humphrey's family motto, as he brought his seven-year-old dapple-grey into line with the rest.

"You may give my fond greetings to my father," said Sir Gui, his nose wrinkling with distaste. "Tell him I will do myself the pleasure of waiting upon him before year's end." He was very fine in Milanese velvet and Antioch silk, his moustache and beard newly trimmed and his hair perfumed with sandalwood. These clothes cost more than deSteny was paid in a year, and all of the men knew it.

"As you wish, Sir Gui," said deSteny.

"Then, you will continue into Sherwood, as we have agreed you will do, and you will retrace the steps of Lady Marian deBeauchamp." He held up his hand in his most peremptory gesture. "Bring me word of her or do not return."

"I will do my utmost to find her, Sir Gui," said deSteny at his most calm.

"You had better, or it will be the worse for you," Sir Gui insisted. "I will not be made a laughing stock. I will hold you accountable for my reputation."

It was an empty threat and both men knew it, but deSteny inclined his head. "I will do my utmost to serve you, Sir Gui." He lifted his hand and called out, "Onward!" and let the big bay head for the gate at a slow trot, his men falling in behind him.

From Nottingham they rode toward Litchfield, keeping on the main road along the river and spending the night at a small castle whose Lord was a veteran of the Crusades and who beguiled his guests with tales of his battles with the Saracens. Most of the men listened eagerly; only deSteny was disinclined to pay attention to his reminiscences, though he took pains to thank Lord Gambert for his hospitality.

The next day they reached the turning for Everhampton and Cannock. The road grew steep and the forest loomed around them, the turning leaves making unexpected brilliance in the deep, green shadows. The men rode steadily, taking care not to wear out their horses, and covered nine leagues before nightfall. They passed that night at a travelers' inn, a squat building hard by the river, with a number of small rooms to let, and a kitchen that provided meat they called goat but was more likely venison, poached by local hunters. It was a pleasant place for the soldiers and they left it reluctantly. The next day was much the same, but the way was harder, demanding more of the company than had been the case the previous day. By the time they arrived at Everhampton, men and horses were worn to the limits. Their host, an earl with a perplexing family tree and an ill-defined fief, took them in, saying, "Not the time to sleep on the road, if you take my meaning."

"No, it's not," the Sheriff agreed.

Two of his men growled agreement.

"And where are you bound?" asked the Earl, leading deSteny and his men into the Great Hall of his keep, an old building with a high, wooden ceiling rising to a point above a cross-hatching of massive beams. Two fireplaces with logs blazing in them kept the chamber from being cold as the branches of a tree.

"To Cannock-Norton," said deSteny.

"That's Lambert deGisbourne's Baronial lands," said the Earl of Darton, mulling this over.

"We are charged by his son to carry a message to him," said deSteny, and didn't enlarge on their purpose.

"Well," said the Earl of Darton, "I wish you joy of seeing him. He keeps to his quarters, as cloistered as a monk."

DeSteny shrugged. "It is our hope that he will see us."

"And hope may be the extent of it. Sir Lambert deGisbourne is not a hospitable man. He keeps himself as remote as his fortress, and title or no, he reserves the right to shut his gates and hold himself to himself. He has been known to turn travelers away on a hard night, and to require his guests to bring their own food. He does not observe any virtue beyond loyalty to the Crown," warned the Earl, and clapped his hands. "These men are cold and hungry. See they have food and drink, and a good bed for the night." He pointed to the gallery where the women of his household had gathered to watch. "If any of you are in need of a companion, I might send you one, to beguile your night." It was an old-fashioned courtesy, and the soldiers hesitated for that reason alone.

"A very generous offer, and one that we may not deserve. Nevertheless, I think we had best sleep alone tonight," said deSteny, and saw two of his men wince. "You soldiers may have women when we are done with our chase, when you have discharged your duty," he offered. "For now, we must cleave to our mission."

"How very . . ." one of the men began.

"You would be wise to say nothing more," deSteny warned, and saw his men turn away from him.

Twitchell coughed. "As you order, Sheriff."

"Well then," said the Earl with false heartiness. "You must have mead, then, to ease your slumbers."

"An excellent notion," said Twitchell, who was the senior of Sir Humphrey's soldiers, and the most experienced man next to deSteny. "We have had a hard ride today, and will want to make the most of our rest."

Although deSteny had doubts about the advisability of allowing his men heavy drink, he knew that another denial might spur an insurrection. "All right. Two tankards, and then retire to the barracks-room."

Twitchell ducked his head. "We will do as you order," he said, as if to make amends for his truculence.

"Very well," said the Earl, and clapped his hands again. "Mead! And take these soldiers to be fed. See there is new bread on the table." He pointed to the long planks at the far end of the Great Hall.

DeSteny went to the nearer fireplace and held out his hands to the warmth; he removed his gloves slowly. His face, lit by the flames, was unreadable. "Tell me more about Sir Lambert, Baron deGisbourne, if you will."

The Earl waved his hand. "There's little I can say. He's a recluse. I don't know why, nor do I want to know."

"Then whom shall I seek out at Cannock-Norton?" deSteny asked.

"I cannot advise you; ask for the Baron. Who knows? He might receive you," said the Earl, amused in some way that deSteny could not comprehend. He swung around as a busine sounded from the gallery. "Ah. My harper has come. At least you shall hear a good singer."

The men in the Great Hall looked up as the craggy-faced musician took his place on the bench at the edge of the gallery in front of the trumpeter. He plucked at his instrument while the man behind him sounded another blast on his busine, then waved the businist away. "I will sing of Isabeau and Roland."

"Oh, good," the Earl confided to deSteny. "I like this one."

The music filled the Great Hall as the harper launched into the tragic tale, singing with more emotion than musicality. The men below watched him as the scullions brought food still sizzling on spits and set out wheaten trenchers that were still warm from the oven. A basin filled with mead was the first offering made to the soldiers, then tubs of butter were put on the table, and, while the harper sang of the hopeless love of Isabeau for Roland, the six men sat down to their meal.

When they left in the morning, it was into a heavy mist that clung to the trees and masked the narrow road. DeSteny ordered his men to hang their spurs on the saddles, so that they would ring and help them stay together.

"It may also bring our foes to us, and we wouldn't see them," said Bayard, deSteny's most seasoned soldier.

"Yes. But if we become separated or lost, then we may as well hand ourselves over to the outlaws now." DeSteny peered ahead into the dim sepia depths of the forest. The cry of a hawk overhead took his attention. "Pay attention to the forest creatures," he ordered, and set his bay into a slow trot.

"Do you expect to reach Cannock-Norton today?"

Mallory asked. He was just nineteen and eager to show his mettle.

"It is six leagues from here, if the Master Sergeant of the Earl's Guard is to be believed," deSteny said as he raised the hood of his cloak.

"Six leagues uphill?" Twitchell's tone of voice revealed his annoyance.

"Oh, God," muttered Mallory.

"It would seem so," said deSteny. "And the sooner we reach our destination, the sooner we may return to Nottingham."

Edhard, the Sheriff's third man, brought his piebald horse in behind deSteny's bay. "You set the pace, Sheriff, and we'll follow."

The fog cleared shortly after mid-day, leaving a glaring sky overhead and anemic sunlight to reveal their upward path. By mid-afternoon the trees were thinning, and here and there broad meadows gave pasturage to cattle and sheep. Occasional clusters of huts indicated the presence of crofters. Once or twice a stone building surmounted by a cross revealed small abbeys at the verge of the forest.

"There!" Mallory called out from the middle of the line of men. He pointed toward the crest of the hill they were climbing. "Cannock-Norton!"

"So we hope," deSteny responded, but as he studied the blocky fortifications fixed on the point of the spur at the end of the crest that spoke of ancient battles, he was certain it must be.

The fortress could only be approached by a narrow track on a ledge so precarious that the men had to ride single-file and at a slow walk, their horses picking their way cautiously. Guards on the ramparts signaled their approach with a series of unmelodic blares on wooden trumpets.

Finally, an officer appeared on the crenellations above them and shouted down: "Ho! Men! Who comes?"

"I am Hugh deSteny, Sheriff of Nottingham, and I am the messenger of Sir Gui deGisbourne, sent with a message for Sir Lambert, Baron deGisbourne. It is urgent. I ask to be received in the name of Sir Gui, whom I have the honor to serve in this mission." He motioned his men to halt, and waited for the officer to admit them.

"Come to the portcullis. We'll raise it so you may enter," the officer called back after a brief consultation with some unseen companion.

"Much obliged," deSteny called back, and rode nearer to the yawning entrance to the fortress. He heard the heavy crump of chains as the soldiers inside began to work the windlass to raise the portcullis.

By the time there was room to enter, a group of officials were waiting to greet them. DeSteny was the first man through, and he waited until all six of his comrades were inside before he dismounted and looked about, trying to determine which of the men gathered around them he should address first.

The problem was resolved when a tonsured monk in Victorine blue stepped forward. "Sheriff, you are welcome at Cannock-Norton." He ducked his head respectfully. "In the name of Sir Lambert deGisbourne, Baron deGisbourne, I welcome you."

"Thank you, Brother—" He waited for a name.

"Oh. Brother Gilchrist," he said, ducking his head a second time. "I keep the chapel here."

"Isn't that work for a priest?" deSteny asked, puzzled by such an arrangement.

"Usually, yes," said Brother Gilchrist. "But Sir Lambert deGisbourne prefers it this way." He indicated the roughvisaged officer next to him. "This is the Captain of the Guard, Nicodemus Upton. He will serve as your host." He tried to pass this off as usual behavior and put his hands together as if in prayer. "Come into the Hall, all you men, and we'll see you fed."

Upton was a stiff man with a puckered scar running from the bridge of his nose to his ear. "I'll convey any message you have from Sir Gui to the Baron," he said in a rough voice. He studied deSteny a long moment. "You seem familiar, Sheriff. Would we have met before?"

"Not that I recall," said deSteny a bit too quickly.

"Um," said Upton, and turned toward the keep. "Come with me." He didn't wait to see if anyone followed him; he walked away, his men and deSteny and his following after him into a long, narrow corridor.

The Great Hall was gloomy, a cavernous room with thick black beams overhead and a few small unglazed windows providing no real alleviation to the dimness. Torches in wall sconces gave off a fitful illumination that only made the darkness more oppressive. A long plank table dominated one end of the chamber, and it was there that Upton led them.

"You may eat here. The servants will bring you bread and honey. If you have ale with you, then you may drink. The Baron doesn't pour his brew for strangers, unless they come at his invitation." He had the decency to look abashed at this lapse in courtesy. "If you will sit, I will send to the kitchen for the bread and a little roasted meat. I think there is butter, too, and some stewed onions. We have half a pig on the spit, and that should assuage your appetites. There is no wine and no soup."

"We'll be glad of whatever you provide," said deSteny with better manners than truth. He climbed over the bench fronting the table and sat down. "We have no ale with us, I am sorry to say."

"It is unfortunate," said Upton, embarrassed afresh.

As the six soldiers took their places at the table, deSteny said, "If you will tell the Baron that the marriage he arranged for his son, Sir Gui, has suffered a blow: Lady Marian was taken by outlaws on her journey from Arundel to Nottingham. Tell him that I am charged with her recovery, for Sir Gui is still eager to uphold the marriage contract for the honor of his House and hers." He took a deep breath, wanting to be through with this. "He will keep apart from her, but he will not repudiate the union."

From the far end of the Hall, an old, cracked voice declared, "Who thought of such a solution? For I wager my fop of a son never came up with so acceptable an answer as that."

A white-haired figure came toward the table. "I am Sir Lambert deGisbourne. What does my son want of me now?"

30.

How Wroughton came to Grief

Now that he had the river between him and the Great North Road, Wroughton had allowed himself to slow down. "At least," he said to his horse, "it isn't raining, and the mists are gone." The fog of the day before had lifted but now the sunlight was fitful, emerging from heavy clouds from time to time but not long enough to make it easy for Wroughton to determine his direction of travel. He had hoped to cover the last few leagues quickly. But the horse was still limping, so Wroughton had been leading him all through the day, with as much of his weapons and equipment tied to the saddle so he would not be too worn out. His feet hurt and his back was stiff from the long hours of trudging on narrow, rutted paths that served as roads. Finally he decided to stop early for the night, continuing the following day as he had done previously, moving slowly as he made his way through the small tracks toward the side-road that led to the south gate of Nottingham. He had yet to find a hamlet he knew, but the speech of the crofters was more familiar, and that reassured him. He was somewhat uneasy, for it seemed possible that he might have become disoriented among the trees. "If we reach the sea, we'll have gone too far," he told the gelding, and did his best to laugh at the notion.

A pair of pheasants burst from cover, flying upward in a daze of brilliant feathers, accompanied by cries of excitement. The gelding reared suddenly, pulling the rein from Wroughton's hands and ran off into the trees, cantering awkwardly on his injured leg.

"Come! Come back!" shouted Wroughton, and tried to run after the animal, certain that the gelding could not go far. Pushing through the underbrush, he tried to keep the horse in sight, and when he could not, he listened for his hoof beats until they, too, faded. He was forced to stop and take stock of himself, going forward cautiously. He had covered half a league in this manner before he realized he was well and truly lost. The horse was gone, with all his weapons but his dagger, his bedroll, and his water-gourd, and he was in no position to continue his search. The track he had been following was behind him, and so he decided to reverse his steps. The day was dying, and soon the forest began to darken. Wroughton tried to make his way through the forest, but he couldn't make out his route, and finally he found himself in a glen he didn't remember passing through as he chased the gelding. He stopped still and looked carefully about, seeing a heap of rubble at the far end of the glen, as if a chimney had collapsed there many years ago. This troubled Wroughton, but he tried to ignore his nervousness as he went over to the tumbled stones, wondering if he could make a shelter for the night. He had a message he had to deliver for His Grace, Prince John, and that was the most pressing obligation of all. Nothing else mattered more than his mission, he reminded himself while he struggled with some of the looser stones. With steady determination he began to pile up a low wall that would give a modicum of shelter.

By the time he had the wall to his satisfaction night had fallen, and the wind had picked up to a steady roar like the sea. Unseen boughs lashed and bent, groaning as the tempest gathered fury. Wroughton pulled his cloak tightly around him and sank down in the lea of the wall he had just built, wishing now he had a small fire to give him a little light and a bit of warmth. He tried to pray, but the storm distracted him and he ended up saying, "Protect me tonight, my God," before trying to find a comfortable position in which to sleep, taking what comfort he could in the knowledge that the denizens of the night were on the far side of the river, and he had nothing to fear from them. Even as he strove to persuade himself that he was out of danger he began to feel fatigue overtake him, and he began to doze fitfully, and gradually he fell into an uneasy slumber.

It was full night when he awakened again, and at first he thought it was because his cloak had soaked through and water was running down his neck and shoulder. A moment later however, he saw someone approaching him across the glen, and he sat up, his hand on his dagger. He wanted to be ready, whatever he had to face. He wished now that he had not kept his broadsword in the scabbard on his saddle, for he would have been glad to have it now, to use against the approaching foe.

"Wroughton?" said Fortesque as he came up toward him. His stride was easy and his manner cordial, as if he had only been out for a stroll. "Well met, Wroughton." His smile showed sharp teeth.

Wroughton stared through the rain. "Fortesque?" he asked, relieved and astonished. "I thought . . . How do you come to be here? I thought you were . . . lost with the others. It's good to know you're alive."

"I've been looking for you," said Fortesque.

Struggling to his feet, Wroughton said, "How did you escape? I was sure you'd been caught by . . . those fell creatures."

"I . . . I ran," said Fortesque, trying not to appear too

hungry. He could feel Wroughton's pulse even at this distance.

"Wise, very wise," said Wroughton, stumbling around the stone walls toward Fortesque. "I wish I had the strength to do the same. My horse bolted and I'm going to have to walk back to Nottingham, once I am sure of the way." He laughed once, a little wildly. "It will be easier for your company."

"It is still a long distance to go," said Fortesque, aware of Hood's men gathering around the little meadow.

"And it will be more easily done with a companion," said Wroughton. "In the morning, we'll set out early and if we keep on steadily, we should be there before they close the gates at sundown." He had to keep his enthusiasm in check. "It's going to be a hard day's walk, but together we should be able to do it."

"Do you want to return so badly? After all that has happened?" Fortesque exclaimed. "What is there waiting for you that you want to return?"

"I want to deliver the message I carry," said Wroughton somberly. "It is my sworn mission."

"You have it with you still?" Fortesque asked, trying to keep from sounding excited.

"Certainly. I was charged to defend it with my life." He placed his hand on his chest, over the place the letter was carried.

"You were," said Fortesque as if remembering something he had forgotten. "How much responsibility has been imposed upon you."

"And I will complete my mission or I will die in the attempt," said Wroughton with utter simplicity.

"As any true soldier must," said Fortesque, and fell on Wroughton, bearing him back against the wall as he savaged his throat. Wroughton let out a shriek that stopped in a heartbeat.

At the sound, Hood's followers burst from the trees and joined in the attack, Scarlet pulling Fortesque aside to take his place.

"Hold!" Hood ordered as he strode up to the bleeding, supine body of Wroughton. "I want to look on him."

"What do you want to see?" Scarlet asked, as close to insolent as any of his men dared to be.

"He has a letter," he announced.

"Can you read it?" Scarlet asked, bending to the torn throat again.

"No. But the Red Friar can," said Hood, and flung Scarlet out of the way before he tugged the front of Wroughton's cote open and seized the flat leather pouch. "Now you may finish with him."

"Do you want him to waken?" Scarlet asked.

Hood considered his answer. "I may. Don't drain him entirely." He turned away, holding up the packet. "Trinitarian! Come here."

The Red Friar trundled toward him, the hem of his habit mired in mud. "What do you want of me?" he asked.

"This." Hood held out the packet. "I want you to read the letter for me. You can do that, can't you?"

"Yes. Yes, I will," said the Red Friar at his most compliant. "But I will need light to see the words properly."

Hood sighed and frowned. "Isn't this enough for your eyes? You're a vampire now. Surely the dark is light enough for you."

"I see fairly well in the dark," the Red Friar assured him. "But not well enough to read this letter."

"Ah, well," Hood said, a nasty edge in his voice. "How much light will you require to read this?" He tapped the letter.

"A candle or two, a torch. The page is filled with

writing, and I will need to pick it out under a lamp, one bright enough to make the writing stand out from the page. Anyone would have the same problem." He rolled the letter and slipped it inside his habit where it would remain dry. "What about Wroughton?"

"Better bring him along. I still want to make him one of us. We can use his talents." He stopped, thinking of something. "Could one of those scholars read the letter?"

"I suppose so," said the Red Friar cautiously.

"Then I shall let them see it. So that you may all agree on its content." There was a smug hostility in Hood's silky voice. "Perhaps I should have brought one of them along with us."

The Red Friar did his best not to shudder. He nodded to show he understood. "I can't think of any reason we should not agree."

Hood kept on walking, going toward Wroughton. He said nothing more to the Red Friar, and instead called out to Fortesque. "You did well. It is wise of you. You didn't get greedy. I don't like my men to be greedy."

He put his arm over the Red Friar's shoulder. "You'll do this for me."

"It is good of you to say so," the Red Friar exclaimed, trying to put a little distance between himself and the fell Hood.

"I honor the men who serve me well." His grip on the Red Friar's shoulder tightened. "You will all do well to keep this in mind."

"Thank . . . Thank you," said the Red Friar. "I am well and truly—"

"You need not busy yourself here. Just prepare to read the letter for me. And remember that you will have to be correct, or the scholars will know that there is an error." He finally released the Red Friar.

"Mercy," the Trinitarian muttered, unable to pronounce the blessings he would have done when he was alive.

"Bring the letter along, and the man," said Hood, turning on his heel and striding back toward the forest; he motioned his men to follow him but hardly bothered to see if they obeyed.

"We had better get Wroughton," said Scarlet, going toward the fallen soldier.

The Red Friar sighed and went to help him.

31.

How deSteny learned of Wroughton's Fate

Sir Lambert deGisbourne leaned on his stick and regarded deSteny and his mounted company of men. "My son is fortunate to have you to serve him, Sheriff," he said, coming as close to praise as his character would allow.

"You are most kind," said deSteny. The morning was bright; the sun glared behind a thick film of clouds that promised worsening weather as the day went on.

"But you will not tell him I said so," said Baron deGisbourne, nodding to show he understood.

"No, I will not," said deSteny.

Sir Lambert almost laughed, but he couldn't bring himself to do anything so undignified, so instead he called out, "I will remember you in my prayers."

"And I'll tell your son what you have pledged to do on his behalf. If you disavow your oath, I rely upon you to inform me so that I will not have to betray your trust or his."

"Do you think he will care?" Sir Lambert asked. He shook his head and gestured to deSteny in dismissal. "He is better served by you than he has any reason to expect. Not that he is likely to acknowledge it, although he has an obligation to those who are his vassals, just as you have an obligation to him."

"It isn't my place to remind him." It was more than he intended to say.

"No," Sir Lambert agreed, turning away as deSteny and

his men started down the narrow track toward the wood below.

DeSteny sighed as he signaled his men to follow him. He was trying to recall what he had seen on the road on their way, for he sensed they would have to find shelter before the afternoon was over. As they made their way along the crest, he signaled Twitchell to ride ahead of him, thinking as he did that they would need somewhere to take shelter. He seemed to recall a travelers' inn some five leagues away, and said to his men, "Not much farther, lads, not today. By the middle of the afternoon, we will rest. We can eat and have a bed for the night and wait for the storm to pass."

"Not an abbey or monastery," said Edhard. "Waiting out the storm in the company of monks is worse than getting drenched."

DeSteny chuckled. "I wouldn't do that to you." Or to myself, he added inwardly. "No, it is an inn, nothing too fancy or obvious, so we won't be noticed by other travelers. We passed it as we came here, in a meadow with a spring; it was of good size—we may not have to share beds. I noticed a barn, as well, so our horses can be stalled instead of being turned out in paddocks to get muddy."

"It may be several days before the skies clear," Mallory warned. "At this time of year, the storms can last for days."

"So they can," said deSteny. "And if we must wait, we will do so. No one will be moving in the forest other than those dire creatures Hood has made." He looked over his men and saw that they were tired and worried. "We'll have a day at least to rest and prepare to travel on to Nottingham."

"Do you think it is safe to do this?" Bayard asked. "Shouldn't we return as quickly as possible?"

"Yes, but there is no reason to take such risks as traveling during a storm would confer upon us." DeSteny was firm on this point, for he knew their dangers were not limited to wet and cold.

"What do you expect, Sheriff?" asked Edhard.

"I think Hood's men are out in force. We have not seen as many travelers as we should, and that means either that fewer travelers are on the road, or they have been preyed upon more regularly than before, which means the number of dead crofters has reached a significant number," deSteny said heavily. "Lady Marian may well be dead by now, or worse, and we must take care that we do not fall to the same evil that has claimed her."

"Are you certain that she was taken by Hood?" Twitchell inquired too sweetly.

"I fear we must think so. If any Lord had made off with her, there would have been a demand for ransom, and since no such claim has been made, it is likely that Hood's men drank her blood. They may even have made her one of their number." He let this sink in, then said, "I do not want the same to happen to us."

His men were silent as they thought over what he had said, then Mallory spoke for all of them. "We will find a place to wait out the storm."

"Ahead. Keep riding. Don't push too hard; we don't want any sprains or splints. We have no reason to hurry." He looked up into the sky. "The clouds are gathering."

"It may still clear," said Bayard.

"It may, and it may rain toads, but I think it would be best to assume that we will have rain before evening. This isn't the Holy Land, this is England." DeSteny heard his men laugh and found it heartening.

"And England rains," said Twitchell, leaning back as far as his high-canteled saddle would allow as the trail began to wind down from the ridge into the heart of the forest.

By the time they reached the inn, the wind had picked up and was moaning through the trees; rain was falling at an angle and the men huddled into their cloaks in the vain hope of finding shelter from the tempest.

"There!" shouted Bayard; he was miserable and the sight of the stockade around the inn was as welcome to him as the walls of Nottingham. He pointed toward the gates as if the rest might have missed them, water flying off his arm with the force of his movement. "We'll be warm in a trice!"

"So we will," said deSteny, who had already signaled to his men to leave the road.

Twitchell rode to the gates and shouted for aid. "In the name of deGisbourne and the Sheriff of Nottingham, open for us!"

Two small men in engulfing rain-cloaks flung open the gates and bowed the company inside, calling for the landlord to come out and greet his guests; the landlord appeared, a blocky man with a blotchy face set in an obsequious grin. "Come in, come in," he exclaimed. "Company is welcome, especially on such a night as this."

"Very good," said deSteny as he dismounted from his horse. "See our mounts are given a handful of oats with their hay. Don't water them until they have cooled. Brush as much of the water from their coats as you can, and see that they are warm in their stalls. They have a long way to go yet, and we can't have them tying up." He stood upright, his back aching from the weather and the long journey. "We'll have ale and beds for the night, and until the storm is done."

"A costly stay, if I may mention it," said the landlord carefully. "If you have no silver in your pockets . . ."

"I have silver, even gold," said deSteny as his men came

out of the saddle. "I will pay you nine silver shillings for two days' care of my men and our horses." It was a generous sum, and everyone knew it.

All but doubling over, the landlord's grin widened. "A most satisfactory sum, very generous of you, m'lord. Better than I had hoped for," he enthused. "It speaks well of you that you will do this during this storm."

"It doesn't," said deSteny, and motioned to Twitchell. "Come. There must be a fire in the taproom. Let's all go in and get warm."

The landlord bustled over to him. "I have a nephew. He fancies himself a singer, of sorts, and he has been in the taproom all afternoon. If you will let him sing to you, I would count it a great concession, and the food I serve you will be the better for it."

"If your nephew wants to sing to us, unless he has no music in him at all, we'll be glad to listen," said deSteny.

The taproom was a low-ceilinged room with blackened beams overhead and heavy wooden panels made dark from years of smoke and grease. There were four barrels standing behind the counter, and a boy of nine or ten was waiting to measure out drink into crockery tankards. By the fireplace, a reedy young man lounged, a harp in one hand, a slab of bread in the other. He looked up as the Sheriff and his men came in, got slowly to his feet, and bowed as if to a great gathering.

"Not those," said the landlord. "I have good pewter tankards for men such as you." He shooed the child away toward the kitchen, then nodded in the direction of the young man.

"My nephew," he said in a tone that suggested he was not completely pleased to have this known. "His name is Alan."

The young man uttered a practiced laugh. "I call myself Alan-a-Dale, for I roam the woods and by-ways to make my songs. I am the singer of the forest, and I am—"

"He is a self-important braggart who would rather amble beside a brook than do honest work here," his uncle went on in ill-concealed disgust. "He would rather hear whispers of Hood's doings than serve a meal or tend a horse." He stopped. "But he does make songs, and if you will listen, he will sing to you."

Alan did his best to ignore the landlord's condemnation, but he said, "I have a new song I have been working on—it isn't finished, but I could sing it for you."

"Not finished?" Edhard asked, as if this admission put the song beneath consideration. "Do you have nothing ready? No song we might know?"

"I prefer to make my own songs than copy others," said Alan stiffly.

"Nephew!" his uncle admonished him.

"I only heard of the events yesterday; I haven't had time to put it all together." There was a shine in his light-hazel eyes, an excitement that went beyond the joy of composition. "I chronicle them, you know," he went on confidentially.

"Whom do you chronicle?" Bayard inquired as the youngster behind the counter handed him a full tankard of ale.

The soldier expected a trivial answer and so doubted he had heard correctly when Alan said, "Hood and his men." The young man leaned forward. "They are bold, brave men, and they are worthy of legends and songs."

DeSteny heard this with a blank expression. "How do you—what manner of songs do you sing of Hood?" He was able to keep the condemnation out of his voice, but his men knew his polite inquiry masked deep dismay.

"You know about how Hood robs the merchants and other wealthy men who travel the Great North Road? It is astonishing how they can set upon groups of soldiers—simple woodsmen with bows and staves—and best them."

Bayard glowered at the young singer. "He and his men also murder crofters, and steal from humble folk."

"Those are the lies rich men want you to believe. They seek to belittle him in the eyes of those he protects, in the vain hope that one of the simple folk will be foolish enough to give him away to the officers of the law—" He broke off, realizing the men he spoke to might well be the very officers he so roundly condemned. "The agents of the merchants, and the dupes of the Lords and Royals," he amended.

DeSteny took the tankard of ale held out to him and did his best to assume a nonchalant manner. "Let us hear your new song, then. We may learn something from you."

Alan shrugged awkwardly, but reached for his battered old harp, tried its strings, which were far from true, adjusted the most egregious of them, and began with an air of bravado:

A spy went out from Windsor on the order of the Prince
Carrying a charge that bold Hood must be taken:
"Bring me this audacious Hood that he may answer
    at once
To all the crimes that have been laid to him.
For I will it, and my word is law everywhere."
Thus it was that armed men did straightly fare.
So Wroughton and a guard set out, bound north as they
    were bid,
And one by one the men fell until but one was left,
To ride on alone, his mission to fulfill. But even he was led
Astray, and wandered on alone, his heart bereft,
His soul forfeit, for Hood came upon him and—

"It needs work, and I haven't got the rhymes right yet, but I think it will make for a fine ballad, eventually."

"What became of Wroughton?" deSteny asked sharply. "Or don't you know that?"

"I have been told that he has decided to join with Hood," said Alan, shrugging. "He must have done, for no one has seen him."

"Why should Wroughton do such a thing?"

Alan gave deSteny a scornful stare. "What do you think? He has seen that Hood is a champion of the forest and all who live within it, and he has turned away from the Court. I've been trying to find the right rhymes to show how he came to join with Hood, rather than stand against him."

"Why praise such a one as Hood?" deSteny asked, his face set in forbidding lines. "Or do you do it to placate him?"

"Why not? Praise him, not placate him." Alan cocked his head defiantly. "Hood has done much that is worthy. He has taken money from rich men and he has protected those who serve him." He moved with a bit of a swagger. "You have heard how he robbed the Bishop of York and gave the gold to the children of the orphanage of York."

"No, I had not heard that," said deSteny. "I have heard that Hood took gold that was going to ransom King Richard from the prison where he is being held, and that Hood then set upon a children's home and drained them all. That was two years ago, when the tales of Hood were only getting started."

"Lies," said Alan. "Nothing but lies."

"I don't think we will agree on that," said deSteny.

"You are a servant of the Prince. You won't listen to me, or anything that is to Hood's benefit, will you?" The young man raised his head, his face set in uncompromising lines.

"It is up to people like me to tell the story truly."

"If only you would," said deSteny lightly, but with a cold sensation in his middle.

"And you think that Hood is a hero," said Bayard, who had been listening with growing incredulity.

"I know he is. Ask anyone who lives in Sherwood. Hood is the one who defends us, he is the one who knows our worth. We all know that he only attacks those who speak against him. None of you care for us but Hood. You may try to shame him as much as you wish, but you are servants of the Prince, and your opinions are his." Alan picked up his harp and struck a twanging chord on it. "We are grateful to him for all he has done for us, or we should be." He cast a meaningful glance at the entry to the kitchen.

The landlord came into the taproom and began to fill tankards with new ale. "You haven't been listening to this rapscallion, have you? He has moonbeams in his soul. Pay him no mind." His hands shook as he passed out the tankards. "He is entertaining in his way, but do not heed him."

"I begin to think I should listen to him closely," said deSteny, the seriousness of his remark silencing the laughter that was burgeoning among his men. Alan beamed as the Sheriff went on, "I begin to think he is saying something very important."

32.

How Hood brought Wroughton into his Fold

Marian deBeauchamp was standing near the dying fire in the center of the clearing where Hood's men lived, her hair clubbed back, dressed as the men were. She had a dirk thrust through her belt, and she rested her hand on its hilt as she turned to Hood as he emerged from his lair. "Have you made up your mind about Wroughton?"

"Yes. I do want to keep him," said Hood. "He has shown his value and it would be useful to have someone in the confidence of the Prince and deSteny to help us in our dealings with them."

"When do you want to change him? I expect you do still want to change him. You might as well. He's already halfway there; why not take him the rest of the way?" She laughed aloud. "I'd like to have a taste of him, and not just because I am hungry. He is one of Sir Gui's men, and it would suit me very well to serve him such a turn. To think that I should be bartered to one such as he! If my father had lived, he would not have required me to marry that fop. But my uncle insisted, and so I had to go to him."

"Which brought you to me," said Hood with great satisfaction.

"Yes," she said, her eyes alight with a passion that was not wholly of the flesh. "And for that I thank him."

"Do you want to have Wroughton before me? Is that what you are asking of me, Marian?" His voice was low and silky, more a purr than speech, and there was a light in his red eyes that made Marian wary.

"With you—with you," she said. "Both of us together. It will be sweet for me, and for you, to drain him together."

Hood put his hand on her shoulder. "If that is what you want, then you shall have it. This once."

"Oh, you are so good to me," she said almost merrily. "When shall we do it? Tonight? Tell me!"

"I haven't decided that yet. I would like to get the most of him. Once he joins us, he will be among us, and live here." Hood put his hand to his brow as if to keep any hint of light out of his red eyes.

There was a moment when the men around them were still and silent. Finally Little John spoke up. "He'll be useful, more than the scholars are."

"The scholars help us with much," said Hood in a tone that brooked no opposition. "I'll hear nothing against them. They know too much to let them go."

"What's the point?" Scarlet asked sarcastically. "They could provide us a little nourishment, if it comes to that, I suppose."

"They can do much for us," said Hood bluntly. "Why should I be rid of them? They haven't been anything but useful. They can record our deeds and show the world that we're not the fiends so many believe us to be. They can tell us what the world is doing, more than the Red Friar can." He looked at Marian, challenging her. "They can be proud of the good they do on our behalf."

"Why should they think that?" Scarlet asked.

"Because it serves our purposes to have us praised in the world. The common folk pay more heed to the tales they hear on market-day than they do to anything the priests say to them. If they learn songs and stories that show us to be their champions, they will aid us because of their faith in rumors," Hood said imperiously. "If the gossips say we are not dangerous, then the merchants will not use so many men-at-arms as escorts and we will feast again, without having to fight for every drop we take."

"Is that why you send messengers to that fool Alan?" Scarlet demanded with as much indignation as he could muster.

"Certainly," said Hood. "And the scholars will do the rest."

"But this is dangerous," said Scarlet.

"It is more dangerous to frighten the merchants so much that we cannot feed," said Hood insistently. "And that's an end to it."

Scarlet spoke up. "It is your decision."

"Exactly," said Hood. "I want to hear no more about it."

The Red Friar, who had been standing in the shadow of a great, blasted oak, stepped toward Hood. "He is yours already, isn't he? Wroughton is."

"I am thankful one of you knows this," said Hood with meaning.

"Where is the man?" the Red Friar looked about.

"He is with the Old Ones," said Hood, his voice dropped down to a near-whisper. "At the barrows."

There was another uneasy silence at this mention of the first of Hood's victims, creatures so desiccated that they were like husks, only their bones left to give them shape. Some were said to be eons older than Hood himself. They lay in a crypt marked by barrows deep in the forest that was said to be the burial place of an ancient King who had ruled long ago; the people of the forest thought the place was haunted.

"He should be safe there," said Hood after a brief consideration. He pointed to Little John. "Go fetch him. And tell the scholars to put a tale together that we may feed to Alan; let it be heroic and grand, so he will want to make many ballads about it. Let the forest ring with his songs, so that many believe they are safe."

"You will have it as you wish," said Little John. "Do you want me to bring him now?"

"Yes. It will take you some time to reach the Old Ones," Hood pointed toward the depths of the forest.

"I can go quickly," said Little John, and turned away from the vast fire-pit where Hood's men were gathered.

"Then do, and at once. Lady Marian wants something to eat." Hood was beginning to be impatient.

"I am going," Little John called out as he disappeared into the shelter of the trees.

Hood folded his arms. "The rest of you had best go scouting—if you want to slake your thirsts, you must find the means to do it yourselves."

Scarlet favored him with an elegant sneer. "You are always the one to determine who shall feed and who shall go hungry."

"In this place, I do," Hood said with an arrogance so complete that some of his men stared in disbelief.

The Red Friar sensed a fight coming and moved to intervene. "Hood is master, Scarlet, and you know it best of all." He leaned on his walking-staff, making it clear that he would stop any disputes that erupted in the clearing, no matter who instigated them. "It was you who taught me that lesson—how is it you have forgotten it?"

"Very good," Hood approved. "You become more worthy with every night." He gave Scarlet a hard glance. "You would do well to learn from this man." He raised his voice. "Bring Wroughton. I want him here now."

"The Old Ones aren't reached in an instant," Scarlet reminded him. "Travel as fast as he will, Little John will need time. He is no bird, to fly there." He sat down. "Where do you want us to hunt this evening?"

"I should think you would go to the cross-roads near the Abbey of Holy Rood." Hood shrugged. "Or you might go to the well on the Ely road. There are always a few men to be found there—pilgrims and other solitary men."

"And that is what you want us to feed on—the dregs of those who travel the Great North Road?" Scarlet asked, and shrugged before Hood could say anything more. "If that is what you have to offer, then it is what I must accept. I will take five or six men with me, and the rest may fend for themselves."

"I thank you, Will," said Hood with silky condemnation.

Scarlet shrugged again. "Those who want to eat with me, come along. There's no reason to wait here." He turned on his heel and started off along the main trail. "We'll be back before dawn, unless it rains."

Hood laughed, the cruel sound echoing among the trees, following those who left with Scarlet. "You and I will have Wroughton to ourselves," Hood said to Marian, his red eyes shining like embers in his white face.

"I thank you for it," said Marian, touching his arm.

The Red Friar watched them, feeling uneasy. "What of the rest of us?"

"I will make an arrangement for you later," said Hood negligently. "Build up the fire, if you would. It is going to be cold tonight, so cold that we will notice it."

"Why should that matter to you?" the Red Friar asked.

"It doesn't," said Hood. "But there are swineherds in this part of Sherwood who would be grateful for a little warmth."

"So you wish to set a trap?" the Red Friar said. "Why should they take such a chance?"

"Because they are cold," said Hood, and went to climb up into the tree that spread its boughs over the clearing, where he could watch for the return of Little John.

"Cold or hot, they will be welcome here," said one of the men whose eyes were hollow with hunger.

"Be sure you drain them and thrust hawthorn down their gullets. We can't manage too many more men," said the Red Friar.

The men in the clearing began to build up their central fire, adding trimmed branches to the rock-bordered pit. The Red Friar supervised their activities and took charge of making their camp appear welcoming to any who might happen upon it. By the time the fire was blazing merrily, Little John appeared, leading a dazed and exhausted Wroughton, whose haggard face no longer expressed any emotion but despondency.

Marian was the first to move toward the soldier, smiling broadly as she approached him. "Welcome, Wroughton," she said.

He looked toward her, but gave no sign of recognizing her.

Hood came to her side. "You may have the first of him, but I must have the last. He will be my servant, not yours." His hand on her shoulder was terribly heavy.

"You are good to me," said Marian as she moved to Wroughton, putting her arms around his neck, the better to hold him in position; after a long moment, he put his arms around her, as if needing her strength to continue standing. "Oh, very good," she murmured as her teeth pulled open the half-healed wounds on his throat. While she fed, he began to sag, his grip on her slipping away as he dropped to his knees.

"Enough," said Hood, pulling her aside. "Now he is mine."

Marian staggered to her feet, swaying a little, her face slack. "Oh, very good. Very good," the words slurred.

Hood paid no attention to her; he was relishing the bounty that poured from Wroughton's neck.

33.

How Sir Gui laid his Plans

"I have hit upon a notion," Sir Gui announced to Hugh deSteny the morning after the Sheriff returned to Nottingham. "I have considered many possibilities, and, after due reflection I think this will serve our purposes very well."

DeSteny paused in his perusal of the message brought to him from York and looked up. "What purposes?" He felt uneasy, for Sir Gui was often attached to his notions and disinclined to turn from them.

"Why, the capture of Hood and the return of my bride. I am agreed with my father: the marriage contract must be honored, for the sake of both our families, and then she may retire to the cloister to live out her life in expiation of her sins and thus restore her good name." He smiled in anticipation of that happy time.

"And how are we to do this?" deSteny asked, troubled and fascinated at once.

Sir Gui waved his plumed hat. "Why, at Nottingham Fair. It is not so very far off," he said as if it were obvious. "Harvest will shortly be upon us, and the Fair will come soon after, on the Eve of All Saints. Think about it. There are contests of marksmanship and strength, and there are games of chance. Everyone comes from miles around for the last festival before winter comes. I think if I were to announce high stakes for the winners in all games, surely the outlaws would hear of it, and they would come with all the rest, in the hopes of enriching themselves, and we could capture them." He lifted his hand. "I cannot think why no one else has hit upon so obvious a solution."

DeSteny did his best to consider the suggestion with as open a mind as he could muster. "It might be possible, but, as you say, people come from miles around: how are we to identify the outlaws? There will be many strangers in the town, and how are we to determine which of them are well-intentioned and which are desperate men?"

"We have some who have seen the outlaws and lived to tell of it. Let them accompany the men-at-arms and pass through the crowds, and that will give them the opportunity to identify such men as they have seen with Hood. Send for that crofter—Hamm, is it?—to point out his missing brother. It is his brother who is missing, isn't it?" Sir Gui paced the breadth of deSteny's study, humming slightly. "It will be an easy matter to find the miscreants and take them into custody."

Although he didn't share Sir Gui's confidence, deSteny said, "It might work, but it would expose all the fair-goers to all manner of danger. And who is to say Hamm Gates would come?"

"They want the outlaws gone, do they not? What, then, is a little risk, when being abroad on the roads is ten times more perilous?" Sir Gui stopped in front of deSteny's table and slapped his hand down. "You cannot tell me that the outlaws cannot be caught this way. They are greedy men, and they are experts with the bow and staff, or so those who have fought them say. They must come to the Fair, and when they do, we shall make the most of their temerity. You know as well as I that they are cowards in their hearts, as all such men must be. All we need is enough soldiers, and they will be ours."

DeSteny could see that argument was useless. And perhaps, with Sir Humphrey's help, he could turn this idea of Sir Gui's into a useful strategy. "What arrangements do you want to have made?"

"First, of course, we must have soldiers, many of them hidden in the crowd. Then we must have the gaols ready to hold them, and guards enough to hold them secure once we have them in hand. If they bring Marian deBeauchamp with them, we must have women to receive her. Nuns, preferably, very discreet ones. And we will need to have a Justice of the Peace on hand, so we may try these criminals at once, and execute them forthwith." He rocked back on his heels. "As you see, I have thought of everything."

"So you have," said deSteny, then put his fingertips together, his eyes focused beyond the half-shuttered window. "And yet, I cannot help but wonder how you plan to bruit about the rewards you intend to use to entice these men in from the forest. This is not the manner of occasion when you can send an invitation or a summons. Yet they cannot learn of it by chance, it must be—" He stopped. "The foolish minstrel."

"What has that to do with—" Sir Gui began, only to be interrupted.

"Calls himself Alan-a-Dale. The outlaws tell him tales, and he makes ballads to them, praising their exploits. He thinks that he is building a noble legend. Well, perhaps he can tell the outlaws a few tales for a change. I want to make him useful." There was a hint of optimism in his manner now, as if he began to think Sir Gui was not completely beyond all circumspection with his plan.

"You will attend to such matters," said Sir Gui, not wanting to be hemmed in by any such considerations that implementation of his idea might impose upon him. "I have done my part by conceiving of a plan."

"That you have," said deSteny, as much in charity with Sir Gui as he had ever been. "And I will begin to do my part, as well. It is still a month until the Fair. I'll see that the first steps are taken at once."

"Very good," Sir Gui approved, beaming. "I will have my clerk inform my father what I have proposed, and my messengers will carry the notice to him—under guard, of course."

DeSteny saw his opportunity. "Yes. And I will want to talk to the guards you select for the journey. I think they can perform a double duty for us, if it will please you, and if you agree to my choices."

Sir Gui was basking in his own good opinion, so he said, "Yes, of course. You may give them your orders, so long as they do not supercede my own."

"Certainly," said deSteny, forcing a note of respect into his voice.

"In the meantime, I am going to spend a day or two with Sir Wilem. We are going to hunt deer. If there is time, we may also hunt wolves." He smoothed the front of his beautiful clothes. "I will visit you upon my return, to find out what progress you have made."

"Very good," said deSteny, and rose to accompany Sir Gui to the door of his study. "You may rely upon me."

"Of course I may. You would not be Sheriff of Nottingham if I could not," he said with formidable hauteur. "See that you do not botch this opportunity," he warned before he turned on his heels and departed.

Left alone, deSteny went to the window and stood looking out on the bright morning. This was going to be a clear, windy day, the sort that still had a little summer in it, where the sunlight fell; in the shadows autumn had already come with its chill. He could smell the ripeness of the fields beyond the walls, and that encouraged him. Gradually a second plan formed in his mind, and he considered it carefully as he weighed his situation. If he went too far afield from Sir Gui's original intent, he would be ordered to abandon his efforts, so his own plan would have to dovetail with Sir Gui's. That could be managed, he decided, particularly if the Bishop would agree to help him. That would be difficult, but not an impossible stumbling block to his burgeoning scheme.

There was a scratch at the door and Nicholas called out, "You have a visitor, Sheriff. A nun."

The Sheriff lifted his head and thought for a long moment. "Who is she?"

Nicholas hesitated then answered, "Her name is Mother Barnaba. She says it is about Wroughton. She is Superior at Saint Gertrude's, or so she tells me. She has the look of her office." This last was not entirely a compliment.

"Mother Barnaba?" He didn't recognize the name. "Have I met her?"

"She says not," said Nicholas. "Do I admit her? She has come a long way."

DeSteny was curious. "Yes. Admit her. And then go fetch bread and mead for her."

"That I will," said Nicholas, and opened the door.

Mother Barnaba came forward, her head lowered respectfully. "My good Sheriff, thank you for receiving me; this is an honor and I will remember your kindness in my prayers. I am the Superior of Saint Gertrude's, and I may have information for you. I pray I have, or I will have come a long way for nothing, and that would vex me deeply." She looked up, the wrinkles strong in her face, her eyes reddened from tears. "You know what has been happening in Sherwood—well, you must!—those creatures who prey on all who enter the forest: I have lost kinsmen to those things—I cannot call them men, or even outlaws—in the forest and I come to you to redress the wrongs I have suffered."

"I will strive to help you," said deSteny, wondering why she had chosen him to petition instead of the Bishop. He could certainly understand why she might not go to Sir Gui, but he struck himself as an odd choice.

"For that, I thank God," she said, devoutly crossing herself and launching into her account. "I have lost my kinsman to what men are calling the forest outlaws. My kinsman was in the company of your man Wroughton, serving as his escort. The outlaws so worked upon him that we have not been permitted to bury him in sacred ground." She caught her hands together. "I don't know what more I can do but appeal to you to deal with the outlaws."

"It has been my purpose for many days," said deSteny.

"Better a plague than these outlaws," said Mother Barnaba. "Ellenby was a good man. It grieves me that he must lie at the cross-roads, his face down in his grave, a sprig of hawthorn through his heart."

"Is that what has happened to him?" deSteny asked.

"Yes. It is all we were permitted to do." She pursed her lips. "I must see him revenged."

"You have pledged to avenge him? A strange vow for a nun, if you do not think it wrong of me to say so." He leaned forward. "Do you insist on vengeance quickly, or will you be content to wait for a while?"

"I want revenge while I live, and I am not a young woman. But as long as God will give me breath, I will be seeking vengeance for Ellenby, and his men, who were lost on his account." She clutched her rosary crucifix that hung from her belt. "I am content to wait so long as vengeance is sure."

"It is as sure as anything on this earth may be," DeSteny wrapped his hand around the hilt of his dagger.

"You place your faith in cold steel." Mother Barnaba noticed his gesture. "I might do the same, were I you." She crossed herself as if to protect herself from her own blasphemy. "You may say that I am wrong to seek revenge when God will do it at the Last Judgment. But he and I are of the same blood, and I cannot leave this completely behind, for that would bring disgrace upon my House, and God would not expect that of me."

DeSteny said nothing. He looked toward the window. "We may find a way to bring these men to justice. It may succeed, but if it doesn't, I will come to you, and it may be that I will have to use you as part of our plan."

"Were it not that it would be a sin, I would wield a weapon myself," she said staunchly. "I have much to expiate, for I have brought shame to my family."

"Would you take a letter to Windsor for me?" deSteny asked impulsively, expecting her to refuse; it would be a very dangerous venture, and Mother Barnaba was not a young woman.

"Yes," she answered without hesitation. "I will pass unimpeded through the forest, for I have a pyx with me, and those creatures will not touch me so long as I have it with me. I am devout enough to be protected."

"They have attacked clerics before," deSteny reminded her.

"I reached Nottingham without any hindrance. I can go to Windsor as safely."

DeSteny allowed himself to be persuaded. "All right. I will make you my messenger, and thank you for the mission you have undertaken."

She gave him a tight little smile. "When will you have the message I am to carry?"

"If you will come to my study after Vespers, I will give a letter for you to take to Windsor for me," said deSteny.

"You will want me to keep this to myself," Mother Barnaba said shrewdly.

"If you would. For your protection as well as the souls of all who travel through Sherwood," said deSteny.

"I will carry your letter, and tell no one. If I can battle these fiends in no other way, this will content me," Mother Barnaba assured him.

"If you can keep your purpose through our efforts, you might do the next thing to using a weapon," deSteny said, thinking that this old woman was more formidable than many captains he had encountered in his years campaigning.

"Good," she said, and used the sleeve of her habit to blot the tears from her eyes. She prepared to leave the study, then said, "I am going to stay at Saint Anne's, if you want to speak with me again."

"I will consult with you before you leave, when I give you the letter. I will make two copies. One for you to keep on your person, the other to go with whomever among your guards you most trust," deSteny promised. "I thank you for all you've done. Simply coming here is a fine thing, and for that I thank you. It is more than many another have done." He had a long moment as he thought that if Sir Gui's ploy failed, he might still have an opportunity to bring about the end of Hood and all his followers.

"You begin to give me some hope, Sheriff, and I had thought all hope was gone." Mother Barnaba bobbed a courtesy to deSteny as she opened the door. "God give us victory over these fell beings."

"You have done the same for me: given me hope, Mother Barnaba. Would there were men with your courage and determination," said deSteny, offering her a salute as she departed.

When she was gone, he rose and paced his study, recalling his ordeal on Crusade that had first exposed him to the evil of undead monsters who preyed upon the living, and whose victims brought the horror to England. He knew what he had to do to triumph over the blood-drinkers, and much as he might wish to avoid it, he could not turn from his duty. He began to steel himself for what he feared was to come.

34.

How deSteny prepared for Combat

"How many arrows and pikes do we have in our armory?" deSteny asked Sir Humphrey as they made their way around the battlements shortly after mid-day.

"Is this for the Eve of All Saints and the Fair?" Sir Humphrey knew that there was a plan afoot to trap Hood during the competitions.

"Among other things," said deSteny. "Do we need to ask the armorers and smiths to make more? What do you advise?" It would be unwise to act without Sir Humphrey's support, for his men would police the All Saint's Fair.

"Do you expect an attack?" Sir Humphrey folded his big arms and glared out toward the vastness of the trees.

"I expect that Hood will become bolder, and I know Sir Gui is becoming restless. I anticipate open battle before too many more fortnights pass. Sir Gui expects us to do something to restore Lady Marian to him." DeSteny laughed his anger. "I have to show my determination in more than words."

"Tell me what you want from me, Sheriff," said Sir Humphrey.

"I'll need weapons and a few men willing to patrol the roads. This will prepare us for the trouble that we may have to face. It's dangerous work, going into the forest, and I have no wish to put any of your soldiers at risk, but my own men are not willing to take on the patrols without others to support them. You can't blame them."

"No, I can't. If it's true that the outlaws have Wroughton among them, then there is much to consider. Wroughton knows a great deal that those creatures will find useful, and it is likely he will give up all to the outlaws, if they have him. And we must suppose that they have him, or the wolves have eaten him, if we are lucky." He sighed heavily and went a dozen steps in deep thought. "I think there are a dozen men who might be willing to patrol for you. I will ask among them, if I deem it necessary. You don't want to leave Nottingham unprotected. I don't believe I can spare more than a dozen."

"I will be glad of any help you may extend to me," said deSteny. He pointed toward the forest, shading his eyes against the glare from high, thin clouds that turned the sun to a bright smudge overhead.

"I'll decide by tomorrow, once I have had a chance to think about this. I want to consider all that must be done." Sir Humphrey put his hand on deSteny's shoulder. "I don't envy you your predicament, Sheriff, that I don't."

"I thank you for that, I think," said deSteny with the suggestion of a laugh.

"Time enough for thanks when I decide what I am to do," said Sir Humphrey, on whom deSteny's irony was lost.

"Tomorrow I look forward to talking with you in the morning," said deSteny.

"After Mass. I will need to consult the Bishop as well as my good angel. In the meantime, leave me, so I can attend to my duties. There is much for me to consider." He had reached one of the stairs down to the inner courtyard. "Is there anything more we need to discuss just now, or can any further discussion wait until tomorrow?"

"Perhaps I should have an accounting of the state of

your supplies. I have had mine inventoried. Nicholas has spent the morning preparing the lists for me. I will be pleased if you will take a copy it, and I would like to have a—"

"—copy of mine," said Sir Humphrey.

DeSteny made a gesture of concession. "Yes. I want that exchange. I know it can be useful to both of us."

Sir Humphrey shook his head as he began to descend the stairs. "You are a persuasive fellow, deSteny, no doubt of that."

DeSteny followed after him. "I will hope that you will accommodate me."

"Of course you do," said Sir Humphrey.

They were almost to the cobblestoned courtyard now, and deSteny knew he only had a few more breaths to set his agreement with Sir Humphrey. "Shall we plan to review our supplies and weapons when we meet tomorrow after Mass?"

"Very well," said Sir Humphrey, giving in. "What you wish is prudent for us to know, and shared knowledge is strong knowledge."

"Yes. It is." DeSteny was vastly relieved. "Well. Until tomorrow, then." He took a step back. "I will await you in my study."

"Fine," said Sir Humphrey, and strolled away toward the marshaling yard, his arms swinging.

DeSteny watched Sir Humphrey, trying to decide how much more he should tell the Marshal. He thought it made more sense to wait, in case Mother Barnaba could not complete her mission, and he would be forced to improvise. When would word come from Saint Gertrude's? he asked himself. He went into the keep, wandering through the Great Hall, his thoughts in a muddle.

"Sheriff," called out Sir Gui's second squire, who was

still at the castle while Sir Gui was away.

"What is it, Osbert?" deSteny asked as the youngster ran up to him.

"A messenger is here, from Arundel, with a letter." He was in a smirched tunic, his hair in need of cutting. He could be an engaging scamp, but just at present he was annoying.

"What does deBeauchamp want?" deSteny asked the air, feeling aggravated by this intrusion: he had too much to deal with, and another screed from deBeauchamp would not be welcome.

"He's asking about his niece, according to the Grey Friar." He chuckled. "He says the language is intemperate."

"DeBeauchamp or the Grey Friar?" deSteny asked, although he knew the answer; the Grey Friar who served as clerk for the garrison was overly nice in his tastes, and Lady Marian's uncle was an intemperate man.

"The Grey Friar," said Osbert.

"What is on deBeauchamp's mind, that he should suddenly send a messenger? Hasn't he heard enough of our situation here?" deSteny wondered aloud, then said to Osbert, "You needn't answer. I wasn't addressing you." He tapped his finger on the hilt of his dagger. "Oh, very well. Bring me the message if you haven't it with you."

Osbert sulked. "I have it in my bed. I'll go fetch it." He scowled as only a boy of nine could.

"I'll be in my study," said deSteny. "Find me there directly."

"I will come, bye-and-bye," Osbert said, and scampered off before deSteny could issue orders to the contrary.

Trouble with deBeauchamp, thought deSteny. This only complicates matters. He knew better than to send word to

Sir Gui, who would dislike any complaints being sent to him. "It has better be sooner than that. Attend to my order at once," he called to Osbert's retreating figure as an afterthought.

There was a scullion near the gaping maw of the fireplace where deer and boar were roasted on grand occasions; at present, the carcass of a goat was roasting over the banked coals. The scullion stared nervously at the Sheriff as if he had been caught pilfering. He got ready to flee, but could not bring himself to move.

"What is it, boy?" deSteny asked.

"I don't know . . . I'm not . . . It's nothing . . ." the youngster stammered.

"It must be something," deSteny said, who was beginning to think the scullion had actually done something he was ashamed of doing. "You needn't be afraid. Speak. I'll listen."

The scullion put down his ladle, paying no attention to the mead that splashed from the pail in which the ladle landed. "I shouldn't . . . My brother was . . . he is planning to . . . the All Saints . . ." He looked around as if wanting to bolt.

"Anyone can participate in the Fair," deSteny said.

"Perhaps," the scullion said. "But he wants to compete in the archery, and . . ."

"Ah," said deSteny, understanding at last. "He is not above poaching, and he fears he will be trapped if he does too well." He laughed. "He may do his all without worry."

"May I tell him?" the scullion asked.

"If you think he won't compete without such a reassurance." He pointed to the corridor leading down to the kitchen. "Does your brother work in Nottingham?"

"He comes to town for Mass. Otherwise, he lives in the

hamlet four leagues from the south gate." The scullion rubbed his hands on the hem of his smock, looking about awkwardly. "I don't think I can tell him anything until Sunday, m'Lord Sheriff." He picked up his ladle again and began to pour measures of mead over the turning goat.

"There is plenty of time between next Sunday and the Eve of All Saints Fair," deSteny pointed out to the scullion.

The boy nodded several times. "This is for tonight's meal," he said unnecessarily. "I have to tend to it, or Silas will beat me."

The invocation of the name of the formidable master-cook brought an understanding nod from deSteny. "Silas does not outrank me, boy," he reminded the scullion. "And so I will tell him, if you like."

Cowering, the scullion shook his head and kept on with his chore, so deSteny decided to show him a little mercy, and left him to it.

As he climbed the stairs toward his study, Osbert came hurtling down toward him, a roll of vellum clutched in his hand. "Hold there, young fellow," deSteny said, blocking the squire's perilous descent.

Osbert stopped his mad rush so quickly that he nearly fell back on his rump. He glowered at deSteny as he held out the piece of vellum. "From Arundel. You can see the Grey Friar's seal is unbroken."

DeSteny took the rolled sheet. "Yes. I see that." It was a dollop of wax dropped next to the Arundel seal, which was broken. "Thank you, Osbert. That will be all."

The boy laughed and shoved past deSteny, resuming his plunge with undiminished enthusiasm.

Was the vellum really hot, or was it only his imagination? deSteny wondered as he carefully broke the Grey Friar's seal and unrolled the sheet, scanning the contents with an anxious frown. When he had finished, he stood for some little while, then went on to his study to draft an answer to this garbled message of accusations, threats, and worries: if Reynard deBeauchamp were so troubled about his niece, deSteny decided, let him come to Nottingham and help find her.

35.

How Hood came to know of the Fair

Alan tripped over a root and put his hand out to keep from falling. He muttered and clutched his harp close to his chest, protecting it from any damage. He had been walking since early morning, hoping to stumble upon one or more of Hood's men. As he walked, he went over his rhymes, planning the song he would offer up to Hood, with the hope that the outlaws would allow him to come along with them to the Fair, where his songs of their exploits would certainly make his reputation.

"So what brings you into the forest?" Will Scarlet seemed to materialize out of the forest, as if the trees and shadows had created him.

"I . . . I was looking for you," said Alan, feeling his pulse pound in his temples as he attempted to conceal his shock.

"And you have found me," said Scarlet, his smile menacing and ironic. "For what purpose?"

"Thank goodness I have," Alan said, faltering. "I have heard something that I think you may want to know of."

"What would that be?" Scarlet sauntered up to him, his hand negligently caressing his dagger.

"Ah . . . there is a . . . a Fair . . ." He coughed and tried to take a step away.

Scarlet backed him up against a tree. "The All . . . All . . . Sacred Ones Fair. It happens every year."

"Not the way this one will happen," said Alan trying to

make this as encouraging as he could. "This one is grander than any they have had in Nottingham in many a year. There will be contests and prizes. Great lords will come, with their households. I've already written a song about it, in the hope that I might win the minstrels' contest."

"You will have to try it on Hood and the rest," Scarlet said, making it more of a command than an invitation.

"Oh. Yes. Of course." Alan clung to his harp as if trying to save himself. "That is what I intend."

"That being the case, you had better come with me now, harper," Scarlet said, as he caught Alan by the scruff of his neck and half-shoved, half-dragged him along.

"I? Now?" His voice rose half an octave. "I thought I should tell you, and you would then impart the news to Hood."

"Did you? Well, my lad, you're wrong," said Scarlet, forcing Alan to keep moving.

"I am expected at the tavern," Alan protested, his voice rising to a squeak. "I cannot be gone much longer without failing my kinsman."

"Then the landlord must be disappointed. We have a prior claim upon you." He forced Alan to move faster as they went deeply into the forest, traveling by trails only Scarlet seemed to read in the tangle of trees and brush. Alan could only pant as he tried to keep up, fear twisting his feet and playing hob with his mind—he would never be able to retrace his steps without help.

"If I don't return . . ." Alan said as they finally reached a ruined stone building.

"The landlord is no fool—in that you are different from him," said Scarlet acidly. "You say you have information for Hood, and if you do, you shall deliver it." He shoved the young harper ahead of him, his attention on the ancient wreck of a house. "Stay here. I will bring Hood to you."

Confused, Alan looked about as if he expected trickery. "Why should I stay here?"

"Hood does not like having the living brought to his hearth, unless he intends they should not leave until they become one of us." Scarlet saw the dismay in Alan's face, and laughed. "You may not think so, boy, but I am being kind to you."

"If you say so," said Alan, looking up at the tree branches where the roof had once been.

"Stay where you are. If you try to leave, you will get lost, I promise you, and when I find you again, I will be in no humor to accommodate you." He touched the quillons of his dagger and left Alan alone in the old house.

Alan held onto his harp as if to keep hold of a floating limb. He could not stop feeling that he had put himself into danger, and that he might still regret what he had done. His fingers shook as he tried to practice his melodies on the harp, and the notes came out badly. He gave up, and found himself a heap of stones to sit upon. This was better, he told himself, because at least he was resting. He began to recite "The Lay of the Bride of Fairisle," taking what comfort he could from the familiar tale. By the time he reached the verses about the dead bride-groom, the floor of the house was in deep shadow and the forest was growing darker. He shivered, and not from cold, and returned to the story of Melusine.

"So this is the singer you described to me," said Hood to Scarlet as they came through a gap in the walls. "Not a very taking example."

Torn between umbrage and fear, Alan concealed his apprehension in petulance. "How would you know?"

Scarlet made a sharp, warning gesture in Alan's direction. "This is no time to make jests, boy," he said sternly, his expression forbidding.

"All right," said Alan, wishing he could leave without depending on Scarlet to guide him home.

"It is said you have information to impart to me," said Hood; he was playing with the short dags on his sleeves, his baleful gaze fixed on Alan.

"I do. Yes, I do." He felt his courage return in a rush. "I do."

"Then out with it. Your assurances mean nothing if I hear only babbling." He came a step closer to Alan, and grinned as the young harper drew back.

"The Fair in Nottingham. On All Saint's Eve?" He looked about anxious, as if hoping to find supporters materializing from the fallen stone walls. "This is to be a grand occasion, finer than in years past. Nobles and gentry will attend, and Sir Gui has stated that he will award prizes—rich prizes—in all the competitions. People will come from all over Sherwood, and they will come with treasure."

"That they will," said Hood. "And so many of them strangers." He stared musingly at Alan. "Go on. Tell me all."

"Well," said Alan, gathering up what courage he could. "The competitions are open to all, not just to the Sheriff's or Sir Humphrey's or Sir Gui's men. The prizes will be given to all, as well, no matter who they may be, or of what station. The Bishop will supervise the judging so it may be fair, and the prizes will be displayed for all to see, so that the awards will be given as promised." He coughed as if to clear his throat. "I am going to make a song about the All Souls' Eve Fair, and sing it in the contest."

"Are you?" Hood chuckled. "Then I must wish you good fortune, I suppose." He turned to Scarlet. "What do you think?"

"I think it is a fine opportunity. So many people on the road, it would be a shame to miss the feast." Scarlet laughed.

"But it may well be a trap," said Hood. "What should we do in that case?"

Scarlet knew the question was a test, and so he considered his answer very carefully. He wished young Alan would go away for this, but it was he who had brought him, and so he was left to deal with this as he could do best. "I think that we must find a way to go, disguised, among the folk, so we may take what we desire. I think we must attack in the forest, but only the stragglers, and take their places in the town. I think we must enter such contests as we may, and claim what prizes we can. I think we can slip away before the fair is at an end, and the soldiers of Nottingham will be unable to chase us if they still have a town full of fair-goers to contend with." He took a deep breath. "And I think we must make traps to waylay the late travelers from the fair."

Hood nodded. "Well-considered, Scarlet. I will say you have considered well."

"I have your example," said Scarlet, trying to hide the relief he felt.

"We will have to plan for the event." He chuckled, and the sound he made was sinister. "When I went on Crusade, I did not plan, and the fell denizens of the desert graveyards made me their kind; when I returned here, I had to subdue all the old undead before I could be sure in my rule in this place. The Old Ones were my first prey. I conquered them, becoming their puissant suzerain. They obey me utterly or they are lost to eternal darkness. Since I have nothing to fear from them, now I hunt only the living, and they give me their strength and their lives so that I may be mightier."

He rounded on Alan. "I am told you have made songs about me before. Well and good: you wish to sing of me—

sing of that, and of my right to rule the forest. I am its lord, no other. Within its borders, I say who lives and who dies, and who rises after death. Make your song of that, harper." He advanced on Alan so quickly that the young man had no time to brace himself for what was to come.

Long, pale fingers fixed in Alan's shoulder, and the force of his grip all but tore the muscles from bone. Hood's red eyes were like flaring embers as he worried at the young man's throat, tearing the skin and exposing the strong muscles of Alan's neck, beneath which the bounty of his artery pulsed. The second bite sank into the shining flood, and Alan lost all ability to struggle, or will to resist. In a few moments, he had become light-headed and was about to faint.

"No, not yet," said Hood, and forced himself to drop his prey, standing over the fallen harper. "You are not dead yet, but you are my creature now, come what may. If you fail me, you will die and go directly to Hell. But serve me, do my bidding, and you will thrive in my favor." He turned away to face Scarlet. "You may have first pick of the travelers for this. Unless that callow youth betrays us, in which case, you will suffer as you cannot imagine." He twitched his hood to conceal his face, which bore smears of Alan's blood about the mouth. "Get the lad home. I will expect you back before midnight." Saying that, he was gone.

Scarlet stood in the stone ruin for a short while, waiting for Alan to come to himself again. Eventually he ran out of patience and nudged the young man's side with the toe of his boot. "Come. You aren't dead yet."

Confused and frightened, Alan levered himself onto his shaking elbows. "What happened?"

"Hood gave you orders. You had best obey them," said Scarlet, reaching down to haul Alan to his feet. "Take your harp and come with me."

"I . . . I'm dizzy." He put his hand to his torn neck and fought the urge to vomit. "What did he do?"

"What he always does," said Scarlet. "He drank your blood."

Alan moaned as much in terror as in pain. "Then—"

"You're tainted, but you aren't one of his group yet. You are between your life and his." He grabbed Alan and forced him to stand up enough to move. "It's going to be dark by the time you're back."

"Oh . . . celestials," said Alan, fighting off an attack of vertigo.

"Don't try to say those words," Scarlet recommended. "You'll only make yourself ill if you do." He continued into the forest, walking confidently along secret by-ways, all but dragging Alan after him.

Although he was fighting confusion, Alan was unable to resist Scarlet's determination. He felt his legs begin to tremble, and his vision swam, but he dared not stop, for fear of what Hood might do if he thought Alan was unable to complete his assigned tasks. But try as he would, he could not think of rhymes for his songs—just now that was as much beyond him as climbing the mountains of the fabled East.

36.

How Mother Barnaba came to Windsor

Her mule refused to go faster than a walk, stubborn after the nature of his kind; he moved along steadily enough, but at the same dogged pace he had set out in, covering the ground inexorably but slowly. Mother Barnaba sat in the saddle, her thighs and backside aching from her long ride. Most of her cheese was gone and only a handful of grain remained in her saddle-bag for the mule, and that would only see her through one more night. Then she must seek shelter and food if she had not yet reached the Prince. It had been several years since she had gone to Windsor, and she was reluctant to do anything more than let the mule find its way, for the woods were much changed from what she remembered. She had been passed by four groups of merchants, each heavily escorted by soldiers, and she prayed for each of them, certain in her heart that some of them would be set upon by the evil that lived in the forest before they came to their destinations.

She had gone through a number of hamlets, making note of the state of the houses and crops, and thinking that the crofters were taking more of a chance in the forest than they had done in years past. Those villages that had a church or an abbey near-by could be much more protected, but there was still the constant chance for trouble. She had made it a point to stop only at walled abbeys and churches within village walls, for she was sure that some of the fell creatures had taken over various religious buildings, and in those places, she would have no protection from them. Her last night had been spent in a fortress, in a stone room that was no larger than her mule's stall. She had not complained, but her back had yet to forgive her the night on the straw mattress.

"Nun!" a small boy shouted as he emerged from the undergrowth, his dirty face set in an angry smile.

Mother Barnaba pulled in the mule, covering her jitteriness with a smile. "Youngster. May God send you a good day."

"Hoo!" The boy rubbed his nose.

"Do you look for birds, or other small prizes?" She was mildly chiding, for even such minor poaching was forbidden.

"You don't know anything." He turned away from Mother Barnaba. "The Prince is hunting today. You shouldn't be on the road."

"Prince John?" said Mother Barnaba, hope flooding back through her.

"And his nobles. You can hear the horns, sometimes. Sometimes they just rush up on you." He capered along the road as if this would be a high treat.

"Don't you worry about being hurt? Out here on your own?" she asked, trying to listen for the sound of horns.

"They don't bother with me. I'm too small for them." He chuckled. "The Prince doesn't mind, either."

"How do you escape trouble?" she asked, truly interested.

"I climb into the trees. I see a lot in the trees." His boast was mischievous.

"Of course you do," said Mother Barnaba. "Perhaps you can climb a tree now, and tell me what you see?"

"I don't have to. The hunt is heading this way. I saw it a while ago." He was about to slip back into the underbrush, but stopped before he did. "I think you should get out of the way of the hunt. You can't keep up on a mule."

"I'll keep your suggestion in mind," she said wryly, but held her mule still while she saw the boy go off to a beech tree. "Do you see anything?"

"Trees," came the laconic answer.

"I mean hunters. Where are they? Do you—?" She stopped as the sound of a horn caught her attention.

"Over that way," said the boy, pointing to the southeast.

"Yes. I hear them."

"Coming this way," he went on, and climbed higher into the branches. "They don't like anyone interfering with their hunt."

"I'm not going to interfere," said Mother Barnaba, a bit mendaciously.

"Don't blame me if they take you in hand," said the boy, his voice fading as he went further up into the boughs.

"I won't," she promised. "Thank you."

"Pray for me," he called down, and then went silent.

She hung onto the bridle, making the mule move to the side of the road. She listened closely to the forest, and once again heard a pair of hunting horns, a bit nearer than before. For a while she waited patiently, but then she grew nervous as she heard the hunting horns getting nearer. She started the mule walking again, wanting to get away from the very thing she wanted. In a quarter of a mile she reached a bridge and was trying to decide whether she should cross it, when she saw four huntsmen on fine, sweating horses break from cover on the other side of the stream. Involuntarily she checked the mule again, and winced as he brayed fulsomely.

Two of the huntsmen drew rein and stared in her direction. "Sister!" one of them exclaimed.

Mother Barnaba straightened up. "I'm Mother," she announced.

Now all four huntsmen had stopped, and one carrying a boar-spear rode up to the bridge. "What are you doing, Mother? The Prince is hunting here."

"I am looking for the Prince," she said with a boldness she could hardly believe.

"He is hunting," the man repeated.

"Then I will go on to Windsor and await him there," said Mother Barnaba.

"No. You might disrupt the hunt," said another of the huntsmen. "You come to us, and we'll look after you."

"Don't you have to ride after game?" Mother Barnaba asked, regarding the men warily.

"We have an obligation to the Prince," said the first huntsman. "We should give you escort."

"Well and good," said Mother Barnaba, making up her mind and kicking her mule to make him cross the bridge. "It is just as well that you will do this for me. I have an urgent message for the Prince alone."

The third huntsman sighed. "Always petitioners." He spoke with a Scottish burr.

"This is not a minor thing," said Mother Barnaba in the same tone she used to rebuke wayward nuns. "For that, I would go to the Bishop."

"That's what every vassal tells his lord," said the first huntsman, lowering his boar-spear. "Bad enough that King Richard should bankrupt the kingdom—the people make no allowances for his burdens."

"I make allowances," said Mother Barnaba, losing patience even as she joined the men on the south side of the stream. "But I am charged by the Sheriff of Nottingham to bring the Prince—"

"Him!" exclaimed the fourth huntsman. "He already sent a messenger, who has long since departed for the north."

"He never arrived," said Mother Barnaba, and saw the four men exchange glances.

"That's different, then," said the fourth man. "You had better come with us."

Two of the men looked at him unhappily. "But the hunt," said the second.

"We wait here for the Prince," said the fourth man. "We would fail him if we do not."

The others had to agree, but did so reluctantly.

"What shall we do now?" Mother Barnaba asked.

"We wait here for the Prince. He should be along in a little while." The first huntsman glanced about uneasily. "It isn't good to linger in the forest too long."

"If you fear the outlaws, then perhaps we should go on to Windsor," Mother Barnaba suggested.

"I fear no outlaws," the first huntsman blustered. "But the Prince is hunting, and I have no wish to ruin his pleasure, or drive away his game."

"I should think," said Mother Barnaba dryly, "that any game you might have flushed is long gone. The hunt has been blundering about the woods for hours, and anything you might have run to ground must have been found already." She could hardly bring herself to admit—even to herself—that she felt safe for the first time since she left Nottingham, and wanted nothing more than to remain in the company of these huntsmen.

The second huntsman laughed aloud. "You may be right, Mother."

As if to add weight to this observation, the sounding of a horn echoed through the trees.

"The Prince will come by-and-by," said the third huntsman. "He will not be best pleased to have his sport interrupted."

"Then he will send me on to Windsor, and I will wait to

report to him there." She was regaining some of her natural air of authority, and the men felt it as well as she.

The second huntsman sighed. "Either way, we won't be in on the kill."

"There will be another time, Botolf," said the first huntsman.

"Easy for you to say, Purvis," complained the third huntsman. "Not all of us are given the honor of riding at the Prince's side."

"I am not there now," said Purvis, slipping the boar-spear back into its sheath.

"We're supposed to protect the flank," said the third huntsman. "How can we do that and escort this Mother at the same time?"

"You have nothing to worry about, Sholto," Purvis told him with a trace of exasperation. "We must give this woman the respect her office commands. There are other huntsmen to do the Prince's will, but if we abandon her, then we will fail to do what the Prince requires of all his household."

"What a lot to say," marveled the fourth huntsman. "No one hears you but us. You needn't come the courtier with us."

"I do not," said Purvis. "Nor do any of you." He ducked his head in apology to Mother Barnaba. "I am sorry these men behave as they do."

"They are men, like my brothers and cousins are," said Mother Barnaba indulgently. "I have heard far worse than that." She was about to say more, but heard the hunting horns coming closer, sounding loudly among the trees.

"We shall learn shortly what the Prince requires of us," said Purvis. "Godey, ride up the road a short way, and signal the others as they come."

The fourth huntsman grumbled, but did as Purvis ordered, spurring his skewbald spotted horse to a canter as a way to show his dissatisfaction.

"Tell me, Mother, how you come to be here alone?" Purvis asked, as he brought his horse in front of her mule.

"I said, I bring a message to the Prince." She did not feel comfortable revealing anything more, not while they remained in the forest.

"But without an escort?" Sholto asked.

"The last messenger had an escort, and he failed to arrive," she said.

"Weren't you afraid?" asked Botolf.

"If God cannot protect me, then no one is safe," said Mother Barnaba, hedging. "I prayed every Office at every Hour, and trusted in Him."

Purvis and Sholto laughed, and Purvis said, "You may say that more than anyone, I suppose." He slewed around in the saddle as the hunting horns sounded much closer to hand; the sound of horses and occasional shouts from men could be heard approaching. "They're almost here. Are you ready, Mother?"

"I am," she said and hoped it was true.

"Then come up the road with us. The hunt will break from the trees near the next bend in the road." Purvis set his horse moving.

Mother Barnaba urged her mule to a walk, aware she would fall behind the trotting horses. As the rest of the hunt came crashing out onto the road, the three huntsmen halted and dismounted, waiting for Prince John to appear. Mother Barnaba remained on her mule, nervous in spite of herself.

It didn't take long for the Prince to arrive, surrounded by men-at-arms and huntsmen as well as courtiers. He was mounted on a fine French destrier, a liver-chestnut with glossy hair and lavish mane and tail. Seeing the four huntsmen and the nun on the mule waiting for him, he drew rein, resigned to the end of hunting for the day.

The four huntsmen went on their knee to him; he motioned them to rise. "What is it, Purvis?"

"We found this nun, Mother—" He stopped, realizing he didn't know her name.

"Barnaba," she said. "I come to you on behalf of Hugh deSteny."

"God's Teeth, what does he want now?" the Prince asked impatiently. "I have done as much as I know to do."

"It is more a matter of what he wants still," she said, emboldened by her purpose.

"This bodes ill," said the Prince; no one laughed.

Mother Barnaba gathered up as much of her courage as she could. "His man Wroughton, who carried a message from you? He failed to return."

"Yes. I remember Wroughton." He rocked in his saddle. "Are you saying he never reached Nottingham?"

"He did not," said Mother Barnaba. "And the Sheriff has learned that the deadly men who live in the forest have taken him captive."

"If that is all they have done," said Purvis, and crossed himself.

"True enough," agreed the Prince, frowning. "Well, Mother," he said after a long moment of consideration, "you had better come along with me. We have much to talk about." He indicated the place on his right. "We will go back to Windsor. Let us go."

With a signal, a pathway to his side opened and Mother Barnaba was actually able to get her mule to trot up to the Prince's side. She was aware of the honor he had done her, and she was determined to be worthy of it.

37.

How deSteny prepared his Trap

It was cold in the mornings now, promising a hard winter ahead. Hugh deSteny stood over the bushel-barrel of water in the corner of his bedchamber. He steeled himself for the icy immersion that was to come. He was prepared for the cold, but he still took a sharp breath as the chill drops struck his face, puffing out his cheeks against the chill. He straightened up, using a length of cotton to wipe the water away, feeling his skin shrink. He would soon have to go to his washtub and take care of his morning ablutions. At least that tub sat in front of the hearth, and a blazing length of oak-trunk would provide some warmth.

A new page—a slight youngster of nine years of age, newly orphaned and brought into Sir Gui's service—came hesitantly to the door of deSteny's apartments. "Sir Humphrey has sent a messenger. Will you see him?"

"Yes, Jotham. Send him to me." DeSteny gestured to the table in the corner. "If he has a message, I can draft an answer here."

"He carries nothing but the words he is told to speak," said Jotham. "He will carry the same back to Sir Humphrey."

"All right," said deSteny, who was growing upset.

"Shall I bring him now?" Jotham asked.

"Yes, if you would," said deSteny patiently. He would bathe a little later; perhaps the water would be a bit warmer.

"Then I will." He bowed awkwardly and withdrew from

the room, only to return a short while later leading a youth of about fourteen, a weedy sort of lad with a hint of a beard on his chin. "This is Garvey deLindley, from Sir Humphrey."

"Sheriff," said Garvey.

Jotham lingered, curious and forlorn.

"Should we speak in private?" deSteny asked Garvey.

"It would be best," said Garvey.

"Wait in the corridor, Jotham," said the Sheriff. As soon as the page had withdrawn, he looked over at Garvey. "Well, what is it then?"

"Sir Humphrey has been informed that he will be provided twenty extra men-at-arms for the Eve of All Saints. Sir Gui's father is also sending ten archers before the celebrations begin. Sir Humphrey asks if you still want them in disguise." Garvey wasn't the least bit curious.

"Of course I do," said deSteny. "I need them to be hidden, to move through the crowd undetected, so they will be at hand when they are needed. They must not bruit it about that they are in the crowd, or their purpose in being there. Let them dress as merchants and monks and workmen. They will do everything to make themselves invisible, to vanish among the various fair-goers. If the outlaws should see an armed camp, they will not enter the gates, and will take vengeance on the fair-goers when they set out for home. The soldiers must be there to spring the trap, and to do this, they must seem to be part of the throng—they must be unremarkable, or their intention will fail. Let them be ordinary, making them no more than a potential prey, so that the outlaws will overlook them. That is the way we will catch the monsters."

"Sir Humphrey says some of his men are not pleased at having to go about without their armor and their badges."

Garvey folded his arms. "He says they want to show their purpose, and so hearten the people."

"Many armed men will not do that," said deSteny.

"But Sir Humphrey says his men think that to conceal themselves is cowardly, and that it dishonors them as soldiers." Garvey's stance dared the Sheriff to contradict him.

"Then they are fools," said deSteny bluntly.

"Why?" Garvey asked, his inquisitiveness finally roused.

"To put their pride in display instead of victory is folly. Vainglory will reap a barren harvest. They may be able to strut and swagger in chain-mail and surcotes, but they will only help their enemies by doing so. There is no value in military array, not in such a campaign as this must be." DeSteny cocked his head. "If they were to hunt the criminals in the forest, would they wear red cloaks and carry polished metal shields? No, they would not. They would wear green and brown cloaks and they would carry shields with their devices painted upon them, because they would know that they must not give any advantage to the foe. This is no different than hunting in the forest, and it will succeed as a hunt in the forest would."

"I shall tell Sir Humphrey you said so." He paused, buffing the sole of his boot on the stones of the floor. "Have you any news for him?"

"Do you mean have I heard from Windsor? No, I have not," said deSteny.

"Do you think you will?" Garvey asked.

"It isn't for me to say," said deSteny.

Garvey shrugged. "As you wish. Will you be supplying the disguises, or shall you leave it to Sir Humphrey?"

"I will tend to some of it, as it is my responsibility and duty," said deSteny.

"Sir Humphrey will be glad to hear of it," said Garvey,

and prepared to withdraw. "How many of your men are you going to put into disguises?"

"Why, all of them," said deSteny as if the answer were obvious.

"Will they comply?" Garvey asked.

"They are my men," said deSteny as if it were all the answer he needed.

Garvey snickered and turned on his heel and went to the door, pausing there to look back at deSteny. "No wonder you're not a knight," he said, and left deSteny to himself.

Had deSteny been less sure of his plan, he might have gone after Garvey deLindley and cuffed him on the ears for his impertinence, but he let the youth go. There was nothing he could say that would change anything that Garvey already thought. He gathered up his clothes and weapons and his drying sheet and went along to have his morning bath, knowing he had more important matters to deal with than the manners of a squire.

As he climbed into the tub, he found his thoughts drifting back to the days in the Holy Land, when he had bathed in the river at dawn every day before beginning his obligations for the day. With that recollection came other visions: some of battle, some of injured men, and of the dreadful, undead creatures who had gone about the Crusaders' camps preying on the wounded. He knew the legends of old, but no story he had heard as a boy in England matched the ferocity of what he encountered on the road to Jerusalem. He winced, not at the cold water, but at the image in his mind of fallen knights rising again, enslaved by the foulest thirst that ever corrupted a Christian. For these men all hope of Paradise and Salvation was lost, and in its place was the degrading, corrupted desire that turned them into creatures of Satan. At first he had fought them with all the strength of his faith, but when that was gone, he had only his duty to his comrades to carry him on in the fight. He clung to that now for purpose and resolve.

"Sheriff?" Jotham asked from the door.

"What is it?" He resumed scrubbing his back with a short-handled brush, almost enjoying the play of cold water and fire-warmed air on his skin.

"You have a messenger in your study, from Sir Gui." He made his report without inflection, and he studied his hands as he reported. "You know him."

"I will be with him directly. See he is given bread and drink for his trouble," said deSteny, nearing the end of his bath. "Tell him I will come directly."

"That I will," said the boy, and hurried off.

DeSteny rose from the tub and stood in front of the fire, letting its warmth restore him. He took the drying sheet and wrapped it around himself, preserving as much heat as he could. As soon as he was dry, he dressed carefully, thrust a dagger through his belt, and buckled on his sword before going up to his study once again. His short-cropped hair was still wet, and occasionally a drop of water would run down his face or his neck, a cool reminder of his bath, but it seemed to him that this was also a reminder of his mortality, and he took it to heart.

Radulph Parr was fiddling with the lavish, gold-piped dags on his sleeves when deSteny walked into his study, a pointed attempt to show the difference in their stations in life, for Parr's clothing would cost more than deSteny could hope to earn in three years. Parr was supposed to rise for the Sheriff, but he only moved forward in the chair, as if to deal with a recalcitrant child. "Sheriff. You kept me waiting." He paused so that deSteny could apologize. When he didn't, Parr went on, "Sir Gui sends me to tell you something."

"I will listen with my full attention," said deSteny. He had met Parr in the Holy Land when he was assigned to the men around King Richard, and had clashed with him then, knowing him for a coward and given to mendacity; he tried to keep this from affecting him now as he stared at Parr, but he was worried that some of his opinion of the man was reflected in his demeanor.

"It may appear somewhat inept of me to receive you in this way, and in your own holding," said Parr. "But you will agree our circumstances have changed."

"That they have," said deSteny and would not elaborate.

"You have certainly altered your life since Crusading," Parr goaded.

DeSteny didn't counter this covert accusation. "What does Sir Gui want?"

"I asked not be given this task, little though you may think so," Parr went on, staring at the opposite wall, unwilling to give up his game. "I told Sir Gui that it would be best to choose another."

"But he didn't," said deSteny, suspecting that Sir Gui enjoyed the idea of making this difficult for his Sheriff. "And he is your liege-lord, so you must comply with his charges, as must all his vassals."

"I didn't tell him why I didn't want to do this," Parr said.

"I suppose I should thank you for that," said deSteny.

"Yes. You should." Parr glared at him.

"Then consider it done," said deSteny.

Parr brushed the front of his long tunic. "So. This is the message: Sir Gui will come to Nottingham in a se'night to make preparations for the Eve of All Saints Fair, and he expects to be received as he deserves. You have notice, and so you have no excuse to be remiss in any appropriate distinction. A courier will be sent when his departure time is nigh. He will bring a suite of perhaps thirty-four, and they must be properly housed and fed. His fighting men will go to Sir Humphrey, who will have charge of their keep."

"Very well," said deSteny.

"Further, Sir Gui will announce a reward for his affianced bride, in the hope that she may be ransomed to her family. He must have a crier to announce his reward throughout the town." Now that he was doing his assigned service, Parr's voice was louder and more assured, but he continued to sit as if to protect himself.

"I will provide him with one," said deSteny.

"He wants, also, the seat of honor for all contests, as is his right," said Parr.

"Providing he is the most noble attendant, he will, of course, have the seat of honor," said deSteny. "The Bishop will share the platform."

"Of course," said Parr.

"And Sir Humphrey, as well, on a lower level," said deSteny.

"That's only right," said Parr, finally rising. "So you know when to expect Sir Gui and his entourage."

"Thank you for bringing me word," said deSteny.

Parr tugged on his dags. "Do you ever miss it, your old life?"

"Not as you might think," said deSteny stonily. He did not like being reminded of the past, especially not by a popinjay in a dagged tunic with parti-colored leggings.

"Then I'm sorry for you," said Parr, as much of a concession as he could make.

"Thank you, but it isn't necessary," said deSteny.

"Until Sir Gui returns, then, Sheriff," said Parr, and left him alone.

A moment later Jotham came through the open door and stood silently for as long as it might take a monk to say an *Ave*. "He is not your friend."

"No, he is not," said deSteny. "But why you should know it, I cannot determine."

The page shrugged. "I listen."

"That could get you into trouble, Jotham," deSteny warned.

"Not listening could get me into more," said Jotham with a cheeky smile.

DeSteny knew that he ought to reprimand the page, but just now he could not bring himself to do so, not with so many grim visions rising in his mind and demanding his attention far more than a charmingly impertinent page. He waved Jotham away, his attention already focused on preparing his campaign against Hood and his minions. "Go along with you."

Jotham, unaware of what occupied deSteny's mind, giggled as he fled.

EPILOGUE

How Summer came to an End

As the moon rose, the Hart emerged from the depths of the forest into the secret glades and meadows, but this brought him little satisfaction: Sherwood thrummed with Hood's malice. This was no longer a haven, and it provided only the illusion of refuge. The Hart picked his way as warily as he would have done if the hunt were still abroad, thinking with each step that the Boar had better be prepared for a battle when he assumed mastery of the forest in three more days, for this crusade was not one that could only be fought by men, but that summoned all the worldly and unworldly powers to the engagement that lay ahead.

About the Author

TRYSTAM KITH is a lifelong student of folklore, fairy tales, legends, myths, superstitions, religions, and cultural anthropology. Kith is a native Californian.